# EMERGENCE

# EMERGENCE

MICHAEL SIMON

Podium

*This book is dedicated to science fiction readers who travel to unknown planets, who unshackle their minds from the mundane, and whose unabashed optimism make this world a better place.*







Cover design by Alexandre Rito

ISBN: 978-1-0394-7569-4

Published in 2025 by Podium Publishing
www.podiumentertainment.com

# EMERGENCE

# CHAPTER 1

*Roads were made for journeys, not destinations.*

DAY 1, 0632 HOURS

The wail of the emergency klaxon cut through his dreams with all the subtlety of a chainsaw, and Ryan found himself on his feet before his brain clicked into gear. His quarters were dark, and the clock by his bed read 0632. He automatically reached for the rumpled uniform lying over the back of his chair. Thirty seconds later, still struggling with the buttons, he stumbled out of his quarters. The lower half of his tunic flapped behind him like a cape as he burst into Operations, prompting a mental image of Captain Tracy running into the room under similar conditions a year earlier. Back then, it was an asteroid on a collision course with the colony that triggered the warning siren and flashing bulkhead lights.

Rani and Chan were already at their stations, hurriedly tapping commands into slate-gray control panels. Each terminal was an extension of thermoplastic fiber that flowed seamlessly from the floor, sprouting like a blossoming flower. Marco's old chair looked like it could swallow Chan in one gulp.

"Will someone shut that damn thing off?" Ryan massaged his temples with both hands before the siren seeded another migraine. Some part of his psyche was aware of the steady hum of server racks at the back of the room and the hologram of the Jovian system hovering below the front portals.

"Got it, Lieutenant." Chan toggled a switch on her terminal and the alarm mercifully ended.

Ryan's ears stopped vibrating. He turned to Rani. "Report."

Rani kept her eyes on her monitor as reams of data scrolled down the left side of her screen. She may have been born and raised on the Indian subcontinent, but an American education had whittled her accent down to a shadow of itself. "Proximity alarm. I'm bringing up the feed from the external camera now."

"Proximity alarm?" A cold fist reached into Ryan's chest. He and Gunner had installed only one such alarm on the moon after the insurrection, and that was beside a certain plague-infested transport. His gaze shifted to the starboard portal in front of Chan. Outside, the laser sat on an elevated ice sheet, its titanium support beams welded to a massive metal piling that plunged thirty meters beneath the surface. The weapon was the colony's only defense against asteroids on an intercept course. But, as imposing as the laser appeared, the Fleet transport parked beside it made it look like a child's toy. "Where's Gunner?"

"In the decompression chamber with Kasim, gearing up," Chan replied.

Ryan gripped the arms of his chair. "Why would anyone—"

"Feed coming in now," Rani announced.

The monitor on the arm of his chair flickered briefly before crystallizing into a static image of the surrounding icefield. The laser and Fleet transport sat in the foreground, and in the distance he could discern the edge of the graveyard. Hundreds of makeshift crosses were hammered into the frozen surface. Guilt oozed into his consciousness. It had been his decision to open the EV door when the rebels tried to storm the Command Center, condemning hundreds of colonists to death. His fingers squeezed the arms of his chair until they turned white. It took a huge effort to shove the year-old memories into an unused corner of his mind.

Now was not the time.

On the monitor, a momentary wind stirred debris on the surface before fading into the thin atmosphere. Nothing else moved. And yet something had triggered the alarm, which meant someone must have gotten within fifty meters of the transport. A thick layer of ice covered the ship, which hadn't moved a millimeter since Gunner pulled it from the ice crevasse with the gator. One of two transports carrying Senator Lecky's marines, it had launched from Florida just ahead of the plague sweeping across North America. Unbeknownst to those on board, a stowaway bacterium had hitched a ride. Only when the passengers were reanimated from cryo-sleep did the germ enter the blastic phase and infect everyone. It was a miracle the pilot managed to land at all. Best Dr. Louis could tell, the last passenger succumbed twenty-four hours after the transport crash-landed in that fissure.

They may have been the last survivors from a doomed planet, but even they couldn't travel far enough to escape the damned bug. It was Ryan's job to make sure nobody got close enough to that ship to unleash the plague.

A small dust devil danced across the surface before disappearing off-screen. With Jupiter loitering on the horizon, dark blue and violet hues played over the ice sheets. The gas giant's immense gravity distorted Europa's tectonic layers, using the moon as a punching bag as it precipitated seismic shifts beneath the surface.

"I see him!" Chan pointed to a figure entering the camera's field of view. A white EV suit, standard-issue backpack with a metallic rod sticking out the top.

Ryan leaned into his monitor. "What's he carrying?"

Rani peered closer, and Ryan couldn't help but notice the subtle change in the specialist. A year ago, her brown skin had been as smooth as porcelain and her long tresses silky black. Now, fine wrinkles covered her cheeks, and streaks of gray shot through her hair like a bad dye job.

She shook her head. "Can't tell. Those ice pillars are blocking the view."

Ryan clenched his jaw. Whatever was happening wasn't good. The fact that a colonist had decided to ignore the golden rule and approach the transport was bad enough. Worse, if his intentions didn't stop there. Ryan had placed the ship under strict quarantine. One tiny bacterium worming its way inside the station spelled the extinction of his species.

Chan touched her earpiece. "Gunner signaled they're leaving the airlock."

"Tell them to hurry," Ryan said. "Why would anyone go near that excuse for a coffin?"

"Crazy," Rani said. "He's heading toward the front hatch."

They watched as the colonist navigated several large pieces of ice on his way to stand under the nose of the massive transport.

"That's it, then," Chan said. Her shoulders relaxed. "He's done, unless he's got a trampoline in his pocket. The door is twenty feet above his head."

Ryan's sense of foreboding settled into his bones. No one would risk a cut in rations and certain imprisonment just to get a close look at a ghost ship.

That was when the colonist pulled the backpack off his shoulder and withdrew a large, cylindrical object attached to what looked to be a kite tail.

"Shit!" Ryan spat. "Get Gunner. Now!"

"What is it?" Chan spun her chair around, eyes wide.

Rani slapped the icon on her screen. "Gunner, the lieutenant needs to talk to you immediately."

The engineer's voice came back slightly distorted, the result of Jupiter's ionizing radiation. "Bit busy . . . Almost . . ."

"Gunner." Ryan leaned into the speaker. "He's got a miner's ladder and he's right beneath the front hatch."

There was a slight pause. Ryan attributed it to shock. "Christ on a cross! We're running . . ." The channel closed, but not before they heard Gunner yelling at Kasim to keep up.

Chan's stare hadn't wavered. "A miner's ladder?"

"Yeah." Ryan's gaze shifted to the hologram at the front of the room and automatically checked for inbound asteroids. The 3-D image remained empty, leaving them with just the single threat on the surface. "Deuterium miners use them to scale ice tunnels. Wire ladders that can be launched using $CO_2$ cartridges and industrial-strength mortar tubes. The cleats are sharp enough to embed themselves in the ice, and the ladder plays out behind. The old cleat-and-sling approach used by climbers used to take hours. Our miners can traverse the tunnels in minutes."

Ryan knew she didn't quite understand, but it didn't matter. On the monitor, the colonist shouldered the cylinder, aimed, and fired. Two metal-tipped brackets shot out and penetrated the external hull next to the transport's front hatch. Attached to the brackets were two thin cables of molecular-hardened carbon linked together by steel crosspieces: steps in a wire ladder.

Chan's hand flew to her mouth. "My God! He's going to open the door."

Ryan didn't reply. It was a game of seconds. Could Gunner and Kasim get there before he released the Four Horsemen?

"Can you signal the colonist?" Ryan asked.

Rani tried several frequencies. "He's not responding."

Ryan grimaced. He resisted the urge to call Gunner again. The engineer would be hauling ass as it was. The space veteran might not be the same person as before the uprising—dying for thirteen minutes does that to a person—but he was still one tough hombre. He knew what was at stake.

Above the transport, a canopy of stars silently watched the drama play out. A few of Jupiter's smaller moons streaked past in high orbit, silent observers at a sporting event. The air in Ops grew thicker.

"I see Gunner," Chan said.

A gray EV suit rushed into view.

"Hurry," Rani whispered.

The colonist had reached the halfway point on the ladder. Thankfully, his progress was slowed by the awkward swinging of the wires every time he took a step and the intrinsic clumsiness of the boxy space costume. It was easy to tell whoever was making this insane attempt was not well versed in using an EV suit. Ryan whispered a thanks for small miracles.

"Stop right there!" Gunner's voice shot out of the nearest speaker. Rani hastily turned down the volume.

The colonist on the ladder hesitated just beneath the door. A second later, he resumed climbing.

"Last warning," Gunner said, panting heavily through the com as he walked up to the transport. A second suit—Kasim—ran into view before dropping to one knee to catch his breath.

"If you'd be so kind as to turn around," Gunner continued. "You'll see I'm holding an industrial-strength laser, something you may recall from an attempted mutiny last year. It's not exactly pretty to look at, but it's got enough energy to flay your suit like a gutted fish. I'm giving you two seconds. One . . ."

The colonist stopped climbing. The helmet twisted slightly and Gunner stepped into his line of sight. The engineer waved the laser like a pom-pom. "Not kidding. Unless you want a closed-casket funeral, I suggest you desist and come down. Now."

The tension left Ryan's shoulders. Worst-case scenario was one more dead civilian. But the colony would live to see another day.

"My son is inside," a female voice said. "I *have* to see him."

Ryan startled. The colonist trying to break into the transport was female? A mother?

He pressed the Transmit button. "What are you talking about? The only thing we know for sure is that there were forty-five people inside that ship—forty-five corpses now. Yes, they're most likely American marines, and, yes, they probably lifted off just before the continent fell. But they could be anybody."

"My son was stationed at Quantico," she said, her sniffling tugging at his compassion. "He was on that ship."

"How can you be sure?" Ryan had a vision of a grieving mother wiping away tears as she stood over her son's grave.

"We hacked into the transport's mainframe and saw the manifest."

Ryan silently cursed. Good old Senator Lecky had brought not one, but two, transports full of marines to conquer the colony. Thank God the laser had damaged this ship before it could land and disgorge the soldiers. Battling marines from one transport had been bad enough; Ryan never would have had a chance against double the number of enemy combatants. He turned to Rani. "Could someone actually hack into the ship?"

She blinked as if processing the question. "It's possible. Although it would take a pretty competent computer wizard to do it."

Ryan grunted. The colony had no shortage of experts. He hit the com. "Everyone on the transport is dead, just like we will be if you open that door. Allowing the bacterium to spread to the moon's surface will kill us all."

"You don't know that," she said. "The germ that caused the plague could have burned itself out by now."

"I'm guessing you're a scientist," Ryan countered. "And if you are, you don't believe that. Microorganisms on Earth can survive for years in hostile environments, just waiting for an opportunity to start reproducing again."

On the monitor, he watched the grieving mother shake her head, putting up that emotional wall that prevented any truths from seeping through. "Please," she whispered. "I just want to see him." She reached up and grabbed the handle.

"Gunner!"

A flash of golden light struck the colonist's helmet. She screamed, hands flying to her head as she lost her grip and fell.

Ryan cringed. He couldn't hear the body striking the verdigris ice, but he knew the impact would be enough to break bones or worse.

"Rani, call Dr. Louis and tell him to meet Gunner in the decompression chamber. He's bringing in an injured colonist."

"Copy that." She relayed his orders to Medical and then hesitated. "The doctor wants to know if he should bring a stretcher or a body bag." The corners of her mouth twitched like she was holding back a smile.

Ryan recognized the macabre humor, a trait the young Hindu had absorbed since witnessing the pain and destruction the last year had wrought. Not to mention the death of Marco, her best friend and lover.

"He says he has a couple of patches left as well," she added. "In case there's a rip in the suit."

Ryan forced a grin. Louis, no doubt, was recalling what had happened to his own arm after a marine bullet had punched a hole in his EV suit. Not many people survived rapid decompression. If Gunner had aimed the laser at the flimsy white fabric instead of her faceplate, the resulting rapid air loss would've ended the mother's life in a few messy seconds.

"Tell the good doctor he'll be treating broken bones this time," Ryan said. Gunner used a scaled-down version of one of the rebel lasers they had confiscated after the insurrection. With any luck, the laser had only stunned the colonist and any resulting blindness would be temporary. Then again, how many photons could human retinas absorb before loss of vision became permanent?

Gunner handed the laser to Kasim before hoisting the unconscious colonist over his shoulder. Europa's gravity may have been only sixty percent of Earth's, but the veteran would be a sweaty sod by the time he entered the airlock.

Ryan heaved a sigh of relief; another catastrophe averted. He stood and stretched. Time to head back to his quarters for a much-needed shower.

The lights in Ops suddenly dimmed.

"Chan?"

"On it." Her fingers pounded the keyboard like a concert pianist. "Isolated the problem. Extractor is still online, but I'm reading zero amperage in the transmission lines."

"Damn." Ryan's brain automatically targeted the new problem. The thermal extractor consisted of a thick titanium tube that plunged deep into Europa's crust. Geothermal heat produced by the shearing effects of Jupiter's gravity became trapped in the form of pressurized water, which was converted into electricity and stored in gigantic magnesium-antimony batteries. If a seismic event had severed the electrical lines, they needed to fix it before the station's backup batteries failed.

"Put a team together . . ."

Something moved on his monitor. Ryan froze.

"Chan, pan the camera back and swivel right."

"Sir?"

"You heard me. Quickly."

The view on the monitor changed as, outside the station, the camera slowly traversed the surface. They saw more blocks of ice, some dirt on the surface and—

"Shit!" Ryan blurted. "Gunner, she's not alone!"

A second EV suit jumped out of hiding and sprinted toward the transport. The ladder next to the cockpit door beckoned like an ancient Greek siren.

Ryan noticed the difference immediately. Whoever was in that EV suit knew how to move on the surface. The strides were longer, surer, and the suit moved without wrinkling, which announced a bigger body. Probably a deuterium miner.

"Kasim!" Gunner's panic carried across the frequency. "I'm too far away. Use the laser!"

The colonist was fast. He reached the ladder in seconds and proceeded to pull himself up two rungs at a time.

"Hit him now!" Ryan hollered.

"I don't know how to fire!" Kasim protested. He sounded hesitant, almost scared, and Ryan understood why. Even during the uprising, Kasim had never killed a man. He was a talker, a politician. But if the colonist opened the door and exposed the moon to the bacterium, it would spell the end of humanity.

"Safety's off!" Gunner shouted. "Just press the damn trigger!"

The miner reached the door and struggled to get his fingers around the handle. Seemingly frustrated, he hauled back and slammed his fist against the hull. Pieces of ice flew off.

A layer of frozen moisture had formed over the body of the ship, filling the depression under the handle. Those few millimeters of ice were the only thing separating the plague from the colony. Where was Kasim?

"What's happening?" he yelled.

"Ryan." Kasim's weak voice filled the com. "I can't . . . do this. To kill someone . . ."

"Kasim." Ryan squeezed his monitor. He'd give anything to take Kasim's place on the ice, to have that laser in his hands. "You have to. There are fifteen hundred people inside these walls. Women, children. I . . . *We* are depending on you. Please. There is no choice."

Outside, the colonist struck the handle again and a large chunk of ice came free.

Ryan held his breath.

The civilian seemed to gather himself before grabbing the handle. His shoulder tensed as he adjusted his weight to haul the metal lever down. It slid out of the locked position, and Ryan dreaded the door starting to swivel . . . just as a beam of white light struck. Kasim wasn't in the frame, but by the way the laser wobbled, the governor had to be shaking like a leaf.

The colonist abruptly straightened. Ryan figured an alarm must have sounded in his helmet, some sensor detecting a sudden spike in suit temperature. He twisted his body around and noticed the laser. Hanging on to the ladder left him with only one hand to try and block the beam. It wasn't enough. His suit split just beneath the oxygen regulator. Every molecule of air escaped in the span of a single heartbeat.

Ryan closed his eyes. He could almost picture the nitrogen in the man's blood vessels boiling and a flurry of hemorrhagic strokes tearing his brain apart, along with every other organ.

He glanced at the monitor in time to see a lifeless corpse tumble off the ladder.

"Gunner?"

"Clear, Ace," the engineer replied. Then, quietly, "I'll take that laser now, Governor."

Ryan sucked in a deep breath. *Thank you, Kasim.* "Sweep the area. We don't need any more surprises."

"Aye."

Ryan closed the circuit. They both knew there would be no one else. The dead marine only had two parents.

Chan glanced over her shoulder, her expression grim. "They were willing to risk all our lives just to see their dead son?"

"That's what families do." Rani wiped her eyes. "Sometimes, that's all we have left."

Ryan's lips tightened into a thin white line. Rani's family had perished when the plague chewed a path through the Indian subcontinent. But every one of the fifteen hundred colonists on the moon had a similar story. "Maybe . . . but in my book, we just killed off another point one percent of the human population." The lights flickered again. "Rani, I need that work crew moving. Tell Gunner to leave the injured civilian with Kasim. He'll have to drag her back. Gunner's new orders are to take a team of engineers to the extractor. We need to fix whatever's wrong ASAP."

"What about the civilians, Lieutenant?" Chan asked. "Do you want me to shut down the concourse and other nonessential areas to save power?"

"No choice," Ryan said. "Medical and the greenhouses get a bye. Nothing else." A shiver crept up his spine as he recalled the last time the extractor had gone down for an extended period. They had gotten the power back barely in time to save two hundred colonists in cryo-sleep.

He gazed out the portal, where Jupiter was beginning its ascent. The conflagration of storms impersonating a planet spared them no quarter, not with the constant bombardment of radiation and frequent magnetic storms. With the Great Red Spot leading the way, Ryan had the distinct impression of a space behemoth checking in on them, silently inquiring if the colony had survived the latest calamity. He pictured the planet regarding them with a bemused look, wondering which crisis would be their last: a deadly germ, an asteroid impact, a mechanical failure . . .

"Not today," Ryan murmured. "Not while I still draw breath." Humans would not go extinct on his watch.

The planet grinned. And waited.

# CHAPTER 2

*We should feel sorrow but not sink under its oppression.*

DAY 1, 1036 HOURS

Before leaving the Command Center, Ryan slipped into his quarters to grab an extra layer of clothes. Since rationing began, the station seemed colder than usual, and he found himself shivering whenever he left Operations dressed only in his tunic and pants. Dr. Louis said it was a result of weight loss, that people required another layer of insulation to replace missing adipose tissue.

Gunner had called the doctor a hypocrite, pointing out that the medical profession had implored people to lose weight for years, and now he was advising the opposite. Louis had rolled his eyes and muttered something about low IQs.

Ryan pulled on the sweater his grandfather had given him the day he lifted off for Europa. The memory kindled nostalgic feelings that quickly faded in the face of the current crisis. He tightened his belt and tucked in the loose end that extended around his hip. Walking along the narrow corridor outside his quarters, he took a second to examine the motifs of home that lined the walls: rich, fertile valleys, gleaming cities, and inviting waterscapes. It was hard to imagine those scenic vistas now, filled with rotting corpses and empty buildings. The admiral never specified if humans were the only reservoir for the bacteria or if animal carcasses also covered the ground.

He drew back the deadbolt and shoved open the door leading into the concourse. A gust of chilly air blew in, the result of Chan taking the heating units offline. Goosebumps formed on exposed skin, and he gritted his teeth until the shock passed.

"Morning, Lieutenant." A gray-bearded man sitting at a small table next to the entrance put down his crossword puzzle. "I heard there was some excitement this morning, and I don't mean the power failure." He gestured to the few lights Chan had left on in the concourse.

Ryan grunted. No secrets on this moon. "Morning, Archie. Who was it this time, Rani or Chan?"

Archie grinned. One of the oldest colonists on the moon, he had been the senior geologist responsible for selecting the best site for a second colony. That was before the plague erased that version of a future. Now, the notion seemed absurd.

"Could have been a bit of both when we had breakfast," Archie admitted. "Or maybe it had something to do with Kasim and some colonists carrying an injured lady into Medical."

Ryan exhaled. With his thoughts focused on the damaged extractor, he had forgotten about the mother. No doubt some of the colonists would remind him, the same ones who never forgave him for his actions in quashing the rebellion.

He realized Archie was still staring, waiting for an explanation. "I had no choice. They were going to break into the quarantined transport."

"You don't have to convince me, Lieutenant. It's Rani who didn't seem happy. But that's why they pay you the big bucks."

Ryan smiled sadly. "Yeah, the big bucks." The plague had effectively erased the need for money or credits or, for that matter, any financial system. There were no items to sell, no products to buy. All that remained on the shelf was survival.

Rani was a different issue. She had come a long way from her idealistic beginnings—a civilian mutiny and the death of a lover will do that to a person—but she still harbored misgivings about his decisions, especially when they resulted in another tragedy.

"She'll come around," Archie said, as if reading his thoughts. "She always does."

The look he gave Ryan was one of understanding, and for a second, it reminded Ryan of his grandfather—his sole surviving kin after the fire—until the plague stole him away. In that instant, he understood why those parents would risk everything to see their dead son.

"You know you don't have to stand guard every day," Ryan said. "There's no one trying to break into the Command Center anymore." Unlike a year earlier, when Governor Bordeaux and his goons had tried to batter down the door.

"Begging the lieutenant's pardon, but Gunner left specific orders when he posted me here. He said under no circumstances was I to deviate from those instructions."

Ryan hesitated. Gunner had "posted" him months before. "You were in the military, right?"

"Twenty years," Archie said proudly. "Served Fleet before turning colonist."

"So, you do realize I'm the senior officer on this moon?"

"Absolutely, Lieutenant."

"And my orders supersede those of anyone else?"

"Without a doubt." The blank stare Archie gave him rivalled that of the best poker players.

"But you're still here?"

"As per Gunner's orders. That's correct."

"Did anyone try to break in this morning?"

Archie scratched his silver sideburns thoughtfully. "Not per se, Lieutenant, but a few civilians shot some angry looks my way after the injured colonist was carried in."

Ryan sighed. It was time to throw in the towel. "Well, if the temperature keeps falling, get back to your hive. At least it'll be warmer there."

"Understood, Lieutenant." Archie went back to his crossword puzzle.

Ryan shoved his hands into his pockets and trudged down the deserted concourse. He recalled the days before the plague when the wide boulevard was full of colonists: families out for a stroll, people shopping for supplies and household items, and teams of miners and workers moving through the decompression chamber. In a small colony like Europa, the concourse was a focal point of civilian life, often hosting public gatherings, parties, and even weddings. That seemed like a lifetime past. Now the stores were empty, the mining and exploration teams out of work, and no events to fill the social calendar. No one wanted to plan a party when the focus was not to starve to death.

Chan's earlier orders to abandon public areas of the station would have sent colonists scurrying into their domiciles, not that they had to be told, since power outages were getting to be a habit.

The white polymer walls lining the thoroughfare remained stained and smudged since the "incident," if you could choose a word to describe spacing five hundred colonists. Besides the graffiti that had been burned into the plastek, blood and bodily fluids left a residue that was impossible to scrub out. And the memories . . . well, they were forever embedded in the fabric of the station. Even the alternating lilac and honeysuckle shrubs had to be cut down after space had sucked the life out of them.

He passed Engineering and a number of closed shops, the entrances damaged by debris when the airlock was opened and the concourse vented to space. One of the pubs, the Event Horizon, was still used for meetings, but the supply of regular alcohol was long gone. Instead, some of the more industrious colonists, the doctor being one of them, brewed a mean moonshine.

The doors to Medical hissed open as he approached, and he exchanged pleasantries with Mabel, one of the nurses, before finding Dr. Louis at his desk, past the row of empty stretchers and large monitors that flowed out of the walls like thick tree branches. The doctor was doing the hunt-and-peck on the keyboard with his remaining hand.

"You know." Ryan slumped into a chair. "They have these wonderful new programs where you can actually dictate notes into patients' charts. I hear it saves oodles of time."

The doctor scowled over the top of his reading glasses. "Look at you, a bully and a comedian. You can rip the eyesight from a grieving mother and murder her husband, and still toss jokes around like Johnny Appleseed."

Whatever wind remained in Ryan's sails dissipated. He fumbled for the right words. "I didn't—"

"No." Louis peeled off his glasses and rubbed his eyes with the back of his hand. His tone softened. "That was wrong. I'm sorry. I just . . . I just wish you could for once stop hitting every problem with a hammer. There was no other way?"

Ryan stared at his feet. He had asked himself the same question when he returned to his quarters. "It was all I had in the moment." He looked up. "The decision was black and white."

"With you, it's always black and white," Louis snapped, an edge returning to his tone. "And for your information, I'm not dictating. I'm trying to calculate the correct synphone dose for our new patient."

"How is she?"

"I think the blindness is only temporary. But she's got four busted ribs."

"Yeah." Ryan rubbed his hands together. "Sorry about that. Does she know about her husband?"

Louis shook his head. "I'll tell her when the time is right."

Ryan wondered if there was ever a "right time" for that sort of thing. "I'm going to install a lock on the hatch of that transport, something I should've thought of months ago."

"Sure." Louis snorted. "Because getting inside that ship is the top item on everyone's Christmas list. Face it: no one could have predicted this. It was stupid and selfish."

Ryan felt the remaining guilt drain away. Once the doctor's bluster faded, his words of wisdom were a balm on Ryan's ragged emotions.

"Tell me about the extractor," Louis said. "Gunner should have arrived by now. When will you know?"

Ryan glanced at the clock on the wall. "Hopefully, in the next ten minutes."

"The longer it takes—"

"The more likely it's something vital," Ryan confirmed wearily. He didn't want to think about that possibility.

"The last time a seismic event cut the transmission line, the Neanderthal said we were down to our last spool of wire."

"It's not just the wire," Ryan said. "We're running out of everything, and what's left has passed its best-before date." The colony had suffered four power outages over the past twelve months—two in the last three weeks. The storage sheds were nearly empty, and Europa lacked the manufacturing capacity to build replacement components.

"Then I hope it's nothing vital," Louis murmured as he turned back to his screen.

It occurred to Ryan how nonchalantly they were handling another life-threatening situation, but even animals became desensitized if constantly exposed to a predator. There was only so much adrenaline in the body, and nerves could only be stimulated for so long. Truth be told, every person on the moon was living on borrowed time.

Mabel stopped by to ask the doctor to read the scan on a patient. Louis paused his calculations, brought up the SPET scan on his monitor, and gave her new orders.

"I heard about your latest batch of supplements," Ryan continued after the nurse left. "Rani said the protein tablets actually taste good, or at least better than the vitamins you've been feeding us these last six months. Some people are even gaining weight."

"Even a broken clock is right twice a day," Louis said. "But yeah, I added sugar to the manufacturing process. The pills are bigger but people can chew them now without gagging."

"Gunner will be happy," Ryan said. "He thought you were going back to an injectable form. You know how much he loves needles."

Louis laughed and rubbed the stump of his arm against his thigh.

Ryan bit the inside of his lip to hide his concern. Even after a year, the wound looked red and angry. Then again, the amputation had been a dodgy effort to save the doctor's life. No member of the surgical team carried the initials *MD* after their name.

"The problem with mankind's evolution is that we ended up omnivores," Louis explained. "We need a bunch of vitamins and minerals to survive. Lack of protein doesn't bode well long-term, especially if you're pregnant."

"Pregnant?" Ryan placed both hands on the doctor's desk as the notion sank in. He would have preferred to wrap them around a cup of coffee, but they had run out of that months before. "How many?"

"About a dozen." Louis shrugged. "Can't stop Mother Nature, especially when my stock of contraceptives has been depleted."

Ryan settled back in his chair. The colony had taken it on the chin with the collapse of civilization and the senator's attempted coup. The survivors had gone to ground, rebuilt, and recovered. Then, a few months previous, they had taken the next step. They started making babies.

"We'll need them if we're going to restore humanity," Louis reminded him.

Ryan nodded weakly. Lurching from one crisis to the next, he hadn't the luxury to think that far ahead. "I feel like the Dutch boy putting his fingers in the dike. And I'm running out of fingers."

"Better you than me." Louis waved his stump in the air.

Ryan stared at the limb too long, and Louis slipped it below the table. In that moment, Ryan felt the need to change topics. "Any other health issues I should know about?"

"Physical-health issues, no. Mental-health issues, yes. These days, I'm dealing with more anxiety and depression, insomnia and PTSD. My guess is one of these factors pushed the parents to break into the transport."

"I didn't know it had gotten this bad."

"That's because you're so focused on keeping us alive, you don't pay attention to everyone's sensibilities. That's for me and Kasim to deal with."

Ryan tilted his head. "I didn't know the governor had a medical degree."

The doctor grinned. "Shut it, smart-ass. Kasim deals with the colonists as a whole; I treat patients individually. Without us working the trenches, your role as tyrant would get a whole lot harder. Now, any other stupid questions?"

Ryan felt like a high school student about to be dismissed. Except for one thing. "Have you come up with any ideas on treating the plague?"

All humor left the doctor's expression. "The CDC tried hundreds of antibiotic candidates. The problem is the plague changes the surface proteins at a prodigious rate. By the time they narrowed down the search to the right antibiotic, the germ had changed markers and the bacteria was unrecognizable to the drug."

"So, all that's left is a vaccine?"

"Unfortunately, yes." Louis's expression hardened. "I've read all the info the admiral sent in his last transmission, including the results of the initial trials."

"You said they didn't go well."

"That's one way to put it. The main issue was growing it in the lab. The damn thing seems to have multiple routes of spread, including airborne. And without basic containment, no way doctors could work on a vaccine. It took them weeks to learn how to create a safe environment. By then, the plague had spread across the globe."

Ryan scratched his cheek. Louis had talked about this before. Something about the unusual properties of the bacterium. "And without inactivating it . . ."

Louis's eyes twinkled like he knew Ryan was struggling. ". . . you can't create a vaccine. Doctors need a stable source of bacteria to experiment on."

"And you can't continue their research?"

Louis jerked a thumb toward the imaging machines along the wall, the SPET, ultrasound, and MRI. "I don't have the right equipment. This place was designed to treat people, not conduct lab experiments. I can tinker, but the time frame to accomplish anything significant is probably measured in years."

Ryan started to give him a snippy reply when Gunner's voice gushed out of the wall-mounted speaker. "Lieutenant, we found the problem."

Ryan opened a channel. "Go ahead."

"Looks like a section of surface ice collapsed into a subterranean cave. It ripped one of the lines off the transformer."

Ryan suddenly felt it hard to breathe. The doctor looked afraid to speak.

"How many feet did we lose?"

"Just finished measuring," Gunner replied. "Forty-seven feet exactly."

Ryan dreaded asking the next question. "How much do we have left in stores?"

"I asked Chan to check." Static invaded the frequency as Jupiter's radiation decided to play with communications. "She said forty . . . feet . . ."

A wave of frustration swept over Ryan, mirrored in the doctor's expression. "Say again, Gunner. Your transmission broke up. How many feet do we have left?"

They heard nothing but static for a few seconds, seconds that bled into an eternity. Without enough wire, they couldn't transmit power. Without power, they would either freeze to death in the next few days or asphyxiate when the oxygen ran out. Louis's red face looked ready to explode.

Finally, the frequency cleared. ". . . forty-nine feet," Gunner said. "Not an inch more."

Ryan didn't realize his thighs had started to cramp until he fell back into his seat.

Louis sagged like a child's blow-up toy with a slow leak.

"That's it, then," Ryan said. "There's nothing left for next time."

"Damn," Louis said, thoughtful. "And I was beginning to like you."

# CHAPTER 3

*The true man does not preach what he practices till he has practiced what he preaches.*

DAY 2, 0900 HOURS

Ryan wrapped his hands around the mug of tea in the briefing room and savored the warm sensation. It was nice to feel his fingers again. That, combined with a noticeable lack of chill in the air, meant the outlook had improved considerably since yesterday. With the extractor back to pumping energy into the colony, room temperature had passed "survival mode" and was improving by the hour. Gunner and the civilian engineers had completed installation of the new wire last night, and Chan's work crew had toiled through the wee hours of the morning, slowly increasing the amperage.

It was fortuitous they had enough wire left to replace what the ice had consumed. And, even better, one of the engineers had found a crate of English tea hidden in the back of the storage shed. Probably smuggled in by the old civilian Board. Now, for a few weeks anyway, they could enjoy not just a cup of tea but good-quality English tea.

Ryan leaned over and sniffed the aroma as Rani and Chan entered carrying their customary water bottles. Since rationing began, every colonist sipped water during the day in an attempt to dull the sharp edge of hunger. There wasn't a person on the moon who hadn't experienced that gnawing ache at night—not since Earth's transports stopped flying and meals were reduced to what they could produce in the colony's greenhouses. Combined with Dr. Louis's supplements, it was barely enough to keep them alive. Ryan would still give his left arm for a steak. Just the thought of a tender piece of meat smothered in mushrooms and onions set his mouth watering.

He waved them to a seat around the white plastek table. "Status on the power level?"

"Eighty percent," Chan replied. "Increasing five percent per hour."

"I initiated the laser," Rani reported. "It'll take three days to recharge."

Ryan sipped his tea and nodded. Just like every other time they lost power. If an incoming asteroid appeared on their radar, all they could do was throw harsh words at it.

He ran his gaze over both women. Just like his conversation with Louis yesterday, neither looked especially choked up about the potentially dire situation. Then again, every human on Europa had lived with the sword of Damocles hanging over their heads for months. At times, Ryan wondered if losing the survival game would actually be a blessing.

Chan took a deep gulp of her water and rubbed her tired eyes. The petite Asian pilot had stepped into Marco's role after the ensign was killed in the uprising. Nobody expected her to replace the talented engineer—no one in the colony had Marco's skills—but she was a quick study. Plus, her background in aerodynamics and years of flying transports gave her a solid foundation.

"How's the training going with our baby pilots?" Ryan asked.

Chan's pleasant visage slipped. "Measured. There's only so much I can do in the classroom. To learn how to fly, you have to sit in the pilot's chair. At least at some point. Rani found an old transport-simulator program, but it can't replicate the real thing."

Ryan glanced out the portal at the far end of the room. With Jupiter setting and the sun a pale dot in the distance, the ice plates appeared dusty gray. After the failed coup, he'd been left with a small fleet of ships: five transports. Six, if they included the infected ship. But only one pilot. If they were ever going to try for the home run and fly colonists back to Earth, they needed to train more pilots. Rani had suggested surveying the colonists, and lo and behold, they discovered two hobby pilots, one of whom was an engineer. At Ryan's request, Chan had started instructing them on the fundamentals of spaceflight, but it was like teaching calculus to kindergarten kids. *Slow* didn't come close to describing the process.

Rani tapped a finger on the table. "You thinking about a plan? To go back?"

"You know we can't," Ryan said. "It's simply not an option." Unless a colony-ending crisis made filling one transport his only option, and he had to pick forty souls to send back to Earth in a final gamble to save humanity.

Chan leaned back. Like everyone else, she had lost weight, but the change was more noticeable because she had been on the pudgy side to begin with. Her thick, black hair had thinned and turned wispy, as though it would blow off her head in the slightest breeze.

"I think you're planning something," Rani continued, waiting until his gaze met hers. "You got that look."

Ryan felt his cheeks flush. In their darkest hour, when the colony's survival balanced on a knife's edge, they had formed a connection. Not a bond in the fraternal sense but rather, in that moment, they had peered into each other's souls.

"We've run out of replacement wire," he said. "And that's not all we need . . ."

The door swished open. Kasim entered wearing a wool sweater over his thawb and had a New York Yankees baseball cap pulled down over his ears. The governor made a beeline for the teapot and poured himself a cup before blowing into his palms. "Damn, it's cold." His gaze found Rani. "How long until the temperature rises above ice-cube stage?"

Rani laughed. "You've been on Europa long enough. I thought you'd be used to it by now."

He slipped into a chair opposite Ryan. "I grew up in Lebanon. The word cold was not in our vocabulary."

Ryan tapped the table thoughtfully. "What's the word among the colonists? Any talk after the transport incident?"

Kasim frowned. "Most are shrugging it off, seeing it as the actions of some desperate parents. At supper last night, a few blamed you for not finding another way to defuse the situation . . ." Chan snorted but Kasim ignored her. "People are just plain tired. Everyone's been fighting this battle for a long time. Emotionally, physically, they haven't got much more to give."

Ryan exchanged a look with Louis, echoes of their last conversation in his head. "At least they still trust you, Kasim. I think that's one of the reasons we've made it this far."

The governor shrugged. He pulled something out of his pocket and slid it across the table. "One of the colonists found it in the back of the storage shed. Must've fallen off the pallets and got wedged in the floor."

Ryan picked up the envelope stamped with the official Fleet symbol and the transport's name. Phoenix. The same transport he was supposed to board after being ordered home by Captain Tracy, days before Fleet shut down and Earth entered palliative care. Which meant whatever this was had been shipped from a time before the plague. Before the universe turned upside down.

He ripped open the seal, and a pic-vid slid into his palm.

Rani leaned over the table. "What is it?"

Ryan turned it over in his hand, a queasy feeling forming in his gut. "It's private correspondence from Earth, from families to colonists." Back when there were families on Earth.

Chan tilted her head quizzically. "I thought each colonist was allocated a certain amount of transmission time each month."

"And they used every second of it," Kasim replied. "But this is different."

"How so?"

The governor shot Ryan a look. "It contains information that families didn't want broadcast on a common channel. Think deaths, divorces, and all manner of personal information that nobody wants heard or hacked. Plus, they could send large files like wills and settlements."

"What are you going to do with it, Lieutenant?" Rani asked.

Ryan fingered the small cartridge. He could release it to the colonists and damn the consequences, or he could pretend it was damaged and unusable, and no one would see it.

"People have a right to know," she continued, looking to Kasim for support.

The governor frowned. "Don't know if I agree, young lady. Spreading bad news at a time like this . . . well, it's never a good thing."

"How do you know it's bad news?" Chan asked. "We can't guess what families send to each other."

"Yes, we can," Ryan said. "People like to broadcast good news to the world. It's the bad stuff that shows up in the mail."

Chan leaned forward, placing her chin in her hands as Ryan's words sank in. No one argued. Even Rani seemed taken aback.

Ryan put the pic-vid in his pocket. "I'll hold on to it for now. We've got more pressing problems at the moment."

As if on cue, Gunner and a young colonist walked into the room. The veteran's face was red and his words angry. ". . . I don't care if the wire is made in Kansas. It can't handle the current!" He ran a hand through his beard and fell into a chair at the table. The girl who followed looked about fifteen, with a pixie face and pigtails.

She sat next to him and wagged her finger in his face. "Stop being so obstinate. Look at the numbers. If we solder the wires and layer them with insulation . . ."

Ryan cleared his throat. "Sorry to interrupt another one of your arguments, but I want to get this meeting started."

"The old fart is being stubborn again," the girl snapped, pointing her finger at the culprit. "He's thick-headed and old-fashioned and won't listen to reason."

"Yes, we know, Sasha," Ryan replied with a brief smile. "But we like him anyway."

"Speak for yourself," Louis said, entering the room on the heels of the last two. "In fact, I'd love to take a poll among the colonists on that very issue."

"Who invited the vet to this meeting?" Gunner growled deep in his throat. "Don't you have some dogs to put down?"

Louis grinned in Gunner's general direction, but it was clear his words were meant for everyone. "Not dogs exactly, but I do have leftover booster shots to hand out. Know anyone who needs to get punctured by some dull and rusty needles?"

Gunner blanched, and Sasha giggled at his consternation.

Ryan rubbed his tired eyes. Sasha might have looked like a rebellious fifteen-year-old, but she was actually ten years older with a dual master's in mechanical engineering and material design. She had arrived on Europa on a transport several weeks before the world went to hell. Sometime, over the last few months, she and Gunner had become a team.

"All right." Ryan focused everyone's attention by tapping his cup. "Let's get started. I called this meeting because it's time we made some decisions—decisions I've been delaying too long."

"I'm not sure about the we part," Kasim said with a wry smile. "As far as I know, there's been a certain dictator in charge for the past year."

Gunner harrumphed. Even Chan chuckled.

"So." Rani stared. "You do have a plan."

Ryan shrugged.

"Don't be modest, Lieutenant," Louis interjected, a veneer of sarcasm coating his words. "It's not like you haven't surprised us before."

The unspoken reference to Ryan's actions in quelling the rebellion hung in the air.

Ryan refused to take the bait. He spread his hands, palms down, on the table. The condensation from the warm mug left a residue on the plastek surface. "Okay, let's cut through the bullshit. We're practically out of replacement parts. Even normal maintenance is being compromised, which means accidents and system failures aren't far behind. It's long past time I made a decision."

Rani leaned back. "You're going to use the transport."

"The transport?" Sasha's eyes widened. She looked at Gunner. "To where? Earth?"

"Don't be daft," the veteran said. "Earth's too far. It's got to be closer."

"What about Mars?" Kasim asked. Ryan noticed the governor's hands stop shaking when he wrapped them around his tea. "It's closer, and they have unlimited supplies."

"Not an option." Louis flashed Kasim a mournful smile. "Our glorious leader convinced you to shoot a man for trying to break into an infected transport. Last thing he wants is to land on an infected planet."

At the mention of what had happened a day before, Kasim paled and dropped his gaze.

Louis put a hand on his arm. "I'm sorry, my friend. I only meant to point out . . ."

The governor shrugged off his hand. "I know what you meant. But it was still my choice to pull the trigger."

Ryan surveyed the grim faces at the table. Nobody wanted to be reminded of the terrible deeds they undertook in the name of survival. Louis caught Ryan's eye and gave him a subtle nod. A small weight fell from his shoulders.

"The asteroids," he said, slicing through the dour mood. "In his last broadcast, the admiral said that when food ran out, the smaller colonies opened their EV doors to end the suffering. They should have the replacement parts we need, and the plague never arrived on their shores. That we know of, anyway. I'm going to take a team and get us those parts."

"Yeah, that's it." Gunner combed his beard with his hand. "The asteroids. Good thinking. They should have most of what we need, and we can cannibalize their primary systems for parts."

"Like transmission wire?" Chan asked.

"Not just that," Rani said, her gaze falling on Sasha and Gunner. "Don't forget about computer modules and mechanical pieces."

The veteran nodded.

Sasha tapped her chin thoughtfully. "The parts we need take up a lot of space." She raised her eyebrows at Ryan. "How do you propose we carry it all back?"

Ryan took a sip of tea to hide his smile. Sasha was bright. His hesitation allowed others to perform their own mental calculations.

"She's got a point," Gunner said, causing Sasha's jaw to drop in surprise. "Even a cargo transport wouldn't have enough storage."

Kasim glanced between Ryan and Gunner. "So, what do we do?"

Louis straightened in his chair. "Two transports. The lieutenant wants to double the carrying capacity."

"Two ships?" Chan asked, looking to Ryan for confirmation. "But, sir, none of them have flown in over a year. God knows what shape Churchill and Atlantis are in since they've been exposed to the elements on the surface. Serenity, Justice, and Phoenix may have been in the hangar, but none of them have had any regular maintenance since they landed."

"Then I suggest you start prepping them," Ryan replied coldly. "Because conjunction between Jupiter and the asteroid colonies occurs in nine weeks. Which means we have to launch in three."

"Impossible," Rani said. "We only have one pilot. Wouldn't it be better to remove most of the cryo-pods from one ship to make room?"

"I ran the numbers," Ryan said. "Even after removing the unused pods, we still need two transports to handle all the gear."

Kasim glanced along the table. "Then how—"

"We pick one of the trainees," Ryan replied before turning to face a stunned-looking Chan. "You said they needed hands-on training. Here's your chance."

"Uh." She struggled to come out of her stupor. "The operative word is training. Neither are remotely close to being able to land or launch a Fleet transport."

Ryan's expression didn't change. "Then I suggest you alter your training schedule. It's roughly a six-week trip, and whoever you pick to pilot the second ship has to be ready."

Chan fell back in her seat as if shot. Her lips moved, but no words emerged.

"How long do ya figure we'll be stayin'?" Gunner asked.

"Not long," Ryan replied. "The plan is to get in, grab what we need, and get out." He shifted his gaze down the table. "Rani, I want you to put together a complete list of what the colony needs. Prioritize the important pieces and make sure everything can fit."

She gritted her teeth. "You're taking two ships?"

"We're taking two ships. I'll rely on Chan to pick the best ones."

"You don't want me to put that list together, Ace?" Gunner said.

"I would," Ryan replied. "Except you're going to be too busy turning some deuterium miners into reservists."

"You're bringing hired help?" Kasim asked.

"We need the muscle. Hired guns to rip apart bulkheads, tear open walls, that sort of thing."

"I thought Neanderthals were bred for that reason," Louis quipped behind his tea.

"We'll need at least four," Gunner said, ignoring the doctor. "And with your timeline, we'll have to shorten the training. It'll take them a week just to learn how to handle the lasers."

"Sounds good," Ryan said. Nobody commented on what had happened to the former reservists during the uprising. Each of the colonists who volunteered to support the military had been killed fighting the rebels. He focused on Sasha. "Do you think you could help Rani? She knows what we need right now, but you can predict what's likely to fail going forward."

Sasha threw a smug look at Gunner. "See, somebody here respects my opinion."

Gunner growled something under his breath.

"What about medical supplies?" Louis asked. "I'm short on everything from antibiotics to analgesics. Do you want me to put together a wish list?"

"Actually, Doctor, I don't," Ryan said.

Louis hesitated. "May I inquire as to why?"

Kasim snorted. "Because you're going with them." He arched an eyebrow at Ryan. "You sure it's wise to take our only physician?"

Ryan's jaw tightened. He didn't like it either. "It's not my first choice, but the fact is we're going to need him more than the colonists. Right now, we're dealing with malnutrition and vitamin deficiencies. The nurses know how to treat that. When the colonies opened their EV doors, sudden decompression would have torn rooms and bulkheads apart. I expect accidents and injuries to occur among the group I bring to the asteroids."

Louis looked like he wanted to argue, but Ryan had sapped the logic from his words. The doctor stared at the table. "I hate cryo-sleep," he muttered.

Ryan touched his fingers as he counted off. "Four reservists, one MD, two engineers"—his gaze landed on Gunner and Sasha—"two pilots. And me." He paused to mentally check his math. "Ten passengers and crew. Two transports."

"Hold it." Rani stared at him. "What am I doing?"

"You're staying," Ryan said, his tone hardening. "You know how the station works and how to fix what's broke. I'm trusting you to keep the power flowing, the laser functioning, and the rest of the systems online until we get back. To help you, I'm conscripting Archie and Solomon, one of the deuterium miners, to be your right-hand men."

She didn't look pleased as she folded her hands on the table.

"What about me?" Kasim asked. "I can help."

"Your job is to keep the colonists in a positive frame of mind," Ryan said. "Up till now, they've been surviving but not living. They need a purpose. To help you find that purpose, I'm suspending martial law."

"What?" Kasim came halfway out of his seat. "You're going to allow civilians to run the colony?" He looked at Gunner. "Is that wise?"

"Not somethin' I'd recommend."

Ryan grinned coldly. After being burned by the previous Board, he had kept the colony under his thumb. None of the civilians liked it, but they were still alive. "Call it a dry run. If we ever bring back democracy."

Kasim hesitated as the full impact sank in. "I don't . . . know if I can do that. Right now, I'm just following orders. I don't give them."

"You'll have to make an example of someone to set the tone," Ryan acknowledged. "The colonists have to be reminded that, no matter who's in charge, mistakes will not be tolerated. Or selfish acts." Like trying to break into an infected transport.

"You're such a hard-ass," Louis muttered, loud enough to be heard.

Kasim looked confused. "What do you mean, an example?"

"The mother," Louis said, tapping the table with his fingers. "The lieutenant wants you to be judge, jury, and executioner for our latest prisoner." He met Ryan's unflinching gaze. "He wants you to be the bad guy."

"Don't you think she suffered enough?" Rani said. It seemed less a question than a statement.

"She damn near killed us all," Gunner reminded them.

"And paid her pound of flesh," Rani said. "She lost a son and a husband."

Sasha glanced between Ryan and Kasim, lines forming on her forehead. Louis kept tapping the table. Chan looked like she wanted to disappear. The tension in the room rose with each passing second. No one spoke.

Outside the portal, Ganymede flew past, a dirty snowball staining the night sky.

"I'll do it," Kasim said, jaw set. He leveled his gaze at Ryan. "Eight weeks in the brig and three-quarter rations."

Ryan started to argue that the penalty was too soft when something in Louis's eyes warned him off. He let out a breath and waited for his thoughts to catch up to his emotions. The doctor was right. Baby steps. Everyone needed to take baby steps. The new brig they had constructed in the transport hangar was akin to solitary confinement and served as a warning to any colonist tempted to break Ryan's rules.

"Very well. Kasim, you'll announce the sentencing tomorrow on the colony net. Dr. Louis, I'll leave it up to you when she can safely leave Medical to serve her sentence."

Louis managed a single nod.

"Three weeks," Ryan continued. "We have to be ready to launch by then." He stood to close the meeting when Gunner raised his hand.

"All good, Ace," the veteran said. "Except for one thing."

"What's that?"

"Our destination. There are a dozen colonies on those rocks. Where are we going?"

Ryan smiled. "Ceres. Pack your bags. We're visiting the largest colony in the Belt."

# CHAPTER 4

*To see and listen to the wicked is already the beginning of wickedness.*

DAY 6, 1930 HOURS

Ryan undid the clips on his wrist before twisting both metal clamps counterclockwise. The joints came apart like LEGO pieces, and he placed the gloves next to his helmet on the aluminum shelf. A petrochemical smell hung heavy in the cool air of the transport hangar. He glanced up at the three behemoths holding court in the cavernous room: *Serenity*, *Justice,* and *Phoenix*. None of the Fleet transports had been started in over a year, and yet the smell of hydrocarbons and creosol hadn't diminished. Chan and her trainees were scheduled to start diagnostics tomorrow in preparation for launch. The petite aviator was going to pilot *Phoenix* while one of the newbie pilots would tackle *Serenity*.

Chan had yet to decide which of the colonists was less apt to get them killed. Despite both vessels being under her strict supervision, Ryan knew which transport he wanted to be on.

He eased out of his EV suit and propped it against the wall. Unlike the decompression chamber in the station, there were no hooks or lockers to properly store individual pieces. Not that he was going to be there long. He pulled two half-frozen beers from his backpack—the result of his ten-minute trek from the station to the transport hangar—before unlocking the door and pulling back the deadbolt. He wondered why Gunner even bothered with a lock. It wasn't like the prisoner could suddenly walk out of the hangar, cross the ice field, and enter the station. Not without a suit. Not in near-vacuum.

The woman sitting on the edge of her bed offered him a smile. "I wasn't sure you were going to come." Sybil wore a slim, pale blue jumper with the top buttons undone. She had tied her blond hair into two long braids that ran down her back. The suggestion of gray roots betrayed her age.

"Why?" Ryan placed the beers on the desk, pulled out the sliding chair from the corner, and sat down. "Am I late?"

She watched him twist off the caps and pour the beer into two coffee mugs. "No, you've never been late. Every Wednesday, nine PM like clockwork. I just thought that maybe the pending mission had upset our schedule."

Ryan chuckled. "Still no secrets on this moon, I see." He stomped out a spark of anger. Even the colonists had found out prior to the official announcement. "Louis or Rani?"

Sybil smiled mysteriously. "If a girl confessed all her secrets, no one would visit her."

"No one is supposed to visit you," Ryan said.

She leaned forward, chin falling into an open palm, exposing a not-so-modest amount of cleavage. "Just you on our date nights?"

"Is that what you call them?"

Except for a brief flash behind her eyes, her expression didn't change. "I remember when our dates were more . . . intimate."

Ryan felt his cheeks glow. He remembered too well.

"It could be that way again." Her gaze flickered to the bed.

Ryan squirmed, spilling beer over her desk. He took a swig. "Not likely, since you're a prisoner and I'm running the colony."

She leaned back. "Dr. Louis says I've suffered enough. He forgives me."

"Yeah, well, Gunner still thinks I should space you and be done with it."

"Tell me something I don't know." She sniffed. "I hear there's a petition circulating that would insist you end my incarceration."

"Really?" Ryan put down his beer. "I wonder what Rani would say about that."

Sybil looked away, and Ryan chalked one up in the win column. Rani's lover, Marco, died in the uprising, killed by colonists who sold their souls to work with Sybil's father, Senator Lecky.

"I haven't asked," she admitted.

Ryan savored the moment. Unfortunately, it did little to extinguish his lingering anger. "Rani drops your food off every day for a year, and you haven't discussed it?" He wasn't sure, but something in her character just revealed itself.

She shrugged and took her first sip of beer. A hard smile formed, like she was forcing it. "An IPA. My favorite. I thought we were out."

"We are. I was keeping these two for a special occasion."

She folded her arms across her chest. "You're leaving on the Ceres mission?"

"In two weeks. Barring any problems, we should be back in a few months."

"Problems like faulty math that would have you heading for Mars by mistake, or plow into an unmapped asteroid, or get fried by a solar flare?"

"You left out mechanical failure," Ryan said. "Or a radiation leak, or maybe there are no supplies waiting for us on the asteroid and we'll return empty-handed. Which means we'll freeze to death when the extractor goes down again."

Her eyes twinkled. "I was getting to those. For now, let's just agree that the odds of you and me seeing each other again lie somewhere between low and nonexistent."

"Rani pegged mission success at ten percent. Chan says that's optimistic."

The prisoner ran a finger around the lip of her cup before taking another sip. She seemed to savor the hoppy taste, giving Ryan a chance to survey the brig. Sybil kept her cell cozy and neat: a single bed, portable toilet, computer, desk and chair. All enclosed inside four titanium walls.

A moment of silence passed.

"I did apologize to Dr. Louis," Sybil said, her voice low. "I . . . I just can't talk to Rani."

"They loved each other," Ryan said. "Eight hundred thousand kilometers from home, those two nerds ended up together. Before they were torn apart." He waited until she met his gaze. "What you did was wrong."

She hesitated. "Which part? His death or the rebellion?"

"Both. We were on the brink—we still are—and your father's greed and ambition nearly pushed us over the edge."

"And for that, you killed him." Sybil's tone was flat, emotionless, making Ryan wonder if she had come to grips with his actions.

"I killed him and his marines before they killed me."

She sniffed. "You don't understand, Ryan. He was my father! My idol. When he told me his was the only way forward, I believed him. In the halls of power, he was never wrong." A sob broke through, and her shoulders trembled. "I'm sorry. Oh, my God, I'm so sorry." Tears rolled down her cheeks.

Ryan didn't move. Didn't trust himself. In his mind, anger and forgiveness battled for dominance. He realized he still harbored feelings for her, and that was partially the source of his pain. But was she playing him again? Like she had in the uprising? He watched for any sign, any clue to tell him what side she was coming down on . . . but his emotions continued to flounder.

After a moment, she reached over and squeezed his hand before pulling back. "Thank you for the beer."

"You're welcome."

She straightened her uniform and looked about to end their "date" when she hesitated. "There was one thing."

"What's that?"

She wiped her eyes with the back of her sleeve. "I don't think you know this, but I spent six months on Ceres before shipping out to Europa."

Ryan stopped with his beer halfway to his lips. "You lived on the asteroid? Doing what?"

"Managing my father's import/export business. He had a factory on Ceres that supplied the colonists with everything from computer processors to nail guns."

Ryan slowly put his beer down on the table. "Well, isn't that interesting?"

*Day 14, 1800 Hours*

Rani didn't realize Chan was speaking until the pilot reached over and tapped her on the shoulder.

"What?" Rani jerked her mind into the present. It took a second to remember she was sitting in her coms chair in Ops, purportedly running diagnostics on the subsystems.

Chan smiled. "I asked if you wanted to grab a drink when we finished, but that's before I realized you were daydreaming."

"Sorry. I was thinking . . ."

"About switching seats?" Chan's gaze shifted to the command chair behind them. "Maybe worried about filling a pair of big shoes?"

Rani's cheeks burned. She tapped her chest in a mea culpa. "Guilty as charged. Truth be told, I'm scared shitless. I'll be the first to admit I'm not his biggest fan, but I prefer it when he's the one giving orders."

"Stand in line, girl. We all feel the same."

Rani's brow furled. "I'm not following."

"It's easy." Chan leaned back and nearly disappeared in Marco's old chair. "Letting the lieutenant make the hard decisions spares us a boatload of guilt. We can wail and protest and blame him for the cruelty and violence. After all, we're just following orders, right?"

"Not sure I agree . . ."

Chan grinned. "There you go, denying it. But the truth of the matter runs deeper. Taking him from that chair removes a buffer that separates us from the gory underside of humanity. Whether it involves shooting a grieving mother or putting her in the brig, you won't be able to scrub the stain from your soul."

"Jesus, Chan. What are you, some kind of sadistic counselor?"

The pilot shrugged. "I was with him when he fought the marines on the surface. Watched him smash the faceplate on one of the bastards before shooting out the transport's window and killing a dozen more. He didn't hesitate."

"It was a battle between good and evil," Rani said, sensing she was losing the argument and not liking what it said about herself.

"It was." All humor left Chan's expression. "But it was also a battle for survival, and Braeder showed his primal instincts were stronger than theirs. Thank God."

A moment of silence passed before she realized Chan was waiting on her. "I don't know if I can do it." She bit her tongue when she realized her true feelings had just slipped out.

The pilot nodded.

"I mean, I'm not trained for this. I'm a bloody specialist. Marco would have been better . . ." She trailed off, her gaze dropping to the ring on her finger. A tear formed and she angrily brushed it away.

Chan reached over and placed her hand on Rani's shoulder. Rani almost shrugged it off, embarrassed like a teenager caught in a lie.

"You think you have it tough?" Chan said in a low, halting voice. "Braeder wants me to fly two ships at once."

Rani sniffed. "You'll have a pilot on the other stick."

Chan snorted and pulled her hand back. "Yeah, some dipshit engineer who I'm supposed to help lose his cherry. What does that make me?"

Rani couldn't help it, she laughed. It felt like a needed catharsis. "He's bad?"

"Come on." Chan shook her head derisively. "You've watched the training. Both of them are shit. Braeder called for anyone with flying experience, and those dumbasses raised their hands." She cursed under her breath. It sounded like Mandarin. "Flying? Really? Flying's got nothing to do with transports. I mean, look at *Churchill* and *Atlantis* on the runway." She flung her hand toward the front portals. "Do you see any atmosphere out there? We don't use rudders and ailerons for a reason. Braeder expects me to work miracles!"

Still chuckling, Rani waved her down. "Easy. You'll give yourself a stroke."

Chan folded her arms across her chest and fumed. "Goddamned dirt-pounders."

"You're a good pilot. That's why Braeder expects you to work miracles."

Chan looked up, hopeful. "You think? 'Cause he never says much at the best of times. Not sure what goes through his head."

"He told me. But you're right; the man doesn't give compliments easily. I think he knows you can handle it."

Chan's gaze flickered to the transport on the other side of the runway, the infected ship that was off-limits. "Maybe you're right. That's probably why you'll be sitting in the command chair."

Rani's first instinct was to deflect, but the hypocrisy slammed her in the face. She blinked and found Chan staring at her.

"This *surviving* thing is a bitch," the pilot said.

"Yeah." Anger tugged at the corner of Rani's lips. "But you're taking *her* with you."

Chan's eyes narrowed at the pronoun. Neither of them wanted to mention Sybil by name. "Maybe we can arrange an accident. They tend to happen in space."

"They do." None of them liked the senator's daughter, especially after she had played on Braeder's heartstrings and left him dangling in the wind. "Try not to leave any evidence."

Chan snorted. "Good luck finding a body."

They laughed and exchanged a high-five.

"Keep this moon safe and boring until we return," Chan said.

"Right back at you," Rani replied. "Get the replacement parts and return ASAP. And ignore Gunner when he gets into one of his moods."

"Pssst." Chan waved a hand. "Me and him got an understanding."

"How's that?"

"Until he can swear better than me, he's not allowed to piss me off."

Rani chuckled. She bent forward and shut down diagnostics.

Chan raised an eyebrow. "We done?"

"Yeah, I just made my first executive decision."

"Which is?"

"You said it earlier. It's time to have a drink."

*Day 20, 1015 Hours*

Ryan watched Sasha leave Engineering before turning to Gunner. "I think she likes you."

The veteran shrugged and went back to checking readouts on the terminal. "She says I remind her of her father."

"Really?" Ryan tilted his head. He hadn't expected that and had a hard time picturing Gunner as a father figure. "Because he was an engineer like yourself?"

"No, because I'm stubborn and grouchy. And she never got along with him, either."

Ryan guffawed. "Well, I see she's got you pegged."

"She's a pain in the ass," Gunner muttered. "Especially with her opinions."

"Only with you." Ryan's smile widened. "She gets along with everyone else. Most of us have been wondering what the connection is."

Gunner stopped entering commands. "Her father served with me in Special Forces."

Puzzle pieces fell together in Ryan's mind. "Did she know that when she arrived on the colony?"

He shook his head. "We ran into each other after the insurrection. Pure happenstance."

"And she hasn't left your side since," Ryan observed. "She's your new best friend."

"Her father was a stand-up guy," Gunner said in a low voice. "Saved my life more than once."

Ryan's smile vanished. "Then her father would be happy to know she's in good hands."

A moment of silence passed before Gunner turned around. "Do you think we need to bring her, Ace? It'll be safer here."

"Sorry, Gunner. Marco may have been the best engineer on the moon, but she's a close second. I'll need her expertise finding replacement parts. Don't worry; I won't put her in harm's way. If anything comes up, that'll be your job."

A wry smile lit Gunner's face. "So, no different from last year."

Ryan checked the computer program. Diagnostics always took the better part of an hour. Thankfully, no errors this time. "Are the transports prepped?"

"Prepped and ready for launch, although Chan is still bitching about the new pilot. She says he's not ready."

"The computer program has been installed," Ryan pointed out. "The guy won't have to touch a button."

"It's not the launch," Gunner said. "It's the landing that's scaring the shit out of her."

Ryan's jaw tightened. They had trained the new pilot, Stoll, for three weeks. There was nothing else Chan could do. Except ditch the second transport. Unfortunately, they really needed that ship.

"You still leaving Kasim in charge?" Gunner asked. "Not sure he's got the gonads to make hard decisions if something happens."

"Rani will step in if need be," Ryan said as the computer chimed its completion. "The military still oversees security issues like the laser and this." He spread his arms to indicate the engineering space.

"It's too much work for one person," Gunner said.

"I've identified civilians who can pitch in. Archie is going to act as her second-in-command until we get back."

Gunner nodded. Everyone liked the geologist, and he had years of experience in the colonies. "Still would have liked to leave more of a military presence on the moon. I don't trust the civilians to toe the line while we're gone."

It was Ryan's turn to shrug. "We have to return to democratic rule, with all its warts and blemishes. Plus, I killed all the malcontents last year." The last was said with a grimace.

Gunner flashed him a stern look. "The bastards deserved what they got, and you know it. What you did was save fifteen hundred decent people. Anyone says different and I'll shoot them myself. You made the right choice then and you're doing it now. So, stop brooding. It's time to step up."

The weight sitting on Ryan's shoulders lessened a smidgen, and he forced a grin. "You say the sweetest things. Don't let anyone ever say you don't have a great bedside manner."

Gunner's brow furrowed in confusion.

Ryan ignored the look. "Any loose ends we have to tie off?"

"Nothing I can think of." The veteran closed the program on his terminal. "Maintenance is caught up. Laser and extractor online. Greenhouses are almost ready for harvest. I added extra supplies to the transport for the additional passenger." He paused. "Are you sure it's a good idea? I don't trust her."

Ryan nodded. "I'll take any advantage I can get. She spent time on that rock, which should translate into less time searching for parts. And returning to Europa quicker. The risk is worth it."

"Weeds keep popping up until you tear out the roots," Gunner said.

"I'm not spacing her. I told you that a year ago."

"She bears full responsibility for what happened," Gunner reminded him. He didn't make eye contact.

"I know. It's just . . . there's been so much death. Ask the doc. He'll say there are better ways to handle these things."

"What does the vet know?" Gunner snapped. "He's barely fired a gun."

Ryan didn't reply. The doctor and several reservists had tried to help when the senator's marines had him pinned on the surface. It cost the reservists their lives and Louis his arm. The weight on his shoulders doubled.

"If you left me behind, I'd make a few decisions," Gunner muttered.

"That's one of the reasons you're coming with me," Ryan said, a smile leaking past his guilt. "God knows the colony would never survive you."

When Ryan walked into Ops, Kasim stood staring out the starboard portal, arms behind his back. Jupiter was beginning its descent over the horizon, and the surface ice reflected a palette of deep purple and blue.

"Thanks for coming on short notice," Ryan said, sitting in his chair.

Kasim turned. "I remember the last time you asked me to sneak into the Command Center unannounced. I was more nervous then."

Ryan recalled those anxious days before the insurrection when Kasim served as their eyes and ears inside the enemy camp. The man had ventured well outside his comfort zone and nearly got himself killed. "This time, I don't mean to put you in harm's way."

Kasim exhaled and took a seat at Rani's terminal. He removed his baseball cap and placed it on the console. "Small miracles. Since the transports are prepped for liftoff tomorrow, I can only assume you want to discuss my role while you're gone."

"You are the governor," Ryan pointed out.

"In name only. You make all the decisions."

Ryan threw up his hands. "I suspended martial law. What else do you want?"

"Relax." Kasim grinned. "I'm jerking your chain."

"Idiot." Ryan gave him the finger.

His friend chuckled and reached inside his thawb to remove a small bottle. He produced two shot glasses and poured an ounce of an amber-colored liquid into each before sliding one across the table.

Ryan picked his glass up and scanned it through the light. "This looks familiar."

"Compliments of the doctor," Kasim said. "Europa's finest rotgut."

"But you don't drink."

"Neither did Louis when he arrived on the moon," Kasim said wistfully. "Things change."

Ryan steepled his fingers. Louis had been a teetotaler before the amputation. And now Kasim had started imbibing. Remorse rose to the surface. He was the common denominator.

Kasim waved a hand. "Not your fault. It's the only thing that warms these cold bones." He leaned forward and clinked Ryan's glass. And waited.

Something between a growl and a snort emerged from Ryan's throat. He threw back the contents of the glass. And scowled. It was just as bad as he remembered from the last time he shared a drink with the doctor. "God, that's rank."

Kasim smacked his lips and refilled the glasses. "I thought you were military."

"Yes, but even we have standards."

Kasim fingered the lip of his glass. "Well, I know you didn't invite me here for a drink, since you usually save that for Sybil—" Ryan started to protest until he remembered there were no secrets on the moon. "So, what dark surprise do you want to impart this time?"

Ryan sighed and withdrew a slip of paper from his pocket. He opened it on the terminal and slid it over to Kasim. "It's my orders in case something happens and we don't make it back."

Kasim's eyes widened as he scanned the page. "You can't be serious. This is crazy."

"As crazy as not doing anything?"

"You're asking me to abandon the colony?"

"Not exactly." Ryan pointed at a paragraph near the bottom. "I want you and Rani to take forty colonists and make a run for Earth."

"Are you going to tell Rani, or is that my job too?"

"I'm leaving her similar orders."

Kasim shook his head. "You're crazy."

Ryan shoved his hands into his pockets, pointedly ignoring his drink. "Think about it. If my mission fails, you lost two transports and two pilots. That leaves just one trainee pilot. On a colony that's two feet of wire away from total collapse. At which point humanity has one last shot at survival—a Hail Mary trip back to Earth."

"And if the plague is still active?"

Ryan shrugged. "You die."

Kasim fumbled for something to say. "I can't choose forty people."

"You don't have to; Gunner did it already. Thirty women, ten men, all with the necessary skills to restart civilization." The part about leaving fifteen hundred behind was left unsaid.

Kasim leaned back in the seat, as if the paper itself was infected with the plague. "This is not my job. Rani—"

"Rani can't do this alone and you know it." Ryan's tone was harsher than he intended, and he silently cursed himself when Kasim winced. "You just killed a man. You know what it takes to save a colony or, in this case, a species. She won't like it, but she won't stop you."

Kasim frowned as the implication sunk in. "I can't possibly . . . and even if I could, how would . . ."

Ryan patted the paper. "Gunner outlined the process: a fake emergency, a fire in the hangar, that sort of thing. No one will be the wiser until the transport lifts off. I even got Chan to download the launch sequence. The landing." Ryan shrugged again. "That'll be up to your pilot. I figure he'll have months to practice."

"What if I decide to stay behind?"

"You won't," Ryan said, and pulled out an object from his waistband.

Kasim's eyes widened as Ryan placed the gun on the table.

"You'll be on that transport," Ryan said. "Because if you stay behind after forcing forty people to take the last ride home, the remaining colonists will kill you."

A moment of silence passed. Kasim snatched up his glass. "Louis was right; you really can be a hard-ass." He downed the contents.

"He should know," Ryan murmured. He pushed the baseball cap toward Kasim. "Thanks for coming."

# CHAPTER 5

*Good people strengthen themselves ceaselessly.*

DAY 21, 0930 HOURS

Rani watched the exhaust plumes fade as the transports departed into the void. Liftoff had proceeded uneventfully, and she said a silent thank-you to Fate. And Chan's launch program. Staring out the starboard portal in Operations, she was mesmerized by how quickly the ion trails blended into the cosmic background. Initially, the transports appeared to be on fire, but with every passing minute, the image shrank until they resembled nothing more than pinpricks of light, indistinguishable from the smattering of stars in the heavens.

"What's the relationship between light and distance again?" Kasim asked. Standing beside her at the portal, he seemed just as captivated. It had been over a year since a transport had left the moon.

"For an object traveling away from you, the intensity of light decreases by the square of the distance." Her gaze retreated to the ice plates on the surface. During last year's uprising, Braeder had ordered Chan and another pilot, Decker, to crater the landing strip with explosives when Senator Lecky's marines tried to land. Now the repaired surface was covered in dirt and small pieces of debris after backwash from the transport engines swept across the ice like an invisible broom.

She sat down in the command chair. It felt strange sitting in Braeder's seat, facing her old terminal. The hum of the servers nestled against the back wall of Operations seemed louder with only two people in the room. She toggled the monitor and scanned incoming data from the transports: speed increasing, trajectory nominal, all systems in the green. She let out a breath, one she didn't realize she'd been holding.

Kasim turned and flashed her a grin, as if he knew exactly what she was thinking. "Flawless. Just like old times."

Rani harrumphed. It wasn't that long since transport landings and launches were both routine and boring. But that was before they had been reduced to one pilot and had to set up computer programs to carry out the most basic of tasks on the second transport. Thank God they lifted off from Europa, a moon with a small gravity well. Launching from Earth would have been something else entirely, and no trainee at the wheel could have managed that.

Kasim walked over and took Chan's chair. A surge of emotion filled Rani's chest, and she bit the inside of her lip to maintain control. She had started thinking of it as Chan's chair several months before. Not Marco's. Not the seat of her boyfriend but someone new. Someone who wasn't Marco.

She focused her attention on the monitor embedded in the arm of the command chair as she switched feeds. In seconds, an interior view of *Phoenix* appeared. Five passengers plus Chan were in various states of disrobing. Six cryo-chambers, with glass doors open, stood ready to receive their human tenants.

"I hope they find everything we need," Kasim said, frowning at the numerous readings and dials on the terminal.

"Yeah, me too." Rani marvelled at the irony. There was no Plan B. As with most decisions they made after Earth went offline, they would either be successful or they would die. "All right. Time to get to work."

Kasim set his jaw. "Wonderful."

Now came the hard part. Rani knew the politician was venturing into unfamiliar territory. His previous life had involved compromise and mediation. But the lieutenant had set the tone: life or death. Survival or extinction. Kasim had to govern the colony with an iron fist tucked in a velvet glove.

"Are you going to deliver meals to the brig?" he asked. Louis had discharged the mother from Medical last night after declaring her eyesight was on the road to recovery, and Kasim had wasted no time transferring her to the brig inside the transport hangar. He didn't say it, but Rani knew he still struggled with the aftereffects of sentencing the mother. And that was just the first obstacle he had to navigate as governor.

"No, I've delegated that chore to the colonists," she said. "I'm going to be busy and frankly don't want to be blamed for starving the prisoner."

Kasim nodded, ceding the reality of Rani's new workload. "If you need help, let me know."

"I will." She turned off the monitor. Watching longer might be interpreted as voyeurism.

The door at the back of the room swished open and a broad-shouldered man walked in. Solomon was as wide as he was tall, like a massive blond-haired bowling ball with legs. She didn't remember him from before the rebellion, but he had earned Braeder's respect over the past year as foreman of a maintenance crew. That was all Rani needed to know.

His gaze sought Rani. "Cap'n, the guys on my crew found something strange in the pit. They're asking if you could stop by and take a look."

Rani arched a single eyebrow. On the off chance some material could be salvaged, Braeder had tasked Solomon's crew with digging out the damaged transmission line that had been sucked into the ice cave. "The transport's barely broken orbit, and some deuterium miner wants me to take an EV walk to the extractor to look at some weird ice formation?"

Cheeks turning red, Solomon shrugged.

"You didn't see it yourself?"

The miner leaned a hip against Chan's terminal. He towered over the smaller, thinner Kasim like a skyscraper. "That's the thing: the guys didn't mention it until we were peeling off our suits in the decompression chamber. It was like they were embarrassed or something. Apparently, Johnson saw it first, and he's my most experienced man. I thought they were joking, but they swear something's in there."

"Miners used to dig tunnels all day, every day," Rani said. "You saw all kinds of weird stuff. What makes this so special?"

Solomon played with the cuffs on his work coveralls. "They didn't say exactly. They just asked me to tell you."

Rani shared a look with Kasim. She had a million things to do and a dozen places to be in the next few days, and all that would have to be pushed back if she were to spend hours trekking back and forth to the extractor just because some dumbass saw Elvis in the ice.

*What would the lieutenant do?*

She glanced at the clock on the wall. "Tell you what: it's too late to start today. Why don't you head out there early tomorrow and check for yourself? If you still think I should go, I'll meet you at noon in the decompression chamber. Will that make them happy?"

Solomon grinned and gave a civilian's imitation of a military salute, to which Rani rolled her eyes. "Sounds good, Cap'n. I'll see you then."

"He does realize you're an ensign, right?" Kasim asked after the miner left.

Rani lay back in the chair and stretched tight neck muscles. "Who knows? I'm just glad he knows where the Command Center is."

Kasim chuckled and patted her arm as he walked out. "Isn't leadership fun?"

*Day 21, 1000 Hours*

Louis wasn't a happy camper. Ryan could see it in his expression: knotted brow, narrow eyes, and bunched cheeks. The doctor held his hand up in a pleading gesture. "I swear I'll get into the pod. Just give me a day or two to get used to the idea."

Ryan's eyebrows rose. "What difference will a couple of days make?"

Behind him, Gunner chortled. "I think the vet will wait until we're in cryo-sleep and turn the transport around. We'll probably wake up back on the colony."

"That's enough," Ryan snapped. He noted Sasha and Chan had already undressed to their skivvies and were in the process of attaching electrical leads to their chests. The reservist, Compton, was a few steps behind. To Louis, he said, "Cryo-sleep isn't that bad. You of all people know there are meds to control symptoms."

The doctor's skin took on a greenish hue, and he shook his head. "Last time, I was sick for twenty-four hours. Nonstop abdominal pains and vomiting despite medication." He shuddered, and Ryan felt a trace of sympathy.

"I'm sorry, Doc. There's really no choice. I want everyone safely sedated and in their pods before Chan sets the automatic pilot."

"I'll gladly hold a bucket for you when we wake up." Gunner grinned. "For every time your stomach twists in your gut and you spew out mouthfuls of yellow bile. I'll even count—"

"Shut up, Gunner," Ryan said. "Get in your pod before I program the computer to perform a medical procedure while you're asleep." He glared at the veteran until Gunner dropped his gaze and retreated to his cryo-pod.

Chan stepped over. Somehow, she maintained her professional demeanor despite wearing nothing more than panties and a bra. "Ship systems in the green, Lieutenant. Course laid in and scans report a clear path ahead. Anything that needs doing before we slip into dreamland?"

"I think we're good, Chan. Get your pod ready. As soon as everyone is asleep, set the autopilot."

She gave him a curt salute, which seemed silly, considering what she was wearing, and marched to the cockpit.

Ryan turned back to Louis. "I need you to do this. More than that, the colony needs you to do this." When Louis didn't respond—the doctor wrung his hands but didn't approach the cryo-pod—Ryan pulled out his hole card. "I don't know if you heard, but Gunner said you wouldn't have the guts to enter cryo-sleep. Rani said Gunner was full of shit and took the bet."

Louis looked up. "A bet?"

"Yeah, when we get back, one month of engineering diagnostics."

The doctor blinked. They both knew that was a lot of work. Louis's jaw tightened, and he reached out one trembling hand to seize the side of the cryo-unit. "You should have told me earlier. If I can saddle that Neanderthal with more work, he'll be too busy to bother me." He took a breath and picked up the electrical patches. "All right. Help me with the leads before I change my mind."

Ryan smiled and grabbed the wires. First problem solved. A small voice in his head warned it wouldn't be the last. Nor would they be as easy to solve. Lies usually only worked among friends.

*Day 22, 1215 Hours*

Rani's EV boots crunched down on ice that had melted and refrozen a billion times in the moon's multibillion-year existence. The bombardment of ionizing radiation from the massive planet peaked during storm cycles and melted millimeters of surface ice, forming tiny puddles that refroze seconds later.

The path to the extractor was punctuated by blue strobe lights embedded in the surface, markers planted by Gunner's crew to serve as guideposts. Unlike Earth's ice sheets, Europa's frozen layers shifted like tectonic plates under the gas giant's immense gravity. And every once in a while, those tidal fluctuations precipitated seismic shifts, which resulted in potentially lethal quakes. One such quake a year before had doomed the outpost on Titan.

Overhead, Jupiter dominated the sky, the Great Red Spot staring down at them like the eye of a cyclopic god. Ancient storms flared deep in its interior, birthing tempests that Earth's atmosphere could never rival.

Solomon stopped and nudged a titanium conduit with his foot. "It's protecting the new transmission line." His words sounded slightly mechanical in Rani's helmet. "Nobody mentioned it, but that's the last of the ductwork. It's not just wire we're running short of."

Rani bit her tongue. It seemed obvious that if they ran out of transmission wire, the shortage of titanium tubes wouldn't matter. She placed her hands on her hips and surveyed the desolate surface. Chunks of ice speckled the hoarfrost all the way to the horizon. "How much farther?"

Solomon walked a few meters ahead and scaled an oblong chunk of ice. "Take a look. We're here."

She climbed up beside him. The extractor building sat two hundred meters away, perched on a rockcrete slab ten meters thick. The white, nondescript shell of a building belied the technologically advanced marvel inside and hid the magnesium-antimony batteries beneath the surface. The shearing effect of Jupiter's immense gravity caused adjacent ice sheets to stretch and bend, generating enough electrical power to run the colony.

"That's where the ice cave formed." Solomon pointed to a circular depression in the surface. "When it collapsed, it hauled the main transmission line down with it, and razor-sharp ice cut it to ratshit."

"You couldn't save anything?"

He shook his head. "Nothing longer than two-foot sections."

*Damn.* Her last hope of salvaging wire sizzled and died. So much for the lieutenant's idea of scrounging remnants.

"All right." She took a breath. Waste of tears to cry over spilled milk. At times like this, she had watched Braeder move on to the next issue. "How do we get down there? I want to see this wonderful ice sculpture before getting back to some real work." She tried to inject just the right amount of sarcasm: enough to make her point, not enough to damage egos.

Solomon didn't say anything and kept his faceplate turned away. Rani smirked. Probably a smart move, knowing this was a fool's errand.

He led her to the depression, a settling of the surface not unlike a sinkhole back on Earth. Yellow hazard tape stretched across the entrance.

"We dug a tunnel to the bottom," he explained. "The guys carved out some steps but it's still slick. Make sure you hang on to the guide rope on the way down."

Rani regretted her decision to inspect the site. She wasn't endowed with an athlete's dexterity, and climbing down the steps looked like it required coordination.

Her hesitation caused Solomon to offer a sympathetic smile. "Don't worry; I'll go first. If you slip, you'll just slam into my back."

Rani took a breath and gestured him forward. "After you."

The ice tunnel was narrow with a low ceiling, forcing them to hunch over as they picked their way down the hand-hewn steps. Solomon had to bend so low, his hands scraped the ice.

It wasn't quite as slippery as Rani feared, but she was still relieved when her feet found the bottom. She calculated they had descended about thirty feet below the surface.

The ice cave was enormous. Solomon's team of miners had set up portable lamps along the walls, but even their combined illumination bled off into darkness. Under the artificial light, the walls appeared blue-green and glistened with a sheen of moisture. For a moment, Rani had a déjà vu sensation, remembering the vast Belum Caves back home. She fought off a sense of nostalgia as she realized she'd never see them again.

Her imagination created fantastical figures out of the shadows. "How deep does it go?"

"Don't know." Solomon helped her navigate a wide fissure in the floor. "The guys said they walked five hundred meters and never reached the end."

She whistled. "How the heck does one of these things form?"

Solomon shrugged, the movement stretching the fabric of his suit. "Sorry, Cap'n. Need a geologist to answer that."

A thought struck her. "Does it extend under the extractor?"

"No, thank God. That would spell the end of the colony." He put his hands on her shoulders and spun her clockwise. "It's easy to get disoriented, but the extractor is that way, several hundred meters through the ice."

Rani heaved a sigh of relief. There was no way they could repair the extractor assembly if it fell into the cavern. "Okay, you impressed me. Now, where is this weird ice formation?"

"Over here." Solomon drew her along the sidewall. "And it's not ice."

"I thought you said—"

"I said it was *in* the ice."

She gave him a sidelong glare. "Now you're confusing me. What's down here if it's not ice? Some weird kind of rock?"

"That's what you're going to tell me," he said, angling his helmet lamp upward. "There it is."

It took Rani a second to realize what he was shining his lamp on. Then she saw it: a thin, rope-like tentacle hanging from the ceiling. The end terminated about ten feet above their heads. She felt a wave of anger coming on. "You dragged me all the way out here for a loose piece of transmission wire? Damn, man, I've got . . ." Her anger petered off when he remained staring, waiting her out. His expression hadn't changed.

"What am I missing?" she asked.

"The wires that got dragged into the ice were on the other side of the tunnel—where we came down." He pointed across the cave. "Nobody laid wire in this area."

Rani fumbled for something to say. "Well, somebody did. Maybe the workmen who built the colony?" She thought the answer was obvious.

But Solomon remained unbowed. "I said the extractor was over there." He held up his hand before she could interrupt. "And no, this is not a stray wire somebody dropped during colony construction."

"How can you be sure?" Rani wanted to end the argument and get back to the station, but a seed of doubt had taken root in her gut.

Solomon selected an instrument from his belt. "This is an infrared scanner," he explained. "It helps identify temperature changes and potential weak points in the ice so miners don't get caught in a cave-in."

Rani's brain fired on all cylinders. Something didn't add up. Her mind desperately wanted to connect the dots, and for that to happen, she needed more information. She fidgeted as he aimed the scanner at the rope-like object.

She leaned in, her helmet only coming up to his shoulder. "What is it?"

He bent over so she could see. The object glowed orange on the screen.

"It's exothermic," he said. "It's producing heat. That's what melted the ice and created this cave . . . over time."

Rani paused as multiple lines of thought converged. "But to form a cave this size from such a small wire—"

"Would take hundreds or even thousands of years," Solomon confirmed.

"How . . ." Rani's second thought slammed home. "How can it be producing heat? If it's not connected to the extractor . . ." She stepped back and readjusted the angle of her lamp. The ceiling loomed twenty feet above them.

"What are you doing?" Solomon asked.

"We can see one end of the rope, but where's the other? What's it connected to?"

His eyes widened, like he hadn't considered that aspect.

"Tilt your lamp to match mine," she said. "Put more light on the ceiling."

He did as instructed, and Rani followed the black wire up to where it disappeared into a small, circular hole in the ice.

Something nagged at her, something on the fringe of consciousness, part of her brain hinting she was missing an important piece of information. At times like this, Marco used to laugh at her, saying there was a delay in her right brain connecting to the left. She waited until the sense of nostalgia faded. "Broaden the beam," she said. "Dial it back to a wide view."

He seemed confused but quickly obliged. Their combined lamps expanded to encompass a broad swath of ceiling ice.

Something between a grunt and a yelp emerged from Solomon's throat, and Rani's pulse quickened. She felt a surge of . . . what? Fear? Excitement?

"Do you see it?" he whispered.

She managed a single nod. *What the hell?*

"What is it?"

She wasn't sure how to answer. Something dark and ill-defined lay frozen in the ceiling. Something that was connected to the heat-emitting wire that, over thousands of years, had melted an immense cave in the ice.

"I have no idea," she murmured. "But no human put it there."

# CHAPTER 6

*Learn as though you will never be able to master it;*
*hold it like you're in fear of losing it.*

DAY 25, 0800 HOURS

As Rani hurried from Ops to the decompression chamber, she wondered how the lieutenant would handle the situation. Something not covered by their training. An alien artifact. Proof of life beyond the solar system. Beyond humans.

She nodded at a pair of colonists passing by the fountain: a couple, judging by the holding of hands and way they folded into one another. The man acknowledged her warily, a reminder of recent events. Of the mother still in custody.

Days past, in normal times, Rani had loved circulating among the colonists, enjoying the camaraderie and light banter. Those days were gone. Now starting a conversation with a civilian was like trying to squeeze blood from a stone. The colonists had turned their backs on Ryan's motley band of heroes, leaving her on the outside looking in. She didn't like it, but she understood it on an instinctual level. In times of strife, people try to minimize risk, and getting too close to the lieutenant often didn't bode well.

She hit the button on the wall and the door slid open, revealing two men in different states of disrobing.

"About time, Cap'n." Solomon grinned. "I was preparing to send out a search party."

"Sorry." Rani sat beside Archie and began unbuttoning her tunic. "A warning light on the laser started flashing, and I had to run a diagnostic."

"Pay him no heed," Archie said. "Grunts think they're funny when they use words that contain more than two syllables."

Rani chuckled. Archie had a dry sense of humor.

"I heard that," Solomon said. "Even though I rarely pay attention to colonists who aren't man enough to fill real suits." He patted his broad chest and flashed a toothy grin.

The exchange turned Rani's expression into a frown. Fleet EV suits came in three sizes: big, bigger, and behemoth, the last used solely by miners. For Chan and herself, it meant always battling oversized arms and legs just to walk across the surface.

Archie didn't seem bothered. He jerked a thumb at Solomon. "Now you know why Fleet attaches oxygen packs to miner suits: to equalize the negative pressure between their ears."

Solomon blinked for a second before slapping his knee. "Good one! Have to remember that." He went back to fastening the clips on his suit.

Archie exchanged a knowing look with Rani. The comradery in decompression chambers had been similar throughout the solar system, a dark humor born out of the ever-present risk that came with venturing into the Big Empty. It remained an unsaid truth that those individuals depended on themselves and each other for survival in an environment designed to terminate life.

"Everyone at the site?" she asked.

Archie dropped the upper half of his suit over his head and adjusted the straps. "Since zero six hundred hours. I'm guessing they're finished by now and just waiting on us."

Rani selected a small pair of gloves and cinched them at the wrist. "You still grumbling about the plan?" Not that anyone was beaming about it. Not the half dozen engineers overseeing the project, not the miners who did the grunt work setting up, and certainly not the scientists who couldn't get a damn reading off the artifact. The lead scientist, Rutherford, had made his position painfully clear at the last meeting. He demanded more time, more equipment, and more power. Rani had triggered his resentment by promising him only one of the three: time. The colony's resources were limited.

*What the heck was that thing?*

After several days of scans, X-rays, and ultrasounds, they had learned nothing except its dimensions. The egg-shaped object was two feet long with a maximum diameter of twelve inches. The wire-like antenna extending ten feet from the base resembled more a rigid stick of titanium than a flexible metal foil.

And it was definitely exothermic. Which meant it was internally powered. And if it had been sitting in the ice for as long as Rutherford postulated—tens of thousands of years—the energy source had to be nuclear. Radiation. But the scientists had recorded exactly zero emissions. No photons or neutrons or energy. No nothing.

Rani noticed Archie eyeing her.

"It's weird," he said, as if reading her thoughts. "But once it's out of the ice, we should be able to get some answers. Several feet of the frozen stuff really interferes with the scanners and monitors."

"I hope so." She picked up her helmet and checked the heads-up display. "Our first contact with ET and we don't have a clue what to do. The colonists are going nuts."

Archie chuckled. "Nobody said first contact came with a user's guide."

Solomon lumbered over. In his massive EV suit, he resembled an abominable snowman. "Testing coms." His voice echoed out of the other two helmets.

Rani gave him a thumbs-up as she secured the last of her straps. She nodded at Archie. "I'll say it again: you don't have to come. It's a long walk and it's going to be a longer day. I can keep you apprised over the com."

His expression remained blank. "Sorry, Ensign, but Gunner left explicit instructions to keep you safe."

She felt a flash of irritation. "Ah, I am a Fleet officer. I can handle myself—"

"And I've been strolling through vacuum since before you were born." His eyes sparkled. "Don't worry about me."

He tested the seals on his suit before moving to hers. In turn, they checked each other's battery, helmet, and straps. It was Fleet protocol—one reinforced by Braeder after they lost a colonist to a cracked regulator a year earlier.

"Ready, Cap'n?" Solomon asked, hand poised over the internal door release.

"Ready."

"Ah." Archie tilted his head quizzically. "You do know she's an ensign, right?"

Solomon's reply was buried in the hiss of the hatch rising.

Rani had descended the steps into the ice cave half a dozen times since the discovery of the artifact, but she still gripped the guidewire with both hands every time. The fall probably wouldn't do much damage, but with a dozen miners and scientists waiting at the bottom, the blow to her ego would linger for months.

The narrow, claustrophobic stairwell didn't bother her as much as that first day, but she still exhaled when she reached the bottom and was able to let go of the wire. One of the miners—the foreman, Jorge—walked up. He was as tall as Solomon but with a noticeable gut that strained the front of his suit. "We were wondering if you got lost."

Solomon snorted and gave Rani a sidelong glance. "Hit a few red lights."

Rani felt her cheeks flush. She wasn't as nimble on the surface as the miners or even Archie. They hadn't said anything during the trek to the extractor, but they kept the pace slower than normal.

"No problems with setup?" Solomon asked.

"Have a look." Jorge tapped the screen on his wrist and a schematic of the cave appeared. Forty meters wide and almost a kilometer long. A flashing red dot indicated the position of the artifact in the ceiling. A squat-looking scissor truck sat directly beneath it.

"How'd you get the truck down here?" Archie asked.

"We found a thin section of ice about four hundred meters that way." Jorge pointed into the darkness. "The boys cut a hole and lowered it down with the gators. It wasn't exactly according to code, but it worked."

Rani noted the presence of several miners along the back wall and, closer to the center of the cave, a gaggle of scientists huddling together. By their subtle movements and gestures, they were conversing on a private channel.

"You sure this will work?" Solomon asked Jorge.

"Not sure about anything, but it was the best we could do." The miner gave Rani and Archie a hooded look.

Rani felt the accusation in his tone. She didn't have to be reminded; this was her call. The miners weren't comfortable working with such little information. Preparing to extract an object of any kind without knowing how it would react made everyone uneasy, especially if *alien* was in the title. On the other hand, the scientists were tearing their hair out, and the colonists likewise waited on pins and needles for *something*. Once again, she wished Braeder were there.

"All right," Solomon said. "Let's do this."

Jorge gestured, and two miners climbed a pair of rope ladders that had been anchored to the ceiling on either side of the artifact.

"Quite the conundrum," Archie said, drawing Rani's attention to the center of the ice cave, where the industrial-sized scissor truck powered up. "I'm sure it will work out." He pointed at a layer of thick mattresses the miners had fastened to the platform.

Rani detected a trace of sarcasm in his tone and said a silent prayer that the man wasn't prescient.

Jorge typed instructions into his wrist unit, and the truck rose on titanium support legs. Behind the *chug-chug* of hydraulic motors, the scissors straightened toward the ceiling before stopping several inches beneath the ice.

"I'm having second thoughts about the weight," Rani admitted as butterflies took up residence in her stomach. "Are we sure the truck can handle the load?"

Rutherford stepped away from his peers. He sported a patchy beard and stood almost as tall as the miners. Unlike them, his suit was creased and slack, revealing a thinner frame. "We discussed this at the last meeting, Ensign." His tone reminded Rani of one of her instructors at the Academy, a chauvinistic son of a bitch. "The lander can handle five metric tons. Based on its size, the artifact would have to have a density of a neutron star to be heavier than that. We're quite safe."

Rani frowned. His exaggeration was intentional. Then again, Braeder wouldn't have asked the question in the first place. Now every person in the cave thought she was a nervous Nellie. The silence on coms confirmed it.

"What about the antenna?" Archie asked. "Could it snap off if the angle is wrong?"

Jorge continued to send instructions through his wrist terminal. "No worries, Grandpa. My colleagues will cut the ice at precise angles. The artifact will fall into those mattresses like a sleeping baby into a crib." He laughed, and the rest of his crew joined in.

Rani's jaw tightened. They were too cocky, too self-assured. That was never a good sign.

Jorge said something over a private frequency, and both miners on the ladders began cutting into the ice using two-handed diamond saws. Rani felt the high-speed whine in her bones, and her teeth started chattering.

A large chunk of ice splintered off and shattered on the floor. The miners stopped and glanced down at Jorge.

"All right." Jorge turned to the group of scientists. "Time for everyone to leave until we finish. Just in case."

Rutherford led his colleagues up the stairs reluctantly, like kids afraid to miss the big moment in a movie.

"You and Grandpa as well." Jorge flicked his fingers at Rani.

"That's a negative," Rani snapped, unable to stifle the veiled anger from seeping into her tone. The man irritated her. There was no way she was going to miss mankind's first contact.

Jorge took a step closer. He towered over her like a tidal wave about to break. "This is my worksite, lady. And I wasn't asking."

Rani braced her fists on her hips. She was glad the misogynist pig looming over her couldn't see her heart going a mile a minute. Her words came out as cold as the surrounding ice. "Perhaps we haven't been introduced. My name is Ensign Singh and I'm in charge of the colony until Lieutenant Braeder returns. And if you don't like my answer, you can haul your ass back to the station, or the brig, whatever suits your fancy, because your order died the moment it touched my ears."

Everyone in the cave stopped moving. The two miners leaning against the wall by the stairs straightened. Solomon wavered, uncertain, his faceplate swiveling back and forth. Out of the corner of her eye, Rani noticed Archie withdraw something from his pocket. After several pregnant seconds, Jorge shrugged. "Your body, your risk." The miners on the ladders relaxed and went back to work.

More chunks fell from the ceiling, and the diamond blades screamed like scalded cats. Rani felt a hand on her shoulder.

"Missy"—Archie's voice sounded hushed in her helmet—"I'd appreciate if you stepped back to the wall with me."

She turned until their faceplates almost touched. Her annoyance vanished when she saw the concern etched in his features, and she allowed him to pull her back a few steps.

Across the cavern, the miners didn't seem concerned. Solomon held court with Jorge and their comrades. They had obviously switched frequencies, as none of the words carried over the com.

"A little nervous, Archie?" Rani asked.

"'Tis true." His gaze rose to the artifact emerging a centimeter at a time from the ice. "I'm a staunch believer in scripted endings no matter the job. Building a house, we know how many nails and what the finished product looks like. Same with mining deuterium: we dig tunnels and use machines to separate isotopes."

Rani's brain clicked into gear, completing the circle. What he said made sense. "And right now, we don't know what's going to happen."

Archie's lips tightened into a fine line. "Our engineering friends can plan till the cows come home, but they're still dealing with too many unknowns. What if it's not a benign artifact but a bomb or a hibernating alien germ?"

Rani hadn't thought that far ahead. She kicked herself. "You think it could be a bomb?"

"A bomb. A watch. Leftover alien garbage. You pick."

Rani desperately wanted to fire back with a sarcastic retort, but his argument oozed logic and, more than that, was downright terrifying.

Solomon cut in, interrupting her thoughts. "We're about halfway through, Cap'n. Figure we got another twenty inches before weight becomes a factor."

She realized the miners beside Solomon were staring at her and had been for a while. They no doubt heard the conversation between her and Archie, which was not very complimentary to the overall plan. Two of the men seemed to be chuckling between themselves, probably exchanging a snide comment on a private frequency.

"Take your time," she said, trying to inject a measure of authority into the situation. "It's not—"

She stopped as the ceiling abruptly cracked. Every person in the cave tensed.

"Archie, is that—"

A second *crack* echoed through the cave. The moon's atmosphere was thin but there was no mistaking the sound. She looked up as a lightning-shaped fissure appeared. A second fracture line emerged, branching off the first. Then a third and fourth. And then a dozen more. Fine slivers of ice fell to the floor like pellets of snow.

"It can't be," Solomon said, his tone incredulous. "The ice is too thick—"

Archie hit Rani like a fullback taking down a tackling dummy. She slammed into the ice hard, the force squeezing the air from her lungs. A small voice in the back of her head told her she'd feel that bruise for days.

"Incoming!" Archie yelled. "Get down!"

Rani twisted her head around in time to see the miners hesitate, like they were waiting for orders from Jorge. That's when the ceiling collapsed. One second, the ice was holding up the artifact; the next, twenty inches of it simply disappeared.

The artifact fell directly into the waiting platform of the scissor truck, just as the engineers had planned. Except it didn't stop. The industrial-strength vehicle could have been made of cardboard for all the difference it made. It collapsed like a tin can under the wheel of a Fleet transport. Titanium girders, duroalloy cross-struts, three-foot-thick vulcanized tires—did nothing to break the fall. In the space of a heartbeat, the entire structure was reduced to the thickness of a sheet of paper.

Not all the mass of the scissor truck was pinned under the weight of the artifact. Bits of tire, bolts the size of a man's fist, and splinters of titanium shot out from the ruptured vehicle like grapeshot fired from a medieval cannon. Small fragments penetrated the walls, stamping the ice like a tattoo artist. Large pieces carved out holes half a foot deep.

One of the miners doubled over as something penetrated his suit. The man standing next to Solomon had his helmet disappear in a splash of red mist. The body briefly teetered on the balls of its feet before falling backward. Blood pooled where his head should have been.

"Jesus!" Solomon breathed as the reverberations faded and the cave became deathly silent.

Rani was already in motion. She keyed the emergency channel in her helmet and activated the colony klaxon. "Medical team to the decompression chamber," she shouted. "Prepare for casualties."

When she reached the injured man, she was surprised to find Archie by her side.

Solomon moved slowly, as if his brain hadn't caught up to events. He glanced down at the beheaded corpse. "He's dead."

Rani shoved him aside. "Not him, you fool! Your other man."

Solomon finally seemed to remember his second colleague and stepped out of her way.

Archie crouched down and rolled the miner over.

Bile surged into the back of Rani's throat. Something had passed right through the miner. A four-inch-wide tunnel ran from his stomach to his back. She could see the ice wall through the fleshy aperture. Blood-tinged frost was already forming along the edges of the wound.

Archie cursed and let the corpse fall back.

"Anybody else hurt?" Rani asked.

Nobody answered. Jorge, eyes wide, managed to shake his head.

Rani took a steadying breath. They were all in shock, and that included the two miners hanging by their fingers at the top of the ladders. The collapsing ceiling had torn off most of the brackets, but they looked unhurt.

"Help them down," she ordered. "And get everyone back to the station."

For the first time, Jorge didn't hesitate in obeying her orders.

In that moment, Rani finally understood what it took to take command: a bellyful of stubbornness and a goddamned tragedy.

After the scientists and miners left, she and Archie stood silently beside the artifact. The bodies of the two dead men lay where they fell, at the front of the cavern. There'd be plenty of time to retrieve the frozen corpses later.

"I guess you're a soothsayer now," Rani said wearily. "How did you know?"

"I didn't." Archie surveyed the debris on the cave floor. "But I've never been one for experts' opinions, especially when they base everything on guesswork."

Rani let out a long sigh. "It shattered twenty inches of solid ice. That's somewhere in the vicinity of twelve tons. On a density scale of one to ten, that ranks as insane."

"If we didn't know before, this confirms the damn thing is alien," Archie grumbled. "'Cause humans got nothing on this."

Rani nodded. The artifact was clearly made of something beyond human technology. Up close, without the obscuring ice, it was dusty gray with fine, white lines that resembled hieroglyphics embedded in the surface. Besides being shaped like one, it was as smooth as an egg with no obvious scrapes, dents, or nicks from the fall. The long antenna lay to one side, snapped off when the main body landed on it.

"Thanks for the push, Archie." She rubbed her ribs and winced. "Even though my chest is going to be paying for your chivalry for a while."

"You're welcome, Ensign." He gave her a wink. "And it's been some time since a female mentioned my name and her chest in the same sentence."

His humor brought back memories of how Gunner and Marco used to banter, and a lump formed in her throat. "We don't have anything in the colony that can handle this much weight. And we certainly don't have a machine to hoist it out of the cave."

Archie clasped his hands behind his back. "I reckon that's true, which leaves us only one option."

"I know," she said. "We'll have to build a lab around it."

Archie tilted his head quizzically. "I was going to suggest we bury it."

"What?" Her eyes widened. "You want me to hide the first and only evidence of alien intelligence?"

He caught her incredulous look and held it. "The thing just killed two members of your crew, and that's after it caused a power failure that almost wiped out the entire colony. Why do I think that keeping this thing around is only going to lead to more death and destruction?"

Rani felt a sinking feeling in her gut. As the senior military officer, there was zero chance she was going to follow Archie's suggestion. But damn if his words didn't strike a sympathetic chord.

*What had they gotten themselves into?*

# CHAPTER 7

*The will to win, the desire to succeed, the urge to reach your full potential . . . these are the keys that will unlock the door to personal excellence.*

DAY 32, 1020 HOURS

Rani wrapped her hands around the mug and savored the sensation. She desperately wanted to sip the fine British tea, the last box of the coveted blend, but drinking it now would limit the warmth soaking into her bones. Plus, she wanted to relish the taste and smell before she consumed what would probably be the last tea she ever drank.

Sitting beside her at the briefing table, Kasim snickered. "Not going to try it?"

She couldn't help but note the governor, with his ball cap and thick woolen sweater, had his hands around a similar cup of tea. "Just treasuring the moment. I want to remember this for as long as possible." She resented the unfairness of it all, something she felt whenever reality reared its ugly head. Which, on this moon, tended to happen on a regular basis.

Kasim's expression fell. "One more obstacle to overcome. Just like the cold and the food and everything else. For the colonists, the accident in the cave was a punch in the gut . . ." His voice drifted into silence.

Rani patted his arm. "We'll get through this. It's just another day." Another day and two more deaths.

Kasim gave her a halfhearted smile and blew over his tea before taking a sip. He sat back and savored the taste. "Rutherford wants to meet with you."

"Already? We haven't even buried the miners yet."

"The scientists have been poring over the artifact the last few days. Maybe they . . ."

Archie chose the moment to walk in. He jerked a thumb over his shoulder. "I bumped into Solomon on my way to the Command Center. He didn't seem happy."

Rani exchanged a knowing look with the governor. "The miners are still pissed about losing two of their own. They want me to contact Braeder so he can decide how to proceed with the artifact."

Archie dropped into a chair next to Kasim. "By his expression, I'm guessing you denied the request."

Rani gave in and took a sip. It tasted wonderful. "The lieutenant doesn't need me complicating his mission. He's got enough on his plate. Besides, what can he do? Turn around and come back?" They both knew that was not going to happen. Not with the colony on life support.

"It's not the ask," Kasim said. "It's the message behind the request. The miners lack confidence in the ensign, and it's their not-so-subtle way of saying so."

"Yeah," Rani smirked. "They'd rather I sit on it until Braeder returns."

Archie chuckled.

"What's so funny?" Rani asked.

Archie shrugged. "Ain't never met a human being who wasn't born with a curiosity streak. It's hard enough for most people not to open a Christmas present early. Here we have an alien artifact in our lap. What are we supposed to do, go fishing until the lieutenant returns? Despite what those miners want, the colonists would probably lynch you if we didn't examine it."

"He's right." Kasim sipped his tea. "I was thinking that maybe we could back off, but there's really no chance. Humans aren't wired that way. You made the right call, Rani. Let the scientists poke and prod for days or weeks, even. At least no one should get hurt."

"Funny, Governor." Archie raised an eyebrow. "That's exactly what they said about removing it from the ice."

*1200 Hours*

The large wooden doors of the Council Chambers had been custom-made on Earth and shipped during the early days of colony construction. Other than that, very little real wood had made it to the moon, as other materials took precedence. And without trees, what they had now would likely be the last any colonist saw of one of humanity's staple items.

Rani paused to check her uniform. After four years at the Academy, it was second nature. Not to mention she was now in charge and had to look and act the part. Braeder had said as much.

The star-shaped portal embedded in the wall revealed a desolate lunar landscape. Jupiter had set hours before, and the shadows born of natural sunlight lent a sinister glow to the emerald ice—hinting that the colony was entering the twilight of its existence.

Braeder had met with the previous Board numerous times in this room before martial law was declared. He always returned from those meetings wearing a scowl.

Rani tilted her head in order to catch a glimpse of the cemetery. Except for Kasim and Sybil, all the old Board members lay buried under those crosses. Or, to be specific, what parts of their bodies that could be found were buried there.

She sensed a presence joining her at the portal.

"Sorry I'm late," Kasim said. "I got cornered by a group of colonists demanding to hear the latest about the artifact."

Rani's lips thinned as her irritation rose. "Did you tell them everything we know was put on the colony web?" It had taken less than half a day before somebody started posting conspiracy theories. Now she was hard-pressed to defend their lack of knowledge.

"It's impossible to prove a negative," Kasim said. "And face it: everyone is just as curious as we are."

"It's in our genes." Rani checked her watch. "I have to run diagnostics on the greenhouses in twenty minutes, so let's get this over with. Tell me why I'm here."

Kasim turned from the portal. "Don't know exactly. The scientists asked for this meeting."

"They didn't give you a reason?"

"They seemed nervous, like they were keeping a secret."

Rani grunted. "That's what we need on this moon, more secrets. Well, let's unravel this one." She pushed open the door and led Kasim into the room. Two men sat at a long plastek table, both dressed in one-piece jumpsuits, and both going prematurely bald. She recognized the one with the thick, coke-bottle glasses.

"Dr. Rutherford, good to see you again." After the *incident* with the artifact.

"Yes, Ensign." He rubbed his hands together. "Terrible tragedy. You do understand it was impossible to predict what happened?" His words sounded more like an excuse than actual condolence.

She slid into the seat at the head of the table and Kasim sat on her right. "Nobody's blaming you or your colleagues. You gave us your best guess." The rest was left unsaid. Their *best guess* was off by a factor of ten. "The artifact is incredibly dense."

"Yes, well." He swallowed. "Turns out that's one of its unusual qualities."

Rani's radar went into active mode. "You learned something?"

Rutherford slid his palms across the tabletop, leaving a wet smear. He gestured to the man sitting beside him. "Ensign, this is Axel Vrabel, a physicist on loan from MIT before the plague hit. He's been part of my team monitoring the artifact since its discovery."

Kasim snorted. "Must be an easy job, since our technology can't penetrate the thing."

Vrabel's cheeks reddened. He had sharp, narrow features and seemed to be all angles and elbows. Rani had a brief vision of clothing-store mannequins that whispered in your ear as you walked the aisles.

"Unfortunately, that's still the case, Governor." His baritone pitch crashed Rani's image and immediately grabbed her attention. "But we were able to analyze what comes out of it."

"There are emissions?" Her hands tightened on the edge of the table. "Like what?"

Vrabel plugged his handheld into the computer interface and selected a file. Seconds later, a 3-D graph above the table.

Rani studied the hologram. "What am I looking at?"

"Neutrino emissions," Rutherford replied, his index finger tracing the sudden rise on the y-axis. The x-axis was broken down into hours and days.

Kasim squinted at the numbers. "The spike corresponds with the *accident* in the cave?"

"Correct." Vrabel picked up the thread. "When the artifact fell from the ceiling, the numbers went off the scale."

Rani shook her head. This wasn't making sense. "Neutrinos are emitted in huge quantities by stars. How do we know you didn't detect a solar flare?"

"Look at the pattern," Rutherford said. "Sure, our sun has that capacity, but we have the ability to triangulate the source." He changed the setting on the computer and a schematic of the colony and surrounding icefields appeared. "The detectors backtracked the signal to its origin." Three lines converged on an area next to the extractor. "There's no debate. The artifact was the source."

"The moment it fell?" Kasim asked.

Vrabel pointed at the timeline. "Exactly. And, more importantly, our computers were able to tease out a mathematical pattern buried in the emission. Two nine nine seven nine two."

Something tugged at Rani's memory. "I know that number."

"It's the speed of light in vacuum," Vrabel said. "A universal constant. And, more importantly, something we would understand based on our science."

"Jesus," Rani breathed, realization dawning. "In order to do that, it must have accessed our computers."

Rutherford scoffed. "That's impossible."

Rani stared at him. "An alien artifact woke up after being frozen in the ice for eons, after traveling untold light years, and you tell me peering inside our primitive computers is impossible?"

"Well, I . . ." Rutherford fumbled for something to say.

She ignored him and tapped the tabletop with her fingernails as her military training kicked in. "So, it reacted to external stimuli?"

Both scientists shot her a look. "We can't say—"

"Spare me," she snapped. "We hit it. It reacted."

Kasim glanced between them, brow furrowed. "I don't understand."

Rani turned her gaze on him. "It's a tripwire. An early-warning system."

"A warning?" Kasim hesitated before he got the next question out. "To what end?"

Rani shrugged. She recalled Archie's words. "No idea. Have to read the mind of whoever put it there. Could be anything from a doorbell to a bomb."

Kasim's eyes widened.

"We can't prove any of that," Rutherford repeated. "For now, all we have is a neutrino spike."

"Which direction?" Rani asked.

Vrabel blinked. "What?"

"The neutrinos. Where were they directed?"

Vrabel threw up his hands. "That's another puzzling part. There were no specific coordinates; it just blasted out a cloud of particles."

"That makes no sense," Kasim said. "Whether it's sending a message or a warning, it's got to go somewhere."

Vrabel paused as the concept took root. "Maybe it malfunctioned. It's been in the ice for thousands of years."

Rutherford nodded in support. "That'd be my guess. No way something that old can be expected to function properly."

"Your guesses are getting to be a problem." Rani's tone sounded accusatory. "I'm thinking there's another explanation."

Rutherford looked down his nose at her. "I have the best minds in the colony studying this, Ensign. The combined weight of their degrees puts any of your explanations to shame."

A slow smile spread across Rani's face. She glanced at Kasim. "What are our esteemed scientists forgetting, Governor?"

Kasim stared blankly for a second before his eyes lit up. "The foil."

"Right." She leaned back and folded her arms across her chest. "It snapped off when the artifact fell. Without the foil, the signal couldn't be focused."

The scientists exchanged a look. "That's only a theory," Rutherford said. He sounded like a petulant teenager. "You can't prove it."

"Like hell I can't." Rani arched her eyebrows. "I've decided I'm going to give your experts time to examine the artifact, Doctor, but if you come up empty, I know just the test."

"What?" Vrabel asked.

Rani smiled. "I'm going to touch it."

# CHAPTER 8

*Ignorance is the night of the might, but a night without moon or stars.*

## DAY 60, 0500 HOURS

Ryan wanted to die. Every muscle ached. Every joint throbbed. It was an effort to peel his tongue off the roof of his mouth. The logical side of his brain informed him he really didn't want to end it all and it was just the vicious headache, gut-wrenching nausea, and body-wide muscle spasms that triggered the nihilistic thought. Waking from cryo-sleep had that effect on most humans.

A soft beep sounded in his ear as IV lines injected a cocktail of drugs into his system.

He had learned long before not to move but rather ride out the immediate effects. Freshmen at the Academy often tried to sit up right away and ended up with their head in the toilet for the next thirty minutes.

The nausea slowly dissipated, along with the drums pounding in the back of his skull. He tried to open his eyes, but his eyelids felt like leather scraping across his sockets. After a few seconds, he was able to focus on the plastek cover of his pod. He raised a shaky arm to hit the release button, and the hatch sprang open. Cool air wafted in, and goosebumps formed on exposed skin.

"Sleeping in, Ace?" a familiar voice asked. "You're wasting the better part of the morning."

Ryan tilted his head to locate the speaker as the drumbeat in his head resumed. It was an effort to get his bearings, and when he finally spied Gunner, he groaned. The white underwear, skinny legs, and frizzled red hair made for one hell of a picture. He closed his eyes before it became ingrained in his memory, and gave Gunner the finger. "Stop acting so goddamn happy."

Gunner chortled. "At least you look better than the vet. His skin is positively green."

Taking a deep breath, Ryan braced his arms on the sides of the pod before pulling himself into a sitting position. His unit sat immediately behind the cockpit. Five more cryo-pods, including Gunner's, stretched along the port side of the ship. The reservist, Compton, slowly got dressed and offered a weak wave. At the far end of the cargo hold, the doctor leaned against the side of his pod and vomited into a bucket Chan graciously held for him.

The pilot caught his eye. "I gave him an extra dose of an antiemetic and a painkiller. He'll be okay."

A bolus of worry tugged at Ryan. Louis had never fully recovered from the sloppy amputation. That, combined with the stress of cryo-sleep, would put him in a bad way. No telling how much damage that body could take.

The door flipped open on the last cryo-pod and a shaky-looking Sasha crawled out. Her skin looked even whiter than Gunner's, and that was saying something. She vomited once on the floor before finding the nearest receptacle, a paper bag from a nearby shelf.

"You okay?" Gunner asked.

She slumped against the cryo-pod and braced her hands on her knees. "Water?" she croaked.

Gunner hurried over and passed her a bottle. "Small sips," he instructed.

She broke the seal and took rapid swallows. Her color began to improve.

After removing the IV, Ryan grabbed the tunic and trousers he had left hanging in his locker. Weeks in stasis left his muscles stiff and sore despite all the peptides, neurotransmitters, and hormones modern medicine pumped into his veins. The regular infusions were supposed to prevent muscle wasting and organ deterioration, but everyone still felt like shit when they woke up.

"Did you check the computer?" he asked Chan. Standard procedure had the pilots waking prior to the passengers. System checks and safety protocols were the number-one priority, and a ship full of sick passengers had a way of distracting pilots.

"Position verified, Lieutenant. Systems nominal. We're forty-eight hours out."

"All right." Ryan rubbed his eyes that were feeling less like sandpaper and more like normal. "We got a lot of work ahead, so let's get everyone something to eat." He caught a glimpse of Louis filling the bucket. "Well, maybe not everyone."

"It's not exactly MIT," Rani said as she unzipped her EV suit, stepped out of the airlock, and surveyed the new lab. It looked like someone had dropped one of the colony modules into the ice cave. Under Solomon's direction, over the past weeks, miners and technicians had constructed the ad hoc facility and equipped it with computers and scanners and all manner of technologically advanced equipment. And all of it was aimed at the artifact sitting in the middle of the room like a spoiled child.

To support the hardware, they had erected a platform supported by titanium girders initially tasked for Delta Hive before the lieutenant converted it to a greenhouse. The floor was a mishmash of aluminum grates and duroalloy planks torn from the concourse during last year's insurrection. Thick plastek walls separated the lab from the lethal realities of space. The final product resembled something Dr. Frankenstein might have dreamed up.

Standing beside her, Archie pulled off his helmet. "Sorry about the finishings, Princess, but the boys have been working overtime to carry out your orders."

Rani removed her helmet. "I never meant—"

"But you're right. In all honesty, they should've thrown on a second coat of paint and polished those electrical connections. I mean, what were they thinking?"

She swallowed a dollop of guilt. "Okay, smart-ass. Point taken." Archie was right. Again. The geologist had a habit of sticking pins into exposed parts of her ego.

His grin faded. "Are you sure you still want to do this?"

"It's been weeks and the scientists have found nothing, Archie. I said I would, and one thing Braeder taught me is to follow through on my promises." She hesitated, looking around. "Besides, they really have built a nice lab."

"Then tell them. Nothing like a little recognition to pump up the troops."

"You win." She was starting forward when Archie snagged her arm.

"And mind the outlets."

She glanced down at the thick, black electrical outlets the engineers had installed for the new equipment. Touching any of the exposed areas would not be a good thing and would shorten her day before she even got close to the artifact. "Thanks." Rubbing nervous hands against her thighs, she cleared her throat. Public speaking had never been her forte, and she avoided it whenever possible. But covering for the lieutenant broke many of her old rules. "A quick word before we start."

Around the cave, people stopped working. Three engineers checking the electrical connections put down their tools. Solomon and Jorge, and two other miners hanging out in the far corner of the lab, turned to face her. Rutherford, Vrabel, and a third scientist she hadn't met stopped punching instructions into a large computer the miners had carried from the physics lab. Vrabel had seemed all arms and legs when they first met. Now she understood why; the man was nearly seven feet tall. How he'd found a suit to fit that frame amazed her.

"I want to say thank you for your hard work setting up this makeshift . . ." She caught Archie's frown. "This *temporary* lab in such a short time. Hopefully, we'll get some answers over the next few weeks." She ignored the smug look on Archie's face as everyone returned to work.

"Jorge doesn't look happy," she said.

Archie grunted. "He hasn't smiled since you undressed him that first day. You insulted his manhood."

"And you say *I* have a big ego."

"On the contrary." He flashed her a blank look. "I never said that out loud."

She snorted and focused on the miners. "What does Solomon think?"

"He's torn. On one hand, he'd like to support his comrades, but on the other, you're doing everything by the book, so it's hard to lay blame."

"You mean blame for the death of his friends?"

"Not your fault," Archie murmured. "My question is, if construction is finished, why are the miners still hanging around?"

Rani surveyed the cave. The geologist was right; the lab setup was complete. They should have returned to the station, where every other colonist, including Kasim, waited with bated breath. "They're curious," she said. "Everyone wants to know what's going to happen."

"You want me to send them back?"

Rani considered her options. She could order them, but that would be like pouring gasoline on a fire. If Jorge didn't hate her by now . . .

A voice interrupted her musings. "If the ensign would care to move, I'd like to take one last reading on the transmission line."

Startled, Rani turned to face the middle-aged brunette who had snuck up behind them and was looking at her expectantly. "Sorry, Ellen." Rani hadn't exchanged more than a few words with the engineer since she arrived on the moon, but she seemed to be a no-nonsense type of girl. And that included dealing with the miners. Even Solomon seemed intimidated. She and her team had worked closely with Rutherford and his colleagues once the order was given to construct the lab.

Rani moved away from the wire and was watching Ellen work when Solomon wandered over with another person in tow.

"Cap'n, you know Nurse Mabel Goguen. I thought it would be a good idea to bring along some medical backup, considering what happened last time."

Rani reached out and shook hands. She recognized the familiar face from Medical. The nurse had wide cheekbones and a friendly smile. She toted a trauma kit in her free hand. "Good to see you again, Mabel. No offense, but I hope we won't require your services."

"No offense taken." Mabel grinned. "And I hope you're wasting my time."

Rani laughed. The nurse had a sense of humor.

A male voice chimed in. "I think we're ready, Ensign." Rutherford glanced sidelong at his colleagues. "Even though, for the record, we're against this."

"Your opposition is noted, Doctor," she said, taking in the collection of instruments on the benches. "But science hasn't provided any answers."

He made a dismissive gesture with his hands, and Rani got the distinct impression he was absolving himself of any guilt if something bad happened. "It's on you now."

A cold shiver ran down her spine when she realized she was the center of attention. Unlike Braeder, her first instinct was to blend into the crowd. It had been a tough slog to change that reflex. She took a deep breath and focused her thoughts. "Sensors up and running?"

"Affirmative," Vrabel replied. "Reading green across the board."

"Power supply and emergency cutoffs?"

Ellen gave her a thumbs-up. "No problem on our end. Try not to screw up yours."

Rani chuckled. Some people could get their point across without adding the weight of an insult. Ellen seemed to be one of those. "I'll do my best."

She picked up a piece of ice, weighed it in her hand, and walked up to the artifact. The white hieroglyphic-like lines beckoned her with infinite promises, until the vision of the man's head coming off in a flash of blood cured her of idealistic thoughts. The thing had killed two colonists.

She stopped when she realized Archie was walking beside her. "I told you earlier, I'm fine with this."

"I still don't like it," he grumbled. "I'm replaceable; you're not."

She smiled at his gallantry. As opposed to several others, his rationale for being the first to touch the alien artifact was born out of concern, not fame. "It's like I told Kasim and why he's pacing back and forth in Ops right now. It wouldn't be right, and you know it."

Mumbling under his breath, Archie stepped back.

The artifact waited. Up close, the surface appeared to be composed of some type of resin, if that meant anything. Broken and crushed pieces of scissor truck peeked out from under the base, like oil leaking from a smashed engine.

In the cave, no one moved. The com remained quiet. She steeled herself, reached out, and touched the artifact with the ice.

After a few seconds, she stepped back. "Anything?"

Rutherford looked up from his monitor. "Nothing. No radiation or emissions of any kind. Every instrument is reading baseline."

*Damn.* Rani feared as much. *Well, time for a leap of faith.* She dropped the ice, took a deep breath, and reached out. As soon as her fingers touched the surface, the white hieroglyphics blazed, and a warm sensation shot up her arm.

There was something else, something that seeped into her veins. A sensation—no, a feeling—of . . . what? Curiosity? Surprise? It grew stronger, like a volcano about to blow. Shocked, she jerked her hand back.

"Got it!" Vrabel shouted. "Neutrino burst!"

Rutherford clapped his hands like a cheerleader. "Same as last time. Computers are analyzing it now."

Archie was instantly beside her. "You okay?"

"Yeah." She examined her hand. No burns, no marks. Normal. "It felt . . . warm."

He eyed her closely. "Nothing else?"

She lifted her hand for all to see. The strange sensation was gone. *Did she imagine it?* "I'm good."

Archie exhaled.

"Another number buried in the emission," Rutherford said. "Six six two six zero seven. Now it's back to playing possum again."

"I don't understand." Kasim's voice on the com. "Does that number mean something?"

"It's Planck's constant," Ellen said. "A universal constant that defines the quantum nature of energy. But don't worry; we don't expect non-scientific people to understand."

Somebody chuckled, and Rani figured Kasim was turning several shades of red.

"Oh." He sounded dutifully chastised.

Rani realized she should have felt elated. She was the first human in history to touch something born of an alien civilization. What did Armstrong feel when he stepped on the moon, or Carol on Mars? Instead, she felt disappointed. This was no eureka moment, no sudden communication with an alien race, and, worse, no new information. Still, it troubled her how easy the artifact had gleaned so much human knowledge so quickly.

"So, what have we learned?"

"Enough," Rutherford said. "We now know there's something about the speed of light *and* Planck's constant that we have to focus on. Maybe we have to bombard the artifact with neutrinos in a frequency based on those numbers."

"Or some multiple," Vrabel added.

"And that will cause it to react?" Rani asked.

"We're just getting started, Ensign." Rutherford was back to using his paternal tone. "I'm sure we'll find the right response in the weeks ahead."

No one argued, but Rani knew they were all thinking the same thing: Did their primitive technology have a hope of finding a key to unlock the artifact mystery? They hadn't exactly succeeded so far. And if this neutrino signal was, in fact, a warning from the aliens as Archie had hinted, what did that say about their ambitions? Humanity already balanced precariously on the edge. Extinction was just a short step away.

"Excuse me." Kasim was back on the line. "But I have a question."

Someone snickered. It sounded like Ellen. "Somebody get him a textbook."

"Enough," Rani said. "Let's hear it, Kasim."

"Sorry," Kasim continued. "But we've stimulated it twice and received two responses."

"Two universal constants," Vrabel corrected.

"Two universal constants," Kasim repeated. "My question is what if the numbers don't matter? Rather, the fact the artifact is responding is all that matters."

Everyone stopped moving. Rani looked over at the scientists, who in turn, were staring at each other. Even Ellen appeared slack-jawed. Until she began to clap. "Very good, Mr. Governor, sir. I take back everything I ever said about you." She turned to Rani. "The man's got a point. Maybe we're focusing on the wrong thing."

Rani chanced a look at Rutherford for confirmation, but the scientist didn't meet her gaze.

"Okay," she admitted. "But it doesn't give us any more insight into its purpose."

"On the contrary," Vrabel said. "Your theory about the foil seems to be correct."

"How's that?"

Vrabel pointed to his computer screen. "I was able to localize the emission pattern. The exact origin of the neutrinos is not the artifact but the broken piece of foil still attached to the base. Instead of it being focused in one direction, the field of neutrinos disperses like a gas."

"So, it was supposed to send a message back to . . . somewhere?" Rani asked.

"Right," Archie said. "Which means it's acting like an early-warning system, and that's not good."

"Time to go?" Archie asked. He picked up the top half of his EV suit and checked the battery. Fifteen percent. Enough to make it back to the station but not much more.

Rani surveyed the interior of the cave. Only Vrabel and Jorge remained, the others having departed over the course of the afternoon. Vrabel was busy switching the detectors and scanners to automatic. Jorge had donned his EV suit before tightening a few staging bolts that had come loose.

After a fruitless, frustrating few hours, everyone was dejected and tired. With no more information forthcoming, the letdown was almost painful. The mood of the colonists would follow suit once they got the news. So much for first contact.

Rani sighed as her hopes for a response from the artifact withered on the vine. "I guess we're done here, Archie." She changed frequencies. "Vrabel, we're heading back. What's your plan?"

Towering over the control panel, Vrabel reminded Rani of an American basketball player, long arms and even longer legs. "I guess I'll join you, Ensign. We've reached the point of diminishing returns. No choice but to let the scanners monitor the artifact overnight."

"'Bout time," Jorge said. "I'm outta here." He pocketed his auto-drill and slung his tool bag over his shoulder before entering the airlock.

"Pleasant sort," Archie muttered on their private channel.

Rani put on her suit and waited for Vrabel and Archie to do the same. Three people in the airlock was a tight fit, and Vrabel had to hunch over as the air was pumped out of the small chamber. After thirty seconds, the outer hatch opened, and they walked to the stairs leading out of the cave.

"Ladies first," Vrabel said with a smile.

Rani hesitated, glancing back at the artifact. "It was probably too much to hope for, some simple message, I mean. Something positive."

"If there's a way to communicate, we'll do our best to find it," the scientist promised. He started up the stairs.

Archie gave her a bemused look. "Our leader wants to be the last person to leave?"

Rani's jaw tightened. The man had an annoying habit of reading her mind. Still, she did feel guilty. Their failure to discern a message reflected poorly on her.

A sudden yelp caught their attention, and a body tumbled down the stairs. Vrabel flailed helplessly before slamming into the unforgiving ice floor. His painful groans echoed over the com.

Archie was on him in a heartbeat. "What happened?"

Vrabel only moaned as he thrashed back and forth, gripping his leg.

"I'll hold him!" Archie called. "You check his bio signs."

Rani dropped to her knees and gripped Vrabel's arm. She managed to tap the right buttons on his wrist, and his vitals flashed across her heads-up display. Pulse and blood pressure through the roof. Adrenaline level peaking.

She tapped another button and the suit diagnosed the problem: a fractured tibia. The AI automatically administered an analgesic and sedative, and Vrabel's painful writhing slowed as he slipped into dreamland.

Archie relaxed his grip and leaned back on his haunches.

Rani keyed the com. "Rani to Kasim. Medical emergency at the extractor site. Send a response team with the gator."

Kasim came back immediately. "Confirmed. Team on the way."

She looked at Archie. "What the hell happened? Did he slip?"

Archie didn't answer. He got up and walked to the stairs. "No." His response was gruff, almost angry. "He didn't slip." He tossed a piece of guidewire into Rani's lap. "See that?" He pointed to the free end. "Someone cut it."

# CHAPTER 9

*By nature, men are nearly alike; by practice, they may be wide apart.*

DAY 62, 0545 HOURS

"The label says *spaghetti*." Louis's face twisted in disgust. "But a better description would be *roadkill*." He took a deep swig of his water in an obvious attempt to remove the taste of his last bite.

Seated on his open cryo-pod, Gunner put down his empty ration bag and snickered. "That coming from a man who spent the last year feeding us something he called vitamins but tasted more like toenail fungus."

Louis glared at the veteran. "Yeah, it damn well kept you and everyone else alive while the solar system starved to death." He hesitated, giving Gunner the once-over. "I guess we all make mistakes."

Gunner made a growling noise in his throat while Ryan, finishing off his own ration pack, chuckled at Sasha's consternation. "Don't worry. Once you get past the insults and the bickering and the petty jealousy, they really like each other." He got up and deposited the empty bag into the recycling bin before brushing crumbs off his pants.

Ryan didn't bother to mention the other inescapable fact: the doctor was right. The stored rations may have tasted like shit, but they were necessary. After weeks in cryo-sleep, even with IV supplements, the organs that comprised the human body required nourishment. Fortunately, two days of light exercise, fluids, and regular food had everyone feeling somewhat normal.

Ryan marched up to the cockpit, where Chan was working the controls. "Update?"

"Almost close enough to initiate scanning, Lieutenant. Another twenty minutes and I'll have some answers for you."

Ryan focused on the gray asteroid in the distance. It might have contained over a third of the mass in the Belt, but it was still less than half the size of Europa. "Diagnostics?"

"Systems in the green. Anticipate a normal landing on whatever pad you choose."

Ryan dreaded asking the next question. "And our sister ship?"

Chan's expression tightened. Ryan knew having a trainee at the wheel of the second transport was keeping her up at night. "Still running on autopilot. I'm hoping I can place it in orbit remotely. The hard part comes when it's time to land."

Ryan frowned. Visions of the second ship erupting in a fireball had haunted his dreams since he made the decision to bring both *Serenity* and *Phoenix*. "Everyone out of their pods?"

Chan tapped her earpiece. "Just spoke to Lecky. The miners had a wee stomach issue." She mimed sticking a finger down her throat. "But they're feeling better now. So much for our macho men."

"And the pilot?"

"Nervous." Chan reached forward to tap buttons on the console, and the nose of the transport dipped several degrees. "He's worried about the landing."

"Aren't we all?" Ryan muttered. He slipped into the copilot's seat. "Put me through."

She keyed the com while he pulled on a headset. "*Phoenix* to *Serenity*. This is Lieutenant Braeder."

"*Serenity* here, Lieutenant. Pilot Stoll."

"Chan tells me everyone is up and about. Congratulations on your maiden flight."

Ryan noticed Chan's grin. No doubt she was recalling her first time.

"Thank you, sir." There was a slight pause. "Uh, Lieutenant, Ms. Lecky would like a word."

Before Ryan could reply, a familiar voice filled the frequency. "Ryan, I think we should land at the Federation colony, New Moscow. That's where my father's factory is located."

Ryan bit his tongue before a parade of four-letter words marched out of his mouth. Sybil had blindsided him. In the brig, she had told him her father had a factory on Ceres. What she failed to mention was the fact it was not in an Alliance colony but a Russian one. A tiny voice in his head whispered, *I told you so.*

"Are you telling me you don't know the layout of the Alliance hives? Because that's what you inferred back on Europa."

"Oh, I know them. Somewhat. It's just I know this one better."

Ryan felt like spitting nails. Europa needed Alliance parts, which meant, in his mind, they had to land at an Alliance colony.

"I spoke to the miners and they agree," she continued. "We can start at New Moscow and move on from there."

"Thank you, Ms. Lecky," he managed between clenched teeth. "I'll take that under advisement." He cut the channel before he said something that didn't play well over an open frequency.

Chan seemed engrossed in her instruments as he turned and climbed out of the seat.

"Why is your face red?" Sasha asked when he entered the cargo hold.

Louis allowed a knowing smile to bloom. "It's the heat, Sasha," he said, winking at Gunner. "Sometimes, our glorious leader struggles with old flames."

Gunner chortled. "What did she want, Ace?"

"To have us land at New Moscow."

The veteran's eyebrow bunched into a hairy knot. "She wants us to land at a Federation station? What the hell for?"

"Apparently, that's where the senator's factory is located."

Louis folded the sleeve over his amputated limb and sealed it with tape. "He built it on foreign soil?"

Gunner snorted and caught Ryan's eye. "Greed knows no boundaries. I'm betting she never mentioned that part when she said she worked on the asteroid."

Ryan sighed and leaned his hip against his cryo-pod. Once more, his naiveté left him scrambling. He bit the inside of his lip and waved everybody in. "All right, Chan's going to initiate scanning in a few minutes. Hopefully, we'll find a prime candidate for supplies and get in and out as fast as possible."

Louis took some shaky steps and sat on the open pod next to Ryan. His color had almost returned to normal. "You should have plenty of choices. There are what, a dozen colony stations on this rock?"

"Ten," Gunner said. "Six Alliance, three Federation, and one Caliphate." He tilted his head. "The Alliance colonies are the largest. Maybe the best candidates?"

"Maybe," Ryan acknowledged, realizing he was second-guessing his initial landing choices. *Damn Sybil.* "But they're also the oldest." His gaze found Sasha. "What do you think about Federation colonies? Since they're newer and probably have the most modern equipment?" He gritted his teeth at the possibility they would follow Sybil's suggestion and land at New Moscow.

The young engineer tapped her chin thoughtfully. "It's not a question of age; rather, it's about the systems."

"What do you mean?" Gunner asked.

"It's a matter of standardization. Europa needs $CO_2$ scrubbers, magnesium batteries, and wire, not to mention parts for our secondary systems. The Alliance stations, even though they're older, use similar components—think computers and mechanical—so that's where we need to go. The Caliphate and Federation colonies were constructed using different engineering standards. Bottom line, their computers may not talk to ours, replacement parts may not fit, and everything from processors to plumbing may not mesh with our systems. I'd recommend we go where the pieces are similar."

"Well, that answers my question." Ryan raised his eyebrows at Gunner. "You good with that?"

"I didn't know the other settlements used different standards," Gunner admitted. "Based on that alone, there's no choice. It'd be a frustrating day for our engineers if they had to jury-rig systems. Don't know if they could do it."

"It would take time," Sasha added, nodding at Chan as she joined them. "And definitely wouldn't be as efficient."

Ryan sucked in a breath and came to a decision. "Okay, first thing we'll do is a flyby of the Alliance stations to get a firsthand view of the damage. Then we decide on which one."

Dr. Louis raised a hand. "Why do we have to settle on just one station? Why not two or even three?"

"Because we have a newbie pilot on the second ship who is scared shitless about one landing," Chan replied. "Making him attempt multiple takeoffs and landings would probably give him a stroke."

"Well." Louis blinked as the realization hit home. "I guess nothing gets easy for this group."

The cockpit of a Fleet transport wasn't designed to hold four people. Not only that, but Chan made it clear her work area was strictly off-limits. The look she gave Gunner when his elbow inadvertently invaded her space was enough to freeze water. The veteran quickly pulled his arm back and squeezed his butt next to Ryan's in the copilot's seat. Sasha sat on his knee.

The redhead giggled when Ryan tried to apologize for the tight quarters.

"Don't sweat it, Lieutenant. When I was a kid back in Iowa, I used to sit on my dad's knee in the cab of the tractor all the time. And he wasn't as ancient as this old fart."

Gunner rolled his eyes.

"Coming up on Ceres now," Chan announced.

"Did you try and hail the colonies?" Ryan asked.

"On multiple frequencies," she replied. "No response."

Ryan nodded grimly. In his last broadcast, the admiral said the colonies had decided to open their EV doors when the food ran out. This only confirmed it. "Just to be clear, it's not a communication problem?"

"Don't believe so, Lieutenant. I even found one functioning coms satellite still in orbit. Fact is, every colony is silent."

"Damn shame," Gunner muttered.

Ryan leaned forward to get a better view of the asteroid. Outside, the infinite expanse of darkness was punctuated only by tiny, distinct points of light. No familiar sun in the sky, no massive gas giant hanging over their heads. Ceres was a spherical rock approaching on the starboard side, ghost-gray and littered with craters that could be millions or billions of years old.

"It's bigger than I pictured," Sasha said, bracing her arms against Gunner's chest to see over the control panel.

"Largest asteroid in the Belt," the veteran replied. "But it's still only about six hundred kilometers across—smaller than the state of Texas."

"What's that?" Ryan pointed to a fuzzy patch of space over the asteroid that resembled webbing on a screen door.

"A water-vapor plume," Chan replied. "I've landed transports here before. The rock has active volcanos that occasionally eject water into the atmosphere. The moisture can stay up there for months or even years."

"Because of the weak gravity?" Sasha asked.

"Exactly." Chan scanned the asteroid. "It can't compete with Europa in terms of the amount of water, but there's still a helluva lot of ice under the surface."

Ryan noted the appearance of tiny reflections on the surface: faint sunlight echoing off a smattering of artificial structures. He steeled himself for what was coming. Since the plague started on Earth, every snippet of bad news about his sister colonies had been received electronically, through Fleet messages. They had accepted the dire updates without seeing the evidence firsthand. That was about to change.

"There's the first station," Gunner said, pointing. "It looks Alliance. Probably one of the original colonies."

Sasha gave him a look. "How can you tell?"

The veteran gestured to an elongated building with several pyramid-like structures radiating from a central hub. "Just like on Europa, those hives are simple warehouses—boxy structures where they could add interior walls as the number of colonists increased. When one building filled up, they simply shipped in another module and connected it through the hub. Since this one has three attached modules, I'm guessing it's one of the earliest constructed. Probably Alpha or Beta."

Chan chuckled. "The computer identifies it as Beta Station."

Sasha elbowed him in the side. "Not bad, old man. Try not to look so smug."

"They named them according to the Greek alphabet?" Chan asked.

"That's right," Gunner confirmed. "The pattern caught on, which is why our hives are named the same way."

The banter didn't lighten Ryan's mood. Details shifted into focus as the transport passed directly over the colony. His breath caught in his throat. "The main EV door is open." He didn't bother pointing. Everyone could see debris spilling out of the open chamber: clothing, pieces of metal, and what appeared to be human bodies half-buried in gray dirt.

"Goddamn," Chan said. "Mass suicide."

Gunner's expression hardened. "I said it before. It was a Hobson's choice: starve to death or end it quick and painless."

"Mostly painless," Ryan muttered. He caught Gunner's eye. "How many?"

The veteran ran his hand through his beard. "Those domiciles handle about two thousand colonists each. So . . . six thousand souls."

A moment of silence passed, broken by Chan. "I need a decision. If we're going to land here, I have to know now."

"Keep going," Ryan said. "There's a lot of debris on that runway and I don't want to take any chances."

Chan nodded and adjusted course, and the transport slowly came about. "The Alliance stations are fairly close together, so the next one should be coming up quick." She tapped a few buttons, checked the monitor, and nodded to herself. "I've got *Serenity* holding on my six. It's . . ." She tapped her earpiece. "Ms. Lecky would like to have a word, Lieutenant. Shall I tell her you're occupied?"

Ryan shifted in the chair. "Tell her I died and can't talk right now."

Sasha snickered, and even Gunner grinned.

"Chan, you have the final say," Ryan continued. "Find a safe patch to put us down. If all the stations opened their EV doors, there could be debris covering every landing strip."

"Already thought of that, Lieutenant," Chan replied. "I'll check it out first. How close to the station would you like to land?"

"As close as possible. The low gravity will help, but there's a ton of supplies we'll have to carry to the transports."

"Understood."

Ryan watched the dull gray surface come into focus as the ship dipped into a lower orbit. He recognized Ahuna Mons, the largest volcano on Ceres, as it passed under their wing. The peak seemed close enough to brush the fuselage.

Gunner scowled as they passed the second station. Debris covered the landing strip like a soiled carpet. "Not looking good, Ace. The admiral said each colony decided on the same course when food ran out."

"Don't worry, Gunner." Ryan extricated himself from the copilot seat. "I have the best pilot in the solar system. She'll find somewhere to park." He turned to Chan. "Notify me when we're on final approach."

"Sir, I . . ." Chan started to reply, but Ryan had already left. She looked at Gunner. "I hate when he does that."

"This ain't all about you," Ryan said, peering over Louis's shoulder as the doctor typed in a list of items on his minicom.

"Mind your own business," Louis snapped. "You asked for a medical list. I'm giving you a medical list."

Ryan's lips twitched. "We still need room for other components like, I don't know, transmission wire."

Louis snorted and shoved his minicom into his pocket. "This is not a Christmas catalogue, Ryan. I'm low on everything from antibiotics to stitches to analgesics. In about a month, I'm going to be forced to perform operations without anesthetic. How do you feel about holding a patient down while I cut them open?"

Visions of Civil War amputations made Ryan shiver. “That’s not funny.”

“Do you think I’m joking?” Louis raised his eyebrows. “Lucky for you, most of what I need can fit in a shoebox.”

Ryan breathed easier when he realized the doctor was right. Bandages and medication vials didn’t take up much space.

A tap on the shoulder stole his attention.

“Chan needs you up front,” Gunner said.

Ryan shifted his focus, glad to be rid of Louis’s horrifying vision. “We’re approaching the next station?”

“Yeah,” Gunner sounded like he had marbles in his mouth, but his stare didn’t waver.

Ryan felt a warning buzzer go off in the back of his skull.

The copilot seat was empty after Sasha returned to the cargo hold, so Ryan took it. Gunner followed him into the cockpit but remained standing in the entrance. Chan had lowered the orbit even more. Up close, the surface of the asteroid bore little resemblance to the ice plates of Europa. It was dull, gray, and monotonous, except for ancient impact craters that scoured the surface like a bad case of acne. Accumulations of rocky material, too small to be called mountains, rose up several hundred feet to disturb the flatness.

An Alliance station was visible out the pilot’s window: four pyramid-shaped hives surrounding a central building—probably a concourse—twice the size of the one on Europa. To one side sat the laser, transport hangar, and several outlying buildings.

“I’ve circled twice already,” Chan said. “The landing strip is clear, but you need to see this.”

“See what?” He placed his hands on the top of the console and leaned forward.

Chan tilted the ship several degrees so he could get a better view. “There’s a ton of detritus outside the airlock.” She pointed. “This side of the laser.”

It was hard to miss. A spray of material, cloth, and metal reflecting the pale glow of the distant sun covered an area about the size of a football field.

Behind him, Gunner murmured, “See the problem, Ace?”

It took a second for realization to sink in. Except for the unnatural contents littering the surface, the overall structure looked intact. Unlike Europa, there were no bullet holes in the walls, no dead Marines sprawled in front of the airlock. He hesitated as his brain registered what his eyes were telling him. "The EV door is closed."

Gunner pressed his lips tight. "Which means someone had to stay behind and close it. And I'm guessing that someone is still in there."

"Christ, Ryan, what are we going to do?" Louis wrung his hands like an expectant father as he paced between cryo-pods. "Could anyone still be alive down there?"

"Are you kidding?" Sasha gave him an incredulous look. "After a year? Unless they have a greenhouse hidden underground, nobody lives."

Sitting on an open pod, Gunner tapped his fingers against the plastek cover. "Not to mention there's been no response to our hails."

"Somebody closed the door," Louis reminded them. "After the fact."

"Slow down, everyone," Ryan said. "We don't know anything for sure. If there are colonists still alive, they could be anywhere. Which is why we're not going to take chances." He stepped over to a closed storage locker and applied his thumbprint to the locking mechanism. It sprang open and stale air gushed out. He reached in and withdrew a heavy metal object.

Sasha gasped.

"You've got to be kidding," Louis said. "You brought a gun?"

"A machine gun," Ryan corrected, handing it to Gunner. He recalled performing the same action with a revolver a year ago. It helped turn the tide of battle. "Doc, one thing I learned the hard way was to be prepared. Before we lifted off, I couldn't imagine a scenario where we would need these, but I brought them anyway."

"Them?" Louis asked. "As in plural?"

"Yes." Ryan removed a second machine gun and checked the clip. "Compliments of our dear departed senator and his marines. And to answer your original question, we're going to do what we came here to do and that's resupply."

Sasha wandered over and took a closer look at the weapon. "I thought so. Upgraded version that handles the rapid cooldown and material stress."

"Yeah." The doctor's tone carried a hefty amount of sarcasm. "They were pretty effective in the hands of Lecky's marines last year."

Ryan leaned his weapon against the cryo-pod and checked his watch. "I spoke with Chan a few minutes ago. She should be starting her final approach right about now. Once we're down, she's going to help *Serenity* land by remote control. Then we'll link up and enter through the closest EV door."

"The one that someone shut?" Sasha asked. She seemed to have gotten a grip on her shock at seeing the guns.

Ryan nodded grimly. "Yeah, that one."

# CHAPTER 10

*He who conquers himself is the greatest warrior.*

DAY 62, 0915 HOURS

Ryan had to give Chan credit: she was one hell of a pilot. He couldn't fall into bed any easier than she landed *Phoenix* on the surface. Now, watching her remote-pilot *Serenity* from *Phoenix*'s cockpit gave him goosebumps. She looked like a teenager playing an old vid game on a fuzzy monitor.

"Don't touch those flaps!" she barked, and it took Ryan a second to realize she wasn't talking to him but rather Stoll, the other pilot.

"Let me handle those. Just lower the speed like I taught you. Gently. That's it. Keep it above stalling."

Outside the cockpit window, Ryan and Gunner watched the second transport make its final approach. The landing gear was down, and the flashing yellow light on the fuselage seemed to mimic the heartbeat of the ship. It would only go out if the transport crashed.

"Pull the nose up," Chan ordered. "No, not that much. Down two degrees. There." She exhaled. "Better."

The rear wheels touched, bounced, and touched again. "Okay, lower the nose."

The front wheel hit the ground hard. Chan grunted like she had been struck herself. "Full reverse now. Brakes . . . No! The other lever! Good."

Ryan felt like he was about to explode. Gunner's hands squeezed the back of the seat so hard, his fingers turned white.

*Serenity* rolled up the landing strip and stopped a full ship-length away from *Phoenix*.

Sweat trickling down her face, Chan slumped in her seat. "Please don't make me do that again, Lieutenant."

Gunner punched the cockpit wall and stomped away. Ryan knew exactly how he felt. The pent-up frustration in his own breast demanded a release. Unfortunately, as leader, he didn't have that luxury. "Have everyone in *Serenity* get into their suits and meet us on the tarmac."

Chan wiped her sleeve against her brow. "You want me there as well?"

Ryan hesitated. He had two ships and only two pilots. Putting either of them in harm's way was not exactly a sound tactical decision. That being said, he had fifteen hundred colonists on Europa depending on him to find replacement parts, and a finite number of bodies to do the work. No, it was all-hands-on-deck time.

"I want every person on this one," Ryan said, his expression set. "Whatever the hell we're getting into, we're doing it together."

As Ryan descended the loading ramp, he felt the weight of irrelevance on his shoulders. In the vast scheme of the universe, were they just a minuscule cog inside an infinite machine? Would their actions affect the rotation of the galaxies, the lifespan of the sun, or the continuation of the species?

And yet, the job ahead wasn't small, either. Before the plague, whenever a transport landed on Europa, it took days for the creaking auto-cats and forklifts to unload the cargo. It also required dozens of men and women to transport foodstuffs, computer equipment, and construction material into the station. On Ceres, he had a sum total of eleven individuals.

The end of the ramp had sunk several inches into the gray, powdery surface. He bent down and ran his glove through the chalk-like substance called regolith, a mixture of powdery dust and broken rock formed by meteorite impacts. Billions of years of collisions. He stared at the bleak background, a carpet of gray nothingness that stretched to the horizon. It was more than boring; it was plain depressing.

"You don't want to leave the ramp down, Ace?" Gunner asked over the com as he descended the metal grating alongside Ryan. "Might be a little quicker on the loading side."

"No." Ryan had learned the hard way not to leave loose ends. It might seem like the easiest route, but Fate had a gift for the unexpected. "I'm not leaving our front door unlocked. Tell Stoll I want the same for *Serenity*."

"Aye, aye."

Ryan surveyed the landscape leading to the station and noticed a reddish tint to the surface. Maybe some iron clay intermixed with regolith? Chan had parked *Phoenix* close to one of the hives branching off the central hub. The landing strip was smooth thanks to human intervention, but impact craters scarred the rest of the asteroid's surface. Several construction vehicles sat parked on one side of the runway: two excavators and a dump truck. Probably used for routine maintenance. He took his first steps and watched his boots sink into the surface. If it wasn't for the abundance of water underground and the rare minerals buried even deeper in the asteroid's interior, mankind would never have built colonies on this godforsaken rock. Given a choice, he'd take the icefields of Europa every time.

He gave his crew a few minutes to acclimatize to the low gravity; it was only three percent of Earth or twenty times less than Europa. Even for military brats like himself with numerous spacewalks under their belts, it took a while for muscle memory to kick in. If someone pushed off with the same strength as on Europa, they might end up floating in the limited atmosphere or, worse, sailing headfirst into the side of a building.

Gunner adjusted quickly, but Sasha took several seconds to come down after each step. The veteran took her by the arm. "Slow down," he said. "Watch me."

She nodded inside her helmet, and after a few minutes, she got the hang of it. He was a little worried about the doctor. Walking in vacuum and low gravity involved balance and dexterity, and Louis had barely put on an EV suit since the amputation. Having only three limbs made it that much more difficult. Fortunately, the medical man seemed to manage.

Chan was the last one off the ramp. "All set, Lieutenant?"

Ryan did a quick headcount. "Close it up."

She tapped a few buttons on her wrist and the ramp began a slow ascent.

The sun was a pale-yellow dot on the horizon, buried in a sky full of stars and a whole lot of nothing. They could have been standing on an island in the middle of an endless sea. The sensation was almost overwhelming.

"Here they come," Gunner said.

Four EV-clad figures descended *Serenity*'s ramp and started walking toward them.

"Are we missing someone?" Ryan asked. *There should be five. Three reservists, Sybil, and the pilot.*

"Stoll thought he spotted something on the side of the runway," Chan explained. "I told him to send someone to make sure there's no debris that could get sucked into the engines when we lift off."

"Who is it?"

"Gonzalez."

Ryan turned and spotted the big miner trudging along one side of the landing strip. "Tell him to hurry. I want to get inside the station ASAP."

Chan quietly relayed the message.

Ryan turned and almost bumped into Sybil.

"What the hell are you doing?" she demanded. It took Ryan a second to realize she was speaking on a private frequency. "You drag me here because of my experience on this asteroid, and then you promptly disregard everything I say? If this is the way I'm going to be treated, I wish you'd left me back in my cell. At least there, only Rani ignored me."

Ryan stared at her hard expression through the faceplate, cheeks tightened into pointed barbs and eyes narrowed to slits. He did his best to maintain a poker face, but the satisfaction that flowed through his veins made it difficult. "Your advice will be heeded at the appropriate time, Sybil. Choosing a landing site was my decision. Besides, you never said your father's factory was in a Federation station."

Her eyes narrowed even further, and Ryan knew she wanted to say something more, probably something caustic or threatening, but she had little leverage. Unlike a year before, when Ryan was a naive lieutenant flying by the seat of his pants.

"What difference does that make? Every station should have what we need."

Ryan shook his head. "Not true. I'm betting only parts in the Alliance stations will be interchangeable with our own. But if that doesn't appeal to you, feel free to return to the transport and wait for us there, because this is not a democracy. The mission will run on my timetable. Is that understood?"

Her mouth worked, but all that came out of his helmet speaker was a grunt.

Chan chose that moment to walk over and pump Stoll's hand. "Congratulations. You just earned your wings."

"Thanks." The colonist sounded like a beaten dog. "Pretty sure I left ten years of my life up there."

Several people chuckled. Ryan wondered what they were thinking during those tension-wracked seconds before the ship touched down. He shifted frequencies. "Gunner, you and Sasha start working on the EV door. Whoever shut it probably didn't leave it unlocked."

"I can bypass it, Lieutenant," Sasha said, holding up her minicom with several wires dangling from the side. "Might take a few minutes, but shouldn't be a problem." She turned and started for the door. Gunner shrugged and followed.

"Cheeky little lady," Louis said over a private line, chuckling. "I think she's adopted Gunner as her newest uncle."

"Seems that way," Ryan mused. In truth, he didn't know what to think about the young engineer. In many ways she reminded him of Marco: smart as a whip but emotionally immature. "All right, everyone," he said over the general com. "Let's grab our gear and get moving."

In ones and twos, they picked up the bags and packs. The reservists were responsible for the heavy boxes that contained their power tools as well as crowbars, cutting saws, and welding equipment. The machine guns were buried near the bottom of one of those boxes. By the time Ryan started walking along the landing strip, Sasha and Gunner had reached the airlock.

Chan grabbed Ryan's arm. "What's that?" She pointed past the transports. "I saw movement."

Ryan stared at gray powder that stretched to the horizon. Nothing . . . until something twitched at the edge of his vision. His pulse jumped. Craters didn't move. He saw it again, reflected light when something shifted position. No, several things. All moving in their direction.

"What the hell? You said *Phoenix* didn't pick up any chatter."

She shook her head. "Just static. All frequencies were quiet."

Ryan stepped away from the others to get a better view. He activated the camera in his helmet and zoomed in. What initially appeared as a smudge on the horizon dissolved into separate shapes: seven EV suits advancing across the surface. His initial surprise and even shock faded as a feeling of trepidation took hold. Followed by fear.

"Lieutenant?" Chan whispered. "They don't look right."

Ryan noticed it as well. Their movements were rough and uncoordinated. Their legs seemed clumsy and awkward, and their arms flailed like marionettes on broken strings. "They don't." He tried to tamp out that spark of dread, but it had grown into a sense of foreboding. Something was very wrong.

What should he do? The question ballooned in his brain. Should he retreat to the ship? He chanced a glance at Gunner and Sasha, who were working on the airlock's external panel. Still oblivious to the new arrivals, the rest of his team dropped their packs and containers by the hatch.

No, he didn't have time. They had minutes at most before whoever was crossing the surface reached the transports. He shifted frequencies. "Gunner, we got company and I'm not sure they're friendly."

The veteran's head whipped around. "Where?"

"Other side of the landing strip. We need to get inside the station. Now!"

"Copy that." Gunner slipped the bag off his shoulder.

Everyone stopped what they were doing and stared.

"What the hell is wrong with them?" Sybil said, her voice dropping into a whisper.

Louis stepped up beside Ryan. "Something strange about the way they're moving."

Ryan blinked. It was more than strange; it was downright unnatural. "Chan, move everyone close to the hatch."

"What about Gonzalez?"

Ryan hesitated. He had forgotten about the reservist. "Call him back."

Chan relayed the order, but instead of retreating, the man stopped and gawked at the approaching figures.

"Move, Gonzalez!" Ryan shouted.

The harsh tone spurred the man into motion. Long strides took him toward the transports.

"He's not going to make it!" Chan blurted.

Ryan intuitively knew she was right. The creatures were on an intercept course.

Gonzalez abruptly changed direction, away from the landing strip. Like a pack of lions, all seven pursuers angled toward him. They weren't fast, but Gonzalez didn't have a clear path. He picked up a rock and hurled it at the group, missing badly.

Each of the creatures carried some type of tool, a section of pipe or metal rod. They fell on him like a pack of carnivores. Sunlight reflected off steel as they landed blow after blow. Gonzalez's screams echoed in Ryan's helmet. The AI automatically turned down the volume, but his painful cries only lasted seconds and ended with a final gurgle. The creatures pawed at him, ripping and shredding his suit well after the body stopped moving.

Sasha squealed and seized Gunner's arm.

Bile surged into Ryan's throat. *What the hell just happened?* "Gunner!"

"I saw it." The veteran tore his gaze off the carnage and focused on the locking mechanism. He kept his tone deceptively calm as he gently but firmly moved Sasha's hands back to the panel. "We're bypassing the circuit now."

The creatures straightened over Gonzalez's ruined body. The man's limbs had been torn from his torso and pieces of his suit scattered like discarded ration packs—if the ration packs had been soaked in blood.

In a single movement, seven helmets swiveled to face Ryan. Fresh stains covered the front of their EV suits.

Ryan's heart pounded against his ribcage. His crew was exposed and vulnerable on the surface, just like Gonzalez. He cursed himself for not having the guns ready. It would take precious minutes to unpack them using clumsy EV gloves. "Running out of time," he warned.

"Something's wrong," Sasha called, her words laced with panic. "The controls won't respond."

Each member of Ryan's team stepped back in tandem until their backs touched the wall of the station. Louis stared wide-eyed at the approaching forms loping across the surface. The surrounding regolith was covered in detritus: ripped pieces of cloth, crumpled papers, and unrecognizable bits of plastek and metal. Like someone had dumped garbage out a second-story window.

Ryan counted down the seconds. Gunner and Sasha had their hands buried in the control panel. Sparks landed on Sasha's arm. Chan and Sybil edged up beside Ryan while the reservists frantically removed crowbars and sledgehammers from the tool cases.

As the attackers closed the distance, Ryan used his camera to zoom in. He shuddered at the sight of scarred and disfigured faces, tongues lolling and eyes bulging like madmen. The unnatural way their limbs spasmed and jerked kindled a visceral fear in his gut.

"Running out of time," Ryan warned. Fifty meters. The reservists formed a line with Ryan in the middle. Sybil and Chan stepped back with Louis and Stoll.

Sasha slammed her small fist against the panel. "The computer is shit. It's either seized or the door is welded shut." Her gaze flickered over her shoulder, and all color ran from her cheeks.

Ryan didn't take his eyes off the approaching horror. "Gunner?"

"She's right." The veteran joined the line. "We're not getting in."

Ryan swallowed. This was not the ending he'd envisioned when he planned this mission: pinned against the wall of a dead colony while a crazed horde descended on his crew. He had a mental image of the African debacle where he lost his entire command. The odds were about the same: three miners, him and Gunner against seven bloodthirsty maniacs. Even a small tear in a suit would be fatal.

"Steady." He kept his voice calm. "Stay tight—"

Thirty meters.

"It's opening!" Sasha cried.

Ryan felt the vibration through his boots as hydraulic motors kicked in and, behind him, the hatch began to rise.

"Go!" Gunner grabbed Sasha and the doctor and thrust them into the large airlock. Sybil dived through the opening alongside Chan and Stoll. The miners almost tripped over each other, scrambling to follow.

Ryan took a few steps before turning around. The attackers were ten meters out. No way the hatch could close before they got in. Somebody had to delay them. He set his boots on the step and cocked his arm. All he needed was a few seconds, enough to protect his people.

Something firm and unyielding seized his shoulder and jerked him inside. His back slammed against the metal side of the hatch, and air whooshed from his lungs. The reservists stepped forward like a row of tanks, blocking the entrance.

The creatures in front took it the worst. Crowbars and hammers smashed into helmets and shields. Glass cracked and split. Air screamed out of tiny fissures, and suddenly, three bodies were down and writhing on the ground. The remaining four hesitated for a fraction of a second, enough time for the reservists to retreat inside before the door cycled closed. Muted bangs reverberated through the metal as fists beat against the exterior.

Air hissed into the chamber, and Ryan's heads-up display confirmed the repressurization process had begun. Gunner threw an arm around a trembling Sasha. Sybil's expression was so tight, her face looked ready to crack.

"What the hell were those things?" she said.

Ryan shook his head. He had no idea.

"Ace, maybe we should forget about what just happened and focus on what's inside."

Ryan turned as the airflow diminished and then stopped. "Why's that?"

"Because Sasha and I didn't open the door. And whoever did is probably waiting for us."

Ryan lunged for the container holding the guns as the inner airlock door started to rise.

The decompression chamber was a mess. It was at least three times the size of the one on Europa, and every square meter was covered in dirty EV suits, smashed pieces of metal, and mounds of soot and grime. Two flickering lights in the ceiling left most of the room in shadow. Boxes of rusted machinery were stacked along one wall.

Ryan waited until Gunner had a machine gun in his hands before taking a step inside. He exhaled when it was clear no threats waited to greet them. "Everyone all right?"

A chorus of ayes answered. Gunner made eye contact through their shields. "Next time the lieutenant tries to play hero, I'm going to hit him so hard, he's gonna wish he stayed back on the colony."

Ryan's lips thinned as the moment rushed back. "Somebody had to delay them."

"That's why you brought us, Lieutenant," Smith, one of the reservists, said, slapping his chest. "Let—"

"I think we have company," Louis murmured. He pointed to an EV-suited figure stepping out from behind the control panel on the other side of the room.

Ryan tensed. "Eyes on, Gunner?"

"Got it." The veteran raised the machine gun.

"Form up," Ryan said. "On me."

Gunner and the reservists stepped up to flank him.

The person in the dirty suit standing by the control panel hadn't moved. When Gunner's gun appeared, he slowly raised his arms and removed his helmet. Ryan found himself staring at a gaunt-looking man with a thin face, patchy beard, and bloodshot eyes.

The man pointed a bony finger at Gunner. "If you're going to use that thing, make sure it's a head shot. We're out of medical supplies."

Ryan motioned, and the veteran lowered the gun.

"Thank you." The man exhaled a cloud of vapor. "Then again, that's a strange way to greet the person who just saved your lives."

Ryan removed his helmet. The air was cool and stale and carried the unmistakable odor of mold. "Thank you for that. You disabled the external panel so we couldn't bypass it?"

"Had to." He peeled off his gloves and jerked his head toward the airlock. "Or they would have gotten in a long time ago."

Ryan gestured and the rest of the party took off their helmets.

The man's eyes narrowed as he studied the insignia on their suits. "You're not from Earth?"

"No." Ryan shook his head. "Europa. We're on a supply run. Last message we received before Fleet went offline indicated there were no survivors on the asteroids."

The man offered Ryan a sad smile. "Not far from the truth. There's only a handful of us left, and little in the way of supplies." He stepped forward and extended a hand. "Name's Max Plante. I'm Governor of Ceres."

# CHAPTER 11

*Real knowledge is to know the extent of one's ignorance.*

DAY 62, 1010 HOURS

Plante led them into an area that resembled more a lounge than the briefing room Ryan was familiar with on Europa. He counted a dozen couches and a score of big puffy chairs surrounding round plastek tables. At the far end, beside a long wooden bar, sat a ten-by-ten-foot portal offering an unobstructed view of the surface: ancient impact craters and a dull expanse of sooty dirt. Ryan felt nostalgic for that massive gas giant hanging over their heads.

Mounds of dirt and piles of debris covered the polymer floor like roadkill on a busy highway. Bags of garbage were propped against a wall adorned with murals of Earth depicting roaring waterfalls and tranquil green valleys. Ryan recalled similar frescos in Europa's Command Center, and just like those pictures, these left him feeling despondent. Louis and Chan sat together on a couch while Sasha, Gunner, and Sybil found single chairs around the table. Gunner had instructed the reservists and Stoll to check their gear and grab a quick bite in a small room next to the decompression chamber.

Ryan dropped into one of the cushioned chairs and a plume of dust shot into the air. "Thanks again for opening the EV door," he said, parking his gloves and helmet by his feet. "I already lost one man on the runway." Gonzalez's death gnawed at him. Another person he was supposed to protect.

Plante took a chair opposite Ryan. His sparse beard matched his receding hairline. Yellow teeth accented his gums when he spoke. "You're welcome, Lieutenant. I'm glad I was able to help."

A tall brunette entered the room. Plante introduced her as Sam Bennett, former member of Ceres's Board. Bennett took a seat next to the governor. She had an angular face made worse by weight loss, and her crew cut failed to cover the skin ulcers on her scalp.

"Truth be told, I thought I was hallucinating when I saw your transports land," Plante admitted. "Sorry I wasn't able to send you a message. We shut down coms months ago to minimize the drain on our solar cells. And it took time to get into the EV room and suit up."

"I understand." Ryan stole a glance at Sasha. He couldn't tell if her gloomy look was a result of her failure to bypass the door controls or from what she had witnessed on the surface.

"You disabled the lock," Gunner said. "I noticed wires hanging out of the panel."

"Did that months ago," Sam replied. Her words carried a Southern accent that reminded Ryan of a certain now-deceased senator. "When the sekers appeared."

"Sekers?" Louis leaned forward and swept dirt off the arm of his chair. "Is that what you call them?"

"One of my former colleagues named them," Plante replied flatly. "Something about an old Egyptian death god. There are other names. Most less complimentary."

"Where did they come from?" Gunner asked. "I didn't recognize the suits."

Plante exchanged a look with Bennett. "They're standard Federation-issue. Best guess is they're from the station two kilometers away. They took us by surprise and killed half my men and women before we barricaded ourselves in the station."

"Did they try to break in?" Sasha asked, shivering.

"Every day in the beginning," Bennett said, her gaze flickering to the portal. "Now they just prowl the surface."

"What about other stations?" Louis said.

"The sekers have probably been through them, although since they showed up, none of us have ventured outside to confirm."

"I can see why," Sybil muttered.

Ryan frowned. "Can you explain something to me? The last broadcast we received from Fleet indicated conditions on the asteroid colonies had gotten bad and . . . steps were taken."

"Fleet wasn't wrong," Plante said. "Things got *very bad.* People were dying from starvation, including the kids. Everyone was suffering."

"That's when you made a decision?" Ryan hesitated. There was no diplomatic way to put it. "To open your EV door."

"And the colonists agreed?" Gunner said. "It couldn't have been easy."

"It wasn't," Plante said. "When Fleet shut down the supply runs, we cut rations and held out as long as we could. However, our greenhouses are small and don't come close to meeting the needs of the population." He sighed. "Eventually, we emptied the cupboard. By then, it was apparent Earth was not going to bounce back. That's when we did it."

Ryan couldn't imagine how something that drastic would play out. "Tell us what happened."

"We had a vote. Ninety-eight percent chose to open the door. So, that's what we did."

"But you're still here," Gunner said. His tone sounded nonjudgmental, but Ryan knew him well enough to recognize the underlying suspicion.

Plante stared at Gunner. "A few of us couldn't go through with it." He applied a smile to a face totally devoid of humor. "Call it an overexaggerated sense of survival. When the time came, we stole EV suits and barricaded ourselves in a large storeroom."

Sasha picked at some dirt on her suit. "And no one stopped you?"

Sam snorted. "Why would they bother? When it was over, we crawled out, closed the door, and repressurized the hab."

"And you ate what, exactly?" Gunner asked.

"We had squirreled away some rations," Plante replied, a hint of defiance in his tone.

"It couldn't have been much," Sybil said. She had tied her hair into one long braid that ran down her back. "Considering everyone was starving by the time they opted for suicide."

Ryan could imagine the wheels turning behind her eyes. Her hard stare revealed what she thought of the colonists giving up.

"Funny thing about that," Plante continued, unperturbed. "We lasted two weeks and were well past the point of regretting our decision when a guardian angel landed."

Ryan wasn't sure he heard the man correctly. "Guardian angel?"

"A transport," Bennett clarified. "An unscheduled visit from a ship that was heading for Mars before the plague struck the Red Planet. It altered course to Ceres."

In a flash of insight, Ryan understood. "It was carrying supplies."

Plante smiled. This time it seemed genuine. "One pilot and a ton of foodstuffs. A guardian angel."

"Except for one thing," Gunner said. "Even a transport's supplies are finite, and it's been over a year."

"Agreed, but we had few mouths to feed, and it gave us time to plant crops in one of the greenhouses." The governor walked up to the portal and pointed to a building attached to the hive. "Behold Ceres's Garden of Eden. It's connected to the concourse via a tunnel."

Ryan stood to get a closer look. "You have seeds?" Something they desperately needed on Europa.

Plante nodded. "Not exactly four food groups, but it kept us alive."

"Obviously," Gunner muttered.

Plante's expression faded into melancholy. "Like I said, we lost half our number when the sekers appeared. That reduced demand. We're down to four. The pilot and another colonist succumbed last month. I figured we had maybe a few weeks before something mechanical failed or malnutrition took the rest of us. Or the sekers found a way in. How many survivors on Europa?"

"About fifteen hundred." Ryan noted the governor's look of consternation. "We built a second greenhouse."

"But that would have taken months. How did you—"

"We starved," Gunner said, spitting the words out like splinters. "But we hung on."

"We lost hundreds," Ryan confirmed, ignoring Sybil's strained expression. "Dr. Louis started producing vitamin supplements and that helped. But we still had to build a graveyard outside the station." In that moment, Ryan didn't feel like elaborating.

Plante shook his head in amazement. "Congratulations. Europa now holds the largest collection of humans in the solar system. Nice to know we're not extinct. At least, not yet."

Louis tilted his head. "So, every station on Ceres followed the same path?"

"They did, but the survival gene isn't just a Western trait. Other groups tried to make a stand after their stations opened their doors."

The doctor bowed his head, ceding the point.

"What happened to them?" Sybil asked. "Did any try to link up with you?"

"Not in time," Bennett said. "Before the sekers appeared, we searched the nearest stations." Her gaze dropped. "There was nothing but bodies left."

"We're the last survivors on the asteroid," Plante said. "Except for the sekers."

"And you don't know where they came from?" Louis asked.

"We have our suspicions," Plante admitted. "Especially after an unscheduled Russian transport arrived several months after the war Earthside began. Best guess is that it launched just before the Baikonur Cosmodrome fell and wandered through the system looking for a safe place to land. We knew nothing about it at the time, but before our food ran out, there were rumors about an outbreak."

Louis's eyes bulged. "The plague hitched a ride on a Russian transport?"

"It's only a rumor," Plante repeated. "But the sekers appeared soon after."

"Well, Ace," Gunner said, "good thing we stopped anyone from boarding the transport on Europa."

Bennett frowned. "You had a similar issue?"

The veteran nodded. "One transport. Several dozen infected bodies."

The governor exchanged another look with Bennett. She inclined her head slightly before continuing. "There was scuttlebutt about Federation scientists performing experiments on infected colonists. But that was before everything went to shit."

"And no word since?" Sybil asked.

Bennett shook her head. "It's been every man for himself."

Ryan recalled those hectic months on Europa when every broadcast from the admiral contained increasingly bad news. "Last message we received said the CDC had gotten nowhere on a vaccine."

Louis held up his hand. "This doesn't make sense. The plague kills people; it doesn't turn them into murdering psychopaths."

The governor shrugged. "We don't have any proof either way."

"So, one Russian military transport." Gunner raised his index finger. "Rumors of an infection." A middle finger. "And the appearance of these sekers." He held up three fingers as if displaying the evidence.

"Makes me wonder if the Russians were working on a cure," Louis said. "Too bad we can't get into their lab."

"Yeah," Plante said. "Bloodthirsty mutants prowling the surface might cut short any trip."

Ryan looked at Louis. "Thoughts?"

The doctor puffed out his cheeks. "I reviewed all the information the admiral sent. The CDC was working with labs across the globe, but they were nowhere close to starting patient trials before civilization imploded. The damn germ mutated too fast to manufacture a functional antibiotic. In the last days, scientists got desperate and tried to design a vaccine by inserting discrete bits of DNA into a person's chromosomes."

"And that would do what?" Sasha asked.

"The theory was it would use the body's own cells to keep up with the changing bacterium. The result would be a kind of natural immunity."

Bennett pointed a finger. "You're the doctor?"

"Yes." Louis gave her a tight grin and lifted his stump in the air. "Though I'm a little shorthanded these days."

When no one laughed, he sat back.

"We could really use your services," Bennett said. "Our two colleagues aren't doing well."

Plante focused on the amputated limb. "EV accident?"

"More like a bullet accident," Gunner said.

Confused lines formed on the governor's brow.

"I'll explain later," Ryan said. "For now, tell me—"

"One second." Louis was on his feet, walking up to Plante. "Open your mouth."

Plante's shocked look only lasted a second. "This is not the time."

Louis wasn't put off, and Ryan recognized the emergence of the no-nonsense professional attitude. "Please, Governor. I want to check something."

Plante looked at Ryan, who simply shrugged. Still obviously reluctant, Plante opened his mouth.

Louis took one look and made a confirmatory noise in his throat. "I thought so. Retracted gums and rotting teeth. You're vitamin-deficient. Tell me, do you bruise easily? Is your vision getting worse?"

Plante smirked. "Sorry, Doctor, but the food choices here are less than optimal."

"Yes, well." Louis rummaged through his pack before pulling out a plastic container. He unscrewed the top and dumped two pills on the table. "Take these now, and I'll get you more from the ship . . . when I can."

"How bad is it?" Ryan asked.

Louis put down his backpack and, without asking, reached up and examined the governor's skin and lips. "Hmm, little adipose tissue, bleeding gums, loose teeth . . . It'll take months to rectify, if he gets the right nutrients. Looks like he's got beriberi."

"Beriberi?" Gunner raised a single eyebrow. "You're making that up."

"You wish," Louis snapped. "This is where the colonists on Europa were heading before I started producing supplements. He's deficient in vitamin B and C, and his organs are starting to fail."

The governor made a face as he swallowed the pills. "Damn, that's rank."

"You have more?" Bennett asked.

"In the transport," Louis confirmed. "Not sure how . . ."

Ryan opened his backpack and pulled out the machine gun. "We'll get them, Doctor."

Bennett picked up the pill container and examined its contents. "Our colleagues aren't doing well. Would you mind checking on them?"

Louis hoisted the backpack over his shoulder and took the container from her hand. "Let's go. Chan, come with me in case I need help."

The pilot got up and followed them out of the room.

Plante watched them go. "I see the good doctor doesn't suffer fools."

"You got that right," Ryan replied. "I've learned to stay out of his way on medical matters. As far as we know, he's the only physician in the solar system, and we're damned lucky to have him." He put the gun back into his pack. "Maybe you're not the only one with an exaggerated sense of survival."

Gunner chuckled, and even Sasha grinned.

Plante dusted some white powder off his fingers, residue from Louis's pills. "Now would be a good time to tell me what supplies you're looking for."

Sasha jumped up and pulled out her minicom. She loaded the file and passed it to Plante. "Scroll down to see the entire list."

Plante's eyes widened the further down he went. "You have enough room?"

Ryan gestured to the portal. "You'll notice two transports on the landing strip. I'm bringing everything back even if I have to lash it to the hull."

Two minutes later, the door swished open and Chan walked in. "Doc's examining the patients with Bennett in Medical. He says he'll definitely need supplies from the transport."

"Not sure about that." Sasha glanced nervously out the portal.

"Don't worry," Plante said. "The good news is, the sekers are still flesh and blood; they need to recharge their suits. Which means they can't hang around the station indefinitely."

"They prowl the surface every day?" Ryan asked.

Plante stood and joined Sasha at the portal. "Mostly in the afternoon. I'm guessing they saw your ships land and came out to investigate."

"How do you keep them out of the station?"

"We sealed the airlocks and welded shut the emergency exits. The only time we venture outside is to repair something vital. The Federation station is two klicks away, so their time onsite is limited." He turned away from the portal. "There's plenty of space in Alpha Hive, Lieutenant. That's where we're holed up."

Ryan leaned forward and began the process of removing his EV suit. He stacked the white polymer upper section along with his gloves and helmet against one of the couches. His eyes automatically scanned the battery and oxygen reserve. Both read ninety-two percent. He detected the musky aroma of body odor wafting in the air and felt a tad embarrassed until he realized he wasn't the source.

"Sorry." Plante removed his own suit and smiled apologetically. "With water in short supply, bathing is a luxury we can't afford."

"Forget it." Ryan dismissed the apology with a wave of his hand. "When we get back to Europa, you can soak all day."

The governor's expression turned wistful for a moment before sliding back into focus. "You won't mind adding a few more hungry mouths to your colony?"

Ryan felt like he was throwing a life preserver to a drowning man. "We can handle it." With both of Europa's greenhouses functioning, food was not the problem. Nor was water, since the ice sheets provided an endless supply. No, it would be the failure of a critical piece of infrastructure that did them in. "We'll have to rotate use of the cryo-pods on the way back. I'll have Gunner draw up a schedule."

"Understood," Plante said. "I imagine your group could use some rest."

Ryan found himself yawning. Cyro-sleep exacted a toll on the human body, and it would take days for everyone to recover. "First order of business tomorrow is to retrieve the medical supplies from the transport. Then we'll begin searching for items on our list. Gunner, get everyone settled and find me afterward."

"Gotcha, Ace." The veteran followed Sasha, Chan, and Sybil out of the room, leaving Ryan with the governor.

Plante pulled on a set of brown coveralls that had seen better days. They were threadbare in places, with numerous holes and few patching attempts. It draped across his body like a sheet, barely concealing the man's skeletal frame.

Ryan jerked a thumb at the portal. "So, we make a run in the morning?"

"It's the best time. The sekers are usually less active then." The governor patted his flat stomach. "Although the sooner my people get a good meal, the better."

A moment of silence passed before Ryan spoke again. "It's incredible you hung on this long. I know what starving feels like, but at least I had an endgame—setting up a second greenhouse. You had nothing to hope for. How did you keep going?"

Plante frowned, his gaze drifting to a sea of stars in the void. "I believe it's our natural state. Humanity, I mean. We refused to go out with a whimper. My group decided to fight tooth and nail to the end."

A sad smile formed on Ryan's face. "*Do not go gently into that good night. Old age should burn and rave at close of day. Rage, rage against the dying of the light.*"

"That old poem?" In the dim light of the wall lamps, Plante looked embarrassed as he sat in one of the chairs. "It does kind of sum it up. What about you? On the way here, Gunner mentioned something about an insurrection and a battle with marines. Care to explain?"

Ryan avoided eye contact. "Our survival came at the barrel of a gun. After I declared martial law, my civilian board staged a mutiny, and a US senator arrived with two transports of marines."

"Goddamn." Plante looked at him with newfound respect. "They tried to force the issue?"

Ryan's expression turned feral. "You could say that."

Plante leaned back in his cushioned chair. "Since you're here and they're not, I take it they were less than successful. How the hell did you survive a marine attack?"

"Not sure *survive* is the right word, Governor. I lost a lot of good people. Fortunately, they lost the war." Ryan hesitated and then realized it was something he had to get out or risk having it fester inside his soul. "The rebels were about to break into the Command Center when I opened the EV door. Unlike you, I didn't allow a vote."

Plante's jaw became unhinged. "How many?"

Deep grooves formed on Ryan's forehead, fueled by a combination of guilt and anger. "Five hundred."

Plante whistled but then nodded approvingly. "Seems we have a similar definition of *survival*, Lieutenant. We both did what we had to do. I saved a few, but you may have saved the human race."

In that moment, Ryan felt a definite bond with the governor. They had both forged similar paths, were beset by similar tragedies, and neither had given up.

An hour later, Gunner joined Ryan in Alpha Hive. The quarters Ryan chose looked to have been a family unit, judging by the pic-vids on the wall. He took a minute to stare at the happy couple and the twin boys. The domicile was small but comfortable: two tiny bedrooms, a single bathroom, and a combination kitchen/living room. Three times the size of his quarters on Europa. Every member of his team would enjoy the excess space since they had their pick of rooms. The hive had been built to hold two thousand people. Ten barely registered.

Ryan sat on the bed, opened his backpack, and removed a few essentials, while Gunner paced in front of the wall-mounted tri-vid.

"I don't like it, Ace. This rock was supposed to be empty. No one alive. Now we've got mutants prowling the surface and survivors in the station."

"I feel the same, Gunner, but that doesn't change our mission. Let's find what we need and get the hell out of here."

"Amen to that. Did you send word to Rani?"

"Just a quick blurb about arriving safely. I told her about Gonzalez."

Gunner caught his eye. "But nothing about the sekers?"

"Her plate is full enough as it is."

The veteran's jaw tightened, like he didn't quite agree with his answer. "Any word back?"

"She said things were status quo. Although the way she phrased it was . . ."

"Was what?"

Ryan recalled the short communication. There was a certain wording that didn't sound like Rani. "Dunno."

Gunner stared at him for a second. "You're not making me feel warm and fuzzy."

"Forget it," Ryan said. "It's probably nothing."

"Okay." The veteran pulled out his minicom and opened a file. "There's a shitload of work to do. Where do you want to start?"

They spent the next thirty minutes putting the finishing touches on a plan. The veteran wasn't happy about Ryan's decision to split up into two salvaging teams, but he recognized the importance of cutting their ground time on the asteroid. Something could go wrong on Europa, and the sooner they got back, the better.

"We'll make a quick run to *Phoenix* first," Ryan said. "Grab Louis's medical supplies before the teams move out."

"Wonderful," Gunner muttered. "More of those foul vitamins."

Ryan grinned. "It's for Plante and his survivors."

"Yeah, it's also a quick way to turn allies into enemies."

Gunner was only gone ten minutes when a knock on the door interrupted Ryan's musings. He had just finished unpacking and was enjoying a peaceful moment of solitude. "Come."

The door swished open, and Sybil walked in. "Sorry to bother you at this late hour, but I need to talk." She took a breath. With her hands clenched behind her back and legs braced, she seemed to be summoning courage. "I . . . I wanted to apologize for my actions. I wasn't trying to usurp your authority. It's just . . . well, anything I do or say, no matter how it comes out, is only meant to help."

Her words of contrition immediately put him on guard. He had heard similar admissions before. Like when the marines landed. "Is this about what happened on the transport?"

She rubbed her palms against her thighs. She had changed into blue slacks and a white blouse. "No, it's my attitude in general. For as long as I can remember, I was taught not to trust anyone, to put my needs first." She leaned back on her heels. "I'm still learning how to be a team player."

Ryan rapped his fingers against the side of the bed. "Is this a new Sybil talking or just a new façade draped over the old version?"

"You don't trust me?" Her eyes narrowed. "Can't say I blame you. But I'm here to tell you that, this time, I've changed. You don't have to watch me twenty-four-seven."

Ryan reclined on the bed. She looked good, like back on Europa when they were dating. She had tied her hair up into a messy bun, and her long legs drew his gaze.

"You're coming with my group tomorrow," Ryan said, gesturing to his minicom. "And we'll start gathering the parts and tools on the list."

"What about my father's factory?"

Ryan gritted his teeth. "Why didn't you tell me the production facilities were on a Federation station?"

She shrugged. "I didn't think it would be an issue, since there weren't supposed to be survivors here or, more importantly, killer mutants on the surface."

Ryan bit his tongue. He couldn't argue with her logic. Although it still would have been nice to know in advance. She had a way of getting under his skin. "With any luck, we'll find everything on the list in this station. The only reason to visit Federation territory would be to obtain something vital, something we can't leave the asteroid without. If that happens, you'll have to lead the way."

Her expression softened when she realized he was letting out the leash, at least a little. He envisioned the wheels spinning behind those blue eyes.

"You want me to escort you?"

He sucked in a breath. The double entendre was not lost on him. "That's the idea. We're on the clock. You said you know the station and the factory. We'll need the safest path. I don't want to risk any more lives."

A smile slowly blossomed, revealing perfect teeth and a single dimple. She loosened a button on her blouse. "Speaking of time, maybe we could share a few moments . . ."

# CHAPTER 12

*Three things cannot be hidden: the sun, the moon, and the truth.*

DAY 62, 1643 HOURS

Rani found Kasim lying on a stretcher in Medical, Nurse Mabel methodically applying a dressing to a fresh burn on his forearm.

"You okay? I was looking all over for you. What happened?"

Kasim snuck a peek at the wound and grimaced. "Solomon was showing me how to splice wires. Turns out I'm a slow learner."

Mabel chuckled.

Rani planted her hands on her hips and assumed a stern demeanor. "I sent the two of you into Engineering to run diagnostics, not fix the wiring. Leave that part to specialists. Like me."

"You were in a meeting with the scientists. I didn't want to bother you."

Rani let her arms drop. "Well, you should have. It was a waste of time."

"Again?"

Her jaw muscles tightened. "They can't even tell me what the surface is composed of or what those strange markings mean. Damn, it's been weeks and we can write down what we've learned on the head of a pin."

Kasim took a breath. "You were looking for me?"

Rani slid into a chair by the stretcher. She wasn't good around open wounds. "Message arrived from the lieutenant. They landed safely."

Mabel stopped working. "Both transports?"

Rani nodded. "Yeah, even Stoll's ship."

Mabel tied off the dressing. "Do you want me to say anything or keep it quiet?"

"The colonists should hear," Kasim said. "They could use some good news."

"Agreed." Rani smiled at Mabel. "Feel free to spread the word, but I think it's best if I make a formal announcement later today."

The nurse picked up her supplies and left.

Rani waited until she was out of hearing range. "He also said they had an accident on the landing strip and Gonzalez was killed."

Kasim's eyebrows peaked. "What happened?"

"Don't know. The message was short and cryptic."

"You think he's hiding something?"

"No more than we are."

Kasim grasped her hand. "To be clear, you didn't tell him about the artifact?"

Rani took back her hand and shoved it into her pocket. "What would be the point? Nothing he can do except worry."

Kasim nodded as her words took up residence. "He'd try to be a backseat driver. Which would distract him from his mission."

"Exactly."

Kasim checked the white gauze on his arm before sitting up. "You're two peas in a pod, neither trying to burden the other. Not sure how that's going to turn out."

Rani shrugged. "I'm still figuring out this command thing."

Kasim gave her a long look before planting his feet on the floor. "I'd better get back to Engineering. Solomon is probably waiting."

Rani took a step, blocking him. "Promise me something first."

"What's that?"

"No more stupid stuff. We've already lost two people. I won't be responsible for losing more. Even if it's only a politician."

She left Kasim with a shocked look on his face as she marched out of Medical. With a list of unresolved issues percolating in her brain, the walk to the Command Center seemed longer than usual.

Since the discovery of the artifact, the mood among the colonists had changed. People she used to chum with seemed more reserved, not quite hopeful, but maybe cautiously optimistic. She wondered if this was what Braeder had experienced when the second greenhouse was finally up and running. If so, he never spoke of it.

As if on cue, two scientists exited the decompression chamber, both barely acknowledging her presence. She stopped in her quarters to grab a blanket before entering Ops. The temperature was always a few degrees colder in the Command Module these days. She made a mental note to perform a diagnostic on environmental. Again.

Pulling the wool blanket around her shoulders, she recalled her early years on the Indian subcontinent and doubted she'd ever feel that kind of heat again. Europa wasn't known for its beaches or balmy weather. She smiled at the absurd thought.

"Something funny, Ensign?" Archie asked when she walked into Ops. Seated at Gunner's terminal, the engineer gave her an inquisitive look.

Rani collected herself. "Just thinking about sandy beaches."

Archie snorted. "Are you sure touching the artifact didn't mess with your head? Don't tell Rutherford; he'll have you committed."

"Ain't that the truth." She wasn't going to tell Archie but, deep down, the artifact scared the hell out of her. Echoes of those foreign sensations still rattled her thoughts and her dreams. "Rutherford wasn't a happy camper this morning. In fact, he stormed out of the briefing room after I turned down his request to divert additional power to the lab."

Archie paused. "He actually asked? What the hell for?"

"Said they needed it for the new analyzers."

"Stupid idiot," Archie said. "Everyone knows the circuits can't handle the additional load. We'd have to strip Medical or the transport hangar for wire, and that's a recipe for disaster."

"The lieutenant would space me if I even considered something that reckless," Rani said, scanning the board. Her gaze came to rest on a flashing yellow icon. "I'm reading a five percent power drop in the laser."

"It's expected," Archie said. "I had to flush the coolant system when Solomon replaced a plugged filter. The manual says it'll take three days to return to normal."

Rani's lips tightened into a thin line. With Gunner and Chan on the supply run with Braeder, it was up to her and Archie and a few volunteers to keep the colony running. Like everyone else who had been pulled into service, the geologist was on the steep side of the learning curve. Rani had delegated other jobs to the civilians—planting and harvesting the greenhouses, for example—but she and Archie were still stumbling through workdays like exhausted sailors. Reservists took shifts in Ops, but the only thing they could do was notify her when warning lights began flashing.

The door at the back of Operations swished open and Kasim walked in, sporting his new dressing. "What did you say to Rutherford at the meeting? The guy nearly chewed my head off."

Rani took a seat in the command chair. "I told him he's got all the power and equipment I can spare. If he's going to decipher the mystery of the artifact, he's going to do it with the gear that's already in the cave."

Kasim sat down in Chan's seat. "He wants more? Every inch of the place is already filled with scanners and ultrasounds and machines I've never seen before."

"And his team has found exactly nothing," Archie said, the suggestion of a sneer on his lips.

"So, he's frustrated and taking it out on you?"

Rani shrugged. "Not my job to keep him happy."

Kasim failed to hide a grin. "The longer you sit in that chair, the more you sound like Braeder."

Rani's face reddened.

"He's got a point," Archie cackled.

Rani leaned forward and placed her chin in her hand. Outside the portal, Jupiter's Great Red Spot swirled into view, a storm so massive it could swallow several Earths whole. She wondered if the vortex served as a metaphor for her new life. Alone. Without Marco. The familiar lump formed in her throat.

Kasim seemed to sense her mood. "With any luck, Braeder should be loading the transports with goodies soon." He hesitated. "Maybe you should tell him about the artifact in your next transmission?"

"Sorry." Rani shook her head. "I'm not about to add to his list of concerns, especially since he's already running into problems."

Archie leaned forward. "You didn't mention that. What kinds of problems?"

She glanced at the hologram at the front of the room. "I didn't want to worry you, either."

"What problems?" Archie repeated.

"He didn't say exactly. Something about the need to keep everyone safe."

"Safe?" Kasim cocked his head. "From what?"

"He didn't specify."

"I said it earlier." Kasim directed his words at Archie. "Two peas in a pod. Neither wants to burden the other."

Rani flashed him a stern look. "It's not Braeder's feelings I'm concerned about; it's the fact he can't do a freaking thing about the artifact until he gets back."

"Same thing," Archie murmured.

Kasim leaned back and cupped his hands behind his head. "I think you're turning into the lieutenant, which means, sooner or later, everyone will hate you."

*Day 63, 0700 Hours*

Rani tugged on the guide rope before starting down the ice steps. Memories of Vrabel's "accident" sent a nervous chill through her bones. The fact that neither Kasim nor Archie had been able to identify the culprit wasn't reassuring.

Archie flashed her a grin through his faceplate. "Don't worry, missy. I checked it already."

"I know," Rani replied on a private channel. "I just had to see for myself. Have you gotten any closer to finding the perpetrator?"

"Not yet." Archie followed as she took slow, deliberate steps. "He or she covered their tracks well."

"Jorge went up right before we did," Rani reminded him.

"He was emphatic," Archie replied. "He said he doesn't use the rope, so he didn't notice anything amiss."

As they descended, towering walls on both sides infused her with a feeling of claustrophobia, and twice Rani had to stop, close her eyes, and take a breath. Archie waited patiently and didn't say a word.

At the bottom, she paused to survey the lab. Bulky lamps from the transport hangar hung from cables drilled into the ceiling, casting plenty of illumination. The plastek walls the engineers had erected to keep the scientists secure were layered with shelves and servers, and papers had been taped to the walls like a child's fridge drawings. A second airlock had been added in the back, along with lockers to hold EV suits. Scientists circulated between desks and counters that surrounded the artifact like stadium seats. Large monitors hung over the strange alien egg, displaying neutrino counts, surface temperature, and a host of other physical variables.

Archie led her through the outer airlock and waited as it closed on hydraulic motors and air was pumped into the small space. Finally, the inner hatch opened and they were able to remove their EV suits and grab a cup of hot water from a nearby dispenser.

Rani shivered. "I should have brought a sweater."

Archie handed her one from his backpack, and she smiled sheepishly. "Thanks."

"Ensign." Rutherford rose from his desk behind one of the large monitors and strode over. "Glad you could make it."

Rani arched an eyebrow. "You did say it was urgent."

"Yes, well." He gestured for her to follow him to his computer. "There's been a development."

A shot of adrenaline caused her heart to skip a beat. "You found something?" The scientist had cancelled their previous meeting at the last minute. Kasim figured it was because they had discovered nothing new and didn't want to admit as much.

Rutherford frowned. "Not exactly."

A second scientist stepped over to join them. He had a mop of dark hair, and the nametag on his shirt said MURRAY. Rani preferred working with Vrabel, but he and his busted leg were still in Medical. Although Nurse Mabel said he was doing so well she'd probably discharge him tomorrow.

"It hasn't responded to heat, light, or any external stimulus. Likewise, it maintains a uniform temperature and is totally impervious to our scans."

"In other words, nothing has changed." Rani did her best to hide her irritation. She had a million things to do back at the station.

"That would be true," Rutherford said. "Except we recorded an emission at zero six fifty-eight this morning."

Archie's head snapped back. "An emission? More neutrinos?"

"No." Murray caught his eye. "Antimatter."

"What?" Rani's gaze swiveled between the scientists. Several questions demanded to be asked. She finally got her tongue sorted around the big one. "Antimatter is dangerous. If it contacts something solid . . ."

Murray raised a hand, reminding Rani of her dad when she protested once too often. "It's okay. The artifact emitted a single antielectron. A positron. It collided with the ice, and we recorded the flash."

Rani exhaled. Last thing they needed was for the artifact to start chucking tiny bombs.

"Why positrons?" Archie asked. "I thought it emitted neutrinos."

"Apparently, it has the ability to emit a host of quantum particles," Rutherford said. "But it still can't focus them."

"Because of the broken antenna?" Rani said.

"Correct." Rutherford tapped a few keys on his terminal and another graph appeared on the screen. "Since the first emission, we recorded a slew of positrons. Note the time interval."

Something in his tone made Rani nervous. She studied the graph until she saw it. "The pattern of emissions has changed."

Archie peered at the monitor. "You're right. It's like a countdown."

Rani froze. "A countdown? To what?"

Rutherford and Murray exchanged a look. The lead scientist shrugged. "No idea, but at the current rate of decline, it'll take about three days to reach what we think is zero. Which means we have that long to figure out how to respond."

Archie scratched his cheek. "It's forcing our hand."

Rani nodded as understanding dawned. "Once it was stimulated, it started a process. Either we initiate the next step or it will."

"Or maybe it'll just shut down," Rutherford said.

A gut feeling told Rani the scientist was wrong, but she didn't have the facts to argue. If the artifact was forcing the issue, it wanted something. "What if we reattach the antenna?"

"Not recommended," Rutherford said. "The risk is too high. It's like leaving your front door open. No way to know who's going to invite themselves in."

"What else can we do?"

"We can fire positrons back," Murray said. "Respond in kind. It may be a test to see if we have the right level of technology."

Rani rested her hands on the edge of the desk. "Can you produce antimatter?"

Lines formed on Rutherford's forehead. "That's what I wanted to talk to you about. It's dangerous, but if we build a containment field and bring in the right equipment, we can minimize risk."

Rani saw where this was going. The man wasn't happy with her refusal to give him the resources at their last meeting, so now he was leveraging this newest development to get what he wanted. "Let me guess. You want me to authorize taking apart the electrical system in the transport hangar so you can manufacture antimatter."

Rutherford didn't have a great poker face, as the corners of his lips twisted in a parody of a grin. "Producing antimatter will require extra power."

Rani gritted her teeth. That was not what she wanted to hear. Many of the colony's subsystems were held together with duct tape and baling wire. "Send me a list of what you need. I'll discuss it with Kasim."

"We only have three days," Rutherford reminded her. "And it'll take time to set up the process. Positrons are not easy to manufacture."

Rani bit her tongue as she spun on her heel and walked over to grab her helmet. She didn't like being manipulated. "I said, send me your list. I'll let you know."

Archie hurried to keep up.

# CHAPTER 13

*Desire to have things done quickly prevents their being done thoroughly.*

DAY 63, 0833 HOURS

The door swished open while Ryan was in the middle of getting dressed. A scowling doctor marched in and plopped down in the nearest chair, throwing up a puff of dust.

"Don't be afraid to invite yourself in," Ryan deadpanned. He pulled clean clothes out of his backpack and laid them out on the bed.

"I'm sick of seeing sick people," Louis said.

"Oh?" Ryan slipped on his shirt and began buttoning it up. "I'm sorry; I thought that was in your job description."

"Not like this," Louis snapped. "We've played this game already: starvation on Europa. I thought I was finished seeing kidney failure and heart attacks in forty-year-olds. We fixed it, remember, with your second greenhouse and my vitamins. Now I'm jumping back into the deep end." He stared at his feet. "I started the survivors here on a vitamin cocktail, but they'll need a lot more if they're going to recover." He hesitated. "When can I get my supplies from the transport?"

"The governor says best time is early morning. We're going to make a run in an hour."

"Good." Louis relaxed in his chair.

The door swished open again and Governor Plante walked in.

"I guess everyone has a key," Ryan murmured.

The governor's gaze landed on Louis. "Thanks for taking care of my people."

The doctor accepted the compliment with a silent nod.

Ryan tucked in his shirt. "Tell me more—"

He was interrupted by Gunner's appearance in the doorway.

"Did someone call a meeting?" Ryan asked.

"I started the reservists working in the concourse," the veteran said. "Figure there's a ton of gear we can pull from shops and stores before we hit Engineering and the Command Module."

Ryan raised his eyebrows at Plante. "Okay with you?" After all, they were stripping down his colony.

"Fine, Lieutenant. We're not using it."

"What's the overall condition of the station?"

Plante found a spot on the unmade bed and sat. "Basically, what you see. Most systems have been offline for a year. The solar panels allow us to maintain power, which is why we still have air and heat." He shivered and blew out gray mist. "Mostly, anyway. Otherwise, everything from electrical to plumbing is intact."

Gunner turned to Ryan. "I figure Engineering and Ops is where we'll strike gold. There will be a ton of replacement parts we can steal. No offense, Governor."

"None taken. But there is one problem."

Ryan stopped dressing. "What's that?"

"The sekers," Plante replied solemnly. "The Engineering module protrudes out of the station proper, which means there's a chance they will hear any banging and crashing. That may give them incentive to try and break through the walls, which aren't thick to begin with."

"That's not good," Ryan muttered. "Gunner, pass the word: we have to keep the noise down. Did you ever get a total count of how many sekers are out there, Governor?"

Plante paused, considering. "Whatever number I pick is only a guess, since we stay clear. At a minimum, several dozen."

Gunner looked out the portal. "Well, Ace, it appears we ain't done fighting yet."

Louis was pacing in the decompression chamber when Ryan and Gunner cycled through the airlock. "No problems?"

Ryan waited until Gunner lowered his end of the storage container before following suit. "All good, Doc. Plante was right; no sekers on the surface at this hour." He didn't comment on the pair of bodies sprawled in the regolith outside the airlock—the result of yesterday's run-in.

In truth, it had been a nerve-wracking trek to the transport for medical supplies. Ryan took a second to let his muscles relax.

Louis motioned to Smith, one of the reservists who waited by the door, and they picked up the metal container. "I'll get these to the governor and the other survivors. It'll be a start."

Plante and Sybil met them in the main concourse by the fountain. Just as on Europa, the white porcelain was stained black, and green algae clogged empty pipes. Only a few lights illuminated the wide boulevard, and they flickered like fireflies on a summer evening. "We have to ration our power," Plante explained. "So, lighting is less than optimal."

"At least the temperature is above freezing," Sybil muttered.

"Not to worry," Ryan said as he pushed a child's tricycle out of his path. "We'll use our helmet lamps." The governor was right. Everything was dark and gloomy, as though hope had vacated the building. Patches of fine gray dust covered the floor, next to pieces of plastek and broken machinery. Sasha, Chan and the rest of his crew waited with the doctor outside Medical.

"It'll take me about an hour to set up IVs for Bennett and the other two survivors," Louis said. "If you don't mind, when I finish, I'd like to go through the cupboards and fridges."

"Don't know how much is left in terms of medicines and equipment, Doctor," Plante said. "We've been picking at it for a year."

"See what you can find," Ryan said. If there was anything useful, Louis would sniff it out. "Sybil, give him a hand. Remember we're on a schedule."

Louis handed the governor two lumpy pills before leading Sybil into Medical.

"What happened here?" Sasha said, staring at the devastation in the concourse. "It's a mess."

Plante grimaced as he swallowed the tablets. "When you open an EV door, wind speed accelerates to one hundred miles an hour in less than a second. That's enough to tear people and things apart."

Sasha winced and refused to meet Ryan's gaze. She had been inside Beta Hive when Ryan opened Europa's airlock and hadn't witnessed the resulting devastation.

Plante raised his voice. "Mind the sharp edges."

The reservists drew closer together, and Chan gave Ryan an anxious look. She remembered what Europa had looked like.

Gunner pointed at rows of batteries stacked along the wall. “What about those?”

“They’re dead,” Plante said. “Used every amp we could find to reboot the main computer when we came out of hiding.” He turned and led them along a boulevard that resembled a combination junkyard and pawn shop.

In the low lighting, shadows teased Ryan’s subconscious. Rusted floor scrubbers transformed into bloodthirsty mutants, and doorways covered in dirt and dust resembled abandoned mausoleums. The darkness hinted at something sinister lying in wait. Scattered among the debris and rubbish, Ryan recognized torn bits of clothing and children’s toys. He was getting a bad feeling about their salvage effort.

“All right, let’s get started. Gunner, take your group to the supply shed. Grab all the tools you can find. The rest of you are with me. We’ll meet back here in three hours.”

He turned and led Chan, Sasha, and Plante toward the Command Center. As expected, they ran into the emergency bulkhead, which had dropped when the airlock was opened. Just like on Europa, a standard failsafe to protect the brain of the colony.

Plante helped Ryan haul on the rusted iron wheel that protruded from the heavy plastek. It took a dozen turns before the door creaked open wide enough for everyone to slip through.

“It looks abandoned,” Ryan said, staring inside. “No one’s been in here?”

“Not since that day,” Plante said. “Nothing we needed.”

The corridor leading to Ops was pitch-black, so Ryan donned his helmet and switched on the lamps before they stumbled into something sharp. The floor was covered in broken glass and dirt, and the walls were stained with something dark and amorphous. As he crept forward, he sensed a singular hope breaking through the constant stream of bad news. If the Command Center was undamaged, they should be able to salvage a treasure trove of gear, including replacement wire.

Chan helped the governor manually open the door to Ops and, once inside, Ryan breathed easy. No bodies and, more importantly, no damage. Sasha and Chan descended on the com and laser terminals, while Ryan used a multitool to dismantle the computer on the arm of the command chair.

“Governor, will the sekers be able to hear us work?” Ryan asked.

Plante shook his head. "It's Engineering where sounds echo against the walls. Ops is better insulated."

Ryan exhaled. "Great. If you wouldn't mind removing the casing from the servers against the back wall, it'll save us time on that end." Ryan pointed to the dust-covered black structures. "Careful with the processors. They're delicate."

"On it." Plante set to work, and in seconds, the air was filled with the buzz and whine of power tools and the screech of metal slats being peeled off the wall.

Ryan took his time removing vital components from the computer on the command chair. Its twin on Europa still functioned, but after several glitches, he had had to cannibalize parts from other terminals to keep it operational.

After two hours, Sasha wandered over. "Lieutenant, we've got a boxful of processors, transistors, and circuit boards. I'm thinking the next step is to start packing the coils and relays from the servers."

Ryan surveyed the back of the room. Most of the servers had been disassembled, and it looked like everyone had a healthy sweat going. "What else is on your list?"

"Circuit breakers. We should strip the bulkheads behind the electrical subsystems." She hesitated, peering at his handiwork. "You need some help?"

Ryan couldn't hold back a grin. He was a soldier, not an engineer. The computer looked like a flayed microwave. "If you wouldn't mind."

Sasha pulled out her power tool and methodically began removing recessed screws. Thirty seconds later, she slipped out the hard drive and placed it in his palm. "Next time, just ask."

A warm glow seeped into his cheeks as his watch chimed. "It's almost time to meet Gunner. You okay to pack everything up?"

"Piece of cake. Tell the old fart I'm going to check his work."

"I'll do that." As he walked the corridor linking Ops to the concourse, Ryan was struck by its similarity with Europa, the familiar images of Earth on the walls depicting green meadows and seascapes. They triggered an unhealthy melancholy that weighed on his mood. Was he just delaying the inevitable? Could this mission really make a difference?

He stopped in front of where his quarters would be, a small two-room living space. On Ceres, a junior officer had probably lived there before the mass suicide. Something inside him revolted at the thought.

Even if things got bad on Europa, he couldn't see himself opening that door. Not again. He hadn't come this far to give up.

*Day 65, 1735 Hours*

"I don't like it." Rani turned away from the 3-D monitor hanging above the door. Gunner had installed it during the insurrection, and Braeder had ingrained the importance of checking it before entering the concourse. Back then, it had served as an early-warning system when rebels tried to break into the Command Center. Now it was just an irritating habit she couldn't break.

The colonists parading outside the door, carrying placards and chanting slogans, only served to open old wounds.

"It's just people exercising their democratic right," Kasim said. He stood beside her, hands on hips, staring at the protest unfolding on the monitor. "Remember, Braeder cancelled martial law. Free speech is no longer illegal."

She ignored the sarcastic aftertaste. Despite the governor's reassurance, Rani detected an unease in Kasim's demeanor. It was evident in his stance and in the way his fingers picked at the cuffs of his thawb. He wasn't immune to last year's memories.

"I'm going to talk to them," she decided.

Kasim raised an eyebrow. "Is that a good idea? Might be safer to let them blow off a little steam?"

"I never agreed with the lieutenant's plan of turning the Command Center into a bunker." She recalled the days when the module was under assault. "I believe most people will act reasonably when presented with the facts."

Kasim tilted his head to make eye contact. "Especially since *most* of the unreasonable people got sucked into space."

Rani's eyes narrowed. Murdering five hundred rebels had been partly her decision, and it still haunted her dreams. Kasim flinched at the look she gave him.

She yanked open the deadbolt and strode into the concourse. Several hundred colonists marched up and down the wide boulevard. A quick survey of the signs revealed AVOID THE ARTIFACT and TURF THE TIMEBOMB as the most common slogans.

At her unexpected appearance, the surrounding colonists stopped marching. She recognized several faces, but none of her old acquaintances made eye contact. The chanting faded, and one of the colonists elbowed his way to the front.

Rani grimaced when Jorge planted his large frame in front of her.

He folded his arms across his chest. "Nice of you to come out of your castle and join us, Ensign. Perhaps you'd be willing to listen to our concerns?"

She made of point of not stepping back. "It doesn't take a demonstration to ask for a meeting. I have no problem speaking to any concerned colonist when I'm not performing regular maintenance. You remember those jobs that you're supposed to be doing? The ones that keep us alive?"

Jorge winced at the subtle jab. "If we keep losing colonists to the artifact, there'll be no need for maintenance."

Rani scoffed at the hyperbole. "We've lost two people, and none since the first day."

"For now," a woman in a blue dress said. She scowled at Rani. "But what happens when the timer hits zero? Will it explode and take out the extractor?"

Rani remembered her from somewhere. Then the image flashed in her mind: one of the nurses who had helped operate on Louis when the doctor was battling for his life. "And what would you have me do, exactly? Because the artifact is too heavy to move."

"Bury it," Jorge said. "Cover it in tons of ice and leave it. Like it had been for thousands of years."

"You think that will stop the countdown? Or protect us when it reaches zero?"

Jorge shrugged. "It's better than nothing."

"You're crazy," Rani said. "Talk to the scientists. The artifact has the power to manipulate the quantum field. If aliens really wanted to turn it into a bomb, a couple of tons of ice isn't going to protect us." She marveled at how Braeder kept his sanity during Board meetings. Especially when people made up their own facts.

Jorge's gaze flickered to Kasim, who had been quiet the whole time. "The governor has the power to shut down research. The military has no say on civilian matters."

Rani turned to Kasim, who shifted nervously on the balls of his feet.

"It would require a vote at the Board level," he said. "And I'm still vetting new members."

The nurse jabbed a finger. "You'd better do it fast, because time is running out. We're not trusting the military on this one. Not after what happened to the miners."

"That wasn't the artifact," Rani said. "That was human error."

"Doesn't matter," the nurse snapped. "Dead is dead." She allowed her scowl to linger before turning away. Jorge dropped his arms and followed her toward the hives. The crowd seemed to sense the change and slowly dispersed.

Rani glared at Kasim. "Thanks for your support," she growled before stomping off.

*Day 66, 1725 Hours*

Rani placed a data slate on Archie's terminal. Outside the portal in Ops, Jupiter loitered somewhere below the horizon, and faint light from distant stars reflected off crenellated ice, casting deep shadows inside fissures and crevices.

He looked up, confused. "What's this?"

"A message to Braeder. It's time I sent him a real update."

Archie fingered the disc. "The artifact?"

"The artifact," she confirmed. "And the boiling discontent among the colonists."

"It's just a few rallies."

"The insurrection started with 'just a few rallies,'" Rani reminded him. "The countdown isn't going away."

When Archie didn't argue, a cold sensation seeped into her gut. She was rapidly learning how much out of her depth she was. "What do you think we should do?"

Archie tilted his head. "About the artifact, definitely tell him, but wait until the timer winds down and we see what happens. About the rallies, let the colonists vent."

"You don't think they'd actually try to collapse the cave?"

"Not unless they're prepared to murder a bunch of scientists in the process." Archie smirked. "With all the research, we usually have people in there twenty-four-seven. Although I might look the other way if one of them was named Rutherford—"

"Thanks for your opinion." She stepped over to the command chair before she said something a leader had no business saying. Her pulse picked up as she remembered why she had decided to send the message in the first place. The clock on the wall told her she had five minutes before the countdown reached zero. "All right, you win. Send the message tomorrow, if we're still here. Any word from Rutherford?"

Archie inserted the data slate and programmed it to send in the morning. "If you're asking if he complained about you kicking him out of the lab, the answer is no."

Rani snorted. None of the scientists or miners had uttered a word of protest when she ordered them back to the station. Vrabel was the only one who'd volunteered to stay behind and monitor the sensors. She didn't like leaving anyone in the lab, but she really needed to know what happened. And it helped if it was someone she could trust.

"Vrabel reported in before you arrived," Archie said.

Rani's jaw tightened. The man still limped like a three-legged dog, but the last X-rays showed his fracture was healing. "What'd he say?"

"All quiet. Except for the positron-emission rate, every other reading is at baseline." He glanced at the clock. "Two minutes."

She rapped her knuckles against the side of her chair. "You don't think it's a bomb, do you?"

Archie leaned back and folded his hands across his stomach. "What would be the point of an advanced civilization leaving the equivalent of a landmine for an up-and-coming species to step on?"

Rani tilted her head. "Unless they wanted to snuff out any burgeoning threats."

"Your logic doesn't work. Even some type of advanced planet-killer would only wipe out one colony and alert civilization to the threat. No, if they were determined to eliminate us, they'd focus on sending a signal back and return with a task force to wipe us out."

"With the broken antenna, the sending-back part is out the window."

"True," Archie acknowledged. "But this doesn't smell like malicious intent."

"So, this is a handshake? An introduction?"

"Call me soft-hearted, but I think any advanced civilization would have eliminated warfare and strife somewhere in their distant past."

Rani stole a look at the clock. Less than a minute. "And if you're wrong?"

He grinned. "You won't be able to say 'I told you so.'"

The second hand clicked on the hour. Rani forced herself to take a breath. A yellow light flashed on Archie's panel.

She reached over before he could react and slapped it with her palm. "Command Center. Go ahead."

"Ensign." Vrabel sounded harried. "Have an update . . ."

Static filled the frequency, and Rani cursed Jupiter's radiation.

"Say again. We lost your signal. Are you okay?"

More static until his voice cut through. "Had a breach in containment, but I sealed the leak. Repressurizing the lab now. Good thing I was in my suit."

Rani exchanged a look with Archie. "What happened?"

"That's why I'm calling," Vrabel said. "You have to see this."

Rutherford and three of his colleagues were waiting in the decompression chamber when Rani and Archie arrived. Each was decked out in an EV suit and held his helmet in one hand. The lead scientist stood when she walked in.

"What happened?" Rutherford demanded. "What did the artifact do?"

Rani ignored him and began stripping off her clothes next to the rack of EV suits.

Archie pulled out the smallest size and laid it on the bench. "Sure you don't want me to come?"

"No, I need you in Ops. Just in case."

"Ensign." Rutherford wrung his hands. "We need to know."

Rani fixed him with a cool glare. "Yes, Vrabel is safe. No, he wasn't hurt when the lab lost pressure. Other than that, I'm on my way to find out."

Rutherford's ears turned red. "Well," he huffed. "We'll come with you."

She held up a hand. "No. Only you and me this time."

Rutherford's shocked look was mirrored in the faces of his colleagues. "You can't order us around. We're civilians, and we don't take orders from the military."

She met his stare and held it. "Except when colony safety is involved."

The scientist glanced around as though the integrity of the walls would pronounce the colony safe. "The station—"

"If Vrabel hadn't had his EV suit on, he'd be dead. Not sure what the artifact did, but I'm not risking more lives. Yours, I'm willing to gamble with." She turned her gaze on the other scientists. "The rest of you can wait here and play solitaire for all I care." She waited until each person began undressing before pulling on the bottom half of her suit.

Archie headed for the exit, wearing his smirk like a medal.

In her next reincarnation, Rani decided she would ask for longer legs. Trying to keep up with the long-striding scientist was an exercise in futility. Twice she had to order Rutherford to stop and wait as she hurried to catch up. Navigating the slabs of ice and deep crevices was dangerous enough for a coordinated person. Her lack of athletic prowess made it that much worse.

Jupiter blazed overhead when they finally arrived at the cave entrance. She let Rutherford descend ahead of her—in his agitated state, he'd probably knock her over if she went down first—and she took her time on the icy steps.

She still had her head down when she bumped into the scientist near the bottom.

"Watch where you're going!" he snapped. The man was rooted in place outside the airlock, staring at something in the ice floor.

She almost blurted something snide when Vrabel limped over in his EV suit. He took her hand and helped her down the last steps. "Sorry to drag you out here, but this time, it's true: a picture is worth a thousand words."

She'd almost forgotten how tall he was until she craned her neck up to meet his gaze. "You said you lost containment?"

He pointed to a circular hole in the tempered plastek that had been covered with an emergency patch. "The exodus of air turned the lab into a disaster area, but that can be cleaned up."

"What happened?"

He took her arm and spun her ninety degrees to the right, and she noted what had caught Rutherford's attention and made him stop at the bottom of the stairs.

A circular hole had formed in the floor of the cave. It lined up perfectly with the defect in the plastek wall.

She had to ask the obvious question. "From the artifact?"

Vrabel nodded. "Right on time. A single pulse."

Rutherford seemed to gather himself. "In the visible spectrum?"

"No, we need to reboot the computers and analyze the data, but I think it was some type of particle beam. Maybe protons."

Rani stepped closer and peered into the hole. "How deep does it go?"

"Not sure, but before you came, I dropped a flashlight down. It fell until it disappeared."

Rani whistled. "You think it's trying to send a signal?"

Vrabel set his jaw. "You mean like ET got tired of waiting and decided to call home?"

"Something like that." She shrugged. "The neutrinos weren't working, so it tried something else in the quantum field."

"Could be," he said. "And this channel through the ice is a random trajectory, since it can't focus the beam."

"There's no proof of that," Rutherford said. "Maybe it was just discharging excess energy now that it's active."

Vrabel stared at him. "Really?"

"I'm glad the beam went in this direction," Rani said. "If it had hit the extractor or the station, it would have spelled the end of the colony."

"Agreed," Vrabel said. "But there's another problem."

Rani didn't like the change in his tone. "Talk to me."

He jerked his thumb toward the lab. "I checked the sensors before you arrived. The countdown has started again."

"What? You mean . . ."

He nodded. "I think because it's not getting a reply, it's planning to send another signal."

Rani's eyes widened as the implication sank in. "That's means it's going to keep firing energy beams until someone talks to it. And sooner or later, it's going to hit something vital."

Rutherford spun and met her gaze. He looked terrified.

# CHAPTER 14

*The object of the superior person is truth.*

DAY 67, 0950 HOURS

It's a short message," Chan said as she remotely downloaded the file from the transport's computer. "Just arrived a few minutes ago."

Ryan sat on one of the packed boxes in the concourse and wiped his sweaty brow. He was beat. Two days of scavenging parts from the station had exhausted everyone. The good news was they had struck gold. Sasha figured they had enough replacement parts to run the colony for another year. All they had to do now was find some wire . . .

Chan joined him. "At this rate, we could be finished by the end of the week."

"Fingers crossed," Ryan said. As long as they didn't run into those sekers again. He waited until a light on his minicom flashed green.

"Message transferred," Chan confirmed.

Ryan stifled a yawn. It seemed Rani had managed Europa well over the past few weeks, but problems on the moon usually came at you sideways. So, past accomplishments were no guarantee of future success. He tapped open the file.

"Anything interesting?" Chan leaned over Ryan's shoulder when he didn't answer. "Sir?"

Ryan had to reread the paragraph three times, and it still took precious seconds for the words to register in his brain. He tilted the screen so Chan could see.

"Holy shit," she whispered.

"Who else knows?" Gunner asked as he paced between the couches and chairs in the conference room.

Ryan felt a weird sense of claustrophobia as he gazed outside the portal. The expanse of regolith hadn't changed, nor had the infinite darkness surrounding the asteroid. The monotonous grayness seemed to hem him in, unlike on Europa, where dozens of moons and a ferocious gas giant provided an ever-changing skyscape.

"Right now, just you, me, and Chan. She promised not to say a word."

Gunner combed his beard with his hand. "And you don't want to tell anyone? Damn, Ace, this is historic."

Ryan ran through the arguments in his head one more time before he opened his mouth. "Which is exactly why we have to keep it quiet. We've got a mission to complete, and that's not even considering the walking threats on the surface. Last thing we need is for people to get distracted."

"But an alien artifact . . ."

"I don't care if it's ET himself; we can't lose focus. That's how accidents happen."

Gunner grunted. The veteran didn't need convincing on that front. Both men had seen lives lost on Europa because of mistakes. He stopped pacing and looked at Ryan. "So, when, then?"

"On our way back. When there's no possibility of a screw-up."

Gunner smirked. "The vet is going to be pissed at you. Not to mention Sasha, and she's got quite the temper."

Ryan settled back into the cushy confines of the chair. "That's okay. I'm used to people hating me."

Rani shivered as she paced inside what used to be a simple ice cave. The artifact sat in the middle of the floor, atop the crushed scissor truck, surrounded by rows of terminals and oversized monitors. Transparent plastek walls separated the lab from the lethal atmosphere outside, although the cold found a way to seep through the thin barrier and battled with the heaters struggling to maintain a hospitable environment.

"It's freezing in here," she muttered, trying to stop her teeth from chattering. She had automatically unzipped her EV suit to her waist once she exited the airlock and now realized it had been a bad decision. She stopped and zipped it back up.

Vrabel offered a sympathetic smile. It was late, and Rutherford and the other scientists had left for the day. "Sorry about that. The station doesn't have any more portable heaters."

She glanced at the small units glowing red on either side of the artifact. It was second nature to step close, extend her arms, and absorb some of that heat. Circulation slowly returned to her fingers. "Rutherford says you should have an answer soon."

Vrabel's smile evaporated. "Rutherford couldn't find his arse using both hands and a map. He still thinks the damn thing will respond to some frequency or particle we haven't tried."

Rani walked over to his station. Despite the scientist being seated, she stood eye to eye with him. "What are you doing?"

Vrabel used his long arms to gesture at the rows of sensors spread across the bench. "Trying to get it to respond by firing every particle known to man at it, including neutrinos, electrons, and even protons."

"And no reaction?"

"Absolutely zero. Rutherford says we haven't found the right particle or maybe the right message. You know, a universal constant replying to another universal constant?"

Rani ran her gloved hand over the edge of the counter. "But you don't agree?"

He shrugged. "My job is to do what I'm told, but I can't see it. An intelligent civilization leaving us a calling card would not intend for us to guess how to answer. There's something we're missing."

"Something like a broken antenna?"

"The antenna is different. It's intended to send a reply. Our response should be something more fundamental. Like accepting a handshake."

Rani shifted her gaze to the artifact resting on the busted truck. The white hieroglyphics glowed silently. The antenna lay on a table beside it.

What Vrabel said intuitively made sense. The artifact was clearly left there for a civilization to stumble across. A doorbell they could ring upon reaching a certain level of technological advancement. But the doorbell was broken and couldn't alert the owners, and humans were too primitive to read the message on the door.

Rani rubbed her chin. "If the artifact is not responding to our signals, the only other information would come from the scribblings on the surface. No luck deciphering them?"

He shook his head. "We need a cipher key."

"Like a Rosetta Stone?"

"Exactly. The computers have been working on it from the beginning. So far, nothing."

"And it keeps broadcasting the same pulse since I touched it?"

"There's been no change."

"Have the colonists seen it?"

Vrabel frowned. "Ah . . . everyone knows about it."

"No, I mean, have the colonists actually heard the signal or seen the markings."

"No, Rutherford restricted the details to scientists only."

Rani recalled her conversation with Archie about advanced civilizations. "Send it out. In fact, put it on the colony net. There's a ton of experts on this moon. I know many are in unrelated fields, but let them see the data firsthand."

Vrabel's jaw tightened. "Rutherford is not going to like it. He thinks science should be restricted to scientists."

"And how well has that worked so far?" Rani asked. "It's been weeks."

Vrabel shrugged. "I'll send it out. Be prepared for an angry call."

Rani slumped into the chair beside him and rubbed her weary eyes. This command thing was draining. She wondered how the lieutenant did it every day. A small voice in her head asked if she could return to her old job, where there was less worry and less responsibility.

"What if we tried to reattach the antenna?"

"And tell them we're here?" Vrabel tapped his long fingers on the keyboard. "As long as they're a benevolent species . . ."

"You just said they left a calling card."

He turned a shade red. "You're right, but it's tough to have the guts to back up that belief. Especially since once you announce our presence, you lose any advantage."

Rani tried to think this through. He was right, of course. It was a gamble. But on the other hand . . . when you considered the threat of the energy beam, the choice became black-and-white. "If we realigned the pieces, maybe the artifact would stop discharging energy beams."

Vrabel stared at the fractured part of alien hardware. He seemed to be wrestling with his thoughts. "Your call, but Rutherford is against it."

She walked up to the artifact and planted her fists on her hips. "We have a few days before it fires again. Let's see what the colonists say about the signal."

He shrugged, and Rani noted the uncertainty in his eyes. Another aspect of command she had learned to accept: nobody was ever completely happy with your decisions.

*Day 70, 1300 Hours*

Rutherford slammed his fist on the briefing room table, startling Rani and cutting her off midsentence.

"That's dangerous talk, Ensign," the scientist growled, gaze flickering to Jorge seated beside him at the table. "We know nothing about these aliens. They could be benevolent beings, or"—he leaned forward—"they could be tyrannical despots bent on subjugating other races or eliminating them completely."

Rani tried to control her irritation. The man acted like a bully, and she hated bullies. She recalled Broscov at the old Board meetings and how the big Slav would throw his weight around. "I was trying to explain why a highly advanced race should have grown beyond warmongering and wanton destruction. Surely, if they climbed this high on the technological ladder, those tendencies would have been discarded long ago."

Jorge snorted. "Or they made it to the top of the food chain by exhibiting exactly those characteristics."

"We can't take the chance," Rutherford said, folding his arms across his chest. "Alerting the aliens to our presence is too much of a risk."

Seated across from the scientist, Archie tilted his head quizzically. "As opposed to letting the damn thing keep chucking grenades?" His tone carried just a sliver of sarcasm, forcing Rani to hide a smile behind her hand.

"It hasn't hit anything vital yet," Jorge pointed out.

"*Yet* being the key word," Kasim retorted. He sat slumped in his seat at the head of the table, and Rani read the frustration in his tight expression. He had called the meeting after the artifact fired the second energy beam, nicking the station and causing a leak in the concourse. Now the sides were shaping up: Rani and Vrabel pushing for action, Rutherford and most of his scientists warning against fixing the antenna. The majority of the colonists, initially excited about the alien hardware, were growing wary and even hostile after the dangerous discharges.

"I'm no expert," Kasim said. "But even I recognize the odds are stacked against us. Sooner or later, our luck will run out."

Rutherford swept his hands across the table. "We need more time, Governor." He ignored Vrabel's eyeroll. "Once we crack the code, we'll be able to see who these aliens really are."

"It's been weeks and you've got exactly nothing to show," Rani said.

Rutherford's eyes narrowed. "Science takes time. We still have experiments to run."

Rani refused to break eye contact. "There's a difference between science and futility, and you're wallowing in the latter. And the colonists are the ones taking the risk."

Jorge pointed a finger. "Last time I checked, we were all colonists. Which means we're all taking that risk."

Rani bit her tongue. The military's job on Europa was to protect lives. She couldn't do that if Kasim tied her hands. A quick glance at the governor confirmed his consternation, as fine lines had formed on his brow.

"How much longer do you need?" Kasim asked.

Rutherford glanced at Jorge. "One week."

"What?" Vrabel jumped up, knocking his chair over. "You want to twiddle your thumbs for seven days while the artifact has another crack at killing everyone?"

Rutherford shifted in his seat. "I, er, should have some answers by then."

Kasim ran his fingers along the table. His glance landed on Rani. "You're convinced it's safe to reattach the antenna?"

"I'm convinced we're dead if we don't do something. What I'm not sure about is if we can actually repair the thing." She looked at Vrabel. "What do you think?"

The lanky engineer righted his chair and took a deep breath before sitting. He avoided looking at Rutherford. "Reattaching it is a nonstarter. We haven't even determined what kind of matter it's made of. What I can do is position it in exactly the same orientation as before it fractured. There's no way to know if that will focus the beam."

"Crazy," Rutherford said. "We didn't survive a year of hell just to get wiped out by an advanced civilization."

"We've got to do something," Rani repeated, looking at Kasim. "The status quo is untenable." At least the scientist couldn't argue with that.

Kasim took a deep breath and turned to Vrabel. "How long until you're ready?"

"I'm ready now."

"You don't need equipment to maneuver the antenna?"

He shook his head. “Funny thing about the broken piece. It only weighs ounces; the rest of the artifact contains the concentrated mass.”

Kasim pursed his lips. “And no idea about the structure of the artifact itself?”

“It’s something we’ve never seen before,” Vrabel said. “The matter is not as densely packed as a neutron star, but it’s definitely got similar characteristics. My guess is some type of super-heavy element that acts as a shield, protecting the guts of the artifact. And there’s no way we’re cutting through it.”

“We could make a hole,” Jorge said.

Archie scowled. “With what? Even a diamond saw won’t scratch the surface.”

“No.” Rutherford said. “Something stronger. We’re almost ready to produce positrons in the lab.”

Rani’s jaw dropped. “You want to detonate an antimatter bomb next to it? Are you insane?”

“Not a ‘bomb,’ a directed beam to cut through the surface. Like a welding torch.”

“You’re friggin’ nuts,” Archie said. “The thing is already firing lethal energy beams and you want to attack it? How do you think it’s going to react?”

“It’s safer than dropping our pants for the aliens,” Jorge muttered.

Rani stared at Kasim. “You’re not seriously considering this? Nothing good can possibly come of it.”

All eyes fell on Kasim. The arguments were on the table. It was time to decide. Rani recalled a similar meeting when Braeder had initiated rationing.

The governor leaned back and rubbed his eyes. “I need to think on this. For now, it’s status quo. We’ll meet back here in forty-eight hours.” He stood. “Thank you for coming.”

Everyone filed out of the briefing room except Rani, who lingered next to the door. “Tell me you’re just playing politics and plan to shut him down.”

Kasim waited until the door hissed shut. “One thing I learned from Braeder is not to make snap decisions. I remember watching him wrestle with an issue for days, examining the problem from every angle. I think you should do the same.”

“You mean like choosing the best way not to destroy the lab and possibly the thermal extractor with an antimatter device. Not to mention declaring war on a technologically advanced species.”

Kasim smiled and patted her shoulder. "Yeah, something like that. Right now, delaying my decision is a compromise." He paused and his expression turned serious. "If you think I'm out of line, you could pull a Ryan."

"What? Eject you into vacuum?"

He jerked as if stung. "No, I meant declare martial law. It worked last time."

Rani thought about it and then sighed. "No, I don't think the colonists could survive another punch in the gut. Rutherford and the miners are going to fight us every step of the way unless we give them a chance to prove us wrong. I hate putting the colony at risk, but . . ." She shrugged.

Kasim stepped up to the portal and stared over the ice fields. "You said each beam has a two percent chance of hitting something vital?"

"About that."

The governor clasped his hands behind his back. "I hate gambling."

# CHAPTER 15

*A lack of patience in trifling matters might lead to the disruption of a great project.*

DAY 71, 1100 HOURS

I'm worried about the timeline," Gunner said as he led Ryan out of the Command Module. "This was supposed to be a straightforward salvage mission. Now the vet is treating sick survivors, we're struggling to locate wire, and even if we find everything, it'll be damn tricky to load the transports with those damned mutants roaming the surface."

A tightness formed in Ryan's gut. The same, nagging doubts had kept him awake most of the night. Despite working eighteen-hour days, they were behind schedule. "I don't know what to tell you, Gunner. Unless you have a magical formula to lengthen the days or kill all the sekers. The colony needs these parts."

"The colony needs to survive," Gunner growled, and Ryan sensed the frustration in his tone. "And that's not going to happen if we don't get back there sooner."

"Hey, Gunner," Sasha called. She had her hands buried in an electrical conduit near Engineering, and metal pieces lay scattered around her like the remnants of a picnic. "You were right about the age of this station. Some of these parts are older than you."

Ryan arched an eyebrow, but Gunner only sighed. "Don't worry, Ace. We're still working on manners." He walked up and inspected the exposed circuits. "The reason it's older is because the Alliance was the first to colonize the asteroids, years before the Federation or the Caliphate. That being said, the layout of the colonies, the modular components, haven't changed in decades. It's like LEGO; they keep adding sections as needed. Which is why there's such a similarity to Europa." He plucked a powered screwdriver off her toolbelt and helped remove part of the external casing.

As the veteran and Sasha worked, Ryan surveyed the main boulevard. Just like Europa, it stretched the length of the station, from the Command Module to the hive entrances. There were other similarities: the closed storefronts lining the street, the dead trees and bushes that had once suffused the air with a sweet honeysuckle smell, and even the detritus covering the floor. The massive fountain in the middle of the concourse was covered in the same green algae as Europa's Trevi Fountain. The unspoken difference: Europa was ten times cleaner and didn't whisper words of doom.

The door to Engineering swished open, and Plante entered the concourse carrying a box of computer parts. Sasha walked over and pulled out some black wire. "How old is this stuff? I'm guessing fifty years."

Ryan shrugged and looked at the governor.

Plante put the box down and wiped his brow. "As a matter of fact, construction began seventy years ago. How did you know?"

"The wire." She turned them over in her hand. "It's four-gauge. The Alliance stopped manufacturing this particular grade fifty years ago. That means this place is ancient."

The governor exchanged a look with Gunner, who was attempting to hide a smile. "I didn't think fifty was ancient."

"Sorry, Governor," Ryan said. "Sasha likes to speak her mind."

"No matter," Plante said, taking the wires from her hand. "Before the crisis Earthside, they worked fine, so we don't comment on their age."

"Well, I will." Sasha touched Gunner on the arm. "The grade doesn't meet our specs."

Plante looked at the veteran. "Is that a problem?"

Gunner puffed out his cheeks. "Yeah, this stuff won't handle the load from our extractor."

"What?" Ryan stepped forward to get a closer look. "Are you sure? What do we use?"

Sasha rolled her eyes. "Magnesium diboride. Even the old fart knows that."

Ryan looked to Gunner, and the veteran gave a perceptible nod. "We typically run extremely high loads through transmission lines. This stuff"—he gestured to the black wires—"would simply fry."

"Damn." Ryan noticed the governor eyeing him. "We ran out of replacement wire," he explained. "It's one of the priority items on the list."

Plante rolled the gritty cable between his fingers. "The entire station was constructed with this grade. Fleet performed some minor upgrades to Engineering a couple of years back but didn't change the wiring."

Ryan turned back to the main concourse as two miners exited Engineering carrying boxes. Sybil followed behind them and gave Ryan a wave.

"Your girlfriend is actually helping," Sasha said.

Ryan felt the tips of his ears redden as Gunner snickered. "Ah, she's not my girlfriend."

"She was on Europa." The engineer stared at him expectantly.

Ryan tried to ignore Plante's inquisitive look. "If we can't find the wire in this station, we have to find another source."

Gunner's humorous expression vanished. "You're talking a different colony?"

"No choice," Ryan said. "If we don't load the right grade, it's a wasted trip."

Gunner glanced out the nearest portal. "Since the Federation and Caliphate were the last to the party on Ceres, I'm guessing their wiring would be the most modern. That means we have to travel across the surface."

Sasha shuddered. "I don't want to go out there with those monsters."

Gunner wrapped an arm around her shoulders.

"There is another option," Plante said. "This colony is connected to the nearest Alliance station by a tunnel. It hasn't been used in a while, but it's a straight run. About two klicks. Might be worth checking it out before venturing outside."

"Any atmosphere?" Ryan asked. "Or will we need suits?"

"Limited in the tunnel, and definitely not in the other station."

"Well, it doesn't sound like we have a choice," Ryan said, feeling a migraine coming on. Last thing he wanted to do was face another bloodthirsty mob. "Sasha, check the wiring in Engineering just in case it's been upgraded. Gunner, put a team together and meet back here in thirty. And make sure everyone double-checks their suits. I'm not taking any chances."

When Ryan returned, Gunner and Sybil were waiting outside Medical, along with three of the reservists, Lucas, Smith, and Compton. Each was big-boned with broad shoulders and a thick beard. Everyone had suited up.

Ryan walked up to Sybil. "I thought you were assisting the doctor." At least, that had been the plan. He glanced at the rows of stacked boxes on the floor and wondered if he had screwed up by not bringing a larger crew to Ceres.

Sybil shrugged. "Chan was there already, and the doctor said he didn't need any help. I figured you might."

"What did Sasha say about the wire in Engineering?" Gunner asked.

Ryan frowned. "The governor was right: wiring is all substandard."

The door linking the Command Module to the concourse creaked open, and Plante walked out, carrying a diamond saw. He passed it to Smith.

"We're going to need this," the governor said. "Follow me." He led the group to the end of the concourse, where the outline of a door was visible under a layer of gray dust.

"Damn, Governor, you don't fool around." Ryan surveyed the wide metal door as he scratched at some nascent whiskers on his cheek. Somebody had welded the edges to the frame and bolted three steel bars across the front. Nothing short of a bulldozer was getting through.

Plante gave a self-deprecating laugh. "We went old-school. It's not pretty, but it works."

"Did the sekers try to get in?" Sybil asked.

"When they first discovered we were in here, they banged on it for weeks. It's been quiet since."

Ryan ran his hand across the top beam. The metal was cold and covered in a fine layer of grime. "So, there's a chance they could be in the other station?"

"I wouldn't bet against it."

Sybil stepped up, her ponytail dangling down her back. "There's no other way in?"

"This place is as secure as Fort Knox," Plante said. "Even the air shafts have been sealed."

"Well, we better get started," Ryan said. "Smith, cut through the welds but, for God's sake, don't open the door."

The reservist put on a set of protective glasses and lifted the diamond saw off the floor. The tool weighed over eighty pounds, yet he handled it like a child's toy. He started with the middle metal crossbeam, and a crescent of sparks shot over his shoulder. "Keep your distance," he warned. "The slivers will burn."

Gunner led the others back a few steps.

Ryan nodded at the machine gun slung over Gunner's shoulder. "I hope we won't need that."

Gunner patted the weapon. "Think of it as an insurance policy."

Plante stared at the diamond blade as it left a molten yellow line in its wake. "I hope no one has claustrophobia because it's pretty tight in there."

Ryan lifted his helmet to his mouth. "Sasha, meet us in the concourse. We're ready to travel to the Alliance station."

Two clicks answered him, and a minute later, the redhead joined them. Her nose turned up when she saw what Smith was doing. "I hate tunnels."

"Sorry about that," Gunner said. "But you're the one who said we need better wire."

She muttered something about "old farts" under her breath before cinching her wrist straps and putting on her helmet.

Lucas and Compton unslung their lasers as Smith finished cutting through the last metal bar. It landed on the duroalloy floor with a dull thud. Plante withdrew a key from his pocket and unlocked the door. Gunner pulled the gun off his shoulder as Smith gripped the handle and yanked hard. It opened with a high-pitched screech.

A blast of cold air washed over them, and Ryan detected a stale smell like moldy laundry. He peered into the darkness and shivered. It looked like a mine shaft: narrow concrete walls and low ceiling. No way he wanted to get pinned in there.

By the silence, he figured everyone had the same thought. Sasha looked the most peaked. "Suit check, everyone." At least their helmets would provide plenty of light.

Gunner took the lead, the reservists tight behind him. Ryan waited for Sasha to enter before summoning his courage and following them into darkness.

It took the better part of an hour to traverse the long passageway, most of the time bent over like hunchbacks. They emerged in a dark subbasement, their EV lamps playing over a dust-covered floor and rows of barren shelves. A single door at the far end of the room stood half open.

"Gunner, take Smith and find out where that door leads," Ryan ordered. "You know anything about the layout over here, Governor?"

"Haven't been here for over a year, Lieutenant, but it should be similar to our station."

"Looks like it's been abandoned at least that long," Sasha said, sounding more relieved than surprised.

Ryan glanced over his shoulder. "Compton, seal that door behind us. I don't want anything sneaking in while we're gone."

"Yes, sir."

Gunner returned and gave him a thumbs-up. "All clear, Ace. I found a stairwell that takes us up to the main level."

Ryan waited until Compton finished wedging the door shut. "All right, take point. And let's get back here as fast as we can."

"Copy that." Gunner slipped off the safety on the machine gun.

Using the lamps on their helmets, they moved single file up the stairwell and exited inside a large storage area. Ryan pulled up the inventory list on his minicom and refreshed his memory while Gunner and the reservists checked out a corridor filled with rusting machine parts, broken furniture, and piles of clothes. Open shops on either side of the corridor revealed more empty shelves.

"Everything's been picked over," Sybil said.

"Yeah." Ryan paused to stare at a smashed glass storefront. "They didn't even close the doors before they pulled the pin."

"Why clean the house if you intend to burn it down?" Gunner asked.

Smith stopped in front of a set of double doors. He cradled the laser in his arms. "Concourse is through here, Lieutenant. Lord knows what state it's in."

Ryan gestured. "Quiet and slow."

Gunner and Smith, weapons in hand, led the way. They pushed through the doors and down a wide corridor that ended in a sealing bulkhead.

"Just like my station," Plante said. "Emergency walls dropped when the concourse depressurized."

"Let me see if I can fix that." Sasha stepped up to a circuit box on the wall. "Strange," she muttered, loud enough for Ryan and Gunner to hear. "There's a small current running in one of the lines."

Ryan exchanged a look with the veteran. "Why would there be power here?"

"No idea."

"Must be the solar panels," Plante said. "Some are probably still operational."

"I can check the source," Sasha said.

"Forget it." Ryan felt the pressure to get moving. "Let's not waste time."

Sasha spliced the wires together, and something clicked inside the bulkhead. It rose grudgingly on hydraulic motors.

"Here we go, Ace."

Ryan waved Sasha and Sybil behind him as they entered a wide boulevard that stretched the length of the station. Under their suit lamps, it resembled the concourse on Europa, except it was double the size.

The governor pointed. The door to the decompression chamber stood open.

Ryan nodded. Unlike Plante's station, no one had remained behind to close it.

Most of the concourse lay hidden in shadow, but what they could see was a mess: busted machinery, torn pieces of clothing, and even children's toys. Everything was covered in a layer of regolith that had leaked through the open door. Europa's concourse had been filled with colonists when Ryan opened Europa's concourse to space, and the results had been that much worse: bodies ripped apart, viscous fluids frozen in organic puddles . . . a human abattoir.

He took a steadying breath. "Let's stick with the plan. Engineering first and then the Command Module. Gunner?"

The veteran yanked his eyes off the surrounding carnage and hefted the machine gun over his shoulder. "Affirmative. Engineering is this way. Lucas and Compton, take point. Sasha, you and Lecky stay close. Keep your eyes peeled."

The reservists nodded nervously as they moved up.

Sasha gave a poor imitation of a Fleet salute. "Aye, aye, old man."

Gunner rolled his eyes, and Ryan turned his head to hide his smirk.

"Where are all the bodies?" Sybil asked. "There should be thousands of colonists in this station."

"They're here," Plante said. "Just not in the concourse. Families opted to spend their last moments together in their domiciles. If you want to see a space-age version of a catacomb, take a trip into the hives. It'll depress the hell out of you."

Sybil clamped her jaw tight and fell back in line as the group walked single file, picking their way through the asteroid equivalent of a scrapyard. Papers and bits of debris stirred in their wake as they approached the

Engineering module. They finally spied two bodies: a man and a woman locked in death's embrace.

Sasha squealed, her hand automatically rising to her mouth before it slapped against her faceplate. She grabbed the closest person—Sybil—and hugged her tight.

Gunner stepped forward and nudged the bodies out of their path. The dried husks slowly drifted away. "It's only bodies," he said, bending down to look Sasha in the eye. "They're long past hurting anybody."

Sasha nodded, but her eyes remained as wide as saucers.

Sybil pried herself out of Sasha's grasp and flashed her a look of irritation. The senator's daughter studied the corpses like a bored pathologist.

Gunner inclined his head toward Lucas. "Move up to the Engineering entrance and stand guard. Smith, keep an eye on our six. Sasha." He took her hand and gently pulled her over to the control panel beside the emergency bulkhead. "Need you to raise the wall so we can get in."

Inside her helmet, her color remained pasty white, but she managed a nod. "I'm okay."

Gunner turned to Ryan. "You got the bags?"

Ryan unzipped his backpack. "Ready."

The veteran stepped back to give Sasha space while Ryan opened a channel on the com. "Chan, we're inside the second station. What's your status?"

Static filled the frequency before she responded. "We're packing up the last of the replacement parts now. Dr. Louis stepped out of Medical a while back. He says he found some interesting records. Something about a vaccine."

Ryan hesitated. "Vaccine?"

"Not sure what he meant either, sir, but he's going over them now."

"Understood. We should be back in a few hours." He closed the channel.

Sasha stood back as the bulkhead retracted, and the Engineering door slid open. She looked at Gunner. "I don't understand it, but there's also a slight current in these circuits."

The veteran glanced at the open control panel as if he could visualize the electrons flowing. "Residual charge?"

She shrugged. "Don't know. It's weird."

Ryan stepped into the room and used his suit lamps to penetrate the darkness. About the size of a basketball court, it housed rows of servers along the back wall and a large workstation in the middle. The place was in a state of disorder but nothing like the concourse. Then again, the emergency bulkhead would have sealed the entrance the second the EV door opened. What he was looking at was simply lack of maintenance.

Sasha slid into one seat, Gunner another. Lucas and Compton stood at the door, their eyes nervously scanning the concourse. With the lighting only reaching so far, their imaginations were left to fill in the missing pieces. Every dark space hid a seker, and every sound was a vile monster waiting to pounce. Plante paced back and forth, seemingly unsure what to do.

"Take a seat, Governor," Gunner said, pointing at the servers. "Pull off the casing and check the gauge of the wire."

Sybil joined Ryan as he pried open the metal casement on the terminal at the front. "What happens if we can't find the right type?"

"Then we keep looking," Ryan said, wincing as a metal flap snapped back on his fingers. The EV suit cushioned the blow. "We may have to visit one of the Federation stations."

She offered him a solemn look. "Trying to cross the asteroid's surface? What about using the transports?"

"Not a good idea," Plante said. "Your initial landing was what stirred them up. Taking the ships closer to the sekers' home station would only be worse. The whole nest would probably react. The risk isn't worth it."

Gunner pulled a power tool off his belt. "Chan's not comfortable wasting what little fuel we have left, either. She says she's barely got enough to launch."

Sybil frowned and switched to a private channel. "What do you think, Ryan?"

"I think we didn't come this far to fail."

Her expression softened and she leaned one hip against his terminal. "Even if you salvage the right parts, what's it going to buy us? Six months? A year?"

"If we're lucky," Ryan acknowledged.

"And after that?"

He caught her eye. "I thought you'd have learned by now: one problem at a time. We're on step two and you're asking me about number twenty. Every day is a victory."

She frowned, age lines deepening on her forehead. "You can only roll the dice so many times before you hit snake eyes. I said it before: you need a long-term strategy."

He stopped tearing down the computer. "And yours is what, exactly? Grab forty colonists and try for the home run back to Earth? And leave everyone else behind?"

Her expression didn't waver. "If it saves the human race."

"Sorry." He pulled a multitool off his belt and began removing the screws. "My job is to save everyone, not just a select few."

Sybil stared at him before shaking her head. "That's not a winning strategy."

He let the screws fall to the floor. "But that's always been the issue, hasn't it? It's the way you think. Just like your father. Everything is a competition where there are only winners and losers. You set your endgame and then maneuver the pieces to achieve it."

"And you don't? Somehow, your words don't match your actions." The reference to murdering five hundred colonists was left unsaid.

"My endgame is survival," Ryan replied, fed up with her arguments. "Yours is more . . . selfish."

"So, altruism justifies your actions? There's no guilt because it's for a greater good?"

Ryan gritted his teeth. Was she right? Was the difference between them a matter of perception rather than a core set of principles? He wondered what Rani would say.

"I've got something," Sasha announced.

Gunner leaned over. "Talk to me."

"I was right. There's power in the uplinks." Her fingers danced along the computer interface, while an exposed side panel revealed a confluence of wires and circuits. A single screen lit up. "It's not much but, after a year, they should be dead."

Ryan noted the blinking lights on the screen. "Could it be batteries?"

"Not a chance. They would have gone dry months ago."

"It's probably nothing," Plante said. "There are panels on the roofs of every station. No one would have bothered to shut them down before they opened the EV door."

"Any way to find out?" Gunner asked.

"I'd need a couple hours to play detective," Sasha said. "But in the meantime, I can do this." She reached out and unclipped one wire before reattaching it to a vacant lead. Behind them, the door to the concourse slid shut. Lucas and Compton relaxed.

Gunner whistled. "That's fine, but can you repressurize the room so we can get out of these sardine suits?"

She gave him a wink. "Piece of cake, old man."

Ten minutes later, they were able to remove their helmets and gloves. The temperature hovered around freezing, but being able to work with their senses unencumbered put everyone in a better state of mind.

Until Sasha slammed the palm of her hand against the metal side of her terminal. It vibrated like a broken bell.

"Something wrong?" Ryan asked.

She slumped back in her seat. "I've examined the guts of three terminals. The wires are the wrong gauge. We can't use them."

Ryan glanced at the gray cable he had hauled out of his server. He hadn't run the scanner over it yet, but it felt exactly the same as the ones in the first station. "Damn."

Gunner wiped his sleeve over a sweaty brow. "I guess we're done here, Ace?"

"Yeah." Their attempt to find replacement wire for the extractor had hit a dead end. That meant Ryan's options had boiled down to a single choice. And no one was going to like it.

"Lieutenant." Lucas raised a hand as he leaned his ear against the door. "I hear something outside."

The air got very thick.

"Helmets on," Ryan whispered. "Check suits."

It took two minutes for cross-checks to be completed. Gunner readied his machine gun, and the reservists bracketed the door.

"Lights out, Ace?"

"Dark and quiet, Gunner."

The veteran peeled back the door and poked his head out. After a few seconds, he leaned back. "Something's moving by the Command Module," he said over the com. "We should be able to retreat the way we came."

Ryan caught a glimpse of Sasha's nervous look. "Take point, Gunner. Lucas, Smith behind him. Compton at the back." He didn't have to say it, but Sybil, Sasha, and Plante sidled up next to him.

"Watch your footing," Gunner said as he led them along the wall of the concourse. He kept his helmet lamps low.

They moved carefully and deliberately to avoid the debris. Last thing they needed was to crash into something and announce their presence. Even in the limited atmosphere, noise would carry.

They reached the tunnel entrance, and Ryan felt more than a little relieved after everyone slipped inside. He slid the door closed and leaned back against it. "Good work. Now, Gunner, get us back to the station."

The veteran gave him a wink through his faceplate. "No problem, Ace. Ready for another hour of creeping through a subterranean channel? Glad no one is claustrophobic."

Ryan took a steadying breath. Oh, they certainly were, but no one was going to admit it.

# CHAPTER 16

*Silence is a friend who never betrays.*

DAY 72, 1810 HOURS

How you feeling?" Kasim asked as he settled into the seat next to Rani in the chilly air of the ice cave. He pulled his sweater tight around his shoulders.

Rani continued staring at the artifact in the center of the room. All the scientists including Vrabel had left for the day, leaving only Rani and Kasim in a lab equipped to hold twenty. "I'm fine," she said. "What are you doing here?"

Kasim peeled open a bag containing carrots from the recent harvest and placed it on the desk. "Well, for one thing, you skipped supper, and having you starve to death before Braeder returns will look bad on my record."

She slowly focused, but it seemed to take precious seconds before his words sank in. "Sorry, I was just . . . thinking."

He snorted. "So I noticed. It's been what, twelve days since you touched it, and something's different. You're acting different."

She flashed him a look. "What are you talking about?"

"You've been coming out here more often, and your mood has changed. More morose and down. Archie's noticed it too. Now, take a bite."

Rani stared at the food as though realizing she was actually hungry. "Thanks."

When she didn't elaborate, Kasim decided to push harder. He hadn't walked all the way out there just to deliver food. "Okay, spill it, Ensign. This is not like you. What happened when you put your hand on it?"

She picked up a carrot and rolled it between her fingers.

Kasim didn't like the vibes he was getting. They needed a strong leader right now, not a vague shadow of one. "Rani?"

She swallowed and forced the words out. "I felt a presence."

He startled. That was not what he expected. "What do you mean by *presence*? Another being?"

"No." Her gaze took on a distant cast. "It wasn't so much a *who* as a *what*, and even then, the sensation was fleeting and confusing."

"You're not making a lot of sense, Rani." But her words did put him on edge.

She threw up her hands. "I know. I'm sorry. It's been keeping me up at night, trying to piece it together. I definitely sensed *something*. Only part I could understand was the emotion."

"Emotion?" Kasim frowned. "What kind?"

"Multiple. In that split-second, I felt surprise, curiosity, maybe even a twinge of disappointment."

"You got all that in less than a second?"

"Yeah," she snorted. "The sensation was instantaneous, like its consciousness traveled at light speed. It reached into my mind."

Kasim's pulse quickened. He didn't like where this was going. "It invaded your thoughts?"

Lines formed on her forehead. "Yes. Maybe. I felt normal one moment and *something else* the next."

"What did it do?"

"It scrolled through my memories. Like it was cataloguing me."

"Jesus, Rani what does that even mean?"

She took an angry bite of the carrot. "No idea, but don't tell Rutherford."

Kasim leaned back. That was good advice. The scientist didn't need to be convinced they might be dealing with an aggressive alien species. "I won't." He turned to the artifact. "But what are we going to do?"

Rani swallowed. "Let's give the scientists a few more days. If they find nothing, I'm going to touch it again."

Kasim wracked his brain for a response, some suggestion that would keep her on an even keel. But all he could focus on were the pulsating white hieroglyphics.

"I wish we'd had guns when the sekers first appeared," Plante said as he chewed on one of Louis's ration bars in the observation room. "Could have saved lives."

"Yeah," Ryan grunted, recalling how valuable his revolvers had been during the uprising. "Too bad Fleet never considered them a necessity on the colonies." He sucked down half his water bottle in one gulp. Working in EV suits was like working underwater, pushing your muscles until they felt like limp noodles. It was good to get back to the station, peel off the thick suits, and grab some food.

Gunner had left to help the miners stack boxes in the decompression chamber. An exhausted-looking Sybil sat back in one of the comfy chairs and closed her eyes.

"Never thought we'd have to defend ourselves," Plante said. "Until the killing started."

Ryan leaned forward. "What happened?"

"We thought they were just survivors from one of the hives, starving and looking for food. We went out to help and that's when they jumped us. I lost some good people that day. Needless to say, after that, we barricaded ourselves in the station."

"How many died?" Sybil asked, opening her eyes to stare at the governor.

Plante grimaced. "A dozen. Each one torn to shreds. Fortunately, that was the last time the sekers got close."

"And you haven't learned anything about them?" Ryan asked.

"Nothing." Plante lowered his head, like it was painful to think about the subject. "There are probably answers in the Federation station, but it might as well be on another asteroid. No way we can get close."

"The way they move on the surface is weird," Sybil said.

"It's unnatural," Plante agreed. "Like out of a horror vid."

Ryan didn't comment. The sekers were *wrong* in so many ways. It was as though their muscles didn't work right or they were rewired in some fashion.

Louis entered the lounge and walked over to join them.

"Anything useful in Medical?" Ryan asked. The doctor had spent most of the past two days searching for supplies.

Louis seemed distracted as he sat down. "Not much. The cupboards were bare, and everything was pretty much picked over."

"Chan said you found some notes on a vaccine?"

Louis hesitated, rubbing the end of his stump.

"Arm okay?"

"Just throbbing a bit." Louis lowered it beneath the table. "Apparently, Medical suffered a fire a few months back, and it destroyed all of the hard drives. All that was left was some hand-scribbled notes."

Ryan's eyebrows rose, and he turned to Plante. "A fire?"

"Right," the governor said. "I forgot to mention that. Probably started by a short circuit. We put it out, but the damage was done."

Louis leaned forward. "The notes alluded to some vaccine trials."

Ryan's ears perked up. "Any details?"

Louis shook his head. "I asked Sasha to check the hard drives in case anything can be salvaged."

Ryan rubbed his whiskers thoughtfully. Replacement parts were why they had come to Ceres, but if there had been some work on a cure . . . "What are the chances the Russians were working on a vaccine before the food ran out?"

Louis stared out the portal. "Unless we stumble on some information, there's no way to know for sure."

"The sekers appeared after the military transport landed," Sybil reminded them. "Coincidence?"

Louis pushed his glasses back up his nose. "Call me crazy, but I think the Russians were doing research on an experimental vaccine."

Ryan tilted his head. "And you think that because . . ."

Louis leaned back and resumed rubbing the end of his stump. "Because those scraps of notes I found hinted at something beyond what the CDC had accomplished, and there are references to the Russian colony."

Plante scoffed. "That's highly unlikely. I know for a fact Federation technology lagged behind the Alliance. And our doctors weren't anywhere close to a breakthrough."

Lines branched out from the corners of Louis's eyes. "But they didn't have a sample of the plague to play with."

The governor waved a hand dismissively. "Impossible."

Louis ignored him and turned his gaze on Ryan. "You said we can't go back to Earth until we're protected from the bacterium. I'm beginning to think there's something on this asteroid that we're missing. We should keep looking."

"Hold on," Sybil said. "You're not suggesting we make a field trip to the Federation station? I'm willing to risk my life for replacement parts but not to satisfy your curiosity."

"It's hardly curiosity when it may involve a vaccine," Louis snapped. Then, in a more-conciliatory tone, he added, "If we access one of their computer ports, I may be able to link into the Federation Medical."

"Impossible," Plante repeated.

“The sekers control the surface of the asteroid,” Sybil said, a thick vein popping on her forehead. “You’re talking suicide.”

Louis glared. “Stop for a second and look at the big picture. We’re on a rock millions of kilometers away from our colony, salvaging parts to buy Europa . . . what, a brief reprieve? Face it: the only chance the human race has of surviving is getting back to Earth. To do that, we need to be immune to the damn plague. And right now, we may be sitting on the only colony that came close to developing a vaccine. Do you want to throw away this opportunity?”

Sybil turned to Ryan. “Tell me you’re not seriously considering this. You saw what the sekers did to Gonzalez. Is it worth the life of our only physician?”

Ryan hesitated. On the face of it, the notion seemed absurd. “You really think they were getting somewhere, Doc?”

Louis threw up his arms. It looked weird with just one hand. “I’ve reviewed all the data the admiral sent us. The CDC was making progress, but I sense the doctors here had taken the next step. I won’t make any promises until I see what Sasha can pull off those hard drives, but, dammit, I think they were on to something.”

Ryan hesitated as all eyes fell on him. “Well, isn’t that interesting.”

“How long?” Rani asked, running her finger along the x-axis on the monitor. The latest computer projections didn’t infuse her with a sense of confidence, and the flashing icon next to the countdown clock only fed her growing anxiety.

Vrabel pushed his chair back. Most of the furniture in the Event Horizon had been shoved against the wall. With no booze, the establishment was rarely used. Not like before the plague, when one had to call ahead to reserve a table. “Thirty-eight hours, six minutes.”

Rani wrapped her arms around herself as cool air formed goosebumps on her skin. With just the two of them in the room, it seemed bigger somehow. “And no idea which direction the beam will fire?”

“Best we can figure, it’s totally random.”

Rani leaned forward, planted her elbows on the table, and rubbed her eyes. God, she felt tired. “Is there any good news you can give me about the damned artifact?”

Vrabel spared her a grin. “We’re narrowing down what quantum particle it’s currently emitting.”

"And that will help us how?"

"Well, if we can respond in kind, it might stop the countdown."

She gave him a stern once-over. "Why do I get the feeling you're reaching?"

"Because I am. But no one has offered anything better." He looked like he wanted to add something reassuring, but the com on the wall went off.

"Medical to Ensign Singh."

*Medical?* She reached over to tap the button. "Go ahead."

"This is Nurse Goguen. I wanted to inform you that the governor collapsed in Engineering. We're treating him now."

Rani jumped up. "What? Damn. I'm on my way."

Vrabel started to stand. "Do you . . ."

She waved him down as she hurried to the door. "Keep working on the emissions. We need to know what we're dealing with."

The concourse was empty as she ran past Engineering. The green algae growing out of the pipes in the fountain contrasted sharply with black marks on the marble.

The nurse met her at the door and directed her to a stretcher in the back. Kasim lay quietly on his side under a white sheet that had been pulled up to his chin. His skin had taken on an unhealthy gray tinge, and dark circles surrounded his eyes.

"Are you okay? They said you passed out." Rani noted the regular waves on the overhead monitor and the yellow IV fluid running into his arm.

"I'm fine," he said. "Just pushing this old body a little too hard."

"Bullshit," a voice said.

Rani turned to see Mabel stepping up to the side of the bed. She checked the IV before focusing on Kasim. "Our governor has been having chest pains for a while and didn't tell anyone. We wouldn't have found out except Solomon was working with him when he collapsed. He carried the governor in here before significant cardiac damage was done."

Rani blinked. "Cardiac damage? You mean like a heart attack?"

"Exactly." The nurse turned down the IV rate. "Stubborn SOB was having angina. Probably would have died if he had been alone."

Rani felt momentary panic—she needed the man to run the colony—before guilt swept it away. "How's he doing?"

"Stable. Dr. Louis left a list of protocols to follow, so the amount of damaged cardiac tissue was minimal. Vasopressors and clot busters seem to have done the trick."

“I’m right here, you know,” Kasim said, frowning. “You don’t have to talk about me in the third person.”

Rani narrowed her eyes. “Yes, we do, especially when you’re acting like a child. Why didn’t you tell anyone?”

He faltered under her stare. “I thought it would go away.”

She tried to look mad, but her concern kept leaking through. “The lieutenant would confine you to bed for a month.”

A hint of a smile teased Kasim’s lips. “Fortunately for me, he’s not here. And, even better, you require my presence at your meetings with the scientists.”

“Not that much,” she growled, savoring the anger welling up inside. “Meetings can wait.”

“You have only hours before the artifact’s timer reaches zero again, Ensign,” he said matter-of-factly. “So, they really can’t.”

Mabel threw a puzzled look at Rani. “You’re not thinking of letting him out, are you? Protocol mandates a course of treatment to rebuild his myocardium.”

Rani ground her teeth together. That was not what she needed to hear in the moment. “Can I steal him for a short meeting, say tomorrow?”

“What? Maybe. But he is supposed to rest.”

Rani spun on her heel. “I’ll be by at noon. Try to keep him alive until then.”

# CHAPTER 17

*It is man that makes truth great, not truth that makes man great.*

DAY 73, 1015 HOURS

Archie caught up with Rani in Engineering. "We have a problem."

Rani lifted her gaze from the readouts. With the circuits beginning to fail with regularity, diagnostics took longer every week. "What is it this time? Environmental controls twitchy again?"

His expression didn't change. "It's not the station."

"Then what—"

"I just returned from the cave. Somebody stole the alien antenna."

Rani forgot about the diagnostic. Her lips formed a curse before her brain kicked into gear. "Bastards. What happened?"

"Vrabel went out this morning to resume the experiments and realized it was missing. He searched the lab before calling me."

Rani stood and closed the program. "So, sometime during the night?"

"Figured they slipped out of the airlock in the wee hours and made the trek to the cave."

"Did you check the recordings?"

"Not yet. Figured I'd tell you first."

She nodded. Last year, she and Marco had used the station's external cameras to discover which colonists were stealing items from the transport hangar. As far as she knew, those cameras were still operational.

"That's our first stop," she said, zipping up her overalls. "Where's Kasim?"

"On his way from Medical."

Rani felt a twinge of guilt. Dragging the governor away from treatment was not the way to care for a heart attack victim, but she needed him. She cursed herself for acting more and more like Braeder.

As if on cue, the door slid open, and the governor walked in. A thick yellow sweater covered the top half of his thawb, but he still resembled a blue popsicle. There were more lines on his face than she remembered, and the skin seemed to hang over his cheeks. His gaze landed on Rani. "Archie told you?"

"Yeah, just now. I want to check the tapes."

Kasim grimaced. "Bad news. I already looked. Someone shut down the cameras."

Archie leaned back against the wall. "So, it was planned. The antenna could be anywhere in the station by now."

"Or they could have buried it in the ice," Kasim said, wringing his hands. "We'll never find it."

Rani caught his eye. "You gave them a week. They waited until now before changing the rules. What does that tell us?"

"That the governor shouldn't have agreed to their demands." Archie gave Kasim the evil eye. "Sometimes, it's better not to compromise."

Kasim blanched. "Are we sure it's Rutherford? Maybe someone else snapped it up."

Rani rolled her eyes. "I understand why people get fed up with the UN. But you're missing the other bit of information."

Archie shifted his weight. "Which is?"

"They weren't getting any answers. Their experiments were going nowhere, so they needed a way to manufacture more time."

Kasim blinked as he processed the information. "I'll put them in the brig. Maybe that'll prompt them to 'fess up."

"Now you're going to break the law?" Rani asked. "Incarcerate without due process?"

The governor glowered at her. "A second ago, he said I was too soft."

"We need evidence," Rani said. "Since we're living in a so-called democracy."

"You could declare martial law," Archie said, a malicious smile forming. "It's been done before."

"Maybe," Rani admitted. "Or I could do one better and follow the lieutenant's lead."

Archie tilted his head quizzically. "Not sure what you mean."

"It means think ahead. When Rutherford convinced the governor to give him another week despite zero success, I got suspicious."

Kasim folded his arms across his chest. "What did you do?"

Rani withdrew a small mechanical unit from her pocket. "I attached a tiny tracker to the antenna. This sensor will pick it up."

Archie grinned. "You sneaky little devil."

"How did you know?" Kasim asked.

"Let's just say I suspected. Call Solomon and tell him to meet us outside Engineering."

The governor walked to the com unit on the wall and made the request.

"If it is Rutherford, he might have friends who won't take kindly to us invading their space," Archie warned.

"Which is why you're going to pick up a couple of lasers," Rani said. "Hopefully just for show."

"And if things go to shit? Two lasers aren't gonna hold back a determined group of civilians."

"Let me worry about that," she said. "Meet you in ten?"

Archie's expression remained grim. "I remember a similar search attempt last year. That didn't turn out so well for a few hundred colonists."

"We're not going to let it get that bad," Rani said, starting for the door. "And if it does, I promise not to space that many."

The concourse was empty as she hurried back to the Command Center. Two reservists monitored the terminals in Ops, and although they understood little about the functioning of the various subsystems, they knew enough to call for help if yellow buttons began flashing. She ran her hand along the dirty walls of the fountain. The layer of algae on the bottom was getting thicker. Like dirt accumulating over a dead civilization.

Before he left, Braeder had told her exactly where to look: behind a loose bulkhead in his quarters. She would have never found it otherwise.

There were only seven rounds in the clip, not that it mattered, since she had never fired a real gun. Even if her life was threatened, she didn't know if she could pull the trigger. She shuddered at the thought of shooting a real person. The weight of guilt after opening the EV door had almost suffocated her soul. More violence would rip off that scab and more.

Tucking the gun in her waistband hid it from view, and she hurried into the corridor before the reservists spied her slipping out of the lieutenant's quarters. Kasim, Solomon, and Archie waited outside Engineering. Archie and Solomon carried small lasers.

"Cap'n." Solomon inclined his head.

"Everything all right?" Archie asked, a strange glint in his eye.

Rani withdrew the small tracker from her pocket and handed it to Solomon. "Turn it on and follow the breadcrumbs. I want to retrieve that antenna and jail the thieves before they undermine our authority."

Solomon nodded, then squared his shoulders, and Rani wondered how he was dealing with the conflicting emotions of having his former comrades on one side, his new boss and common sense on the other. She had gone with her gut when she decided on including him in the hunting party. If she'd misjudged, she had just squandered any hope of ending this peacefully.

He powered up the device and waited for the signal. "It says Beta Hive."

Rani kept her voice calm. "Take point."

The damaged sections of Beta Hive had been cleared away after the insurrection, but laser scorch marks still peppered the walls like pock-marked skin. There were other, darker stains that Rani refused to focus on.

They walked through a small park, the stone markers covered with dirt, the plastek benches dented and broken. Small trees and bushes struggled to survive after too many cold nights while the extractor was offline.

A few colonists stretched their legs on the walking paths, giving Rani puzzled looks as her group passed an abandoned tennis court. Six separate walking paths led away from the park, and Solomon hesitated until the tracker locked on to the signal. "This way." He led them into a corridor nestled between tightly packed domiciles.

Heads appeared in windows, and doors cracked open as they passed. The corridor was only six feet wide, and Rani cringed as their footsteps echoed off plastek walls. Solomon took them along a twisting route until they reached a door with the number B102 imprinted in bold red letters.

He turned to Rani, jaw set. "It's in here."

Archie stepped forward and rapped his knuckles on the door. "Open up. The governor wants a word."

His voice bounced off the walls and settled into darkness. He waited a few seconds and repeated the knock. "If you don't open this door, we have the legal right to force our way in."

Something stirred inside. Rani closed her eyes and listened. Did she hear voices?

The door cracked open. She recognized that face. Rutherford.

The man's eyes landed on Kasim and widened. "Governor?"

Rani stepped in front. "Open up. I believe you have something that doesn't belong to you."

Rutherford hesitated, his gaze shifting from Kasim to Rani before he complied. Jorge and another burly miner stepped around him and entered the corridor, practically filling it. Rani felt like she was looking up at a pair of mountains.

Rutherford slid between them. "I don't believe you're welcome here, Ensign." He looked down his nose at her. "Best if you leave before something ugly happens."

Rani squeezed her hands into fists to stop them from trembling. It took a supreme effort to hold her ground. "Perhaps you've forgotten, but my job is to protect the colony, which means I have the right to examine any domicile that may harbor a threat. Now stand aside so we can perform a search of the premises."

Rutherford's smile had all the warmth of a reptile, thin skin stretching across his cheekbones until he resembled a corpse. "And what, pray tell, are you looking for?"

"As if you don't know." She tried to step between them but the miners didn't budge.

Archie and Solomon pulled the lasers off their shoulders. Kasim paled.

"Do what the lady says," Archie growled. "I'm not going to ask again."

Doors in the corridor behind them screeched open, and four more big bodies crowded into the narrow space.

Rani forced down a volcano of panic. They were trapped. Six deuterium miners, each tipping the scale at three hundred pounds, glared down at her. Kasim looked about to faint, and even Solomon's gaze flickered nervously.

"I think you better hand over the lasers," Rutherford said. "Those popguns aren't going to stop the inevitable."

A miner made a grab for Archie's weapon. Archie slapped his hand away and pointed it at the man's face. "Try it again and I'll take out your eyes."

The big miner leaned in and growled.

"Last chance," Rutherford said. "Pass them over or we're taking them."

Rani's heart pounded against her ribs. Her old self pined for a peaceful solution, but the new, scarred version realized that option had disappeared.

"Ensign?"

She reached back, wrapped her fingers around the gun, and whipped it out. "Back off! Right now."

The miners on either side of Rutherford recoiled, almost squishing the scientist into a pretzel.

He shoved them away. "Idiots. She's got one gun. There are seven of us. What can she do?"

"What can I do?" Rani stepped forward and thrust the gun into Jorge's chest. "I can shoot him, and maybe him, too." She twisted the weapon and pointed at his partner's face. The miner blanched. "Now get back inside!"

The moment balanced on a knife's edge. The miners facing her hesitated, uncertain. Rutherford looked scared, like he was dealing with a madwoman.

A thud sounded behind her.

"Look out!" Archie shouted.

Blood pounding in her ears, Rani wasn't sure if she heard the whine of a laser before someone grabbed her shoulder and squeezed. She cried out in pain as she was lifted off her feet. Her finger twitched and the gun belched flame and smoke. A roar swept up the corridor. The grip on her bones lessened and she fell, landing hard on her side.

Reality splintered into shards like a shattered mirror. A foot grazed her chin, snapping her head back. Kasim slammed against the floor, his expression dazed, his forehead dripping blood.

She aimed and the gun roared again. Some part of her mind was aware of lasers buzzing in the background. Of screaming and cries of pain. A heavy boot stomped on the duroalloy plate beside her head. She fired blindly once and then twice. Another shriek and a body fell, pinning her to the floor.

Panic! She couldn't move, couldn't breathe. Her arms scrambled for purchase, but the weight was too much for her to budge. She was trapped . . . suffocating . . . She tried to scream, but her lungs refused to obey.

The weight on her chest abruptly lessened, and she sucked in gobs of air. Bright lights. Somebody hauled her to her feet, and her vision fell into focus. Archie, his split lip dripping blood and one eye rapidly swelling shut, gently pried the gun from her grip. His lips moved but she could hear nothing over her pounding pulse. She wanted to throw up. Two seconds later, her stomach complied.

Archie held her as she retched up mouthfuls of yellow bile that splattered the floor between two prone bodies.

"It's okay, missy," he whispered in her ear. "We're good now."

She wiped one sleeve across her mouth. Her breath was foul, and her voice came out in a croak. "What happened?"

Archie held her upright with a strong arm. She didn't protest because her quivering legs weren't up to the task. She saw Solomon kneeling over Kasim, pressing a ripped piece of cloth against his forehead.

"Your bullets evened the odds," Archie said, gesturing at the two miners lying in the doorway. Their dull eyes stared into the afterlife, and dark blotches slowly spread across their chests. "Solomon and I hit one with the laser and the rest made a run for it."

Rani focused on the third miner moaning on the floor.

"Where's Rutherford?"

"Ran back inside with Jorge." Archie checked the magazine before slamming it back into the gun. "If you'll wait here, I'll go and retrieve him."

She sagged against the wall. "Don't forget the antenna."

Archie's split lips separated as he grinned. "Don't worry, missy. There's no chance of that."

The butcher's bill was two dead and one injured. Critically. The nurses worked on him in Medical, but without the doctor's guidance, Rani didn't expect a favorable outcome. She waited for the usual flare of guilt to invade her senses—punishment for inflicting pain on fellow human beings—but the only emotion that declared itself was anger. And, later in her quarters, as the tears fell, cold satisfaction.

*How dare they.*

For the first time, she truly knew how Braeder felt. How primal instinct took over in times of crisis. She'd never admitted it until now. Even in the darkest moments of the uprising, she'd convinced herself what she was doing was only temporary. That the true nature of mankind would emerge if left unfettered.

Rutherford and his goons had put paid to that naiveté. Greed, selfishness, and narcissism were not traits that died with individuals—Bordeaux's and Grimes's faces flashed in her mind—but persisted in the air like miasma over a swamp. What Rutherford had planned for her and Kasim was a big unknown, but it wasn't good. They deserved what they got. Even the dead ones.

The icing on the cake was when Archie returned from searching Jorge's domicile with a pair of wire cutters, the type that could be used to cut a guide rope. Vrabel's expression said it all when he found out. The scientist with the healing fracture offered to escort Rutherford and his goons to the brig. Rani politely declined, unsure if any of the new prisoners would survive the trek across the surface.

She stared into the mirror and wiped the tears off her cheek with a facecloth. Her eyes remained puffy, her color off, but she didn't care. How she looked mattered little. Doing her job and keeping the colony safe remained the top priority. She scowled as a half-hidden truth infiltrated into her brain. Braeder had planned this. He knew she would have to stand up to her demons at some point, and no amount of tears would ease the pain.

"Bastard," she muttered. But anger that she aimed at the lieutenant dissolved under a tide of satisfaction. She had passed the test, and she would shove it in his face when he returned.

A thought struck her. What if Braeder didn't return? What if something happened to the away team? How could . . . She tossed that thought aside. No, she would do her part in the colony, and Braeder would complete his mission on Ceres, and it would all come together in the end.

She fought an irresistible urge to laugh. Like that ever happened on Europa.

# CHAPTER 18

*The thousand-mile journey begins with one step.*

DAY 73, 1145 HOURS

Ryan stepped up to the portal and stared at the fields of gray regolith. Dull, monotonous, extending all the way to the horizon, until it slammed up against a wall of darkness that was itself endless and impenetrable. Why colonists had chosen to live on this rock boggled his mind. At least on Europa they orbited a massive planet with hellfire colors and swirling storms. He hesitated, bathing in the irony. Maybe he was the crazy one. On Ceres, no one was assaulted by waves of radiation or random seismic events that could sever any number of critical systems.

He took a breath to focus his thoughts. The tavern that served the hive wasn't large, but at least it had comfortable couches and chairs, if one didn't mind the dust that floated in the air like morning fog.

Gunner and Plante sat across the small faux-wooden table in the center of the room. Louis squirmed at one end of a blue couch and kept glancing at the notes in his hand. Two additional days foraging through the ashes of the fire in Medical had proven rewarding. Last night, he'd stumbled on a trove of documents that somehow escaped the flames, and his excitement was palpable.

"You're absolutely sure about this?" Ryan asked. "It's not just some scientist tilting at windmills?"

Louis waved a mittful of papers in the air. "It's all here, Ryan: lists of reagents, sample components, mean inhibitory concentrations . . . you name it. And yes, they were making progress, more than the CDC."

"And you say the two groups were working together, Alliance and Federation?" Gunner said. "That's hard to believe."

"Actually, all three political factions," Louis replied. "Including the Caliphate station. Until they ran out of food and opened their EV door."

"So, two remained." Ryan turned away from the portal. "Why did their collaboration stop?"

"Because the Federation went quiet. According to the information I found, one day they simply stopped answering the com."

Plante's expression hardened. "I'm guessing that was about the time the food stocks were running out. Research took a back seat."

"Could be," Louis acknowledged before picking out a page. "But one guy, his name was Marie, suspected the Federation scientists had made a critical discovery and were holding off on sharing it."

"They got selfish?" Gunner snorted. "Typical Federation move."

"Any way to find out what they learned?" Ryan asked.

Louis shook his head. "I'd have to access their computers or their lab."

Ryan walked over and sat down on the other end of the couch. He rubbed the bridge of his nose. It was decision time.

Gunner stared at him expectantly. "There really isn't a choice, Ace. We need that wire."

"I know." The air came out of Ryan in a long sigh. "We can't use the transports because the governor says they'll stir up the sekers. There's no point searching the other Alliance stations; they're probably wired with the same obsolete grade. The Caliphate colony is too far away. Which leaves us with only the Federation station. It's close enough to reach with the gators. And these hints about a possible vaccine only make the case stronger." He racked his brain for another option but came up empty. "Needless to say, it'll be a dangerous trek across the surface. We need a plan."

Something between a snort and a grunt emerged from Gunner's throat. "Amen to that. Just don't know what that would be."

"You really think the Federation station will have upgraded wire?" Plante asked.

"It was built decades after ours," Ryan reminded him.

"And the sekers? They're not going to stand by and allow us to stroll over."

"That's why we need a plan, because nobody wants to play with our new friends."

The governor looked like he still wanted to protest but, instead, grudgingly fell back in his seat. Something about his attitude bothered Ryan.

"Have you visited that station before?" Louis asked.

"Only on diplomatic missions," Plante said. "The animosity between political blocs on Earth extended to the colonies. We were discouraged from significant interaction."

Ryan leaned forward, hands on knees. "So, we need to get over there safely, pull out several hundred feet of wire, and make it back, all without attracting the attention of the sekers."

Plante scoffed. "And for your next miracle—"

"We need weapons," Ryan said, ignoring the governor. "Something to keep them off our backs."

"I hear you, Ace, but our machine guns have only so many bullets. From what the governor says, there's more targets than we can shoot." He looked at Plante and raised his bushy eyebrows.

"At least that many," Plante confirmed. "We never got an exact number, but I'm guessing two, maybe three dozen. Trying to make a run over there would be suicide."

Ryan took another look out the portal, this time with a tactician's eye. With the enemy outnumbering his crew, he needed an edge. But the surface of the asteroid was flat, which meant there was nowhere to spring an ambush. And gators were designed to haul supplies, not elude pursuing madmen.

A knock on the door preceded Sybil walking in. "Doctor, Bennett says she's running out of vitamin shots and nutrients. She wants to know if you have more."

Gunner snickered. "Looks like Ceres's survivors need the vet more than we do. What say we load up the replacement parts and maroon him here? I don't think anyone will mind."

The doctor's jaw tightened. He scratched his nose with his middle finger.

Plante gave Gunner a strange look but didn't comment. Ryan figured he'd probably ask about the odd relationship later.

"I'm open to ideas," Ryan said. "To get to the Federation station, we have to cross the surface, which means we have to deal with the sekers."

Sybil's eyes widened. "You're not serious. After what happened to Gonzalez?"

"It's suicide," Plante repeated. "Better to stay behind these doors."

"Too bad the transport doesn't have a weapon," Gunner said. "We could get airborne and take them out from a safe distance."

"Not a bad thought," Ryan said, his mind going to a new place. They couldn't make more bullets, but that didn't mean they couldn't build something useful.

Gunner cocked his head. "What are you thinking?"

Ryan drummed his fingers on the table as Sybil slid into a seat beside him. "Remember how we stopped the senator's transport from landing on Europa's runway?"

"You cratered the ice," Gunner said.

"Right." Ryan noted Sybil's sudden consternation. Her father had been on that transport. "We used explosives."

Gunner ran his hand through his beard. "Not sure how it applies here. Since the mutants aren't coming in for a landing."

"No, but what if we buried explosives and drew them to us?"

Plante blinked. "Like IEDs?"

Gunner straightened. "Suck them into a kill zone? Damn, Ace, that could work." He turned to Plante. "What do you have in terms of raw materials? Any cordite or manganese?"

"Ah." The governor seemed at a loss for words. "Not sure."

Gunner turned to Ryan. "We'll have to search for fuel and an oxidizer, not to mention some sort of container and switch. Could really use Marco on this one."

"Talk to Sasha," Ryan said. "See if you can get a start building detonators. I'll take care of the explosive."

Gunner's eyebrows rose, but he didn't comment.

"I still say this is a bad idea," Plante said. "Why don't we just load the transports with what we have and head back?"

"Governor, all the parts and supplies we've accumulated won't mean shit if we don't bring back the right wire. Our stores on Europa are empty. On top of that, the doctor is right. If there's even a small chance the Federation made progress on a vaccine—one that allows us to return to Earth—we have to check it out. The information we find may allow him to develop a cure."

"What about the plague?" Sybil said. "You won't let anyone near an infected transport a year after it landed, and now you want to play with the actual bacterium?"

Ryan met her worried look. "Even the damn bug can't survive vacuum, and we're going to be in our suits. And even if we remove our helmets, I don't plan to go anywhere near the sekers."

Gunner gave him a barely perceptible nod.

Sybil shrugged. Ryan knew she wasn't happy with the answer but couldn't argue with his logic. "Governor, meet me and Louis in Medical in an hour. Sybil, stay behind for a minute."

Ryan waited until the other two left the room before he swiveled around. "Two things. First, tell me how familiar you are with your father's factory. Did you visit once a month, or were you walking the corridors every day?"

She gave him a wary look. "I practically ran the production line. I know the layout like the back of my hand. Why?"

"So, if we snuck into the Federation factory, you could keep us hidden?"

Her face seemed to lose its pigment. "You want me to go with you? I don't—"

"Sorry," he said, ignoring her protest. "But without a map, we'd probably get lost or run into a horde of sekers. I need you to help us find what we're looking for and lead us out of there. Think you can manage that?"

Her mouth opened, but for a few seconds, no words emerged. Ryan figured she was trying to formulate an adequate response. "You're putting everyone's lives in my hands? After what happened last year?"

"I want to stack the odds for a successful mission. So, yes, we'll follow your lead."

"Even Gunner?"

Ryan's expression hardened. "Gunner follows orders."

She shrugged.

"Second thing," Ryan said. "Tomorrow, I want you to take me on a tour of your father's facilities on the concourse."

Sybil scratched her cheek, confused. "Ah, you walked past them several times over the past week while we worked. Remember the carpet and furniture stores?"

Ryan recalled seeing them as they carried boxes to the decompression chamber. The retail stores displayed the type of luxuries his colonists had longed for before the plague swept away that future. "I'm not talking about what's in the showroom. I need to see the manufacturing process in the back."

"And that's because . . ."

"Because most of what we saw in the store was constructed using polyurethane."

She gave him a blank stare. "My chemistry is a little rusty. Enlighten me."

He smiled. "It's one of the essential ingredients in TNT."

"Goddamn, Gunner, he really wants us to do this." Sasha stood five feet away from the box of flexible foam the lieutenant had dropped off. Like it contained a sample of the plague.

The veteran chuckled and started emptying the box, stacking individual pieces on the lab counter. The back of Medical wasn't large, but it had most of the equipment they needed and plenty of space. His first instinct was to put a reassuring hand on her shoulder, but that would have sent the wrong message. "This stuff ain't going to hurt ya. All we have to do is extract dinitrotoluene."

"That's only the first step in the process." Her gaze flickered to bottles of sulphuric and nitric acid sitting inside a glass fridge. "Converting it to trinitrotoluene is the dangerous part. And with the medieval equipment we're using, we might as well be working in the Middle Ages. Give me flow cytometry over old-fashioned synthesis any day."

Gunner grinned. "So, we go back to the basics. It's not like we have a choice. Not if we want to find a way past the sekers and allow the vet to get a look at a possible vaccine."

Sasha tilted her head. "Why do you keep calling him that? Did he change professions?"

"Because animals is all he should be treating," Gunner said. "With his cursed needles and his pills."

Sasha's eyebrows rose. "So, it's true. Rani said you don't like needles."

Gunner waved a hand, dismissing her words. "We got work to do. Are you going to stand there and watch or pitch in?"

She took a hesitant step toward the foam on the counter. Screwing up her courage, she reached out and rubbed a piece between her fingers. She seemed relieved when it crumbled on the counter. "I'm having second thoughts. Not sure if we blow ourselves up, it'll be worth it."

Gunner stopped organizing the countertop. "And what kind of thoughts will you have when Europa's thermal extractor calls it quits or a greenhouse fails? Face it, kid: if we're going to survive this nightmare, we have to take risks."

The freckles on her face merged as she struggled to find an appropriate retort.

"Come on." Gunner pointed to the pile. "The governor will be by shortly with some heaters and glass decanters. We need to free up counter space."

Sasha's lips twisted into a frown. "I don't like him."

Gunner turned. "The governor? Damn, he kept his people alive for the year. What's wrong?"

"It's the way he looks at me. Makes me feel dirty."

The veteran scratched his beard. He hadn't noticed anything untoward. The man wasn't exactly the friendly sort, but Gunner wasn't one to throw rocks at glass houses. "Has he ever said or done anything?"

"Didn't have to. I could read his eyes."

Gunner considered her words and shrugged. He wasn't sure what vibes she was detecting but resolved to keep his radar on. "Noted. Now can we get back to business?"

Sasha folded her arms across her chest. "All right, but you stack the foam in the heater. I don't want to be around when those molecules get excited."

Gunner snorted. "What are you going to do?"

"I'll set up the extractor and program the computer. I'm better at the technical stuff, anyway."

"And you're leaving the grunt work to me?" He couldn't stop a suggestion of a smile from creasing his cheeks.

She giggled. "If the shoe fits . . ."

Gunner stepped over to the autoclave and began shoveling foam pieces into the open shelf. "You win. Just tell me what to do."

"It's still going to take time," Sasha cautioned. "And there's no way you can convince me to cut corners."

"No worries, young lady. It's going to take Ryan's group several days to load the transports." The decompression chamber was full to bursting, and that didn't count the stacked boxes in the concourse.

She hesitated, her eyes darting back to the bottles in the fridge. "You'll handle the acid, right?"

He sighed. "Yeah, I'll handle the acid."

*Day 74, 0900 Hours*

"Are you sure it's okay to let him out?" Mabel asked, her skepticism percolating to the surface. "It won't matter how many shots I give him; his myocardium is not going to regenerate if he keeps pushing the envelope. His body needs rest."

Rani glanced at the stretcher visible around the corner in Medical, and the pair of feet sticking over the end. "His heart isn't healing?"

Mabel pulled out her minicom and showed Rani the results of his latest blood tests. "Troponin levels are still elevated, which means cardiac cells are still dying. And we can't put a stent in the left anterior descending artery until Dr. Louis gets back."

"You can't do it?" Rani asked.

The nurse snorted. "And for my next trick, I'm going to do a brain transplant: yours for a turnip."

Rani felt her cheeks burn. "All right. You win. Keep him as long as it takes to repair that ticker. Tell him he's officially persona non grata at future meetings."

Mabel arched a single eyebrow. "And he's going to believe me?"

"If he causes a scene, use one of those belt restraints."

Mabel snorted. "Oh, that'll go over well. Are you trying to give him another heart attack?"

Rani threw up her hands. "Okay, tell me what to do, because you're leaving me hanging right now."

Mabel took her by the arm and directed her toward Kasim's stretcher. "Just tell him the truth. Things usually work better that way."

Butterflies filling her stomach, she allowed the nurse to lead her into the other room.

Kasim looked up. "How did my tests go?"

Rani glanced at Mabel before summoning her courage. Throwing Rutherford into the brig was easy compared to delivering bad news to a friend. "Not good. Your heart is still under too much strain. Mabel says you need at least a week of bed rest."

His eyebrows rose in unison. "And what do you say?"

"I say I can't govern the colony with a dead man. Do what she suggests."

"What about my Ops shifts?"

"I'll handle some, or Solomon will. Your job is to get better."

"Solomon will need help to conduct diagnostics."

"I'll send Archie." She nodded at Mabel, who jotted down a note on her minicom.

Kasim leaned back and massaged his cheeks. "Well, okay."

Rani blinked. "Okay?"

He looked at her. "What's wrong? Didn't you hear me?"

"Ah, no." She fumbled to right herself. "It's just, well, that's good." She stepped toward the door before reality slipped back into focus and he protested her decision.

"Hold on." He raised a hand, and Rani's hopes for an uneventful exit vanished. Mabel found something interesting on the floor to stare at.

Rani exhaled. "What?"

"I had a chat with Ellen about the artifact."

Rani tried to put a face to a name and failed. "Ellen?"

"The engineer," Mabel said. "Brunette. You met her in the ice lab."

Rani remembered. "You discussed the artifact with her? Any reason?"

Kasim laid his head back on his pillow. Rani couldn't help but notice his paler-than-usual skin. "She's an engineer, but she's also part of a musical group here on the station. Plays several instruments. She's quite good, I'm told."

Rani rubbed her aching eyes. It had been a long day, and without Kasim's help, tomorrow was going to be even longer. "Is there a point to this?"

"The point is, kudos to you. Once you put the artifact information on the colony net, everyone started talking about it, especially those weird markings on the surface. Not only do people feel they're involved in deciphering the mystery, they're no longer bitching about all the bad things that can happen."

"What's this got to do with Ellen?"

"Well, it seems she, along with several members of her group, recognized a pattern in those markings. They say it resembles notes on a music sheet."

Rani's confusion was mirrored in Mabel's expression.

"Not sure I'm following," the nurse said.

Kasim smiled. "That's because you don't know music. According to Ellen—who, don't forget, is also an engineer—says when you boil it down, it's basically math. They're going to correlate the markings with specific notes and see if they can write a musical reply."

Rani hesitated. *A musical reply*? "Is that even possible?"

"Ellen says it is. And more to the point, if it's true, it answers the big question about the intentions of the aliens."

"You mean whether they're hostile or benevolent?" Mabel said.

Kasim pointed a finger. "Exactly."

Rani struggled to tie it together. Then something sparked in the back of her brain, and she felt the flush of excitement. "They wanted to ensure we were a benevolent species. Because any race that had a creative side was less likely to be hostile."

"That's my feeling as well," Kasim said. "Although I don't think Rutherford would agree."

Rani's enthusiasm waned. "You're probably right."

"So, what happens now?" Mabel asked. "Is Ellen going to host a concert in the ice lab?"

The undercurrent of sarcasm didn't affect Kasim. "Maybe not a concert," he conceded. "But definitely a string of notes."

"How long do you think?" Rani asked.

Kasim scratched his chin. "Not sure. She said the markings were pretty complicated."

"I'll talk to her," Rani decided. She glared when Kasim started to sit up. "I said *I'll* talk to her. You have a job to do, remember?"

Kasim seemed about to protest when the nurse pulled out a restraining belt and waved it in his face.

"Damn, Mabel, I was just kidding," Rani said.

Mabel smiled sweetly at the governor, who quickly fell back. "Yeah, we were just kidding." She placed the belt on the shelf beside the bed.

"What about your decision to touch the artifact again?" Kasim asked. "That still on the agenda?"

"It's on hold," Rani admitted. The episode with Rutherford had unnerved her, and now with Ellen's pending recital, she could wait a little longer. Despite the two percent risk every time it discharged. Or the risk she would make the situation worse.

"Probably a prudent decision," Kasim said, lying back as Mabel took his blood pressure.

Rani seized the moment to walk out of Medical and count both her blessings: a possible answer to the riddle of the artifact, and a governor too sick to give her any grief.

# CHAPTER 19

*One joy dispels a hundred cares.*

DAY 76, 0925 HOURS

We'll bury the IEDs at these locations." Ryan pointed to three spots on the rough map he had sketched on a piece of paper. The briefing room in Ceres's Command Module reminded him very much of the one on Europa, except for the layer of dust and lack of power.

Gunner rose out of his seat and peered at the three X's. "I'm guessing you're planning to draw them in, 'cause they sure as hell aren't gonna to wander over by accident."

"That's my plan. Somebody has to wave a red flag. Just like a bullfight."

Gunner harrumphed. "Not sure I agree with that analogy. But okay."

The governor tapped his finger on one spot. "This is awful close to the station. When it goes off, it might damage the walls."

The fourth person at the table leaned forward. "I reviewed the calculations," Sasha said. "Based on the amount of TNT, the lack of atmosphere, and the distance to the station, the force of the blast shouldn't even scratch the paint."

Ryan grinned. He didn't know if there was actual paint on the walls of the station, but her response hit the right note. Even Gunner looked satisfied. "I want to spring the ambush close to the exit. Just in case something goes wrong and we have to get inside in a hurry. The airlock is thirty seconds away."

"So you say." Plante still didn't look happy. He hadn't stopped complaining since Ryan convened the meeting. "When do you want to put this mad plan of yours into effect?"

"Tomorrow. Gunner will bury the IEDs early in the morning, before the sekers become active. The away party will suit up at noon and take position in a semicircle behind the charges. That's when we'll lure them in."

"Using sacrificial volunteers?" The governor's tone was pure sarcasm. "Who do you not like the most?"

"I'll decide tomorrow," Ryan snapped. He was getting fed up with Plante's constant griping. The governor looked away.

"What about the gators?" Sasha asked. "Where are you going to place them?"

"Around the corner where they won't be spotted. Chan went over them. She says they're good to go." He paused and scanned the sketch one last time. "Okay, that's it for now. Check your gear before bedding down. Gunner, stay behind for a minute."

Sasha raised a single eyebrow as she and Plante rose to leave.

Gunner gave her a nod before leaning his hip against the table. "What's on your mind, Ace?"

"I'm going to send Rani an update. A real update."

"About time, Ace. She'll worry, but she should know."

"Agreed. One more thing. Did you see the condition of the station's EV suits?"

The veteran's brow furrowed. "In the decompression chamber? Didn't notice. Why?"

Ryan rubbed his palms along the surface of the table. "I examined them earlier today when Chan was checking the gators. They're pretty worn. Lots of patches."

"That's to be expected," Gunner said. "Ceres is an older colony. Mining's been going on for decades."

"True, but do you remember when Wilson's oxygen regulator split on Europa?"

Gunner grimaced. He had been the one who dragged the body inside. "Hard to forget."

"Well, I found similar cracks in these suits. And there were no signs of repairs."

The veteran straightened. "You're saying these defects appeared after Earth cut off contact." He hesitated as his thoughts reached their natural conclusion. "Plante's group have been making excursions onto the surface."

"He told us they ventured out rarely, only when there was an emergency."

Gunner frowned. "It makes no sense. We're his ticket off this deathtrap. Why would he lie?"

"I have no idea, but it makes me think we're not getting the full story. He's hiding something."

"Are you going to ask him?"

Ryan paused to weigh the pros and cons. His gut told him they were deliberately being misled, but this didn't feel like the time to tip his hand. "Let's just watch and listen for now. If there's more inconsistencies, I'm sure they'll show themselves."

Gunner shrugged. "Your call, Ace. Just don't turn your back until we know who we're dealing with."

Rani stopped by her quarters on the way back to Ops to pick up the envelope sitting on her desk. Braeder had given her sealed orders before he left, and she wasn't supposed to open them unless something dire happened to the colony. She, of course, had opened them ten minutes after the transport launched . . . and what was inside had shocked her.

His instructions to take forty survivors back to Earth in a Hail Mary attempt to save humanity seemed insane. But the more she thought about it, the more it made sense. It was a terrible decision, just like opening the EV door had been. But it was also a necessary one.

Orders in hand, she walked into Ops and relieved the reservist on duty before calling Archie and settling into the command chair. Rereading the details made her sick to her stomach.

Twenty minutes later, the door swished open.

"'Bout time you got here," she said.

"Sorry," Archie said, walking up to Rani's old terminal. "I stopped to see Kasim in Medical after we finished diagnostics."

"How's he doing?"

Archie smirked. "He's still pissed at you, but Mabel says his numbers are improving."

"Everything good in Engineering?"

"All systems in the green." He noted the papers on her lap. "Some light reading?"

"Orders from the lieutenant. Contingency plan in case everything goes to shit."

Fine lines appeared at the corners of Archie's eyes. "I'm not following."

"He left me explicit instructions what to do if the colony experiences a catastrophic failure."

"Like an asteroid strike?"

"Or an alien artifact burning a hole in the station."

Archie's somber expression didn't crack as he sauntered over to the starboard portal. "I'm guessing it's got something to do with using one of the transports and our last trainee pilot. And making a run to Earth."

Her eyebrows merged. "How'd you know?"

He turned around. "Because that's what I would do. Did he identify the chosen ones?"

Rani waved the paper. "Right down to their colony IDs. And a plan to sneak them onboard before the colonists find out and panic."

"And your trainee pilot? How would he manage?"

"Chan downloaded a launch program before they left."

"Bugger thinks ahead," Archie muttered. Then, louder: "Somebody still has to use the gator to tow *Justice* out of the hangar."

"That's your job," Rani said. "And I was supposed to tell you just before it had to happen."

Archie took the paper and scanned it. "Maybe less of a bugger and more of a bastard. I don't suppose I'm on the list?"

Rani shook her head.

"Didn't think so." Archie turned to stare at the gas giant hanging high in the sky.

A moment of silence passed before Rani summoned the words to continue. That they were even talking about this scenario seemed surreal. "So, you'll handle that part?"

Archie snorted. "Braeder knew I would, or he wouldn't have included me."

"I'm sorry, Archie."

"The fact that you're telling me now means it's on your mind. Does anyone else know?"

"I'm thinking maybe Kasim, although he's never mentioned it."

"Wouldn't surprise me," Archie said. "He and Braeder are pretty tight."

Rani stood and joined him at the portal. "I'll check with him in the morning. It's not information one can post on the colony net."

"Strange duck, that lieutenant of yours," Archie said. "Including me in the plan despite not being on the list."

"I think he was only informing people he trusted," Rani said. "He didn't want me to know until it was too late to change the plan."

"He needed you to be the badass for a while. If things were going to shit, you had to live the role in order to make the decision." Archie paused. "So, here's the big question: why are you bringing it to my attention now? You said there's only a two percent chance that each alien discharge will hit something vital. Are you sure it's time for a Hail Mary?"

"I'm telling you because I've got a laser with a bad attitude, a power cable that's one foot of wire away from disaster, and a governor who's got a bad heart and could die on me at any time. How long do you think this house of cards is going to stand?"

"The colony is still functioning."

"I'm not executing the plan, Archie. I'm just putting all the chess pieces in position. I haven't slept the past couple of nights, thinking about this. If something catastrophic does happen, there's no way we can launch a transport in the moment. We need the pieces ready to go. Which means you, me, and Kasim have to be on the same page."

"You going to drag him out of Medical to talk about it?"

"Like I said, we have to be on the same page. And Medical has too many ears. No way this can get out."

"Mabel won't be happy."

"Not my job to keep her happy."

Archie folded his hands behind his back and continued to stare into the void. They both knew the future didn't bode well for the colony. If not the artifact, then something else, like the thermal extractor or a crop failure.

By any definition, the sword of Damocles.

*1700 Hours*

Rani waited until Archie plopped down next to Kasim in the briefing room. The most senior colonist on the moon wore a scowl like a badge of honor. "When you said we were going to call a meeting, I didn't figure it was going to happen today. I was in the middle of running diagnostics. What's so damned important?"

"That's exactly my question," Kasim said. "I thought my job was to be a good boy in Medical."

Rani kneaded the edge of the table. She would have liked to wait until Archie finished his work and Kasim had more time to rest, but that was no longer an option.

"I just received a message from the lieutenant," she said, staring at her hands. "There's been a complication on Ceres."

Kasim straightened. Archie's glower disappeared.

"Did something happen to the transport?" Kasim asked.

"No, they found survivors."

Archie's eyebrows fused. "After a year? That's impossible."

Rani didn't have the energy to argue. "Some Alliance colonists. They're on their last legs. Dr. Louis is treating them."

"So, what's the problem?"

"Braeder says there's other survivors as well. Probably Russian."

Kasim's eyes narrowed, as though he detected an edge to her tone. "And?"

"There's something wrong with them. They attack and kill on sight. That's how Braeder lost Gonzalez."

"What do you mean, 'something wrong'?" Kasim asked.

"Dr. Louis compared it to rabies. Whatever it is, it turned them into murdering psychopaths."

"Christ," Archie muttered.

"Why tell us now?" Kasim asked. "Since he's obviously been keeping it a secret."

"Because they had been safe inside the Alliance colony," Rani said. "But now they have to travel to the Russian station to find transmission wire."

"And the surface is where the psychopaths prowl?"

"Exactly."

"That's . . . crazy," Kasim said, exchanging an incredulous look with Archie. "How's everyone else?"

"Fine. No other injuries. Or deaths."

"What about the items on the list?" Archie asked.

"They've found most of what we need. Except the wire."

Kasim fiddled with his sleeves. "Will he be able to lift off on schedule?"

Rani shrugged. The lieutenant had been less than forthcoming on that part. In fact, she was sure Braeder was holding back. "He says he'll update us when he can."

"We need that transmission wire," Kasim said.

Archie stared at her through narrowed slits. "You didn't call us here just to tell us Braeder's in a bad way. There's more, isn't there?"

Rani didn't flinch from his hard gaze. She had gotten good at delivering bad news. "The laser is down again. This time, I pinned down the cause. The pump that runs the coolant shorted out."

"Well, that's not helpful," Kasim said.

Archie gritted his teeth. "And if an asteroid comes calling?"

Rani shook her head.

"What?" Kasim's eyes bulged as he seemed to realize the implication. "Can you fix it?"

Rani sensed the governor's panic. With the colony's only defensive system offline, Europa was vulnerable to any heavenly body with the moon in its crosshairs. "Marco fixed a similar problem last year, but back then, we had extra parts. The only solution now is to switch out a pump from one of the hives."

Kasim spread his hands on the table. "And that's a problem?"

Archie snorted. "Only if you mind the smell of raw sewage. Once we remove one of the pumps, the system will back up sooner or later."

The governor grimaced.

"Pressure in the line will drop by fifty percent," Rani acknowledged. "It won't be pleasant."

Kasim hesitated as the implication sank in. "We don't have a choice, do we?"

"Not unless you can sign a truce with several thousand asteroids," Archie said.

"I'm guessing you want me to deliver the bad news to the colonists?" Kasim said. He didn't look happy at the prospect.

"You are the governor," Rani said, feeling a shadow of guilt at delegating the task.

Kasim exhaled. "I'll announce it over the colony net."

"I'll put together a work crew," Archie offered. "And remove the pump."

Rani held up her hand. "Sorry, Archie. I have another job for you."

The geologist tilted his head. "I don't like that look. What are you thinking?"

"The laser leak isn't the only malfunction. The greenhouse harvesters have stopped working."

"Did you run diagnostics?"

She nodded. "Processors are fried. Excess radiation from the gas giant. It's a common problem, and usually, Fleet sends replacements every year. Except—"

"Except there is no Fleet," Archie said. "We'll have to harvest by hand, which means we're going to lose a percentage of the yield."

Kasim squeezed his eyes shut. "Now you want me to tell the colonists we're going to cut rations?"

"No." Rani tried to wave down his concern. "Let's wait until we run the numbers. People will need time to digest the information on the pump."

Kasim sagged in his seat, relieved.

"So, why the meeting?" Archie asked. "We could be working on the pump already."

Rani interlaced her finger on the table. "Because I wanted to discuss Braeder's plan."

The governor raised his eyebrows. "His plan?"

"His Hail Mary proposal," Archie scoffed. "Don't pretend like you don't know."

Kasim looked like he was about to protest and then shrugged. "He told me in confidence."

Archie caught Rani's eye. "Yeah, well, you should know, there are no secrets on this moon." He folded his arms across his chest. "She wants the three of us on the same page."

"I also said I wanted everything ready in case we had to pull the trigger," Rani continued. "Except, after getting this message from Braeder, I have a notion to change his plan."

"Change it?" Archie asked. "It's complicated enough with trying to herd the right people into the transport without the rest of the colonists noticing."

"Or getting the chosen ones to agree," Kasim added. "It's not like people are going to jump at the idea of leaving their families to travel halfway across the solar system."

"Tell me about it," Rani said, sucking in a deep breath. "After the hellish year we've had, all people want to do is hunker down and wait for Braeder to save them."

Archie stared at her with lowered lids. "I'm getting the feeling you're not quite of the same mindset as the colonists."

Rani bit back a smile. Her *lieutenants* were learning how to read her mind. "I'm not saying it's going to happen, but like we discussed, we have to be ready just in case."

She watched their jaws drop as she outlined her plan.

# CHAPTER 20

*It is better to light a candle than curse the darkness.*

DAY 77, 1200 HOURS

Ryan placed Gunner and the reservists in an inverted V with the apex touching the wall of the station, and the sides stretching out like a pair of long arms toward the horizon. To remain hidden, they dug shallow pits in the regolith, prompting Gunner to make a snide comment about World War One foxholes.

Ryan passed out the weapons—Gunner the machine gun, Lucas and Compton the lasers—and kept the second machine gun for himself. Smith carried a heavy iron pipe he had picked up from one of the supply rooms. The five of them formed the arms of the V, while the governor, Sybil, and Dr. Louis huddled behind the station, out of sight.

He opened a channel. "Coms check. Gunner?"

"Ready, Ace."

"Smith, your group set?"

Two clicks from the reservist.

"Governor?"

"Waiting with the doctor and Ms. Lecky."

"Okay." Ryan checked the time in his helmet's heads-up display. Twelve hundred hours. "Time to send out the bait." He heard Gunner grumble through the com and ignored it. The veteran was never happy with Ryan putting himself in harm's way. "That's supposed to be my job," he had said when Ryan revealed the details of the plan.

But Ryan wasn't having it. The last time he was sidelined by the veteran, Marco got killed and Gunner died for thirteen minutes.

He checked the safety on the gun and surveyed the approach. The surface was deserted as far as the eye could see, nothing but boring grayness stretching to the horizon.

"Governor, you said they usually appear in small groups?" Plante was even less excited about Ryan's decision than Gunner, and he had argued strenuously against it until the veteran shut him down.

"That's right," he mumbled, and Ryan was reminded of a moping teenager. "They hunt in packs, and usually appear about this time. But sometimes, we don't see them for days. There's no predicting."

Ryan took one last look at his crew before walking away from the station. Sol was a faint light in the distance, slightly brighter than the other flickering stars in the heavens. "Doctor, I don't think we're going to need that extra IED. Hang on to it for now."

Two clicks sounded in his ear. Sasha had produced enough TNT to make an additional IED, and Louis carried it just in case. During his training, Ryan had learned there was no such thing as too many bullets. Or, in this case, bombs.

"Not too far, Ace," Gunner cautioned after Ryan advanced about fifty meters in front of the station. "You saw how fast they moved when they swarmed Gonzalez."

Ryan shuddered at the memory. It was like something out of a B-grade horror vid. A flash of light in the corner of his vision focused his thoughts, and his heart skipped a beat.

Dirty EV suits coming over the horizon.

"I see them. Looks like four approaching from the Russian sector."

"Better get back, Ace."

"I don't think they've seen me yet." He took a few more steps and raised his arms.

"Goddamn, Ryan," Sybil muttered.

The sekers seemed to freeze before altering course. Ryan's pulse skyrocketed as they accelerated toward him.

"They're coming. Get ready." He returned using slow, measured steps. Now was not the time to push off so hard he ended up floating above the surface.

"Looks like a second group at three o'clock," Gunner said. "Would it be crazy to suggest they're talking to each other?"

Ryan glanced over his shoulder. Gunner was right. "Governor, can they communicate?"

"That's not possible," Plante scoffed. "They're sekers."

Ryan reached the line of reservists and settled into a small depression. Cradling his heavy pipe, Smith moved up beside him.

Ryan could see all the sekers now. "Gunner, first group is going to pass by my side of the station. Are you good?"

"Ready on your mark."

Ryan's training took over. He crouched low to present less of a target and slid off the gun's safety. Red stakes hammered into the surface identified IED sites. The first sekers reached the target.

"Now!"

A section of regolith disappeared in a cloud of gray mist. Ryan felt the vibration roll through his legs, reminding him of seismic tremors on Europa. Bodies were hurled off their feet, and one was propelled upward. Faceplates cracked. Jagged tears appeared in EV suits moments before the air was sucked out. He raised his gun, but none of the sekers remained standing. Three lay unmoving on the surface, scattered like a child's doll set.

Gunner's voice hauled him out of the moment. "Second group is veering off."

Ryan peered through the cloud of gray fog. Four sekers had swerved away from the explosion and were heading toward Gunner's side.

"You got this?" Ryan resisted the urge to run over.

"Hold tight," Gunner said as if reading his mind. "It's my turn."

Seconds later, a second patch of surface dust and rock erupted. Two sekers were caught in the middle of the blast, the force shredding their suits. The other pair were hurled backward, one skidding through the powder like a snowplow. The other tried to stand, but Gunner shot it in the chest. Compton punctured the second seker with a laser beam. The suit constricted like vacuum wrap, and it pawed frantically at the ripped fabric for several seconds before its anoxic body began convulsing.

The veteran was checking his magazine when Ryan walked over. "It worked, Gunner."

"Aye, even better than Sasha predicted."

Ryan glanced at the bodies. "How's that?"

Gunner pointed. "She never figured for this."

Confused, Ryan looked up to see a figure steadily rising off the asteroid. It writhed desperately in the gravity well, as though its struggles could reverse its climb.

"It has escape velocity," Gunner said. "There's no coming back."

Ryan grimaced at the thought. Floating away from the surface, to drift forever in a cosmic ocean. To live until the oxygen ran out.

Sybil joined them. She glanced at the flailing body and shivered. "Damn."

Ryan surveyed the asteroid. Nothing moved. It was time to go. "Braeder to Louis. Surface is clear."

Two gators swung around the corner of the station with Plante and Louis each at a wheel. Both machines were carbon copies of the ones on Europa, the same type Chan had used to ram one of the senator's marines before he could put a bullet in Ryan's brain. Oversized, weighted, rubber tires for traction on the loose surface and a wide aluminum frame. Unlike grav-cars, the engines weren't designed for speed but rather durability. There were no roads linking the colonies.

Ryan and the others piled on and headed out across the surface at the dizzying speed of ten kilometers per hour.

"I still don't think this is a good idea," Plante muttered. "There may be more out there."

Ryan bit back his irritation and swiveled his helmet to catch the governor's eye. "Europa needs the wire. We're not leaving without it."

Plante shrugged, his bony shoulders barely denting the suit fabric. "I would never put my people in harm's way."

Ryan's first instinct was to ask him how successful he had been, since most of "his people" had succumbed to starvation. But that wouldn't have been the politically correct thing to say. Instead, he watched for movement on the surface as the gators pushed through the dirt and small rocks.

"Another ten minutes," Gunner announced on a private channel, pointing to a white smudge on the horizon. "Still want to head around back?"

"That's where Sybil says the other entrance is. We'll work our way to Medical from there."

Gunner's expression tightened, but he managed a nod.

Ryan held on as the gator bounced across shallow craters in the surface. Something in the back of his mind nagged at him, and it was only after looking up into the void that he put a finger on it. It was the planet, or lack of it. After more than a year staring at the monster in the heavens, space seemed empty with just faint specks of light flickering in the distance.

The white smudge grew into a three-story nondescript building, square modules lumped together by engineers rather than artists. As opposed to Europa, only a few portals punctuated the drab exterior. Plante's gator led the way around the side of the station, and Louis followed in his tracks, doing his best to keep the vehicle steady with his one hand. They passed the runway, and Gunner pointed to a greenhouse nestled against the side of the station. Both front hatches were open to space.

They found the airlock exactly where Sybil said it would be, bolted to a connecting module that led directly to the fusion reactor. In the distance, Ryan spied a solar farm, rows of large panels that reminded him of cornfields on Earth.

"Any chance the reactor is still operating?" Ryan asked.

Plante shook his head. "There's no vapor in the vents, which means it's offline."

They parked the gators next to the station, and after everyone disembarked, Gunner threw a gray tarp over both vehicles.

The veteran shrugged when Ryan gave him a look. "Found it in one of the storage rooms off the concourse. Figured it might hide them from the sekers."

Ryan hesitated—the tarp did help them blend into the gray background—before returning to the plan. "Sybil, your turn."

Sasha had called them "cheat codes" when she wrote them down. Something about hacking administrative buildings when she was a student. When pressed by Gunner, she brushed it off as innocent pranks. The sparkle in her eyes hinted at something more.

Sybil hurried to the control panel on the side of the hatch and pulled down the cover. Dust drifted in the thin atmosphere. "What happens if the codes don't work?"

Ryan didn't answer. The backup plan was to head to the front airlock, but that was the one the sekers seemed to use.

"Nothing ventured," Gunner muttered.

The three reservists bracketed the door as she plugged numbers into the computer interface. Gunner pulled the machine gun off his back and scanned the surrounding landscape.

Sybil hit the Execute button and stepped back. She seemed shocked when the light switched from amber to green and the circular door hissed sideways, exposing an empty airlock.

"It's not very big," she said dubiously.

"Doesn't matter," Ryan said. "Gunner, check it out."

The veteran tapped Smith and Lucas on the arm and led them inside. "Back in a minute." He touched a flashing light on the inner panel and the door rotated shut.

No one said a word as Ryan cradled his gun and paced in front of the door. Even Sybil remained mute until the red light shifted to green and the airlock opened.

Ryan relaxed when Gunner gave him a wave.

"All clear, Ace. Place doesn't look like it's been used in a while."

It was a tight fit, but the group wedged themselves inside the airlock. Ryan felt like a sardine until the inner door cycled open and they fell out.

The room was about half the size of its equivalent in the Alliance station, with several racks of EV suits along one wall and rows of shelving containing dust-covered helmets and gloves.

"Damn, Ryan." Dr. Louis eyed the flickering lights in the ceiling. "There's power here." He checked the scanner on his belt before removing his helmet. "I'm reading an oxygen atmosphere. Little on the chilly side."

The group followed suit. Ryan felt the bite of cold, stale air and shivered. "Smells like mold."

"Better than vacuum." Gunner walked over to check the nearest computer. "The vet's right; there's power running in these circuits. Must be solar panels."

Ryan gripped the gun tighter as realization sank in. "Which means someone must be doing maintenance." He looked at Plante. "You had no contact?"

The governor threw up his hands. "My job was to keep people alive and avoid the sekers."

Ryan frowned. Something didn't add up. By Gunner's expression, he was thinking the same thing. "Sybil, does this part of the station look familiar?"

She tightened the elastic holding her ponytail. "I vaguely recall being down here once or twice. If we can get to the concourse, I'll have a better idea."

"Doctor, where's the infirmary?"

"I'm guessing somewhere public. Probably the concourse as well."

Ryan glanced out through the narrow window in the door. He couldn't see much from there, but his mind was already made up. Sneaking into Medical solved two problems. The wire in the walls should be the most modern in the station, and Louis would gain access to any information on the vaccine.

He sucked in a deep breath. There was a point in every operation where things got tricky. "Okay, we do this by the numbers. Clear each room as we go and mind the corners. Gunner and Smith, take point. The rest, single file."

Sybil walked up to the exit and keyed in Sasha's code before stepping back. Gunner led them into the next room, some type of storage area with dust-covered boxes and metal containers stacked along the walls. No ceiling lights functioned, so they put their helmets back on and used the lamps to navigate a path through the debris.

The storage room funnelled into a wide corridor that stretched into darkness. Rows of doors occupied one side, facing a solid wall on the other. Gunner stopped in front of the first door. "What do you think, Ace?"

Ryan turned to Sybil. "Best guess."

She lifted her hand like she wanted to bite her nails and then dropped it. "I think we're below the hives. I remember laborers taking supplies down a flight of stairs."

Ryan nodded at Gunner. "One door at a time. Find us a stairwell."

The veteran and Smith took the lead. Gunner stood to one side with his machine gun ready while the reservist yanked the door open. Most turned out to be additional storage rooms containing machine parts or discarded pieces of old computers. Others held cleaning supplies and stacked pieces of furniture.

Halfway down the corridor, Gunner hesitated. "Found it."

Ryan led the group to the stairwell, a dust-covered set of concrete steps leading up. "No footprints on the floor."

"Probably because there's nothing of value down here," Plante said. "I bet the sekers don't even know this part of the station exists."

Ryan caught Gunner's eye and the veteran nodded. The governor sounded too sure in his pronouncement. "Smith, take point."

They ascended the stairs quietly. Ryan strained to hear anything, but only the soft echo of their steps vibrated his eardrums.

One flight up, a locked fire door blocked the exit.

Ryan opened the circuit box mounted on the wall. It took all of two minutes to remove the casing, cut and splice a wire, and hit the Execute button.

The door ground to one side and a blast of warm air blew in.

"We've got light," Sybil said as she leaned through the doorway. A few scattered lamps on the wall cast a weak glow over what appeared to be a workout room: stationary bikes and free weights next to a gym floor. "I recognize it. This is where they held ceremonies for visiting dignitaries."

"That explains a lot," Gunner snorted. "A US senator playing footsie with the Russians."

She glowered at him. "It was a business arrangement. Nothing more."

Ryan pointed to a pair of closed metal doors across the room. "Where does that take us?"

"Into the main concourse," she said, ripping her glare off Gunner. "They call it Stalin Drive, and it runs the length of the station."

Louis stepped up. "Where's Medical?"

She paused. "Left. The concourse is lined with stores and repair shops. It's behind some kind of statue."

Ryan joined Gunner on point and led the group across the room. Everything from the exercise machines to the towels to the reception desk was covered in a layer of dust.

"How do you want to play this, Ace?" Gunner asked, running his hand along the door's push bar.

Ryan put his ear to the door. Nothing. "The target is Medical. Once we get in, Gunner's team will check the wiring. Doc, do your thing. We stick together at all times. Any noise, we go to ground. Worst case, we retreat back to the stairs. Understood?"

Everyone nodded. Gunner kept his weapon leveled when Smith pushed the door open.

Despite his gentle touch, a high-pitched screech leaked into the concourse as rusted metal pieces slid over each other. Inside, several wall-mounted lamps flickered weakly, creating a maze of shadows.

Ryan motioned and they shut off their suit lamps. He closed his eyes and listened. Nothing but the sound of his own heartbeat.

"All quiet," Gunner said over the com.

Ryan reached out and took the weight of the door. "Single file. Quietly."

Gunner led them out. He stayed tight to the wall, his head on a swivel, his eyes in constant motion.

They moved as a single entity, crouched over, placing their feet between pieces of glass and bits of broken machinery. Sybil was right; the main boulevard was huge, three times the size of the concourse on Europa. The weak glow of the lamps infused the air with an ominous, oppressive feel. The ceiling arched twenty feet over their heads: plastek with glass inserts. Stars flickered in the heavens. Multiple storefronts lined the concourse, their entrances smashed, their signs defaced with Russian graffiti. The floor was covered in debris and refuse, reminding Ryan of a garbage dump.

"Just like home," Gunner muttered.

# CHAPTER 21

*Time flows away like water in a river.*

DAY 77, 1255 HOURS

Rani slumped back against a slab of ice and listened to the hum of the fans in her helmet. She desperately needed to catch her breath. Environmental struggled to maintain a constant temperature in the face of increased pulse and respiration, while sweat dripped down her back like a leaky faucet. Taking the long trek to the artifact was turning into a test of endurance, and she wasn't built to be an athlete.

Solomon towered over her, his face a mask of concern. "We can't stop, Cap'n. We're too close."

She tilted her helmet to catch his eye. Beyond him, Jupiter filled the sky, a conflagration of storms that could have inspired Dante. "You think several hundred feet of ice is going to make a difference? The last energy blast from the artifact burned a hole in the moon nearly a mile deep."

Solomon glanced at the cave entrance barely visible in the distance. He shrugged.

Rani knew how he felt. It was in their genes: get as far away from a threat as humanly possible. Except their genes didn't take into account random antimatter beams emitted from alien artifacts. She checked her watch. Vrabel had it timed to the millisecond. "Five minutes isn't going to make a difference. You want to sit?"

Solomon shook his head and paced in front of her like an expectant father.

Rani glanced in the direction of the hives. She pictured colonists huddling with family, praying the energy beam didn't punch a hole in their domicile. Or their extractor. Or their greenhouse. Ellen and her fellow performers were working diligently to decode the strange alien hieroglyphics on the surface, but that was going to take a while. The female engineer said teasing out the right response had turned out to be painstakingly complicated, with many of the notes beyond the range of human hearing.

Only Vrabel had the courage to stay in the cave and man the sensors. She didn't argue. If it was your time, it was your time.

Solomon spun on her. "You said there was a two percent chance of the beam striking the station?"

"That's what the numbers say." Rani tried to inject the right amount of confidence into her tone. After weeks leading the colony, she had learned that telling a lie was better than staying silent. Solomon was just like the other colonists; they needed reassurance. And answers. The facts hardly mattered. Tell them they would be safe, and they'd sleep better at night.

No one needed to know that after the first antimatter discharge, she had lain awake in her quarters, unable to sleep until she satisfied the nerd side of her brain and calculated the probability of the beam striking something vital.

Solomon set his jaw but seemed mollified by her answer. Colonists were just as relieved when she posted the numbers on the net. Nobody asked the next logical question: how long would they keep being lucky? How often could you roll the dice before coming up snake eyes?

She checked her heads-up display. "Thirty seconds."

Solomon took a seat next to her on the ice. He hunched over like he wanted to shrink his big body into the smallest fissure.

Rani remembered Marco slouching the same way when the lieutenant ordered him to do something outside his comfort zone. Like an ostrich burying its head in the sand.

The counter on her display clicked on *ONE* and she held her breath.

Something flashed overhead.

"Holy shit!" Solomon exclaimed. "That just missed us!"

Stunned, Rani took a second to connect the dots. "It went toward the station." She jumped to her feet and started moving. "Singh to Kasim. Come in."

The channel opened and she heard the whine of an alarm in the background.

“Rani!” Kasim sounded like he was shouting. “Beam punched a hole in the wall. Air is leaking out.”

“Anyone hurt?”

“Negative. Emergency bulkheads dropped in front of the hives and Medical. No one was in the concourse.”

Rani exhaled and slowed her pace. A bullet had just grazed their collective cheek. “Send out a repair team to find and patch the hole. We’ll be back in twenty.”

She heard two clicks before the channel closed.

Solomon gave her a sidelong look. “We got lucky.”

“Yeah.” The fans in her helmet increased their pitch. “And only days until the next one.”

The Federation concourse rekindled memories of how Europa had looked after he opened the EV door, right down to the flickering lights on the wall and the dead plants surrounding the fountain. Even the bodies wedged beneath detritus had that same lifeless color.

“Keep the suit lamps off. Mind your steps.” If there were sekers around, they didn’t need to draw unwanted attention.

The governor looked nervously over his shoulder.

“Everything all right?” Ryan asked as Gunner led them through the combination morgue and salvage yard. The veteran stopped behind a pile of metal staging and surveyed the darkness.

“Yeah.” Plante was sweating profusely behind his faceplate. “Just a little tense. Can’t wait to get out of here.”

Ryan couldn’t argue with that. He nodded, and Gunner continued down the concourse.

The entrance to Medical was as damaged as everything else. Busted windows and smashed plastek beams. Stepping through broken doors, they entered a reception area filled with upturned chairs and empty shelves. Small piles of dirt and garbage lined the floor.

“Doc?”

Louis moved to the head of the line. “This way. Through the double doors at the back.” He led them past wrecked furniture and an upturned secretary’s desk, into the examination rooms.

“Looks like the aftereffects of a riot,” Sybil said. “They even tore the blood-pressure cuffs off the wall.”

Ryan didn't answer. He could only imagine how conditions had deteriorated by the time they decided to open the colony to vacuum. Was there civil unrest? An uprising when medical care disintegrated? The damage spoke for itself. He followed Louis to where imaging machines sat nestled against the wall. Total darkness greeted them.

"Lamps on," Ryan ordered. This deep inside Medical, their light shouldn't spill into the concourse.

The area brightened as multiple EV lamps flashed.

"Oh, God!" Sybil recoiled as if struck. Her face turned white.

Louis seemed stunned. "This . . . this is barbaric."

Ryan couldn't tear his eyes off the macabre scene. It was something out of a nightmare: bodies stacked like cordwood along the back wall. Two desiccated corpses lashed to gurneys, stomachs peeled open to reveal internal organs. Crusted bloodstains on the floor.

The reservists spun away. Smith whipped off his helmet and vomited on the floor.

"It's a bloody abattoir," Gunner whispered.

Ryan stepped back and his heart slammed against his ribcage. "Is this the plague?" His ultimate nightmare coming true. He gripped his chest. He shouldn't have brought them there.

"No." Louis made a dismissive gesture with his gloved hand before running his scanner over one of the corpses. "This is not how the plague works. Something else killed these men."

Ryan relaxed his grip and peered closer. He realized both corpses on the gurneys were male. "Then what the hell happened?" He had to keep telling himself what he was seeing was real, not some backstage prep for a horror vid. "Were they tortured?"

"I don't think so." Louis stepped over to the second corpse. He took several long seconds to complete a scan. "This is strange. There's something wrong with the organs."

Ryan swallowed the rising bile in his throat. "In what way?"

"They both died from the same cause: an acute immunological reaction."

"An acute what?"

"The body rejected itself," Louis said, pulling off his helmet. "I've never seen anything like it."

"Maybe the vet could explain it in English," Gunner growled.

Louis glared at the veteran. "If you ask nice, I'll use small words . . ."

Ryan held up his hand. "Not now. We're on the clock."

Louis exhaled. "Normally, to fight infection, the body ramps up production of white blood cells and immune agents to destroy the invader. It seems in these patients, the immune system, for some reason, went into hyperdrive. It attacked everything, and by *everything*, I mean every cardiac cell, every nerve, every organ. This is what killed them."

"Why would their own systems to do that?"

"Some type of foreign stimulus," Louis surmised. "What exactly that would be, I haven't a clue."

"These people weren't brutalized?" Sybil asked. "This is not a torture cell?"

"Oh, no." Louis picked up an empty vial and syringe from the nearest counter. "It seems at least one doctor was trying to save them."

"Would the patients know it was happening?" Sybil asked. "Would they be in pain?" She slid up to Ryan's elbow. Her color was returning to normal.

"Oh, yes, they would have known something was wrong. For starters, each person would have swelled up like a blowfish. Lung tissue would disintegrate, filling the chest cavity with blood and making it nearly impossible to breathe. The pain would have been unbearable." He laid his hand on the restraining straps. "Which is why they were tied down. My guess is that most of those vials on the counter contained painkillers like synphone."

"Then it's not the plague?" Compton asked. The other reservist, Lucas, kept his gaze averted. Smith remained on his knees as he wiped his mouth with his sleeve.

"No." Louis straightened over the corpse. "This is something else."

Ryan's gaze shifted to the other bodies stacked against the wall. "And them?"

Louis walked over and took a cursory look. "Same process. I see subtle differences, but it's the same root cause." He paused, and Ryan could envision the wheels turning behind those wire-rimmed glasses. "Not sure what could trigger such an extreme reaction."

Sybil seemed hesitant to leave Ryan's side. "No disease you ever saw?"

"Or read about." The doctor looked to Ryan. "If we could find some notes, patient charts, or even test results, I might be able to follow the breadcrumbs."

"What about you, Governor?" Ryan turned to face the man, who had remained strangely quiet since they entered Medical. Even now he loitered close to the door. "Any thoughts?"

Plante kept his eyes on the floor. "I told you. We haven't crossed the surface since they opened the EV door."

"But you said you did go outside to make emergency repairs."

"Yeah, well, we never ventured this far."

Ryan made eye contact with Gunner. "Okay, Sybil help the doc look for notes, files, anything that can tell us what happened."

"And not just related to these poor bastards," Louis said, nodding at the corpses. "Anything on the plague. Find me some hard drives. I'll take them back to our station."

"Gunner, you, Compton, and Smith check the wire in the wall," Ryan said. "Tell me if it's the right gauge to make Sasha happy. Lucas, stand guard at the entrance, but keep your helmet lamps off. We don't need anyone, or anything, sniffing out our presence."

Ryan started for the computer sitting on what appeared to be the doctor's desk when he noticed Plante hadn't moved. "Be a good time to pitch in."

Plante slid down to the floor. "Sorry. Feeling sick. Need a few minutes."

Ryan bit his tongue. For a guy who survived the nightmare of the last year, the governor seemed easily spooked.

"Ryan." Louis's voice in his ear. "Look at this."

"Found something?" The doctor hovered over some printed images.

"SPET scans from one of our victims." He jerked a thumb toward a gurney. "They're impressive. The brain architecture has been distorted by severe cerebral edema. Even the fissures have completely disappeared."

"In English, Doc."

The lines on Louis's forehead deepened. "Whatever stimulated their systems was able to cross the blood-brain barrier, which in turn caused the hyperimmune response. Not only were the patients writhing in agony, they were also suffering from acute delirium." He paused, massaging his chin. "Which makes me wonder . . ."

Ryan stopped and pulled off his helmet. The air was rancid, forcing him to breathe through his fist. "What?"

Louis straightened like he had just come to a decision. "The cognitive part of their brains are severely damaged. I think this is where the sekers came from."

Ryan's eyes widened. "They're a result of medical experiments?"

"Experiments or treatment. It's what turned them into raving psychopaths, disconnected from reality and driven by primitive instincts."

The doctor paused and shifted his gaze to the corpses along the wall. "I need more information on how it happened."

Ryan picked up one of the scans as pieces of the puzzle fell into place. The link between the sekers and the Federation . . .

"Ace." Gunner had removed his helmet. He walked up to Ryan carrying a two-foot section of blue cable. "I pulled this out of the wall. It's part of the electrical system in Medical." He flashed Ryan a smile. "Sasha is going to blow a gasket when she sees what we found."

Ryan was careful not to get his hopes up. "The right gauge?"

"Exactly," Gunner confirmed. "All we have to do is rip out a couple hundred feet and carry it home."

Ryan started to respond when Lucas hurried into the room "Lieutenant, there's something outside."

Gunner's expression tightened. "We don't want to get pinned in here. Medical is a dead end."

Ryan picked up his helmet. The veteran was right. Tactically, it was the worst place to be if someone attacked. Decision time. "Smith, with me. Gunner, get ready to move."

He looked around. Something was amiss. "Where's Plante?"

# CHAPTER 22

*Our greatest glory is not in never falling but in rising every time we fall.*

## DAY 77, 1449 HOURS

Ryan turned off his suit lamps before edging up beside Lucas. The flickering lights in the concourse turned shadows into monsters. "Which end?" he asked, voice low.

Smith slid back to give him room as Lucas pointed. "Behind the piles of garbage."

Ryan craned his neck around the edge of the broken door. He saw nothing for several seconds, then something twitched and a cold hand gripped his heart. *Shit.* They weren't alone. He backed away from the door. "Stay here and keep watch."

Eyes wide behind his faceplate, Smith swallowed nervously. He picked up the large steel pipe and braced it against his chest.

Ryan hurried back inside. "Gunner, we got company. Time to leave."

"What about the wire?"

"We'll have to come back for it."

The veteran's eyes narrowed. "Copy that."

"I could use more time, Ryan," Louis said, waving a hard drive in the air. "The doctors here were on to something."

"Feel free to stay, Doc, but we're leaving." He tried and failed to keep the irritation out of his tone as he picked his machine gun off the floor.

Louis flashed him a scowl and shoved the drive into his pocket.

Ryan returned to the entrance as Gunner herded the group toward the front. The cloying putrefaction smell seemed stronger, and he wondered if his senses were ramping up to deal with the newest threat.

Smith fidgeted as Ryan crawled up next to him. "Anything?"

"I think they're close, sir. Can't see them yet, but they're getting louder."

Ryan looked around. "Anybody see the governor?"

"I'm right here." Plante emerged from the shadows. "What's wrong?"

"The sekers are in the concourse. We have to vacate." He turned as Gunner approached. "Single file. Back the way we came."

"Understood." Gunner pulled the gun strap over his shoulder. "If I hear anything?"

"Go to ground. We're not here to fight. Get us back to the gym."

The veteran nodded, checked the concourse in front of Medical, and slipped out. Lucas and Compton followed. Ryan grabbed Sybil's arm to keep her next to him. She was the closest thing to a map. Just in case. Louis gave Ryan a nervous look as he and Plante followed Gunner.

Ryan's hyperactive senses noted every sound: each breath, the crunch of broken glass, even the swish of suit fabric.

Something fell and smashed behind them.

Everyone froze.

Ryan waited. Nothing. He caught Gunner's backward glance and gestured. *Go. Faster.*

They passed ruined storefronts and the algae-covered fountain. The concourse seemed darker, like some of the flickering wall lights had failed since they arrived. Louis stumbled, and Smith caught him before he fell.

They were halfway back to the gym when a scream erupted from a nearby shattered storefront. Something stepped clear of a ruined doorway, and Ryan's blood ran cold. A limping form, covered in blood and ripped tatters of cloth. The man lifted his head and howled again.

"Run!" Ryan shouted.

Eyes wide, Sybil and Louis broke into a sprint. Plante was right on their heels.

The man's wild eyes landed on Ryan. He resembled the sekers on the surface: bearded face covered in scabs and ulcers, dried blood under his nose, and some tufts of straggly hair on his scalp.

Ryan raised his gun. "Stop!"

The man screamed. Something answered from farther down the concourse.

The seker charged.

Twenty feet. Ryan aimed at center mass and pulled the trigger.

The recoil knocked Ryan backward, and he cursed himself for forgetting about the low gravity.

The bullet struck just below the breastbone, knocking the seker into a pile of rusted pipes. Blood seeped from a new hole in his chest.

Ryan didn't hesitate. He turned and chased down the group. Screams echoing off the walls hastened his pace.

Gunner was holding the door open when he arrived. "Was it—"

"A seker." Ryan ducked through the door and Gunner scanned the immediate vicinity before pulling it shut. "They're coming from both sides."

Smith shoved a metal rod through the push bar while Lucas and Compton piled heavy weights against the inside of the door.

"Don't know how long these will hold," Compton said, dropping a fifty-pound iron barbell into position. "But it's all we have."

Everyone had switched their helmet lamps on, and Ryan followed suit. The time for stealth had passed. He had barely taken two steps when something slammed into the door and the narrow window shattered. An arm clothed in some kind of ripped uniform reached through, scratching for the locking mechanism. Another violent blow and the door rattled on its hinges.

By the time Ryan reached the stairwell, Gunner had funneled Sybil and Louis through the fire door and down to the first landing. Lucas and Smith cast nervous glances as the entrance rattled a third time and a large crack split the center.

"Hurry!" Gunner urged. "They'll be through any second."

Ryan squeezed past just as the door exploded in a wave of plastek splinters. Gunner slammed the fire door shut. The metal was strong but not impenetrable.

He took the steps two and three at a time. "They're in! Keep moving!"

The group paused on the first landing and Gunner leapfrogged to the front. "I'll cycle open the airlock," he shouted over his shoulder. "Compton, Smith, on me."

Ryan didn't realize he had his arm around Sybil until she tripped and nearly took him over the railing. "Get going!" he urged when she seemed ready to stop.

"Leaving the stairwell now," Gunner called. "Airlock is just ahead —Christ!"

"What?"

Machine-gun blasts echoed up the stairwell and through the com in Ryan's helmet. He let go of Sybil and took the last six steps in one leap. Some part of his brain noted Louis crouching by the bottom of the stairs.

He burst out of the doorway, gun leveled. Two seker bodies lay twitching on the concrete floor. "What the hell?"

Gunner lifted his machine gun, the barrel oozing smoke. "They were standing in front of the decompression chamber."

Ryan realized the door leading to the airlock was shut. "How did—"

"No time." Gunner shoved him down the hallway. "It's locked. We need to find another way out of this place."

"Damn." Ryan had seconds to decide. Louis and Sybil spilled out of the stairwell.

"They're banging on the fire door," Louis warned.

Ryan only had one option. "Gunner, Lucas, keep them off our ass. The rest of you, with me." He hesitated. "Where's Plante?"

Louis bit his lip as he glanced around, dumbfounded. "He was behind us a second ago."

"No time." Ryan hauled Sybil down the corridor and began ripping open doors. "Tell me if you recognize anything."

Her response was buried in the echoes of more gunshots. More screams.

The hallway ended in a dead end, a wall of concrete. Ryan checked the last door on the left. His heart sank when it opened into a broom closet.

"I got one!" Louis exclaimed behind him.

Ryan spun. The doctor held open a door that led into darkness. No choice. He jumped inside, machine gun leveled, as the twin beams of his suit splayed across the room. Desks and chairs furnishing an office . . . and a glass exit at the far end.

"Gunner, last door on the right!" he yelled between machine-gun bursts. Gunner was battling something. "Move it!" He heard two clicks on the com followed by another blast of automatic fire.

Louis grabbed Smith when he nearly tripped over an upturned chair. Sybil used her long legs to match Ryan's pace while Compton kept a wary eye on their six.

Ryan slammed his shoulder into the glass door . . . and bounced back. Locked. Smith picked up a metal file holder from a desk and rammed it against the bottom pane. It shattered. Ryan regained his balance and reached through the busted glass to unlock it.

Sybil shoved the door open. "Some kind of warehouse," she panted, aiming her beams along the rows of shelves that bracketed a wide aisle.

"Keep going!" Ryan led Louis and Compton through before looking back. No sign of the others. "Gunner, where are you? We're leaving the offices and heading into some type of warehouse."

"They're all around us," the veteran wheezed. "Lucas is down, and I'm almost out of ammo."

"Shit." Ryan scanned the area. Nowhere to set up a defense. He checked his magazine. Half-full.

"Coming to you now," Gunner shouted through the com. "I see the desks."

A small weight fell off Ryan's shoulders, and he picked up the pace.

Sybil's voice in his ear. "We reached the end. It looks familiar. I think there's an exit around here somewhere."

Five seconds later, he spied Sybil in front of a pile of boxes and iron beams. Louis was bent over, hand on his knee, trying to catch his breath.

"Are you sure there's a way out of here?" Ryan asked. The screams behind them were growing louder, and there was no sign of Gunner.

She nodded. "We used this part of the station for storage. There's a door behind this pile."

Ryan sucked in air. "All right, clear a path."

They started pitching boxes. Even Louis, with his single arm, shoved away as much as he could. In seconds, they had cleared a small space, and Ryan spied a door handle and a padlock that hung down like a coffin nail.

Automatic fire echoed off the walls. Gunner was getting close. Smith cast a nervous glance into the darkness.

Sybil kicked the metal hasp in frustration. "We need a crowbar or something."

"No time," Ryan said. "Stand back." He pointed the gun at the locking mechanism, shielded his eyes, and fired.

One side of the hasp came apart. Ryan kicked it once, twice, and the metal pieces scattered across the concrete floor. He sucked in a breath. "Open it."

Smith gripped the handle and yanked on the door. It fetched up against the iron beams.

Ryan nearly panicked. The opening was too narrow.

"Come on! Help me move them." He picked up one end of the top beam, and Smith folded his hands around the other. The screams behind them merged into a continuous, maddening cry.

"Now!" Ryan heaved, and the beam scraped across iron and fell off the pile.

He flexed his fingers when they threatened to cramp. "Next one."

His muscles protested, but they managed to slide that one off as well. Heavy footsteps made him spin around, his gun rising, until he recognized Gunner sprinting down the center aisle.

His EV suit was stained and ripped, and his helmet was gone.

"Lucas?" Ryan asked.

Gunner shook his head. The non-answer spoke volumes. "I dropped some shelving in front of the doors. It won't slow them for long."

"How many?" Ryan asked.

"Maybe a dozen." Gunner focused on the iron beams as Compton pushed the last boxes off the pile. "The door?"

"Yeah, we have to move them."

Ryan wrapped his hands around the next beam and, with Smith and Gunner helping, shoved it to one side. Two more quickly followed.

"I can get through!" Sybil declared, squeezing her thin frame through the opening as Louis and Compton put their shoulders into the door.

A large crash echoed off the walls. Gunner caught Ryan's eye. "They're coming, Ace."

"One more," Ryan grunted. His forearms spasmed as he wrapped his fingers around the next beam. It hadn't hit the floor before he had his gun out.

"I'm good!" Louis blurted. He removed his helmet and scrambled through the narrow doorway.

"Smith!"

"Sir!"

The reservist thrust himself into the space. His suit fabric caught and ripped, but he somehow got through.

"Gunner, you're next!"

"No time, Ace," the veteran replied, pulling the machine gun off his shoulder. The screams rose in intensity before a figure burst into the light. Ryan had a momentary vision of a scraggly beard, wild eyes, and a large scar that split his nose down the middle. Gunner's bullet punched a small, circular hole in his forehead and he was down.

Two more bodies came rushing down the main aisle. Gunner aimed and fired. Three bullets. "Almost out."

"Compton, move!"

The reservist grabbed the doorway with both hands just as a body came flying out of the darkness, bowling him over. Ryan moved to intercept when Gunner yelled, "On your left!"

Ryan spun, and his gun barked twice before the thought reached consciousness, and a scruffy woman rolled to the side, clawing at her stomach. Another shadow launched itself at Gunner. Ryan fired but the bullet only grazed his skull, and the seker knocked the veteran into the pile of iron beams. Something hit Ryan in the head, and his world disintegrated into a maze of flailing limbs and subvocal grunts. A clawed hand ripped his suit, and then swung at his eyes. He brought his gun up and rammed the muzzle into a grizzled face. Four teeth disappeared. The dazed creature rolled off, and Ryan brought his heel down on its throat.

Gunner used his machine gun like a baseball bat, crushing the skull of a tall, emaciated female. A bald man seized his gun by the barrel and tried to yank it away.

Ryan shot him in the chest. He bent over Compton, but the man's eyes had already glazed over, and blood had stopped pumping from the open gash in his neck.

"He's gone!" Gunner pushed Ryan toward the door.

A seker screamed as it hurled itself at Ryan. Gunner swung low and Ryan heard a loud *crack* as the gun barrel fractured bone.

Ryan yanked the door hard, gaining another inch, maybe two, and squeezed into the opening. Metal splinters dug into the skin on his back. He grunted and forced his way in. Blood dripped down his leg.

Gunner was right behind him. On the other side, Louis slammed his shoulder into the frame. The opening widened another inch.

A hand reached out and snagged Gunner's foot. He kicked the seker in the jaw. Another skeletal hand got a grip on his shoulder. Ryan leaned over the veteran's head and fired his gun into its face. Blood and bits of gray matter peppered his EV suit.

Gunner had managed to squeeze his thick frame halfway through when the fabric fetched up on one side. Two mutants clawed at his back. Ryan fired into the body of the first. It sagged boneless to the concrete. He swiveled to the other, but the hammer clicked on air. Empty. He threw the gun and hit the seker in the cheek. It stumbled back, and Ryan hauled on Gunner's arm. The suit material gave with a jolt, and the veteran fell on top of him.

"Go!" he shouted, but Gunner was already rolling off.

A seker tried to squeeze into the opening—black-rimmed eyes, mouth wide in a soundless scream—when Ryan slammed his foot into its face. Something crunched under his heel and blood poured out its nose.

"Come on!" Gunner grabbed his arm and hauled him up. "We have to leave."

They staggered through a narrow corridor that sloped upward. Gunner's suit lamps were out, the glass fronts smashed, so they felt their way along concrete walls. Sekers scrambled through the door behind them, their high-pitched screams echoing in the darkness.

"Hurry!" Louis's voice from somewhere ahead. "Last door on the right."

*What door?* Ryan couldn't find an exit. Then he saw lights: the doctor's suit lamps. The man held a door open with his back and gestured frantically. Gunner practically threw Ryan inside, and the doctor slammed the door shut. Smith shoved an iron bar under the handle and wedged it against the floor.

Something crashed into it, shaking the frame.

"This way," Sybil said, appearing out of the darkness. "I remember there's a stairwell on this side of the room."

Ryan found it and took the steps two and three at a time . . . until the stairs split into two sets, and he ran into a barricade on the second landing. Metal beams covered by sheets of heavy plastek and aluminium fencing that stretched up to the concrete ceiling. "What the hell?"

Gunner ran up and gave it a shove. "Welded and bolted. Somebody was determined." He glanced at the set of stairs that bypassed the blockade. "Which way, Ace?"

Ryan eyed the primitive barrier. "If we can get behind this, we'll be able to hide. There's a small gap at the top. I'll bend back the fencing and make a hole."

Louis cast a dubious eye over the structure. "How the hell can you balance up there?"

"We'll hold him," Gunner said, grabbing Smith and hauling him close. They linked hands. "Step on, Ace, and be quick."

Ryan used their shoulders as leverage, placing one foot on their hands so they could hoist him to the top of the metal barrier. He hauled on the fencing until it bent back with a high-pitched screech and a small opening appeared. "It's tight. Let me get through and then send up one at a time."

He wiggled his frame between knife-like flanges of corrugated aluminum and grunted every time something punctured skin. After a brief struggle, he pulled himself free and wiped bloody hands on his suit. He swiveled around and reached for the doctor as Gunner and Smith lifted him up. Louis flailed before grabbing Ryan's hand. It took several precious seconds to drag him through the opening and lower him to the concrete floor on the other side of the barrier.

"That door ain't gonna hold long, Ace," Gunner warned, looking down the stairwell.

Ryan bit his tongue as something sharp jammed into his thigh. Another edge of metal fencing. "Sybil, you're next—"

A crash sounded, followed by the sound of scrambling feet.

"Shit!" Ryan leaned over the edge. "Hurry!"

Sybil was reaching for his hand when Gunner and Smith abruptly dropped her.

"No time. Have to move." The veteran wrapped an arm around Sybil and they ran up the other flight of stairs. "Hide yourselves, Ace," he called over his shoulder. "We'll try and circle back."

Ryan watched helplessly as Smith bolted after Gunner and Sybil. There was nothing he could do. Footsteps on the stairs. He and Louis dropped to the floor and hid behind a thick metal sheet. A mass of bodies reached the landing platform. Hands rattled the barricade, wild dogs pawing at the fence. Several tried to scale the barrier but lost their grip and fell, landing hard on the concrete. Seconds later, the horde scrambled up the other set of stairs.

Ryan exhaled and hauled Louis to his feet. "Hurry! Before they come back." He didn't want to admit it, but there was nothing he could do for his crew. They were on their own.

The stairs led up to another fire door. No handle. The metal plate meshed with the exterior frame. A wave of frustration threatened to steal Ryan's thoughts. He pounded on the door. There was no way to open it without a laser saw.

Something creaked on the other side, metal sliding against metal, and it suddenly swung open. Ryan found himself staring down the muzzle of a gun.

"Jesus, mate," a voice said. "You trying to get yourself killed?"

Ryan recognized the uniform. Alliance. "Who are you?"

The man blinked. "I'm Max Plante. Governor of Ceres. Who the hell are *you*?"

Gunner peered around the corner and gritted his teeth. At the end of the corridor, the door to the decompression chamber lay open. Which meant someone had been there since they sprinted past earlier. Taking a deep breath, he stepped back into the storage room.

Sybil was on him before his eyes adjusted to the darkness. "Anything?"

He shook his head wearily. He didn't like talking to the traitor at the best of times, like when she had been in Europa's brig. Here was worse. "Somebody opened the door, but the coast is clear. I'm guessing they're searching for Braeder."

At the lieutenant's name, Sybil's face reddened. "If the sekers haven't returned—"

"Then he's still alive," Gunner acknowledged. Or—a second thought tugged at his mind—they were ripping the bodies apart.

"If they are alive, it won't be for long." Plante grunted. "He doesn't know the station, and the sekers control every square inch of the place."

The sound that oozed from Gunner's throat mirrored the anger on his face, and Plante hurriedly looked away. Gunner didn't know where the governor had gone during their frantic escape or how he miraculously reappeared when they circled back to the airlock. But if they survived this fiasco, he was going to get answers.

Smith limped over. Gunner had tied a crude bandage around his shoulder, but blood still leaked through. "What's the plan, sir?"

Gunner fisted his hands. This was the part he hated. Following orders was his forte, not giving them. But right now, he had no choice. He fingered his ripped sleeve. "If we're going to get out of this shithole, we need suits, and the only place that's got 'em is right down that hall. Which means our escape plan runs through that room."

Smith swallowed nervously. "The sooner, the better? Before the sekers come back?"

"That's right. We spied suits when we arrived. I say we sneak down, grab them, and get the hell out of Dodge."

"What about the lieutenant?" Smith asked.

Gunner flashed him a cold smile. "Oh, have no fear, we're coming back. We just need to load up on weapons first."

Sybil stepped to the door and peeked out. "There's a lot of open space between us and that room."

The tremor in her tone almost made Gunner laugh. Now she needed him. "Stay tight behind me. If I start to run, don't hesitate." He looked at Plante. "That goes for you as well."

The governor nodded.

"All right." Gunner scanned the escape route. Two wall-mounted lights flickered, casting shadows that danced across the floor. No sound. He would give his left nut for a gun.

Sybil was on his hip as he stepped gingerly into the corridor. Their goal was one hundred feet past a half-dozen open doors. His footsteps were silent on the duroalloy floor, and he pointed at shards of broken glass so the others would avoid them. He tilted his head around the first doorway. Some kind of water pumping station, with pipes and conduits leading into darkness. He sucked in a breath and hurried past, and waited for a warning scream that never came. He exhaled and kept moving. Two more open doorways. Twenty more nail-biting seconds. Forty feet.

Sybil tripped over a metal sheet. The screech echoed down the corridor.

She looked up at him, eyes wide.

*Shit.*

An answering howl erupted from deep within the rooms. Something fell and smashed against the floor.

"Run!" Gunner shouted.

They sprinted past the last three doors. Shapes appeared in the corridor, distorting the light as they burst into the decompression chamber.

"Help," he grunted, swinging the heavy metal door around. The thick titanium hinges creaked in protest. Smith appeared at his side and added his shoulder.

The door clicked into position just as something slammed into the other side.

Gunner gripped the handle with both hands. "Find something to wedge it with!"

Sybil and Plante searched the debris on the floor and came up with a piece of plastek. They shoved it through the latch, and Gunner slowly removed his hands. The handle twisted but not enough to disengage the pins.

He pulled off his ripped suit and pointed to the EV rack. "Change quickly." No telling how long their impromptu lock would hold.

Sybil helped the injured reservist into a new suit and double-checked the straps. They had all lost their helmets in the mad dash through the station and had to find new ones. Gunner hurriedly switched suits and batted away Sybil's hands when she tried to check his connections.

"No time," he grunted. Truth be told, he couldn't stand her hands anywhere near him. He didn't know how Braeder did it. He pulled on his gloves and tightened his helmet before stepping over to the control panel. The power button pulsed green.

Something heavy rattled the door.

"Get in," he ordered, and waited as three more bodies squeezed into the chamber before hitting the switch. The door rotated shut and a chugging sound filled the room as air was pumped out of the chamber.

"Make a beeline for the gator," Gunner ordered. "There's other exits out of this hive, and we need as much of a head start as we can get."

Smith nodded. Plante's expression was unreadable, but he certainly didn't look happy.

Gunner figured they had at best a fifty-fifty chance of making it back. The gator wasn't fast and they were out of guns and lasers. He set his jaw. They may be leaving, but it was only temporary. He was sure as hell coming back to get the lieutenant.

# CHAPTER 23

*Wherever you go, go with all your heart.*

DAY 77, 1458 HOURS

"Who am I?" Ryan asked, incredulous, as he stared down the muzzle of the gun. During his time in Fleet, he had had multiple weapons pointed at him, especially in the African debacle. Fortunately, most of them missed. And since he wasn't dead already, he figured the guy holding this gun preferred not to use it.

"Yes, who are you?" the man demanded. "And why did you stir up a hornet's nest?"

Ryan leaned back against the wall. He chanced a glance at Louis who, despite panting heavily, also stared wide-eyed at the weapon. "Yeah, well, 'stirring up' the sekers wasn't our choice. We were trying to find information on the plague."

Ryan knew he had said something wrong when Plante's grip tightened and the barrel rose to meet his face.

"You from Earth?" the man asked.

"No." Ryan raised his hands before Plante's finger twitched on the trigger. "We're from Europa."

"What? That's impossible."

Ryan pointed to the insignia on his shoulder. "We came here in search of supplies. The last message we received said everyone here was dead."

The grip on the gun lessened. The man seemed to waver.

"And I'd really appreciate if you pointed that thing somewhere else."

Plante seemed to realize what he was doing and let his arm fall. "Sorry." He shoved the gun into his waistband. "It's empty, anyway. I ran out of bullets months ago."

Ryan's anger drifted away. His new friend was as defenseless as he was. He gripped the door handle. "Thanks for letting us in."

The man pointed to a monitor on a nearby table. It showed separate views of the stairwell and several sekers milling around outside the barricade. "They would have torn you to pieces. I had to do something."

"You have cameras outside?"

"I installed them after I built the fence." He peered at Ryan. "How did you get past that, anyway?"

"Pulled back the aluminum at the top and squeezed through."

The man winced. "That's not good. It'll have to be repaired."

Louis caught Ryan's eye before stepping forward. "You said your name is Plante?"

The man gave him a strange look. "Ah, yeah."

"Plante, governor of Ceres?"

"Last time I checked."

"That's weird," Ryan said. "Because we've been working with another fella by the same name in the Alliance station."

Plante let out a sigh. "It's a long story. Come with me and I'll explain." He double-checked the locks on the fire door and scanned the monitor before leading them through a small archway.

Louis raised an eyebrow and Ryan made a subtle gesture with his hand. *Don't say anything.*

They entered a large room illuminated by several wall-mounted lights. At the far end, a large plate-glass window overlooked the asteroid's regolith-covered surface. Next to it, a vegetable garden complete with heat lamps and water pipes occupied most of the floor space. Ryan recognized several rows of carrots and tomatoes growing in about twelve inches of soil.

"My version of a greenhouse," Plante explained, running his hand over the leaves. He gestured to the sunlamps overhead. "It's not much, but it's kept us alive."

Ryan glanced around. The room itself seemed to be some sort of converted lab with countertops, sinks, and multiple computers. Much of the equipment had been pushed against the walls. Black cables crisscrossed the room like ancient clotheslines. Ryan stepped over and touched one. "Power supply?"

"Solar panels on the surface," Plante explained. "Started off with plenty of amps, but I keep losing panels." He shrugged. "Can't get outside to do routine maintenance. Not with sekers patrolling the station."

Louis looked over. "You said *us*?"

Plante turned toward a closet at the far end of the room. "You can come out now. It's safe."

A door swung open and a small person peeked out. Ryan was shocked when a young boy wandered over to Plante. He looked all of three.

The man picked him up. "It's all right, Jason."

Two more children entered the room. Hesitantly. The girls looked about four or five years old and each clutched a stuffed animal tightly to their chest. Their eyes never left Ryan.

"Lieutenant?" Louis approached the children and dropped on one knee as he ran a critical eye over them. "Malnutrition," he pronounced. "Just like the survivors in the Alliance station."

"Thanks for that vote of confidence." Plante snorted. "At least we're still here." His expression relaxed. "You a doctor?"

Louis pulled a scanner out of his pocket. "I am."

Plante watched silently as the doctor ran his instrument over the boy.

"Damn, Ryan," Louis said as he checked the other two. "Liver and renal failure. They need medicine from the transport."

"But at least they're alive," Plante repeated, irritation creeping into his tone.

Ryan offered him a tight smile. "Pay him no heed. He acted the same way on Europa when we instituted rationing."

Plante's eyebrows rose. "Europa is still . . . there?"

"Smaller in number, but yes. Problem is, our infrastructure is breaking down, which is why we're here. To find replacement parts." He paused as he tried to piece together the facts. And failed. "Tell me about the *other* Governor Plante."

The governor put the boy down. "That would be my former executive officer, Wilshire. Harold Wilshire."

"And he's claiming to be you?" Louis said. "What happened?"

Plante stepped over to adjust the water dripping over a row of tomatoes. "Let me back up. When the plague hit Earth and all transport flights were grounded, we introduced rationing. All colonies on Ceres did. Problem was, we had too many mouths and not enough greenhouse space. Still, we hung on in the hope Earth would eventually bounce back."

Ryan exchanged a look with Louis. "Yeah, hope springs eternal."

"After several weeks, things were looking bleak," Plante continued. "That's when I received a call from the Federation. Apparently, they had a sample of the plague."

Louis slapped his palm against the countertop. "I knew it! They were working on a vaccine."

"Plante, er, Wilshire told us the Russians had shipped in the bug on one of their transports," Ryan said. "Or, at least, it was a rumor."

"It was no rumor," Plante said. "They were making progress in designing a vaccine, but they needed our help to produce large quantities so they could begin experiments."

"Why'd they ask you?" Louis said. "Why not do it themselves?"

"Because they didn't have the production capacity or the proper equipment." Plante swung his arm at the machines on the counter. "This was one of their labs. It's pretty rudimentary compared to what we have in our station."

"So, you agreed," Ryan said. "What happened?"

"We mass-produced the vaccine in one of our vats and sent it back. In fact, we collaborated with their scientists for a while. Until they stopped answering our calls."

"And you didn't try to find out why?"

"At that point, nobody cared what the Russians were doing, because we were all starving."

"Wilshire said you had a vote on opening the EV door. But not everyone agreed?"

"There were about twenty of us, including Wilshire, who couldn't go through with it. We barricaded ourselves in one of the storage lockers and emerged afterward to close the door."

"So, he told the truth about that part, at least," Ryan said, pissed at himself for being duped so easily. "How did you get stuck here?"

"Happenstance. We discovered there were still colonists alive in this station." Plante's gaze drifted to the kids who huddled around him. "I suggested we send a rescue team."

Ryan saw where this was going. "Wilshire didn't agree."

"Said we already had too many mouths to feed. Most of our group came down on my side, so I overruled him. We found survivors in one of the Federation hives, including a dozen Russian scientists working on a vaccine."

Louis tilted his head. "They didn't open their EV door?"

"Oh, they did, but the scientists had squirreled away foodstuffs and decided their only chance for survival was to finish their work. They had enough supplies for themselves and about fifty 'volunteers.'"

"Why so many?" Ryan asked.

"Remember Medical," Louis said quietly. "What we saw in Medical."

Ryan hesitated. *What about it? The bodies!* "They kept them alive to experiment on?"

Plante met his gaze, and Ryan saw his disgust mirrored in the governor's eyes.

"We found corpses in Medical and in a locked room on the second floor. That's where they kept the sekers. When we confronted the scientists, a fight broke out. Wilshire teamed up with the Russians and released the sekers before hightailing it back to my station. That's when all hell broke loose."

"They killed your people?" Ryan asked.

"I'm the last," Plante confirmed.

"And you had no idea what they were doing until you arrived here?"

Plante grimaced. "Believe me, my entire crew was shocked by what we found. Except for Wilshire."

Louis snorted. "He thought the ends justified the means, and the Russian methods didn't bother him as long as they developed a vaccine."

"Sounds like you're familiar with that type of mentality," Plante said.

The doctor nodded.

"We had similar people on Europa." Ryan had a brief mental image of Grimm and Bordeaux. "They lacked morals as well."

"Wilshire marooned you here?" Louis asked.

"He left us to die," Plante snarled. "The kids are all that's left of the Russian colonists. Except for the scientists and criminals."

Ryan frowned. "Criminals?"

"Where do you think the scientists got their volunteers? By the time the food ran out in this station, the jail was full. They had their choice of candidates."

"Wow," Louis muttered. "This keeps getting better."

"How long have you been here?" Ryan asked.

Plante pointed to a calendar pinned above a sink. Individual months had been ripped out and taped in a straight line. "Four months, two weeks, five days."

Ryan surveyed the makeshift garden again. "But you hung on."

Plante shrugged. "Thankfully, the Russians had already started building this greenhouse. Power cables had been hooked up and water pipes installed. There's enough seed to keep going, at least for a while. It didn't hurt that I was a biologist in a former life."

One of the young girls edged closer. Plante picked her up and deposited her on his lap. "After they massacred everyone, the sekers began to roam the surface. The kids survived by hiding in that closet. I found them when I fled up to the second floor and barricaded the stairwell."

Ryan's anger simmered beneath the surface. Wilshire could have been a reincarnated Bordeaux. "The sekers don't try to break in?"

"They don't know I'm here. Although . . ." His gaze shifted toward the fire door. "That may have recently changed."

"Sorry about that," Ryan said. "We were running for our lives."

"I know the feeling."

Louis got up and walked over to the lab counter. "Wilshire never came back?"

"He probably thinks I'm dead. The bastard took the opportunity to get rid of me and chart his own course."

"Don't think that worked out so well," Louis said. "Since there's just four of them left."

"Is that all you saw?" Plante shot the doctor a look. "Because he left here with about twenty, including the scientists."

Ryan gripped the edge of the counter. Hoodwinked again. Rage threatened to burst from his chest. "Besides Wilshire and Bennett, I don't know how many of those twenty are still breathing."

Louis nodded as the facts filled in the puzzle. "The other survivors must have been hiding in the station, which was why Sasha detected those electrical currents."

"They planned it from the beginning," Ryan growled. "They saw our transports land and squirreled away the survivors, all but four. Wilshire has been playing us the whole time. Letting us do the work of salvaging parts and loading the transports. And, at some point, he planned to take over."

"He was waiting for you to turn your back," Louis spat, exchanging a look with Ryan. "And if that son of a bitch really has a vaccine, he can take the transports anywhere, including Earth. That also explains why he tried to talk you out of coming to this station. He didn't want us to discover what happened."

Ryan slammed his fist against the wall and silently cursed his ineptitude. "When we get back to that station, I'll feed him to the sekers myself."

The doctor's eyes narrowed. "I'm hoping Gunner beats you to it."

"Gunner's still blind to the traitor in his midst," Ryan said.

Lines formed on the governor's forehead. "Your man?"

"As long as he's still alive."

Plante put the child down. She seemed more settled as she went back to the closet and pulled out some broken toys. "This stairwell leads back to the decompression chamber. If your people made a beeline for the airlock, they would have a clear run."

Ryan nodded, relief dousing his anger. Knowing Gunner like he did, if the veteran had the smallest chance at surviving this mess, he would seize it. "You never tried to escape?"

The governor gestured at the kids playing with their toys. "With them? How do you think we would do on the surface?"

Ryan sighed. "Stupid question."

"We do have extra suits stored in one of the closets," Plante continued, nodding toward a narrow door beside the greenhouse. It's just, well"—he shrugged—"we never got an opportunity."

"Tell me more about the vaccine," Louis said. "I reviewed the data from the CDC, and they were nowhere close to cracking the code."

Plante stood and walked over to a pile of blankets in the corner. Sometime in the last few minutes, the young boy had drifted off to sleep. "Best we can figure, the Russian doctors on Earth made some kind of breakthrough before the Cosmodrome fell. The scientists here continued their work and took the next steps."

"And those *next steps* included human guinea pigs," Louis grumbled. His lips twisted in disgust.

"Yeah, the scientists didn't tell us that part of the plan when they asked for help."

"What about the vaccine? Did any of the subjects develop an immunity to the plague?"

The governor gently laid a blanket over the sleeping child. "That's the confusing part. I'm not sure what happened after we shipped over the vaccine prototype. We discovered the sekers when we arrived, but I was too busy running for my life to find out about their experiments."

"How are the sekers still alive?" Ryan asked. "Other than yours, we didn't see any greenhouses inside this station."

"They're not totally insane, Lieutenant. I watched them complete simple tasks, and learned behaviour seems to be maintained, like charging batteries on EV suits."

"What about food? It's been months."

Plante grimaced. "They're carnivores. There's a station full of dead bodies."

Ryan felt like throwing up. He recalled what they did to Gonzalez on the runway. "They can't survive forever."

"No, you saw the condition they're in. I figure they'll all be dead in a few months." He grinned coldly and gestured to the vegetables growing under the sunlamps. "The problem is, we'll probably be joining them."

Plante turned away from the sleeping child. "Did Wilshire ask for passage to Europa?"

"He didn't have to," Louis snickered. "Our glorious leader offered him a ride."

Guilt oozed into Ryan's veins. He fumbled for something to say. "Yeah, we were supposed to leave right after we gathered the needed parts. This side trip was a last-minute attempt to gather wire and find out about a possible vaccine." He hesitated and then added, "A stupid decision on my part."

"Sounds like a humane decision. You were looking for wire?"

"Yes, for our extractor. We ran out."

Plante scratched at some scabs on his scalp. "Not sure if I can help you in that department. This place"—he spread his hands wide to encompass the entire room—"was some kind of vaccine lab before they transformed it into a greenhouse."

"Actually, Medical had wire—"

"What do you mean, 'vaccine lab'?" Louis interrupted, his expression serious. He walked over to the counters beside the heat lamps.

Plante shot Ryan a puzzled look. "Not sure. I'm no doctor, but there's a bunch of written notes by the sink."

"Indeed." Louis hauled out a package wrapped in cloth from his pocket and deposited it on the counter before walking over to examine a pile of loose-leaf.

"What do you have there?" Ryan asked.

The doctor jerked a thumb at the fist-sized item. "The last IED."

Ryan blinked. "You hung on to it?"

Louis shrugged. "You were kind of busy keeping us alive, so I wasn't exactly going to bother you."

"Well, a lot of good it is now." Ryan shifted his gaze to Plante. "What do you think Wilshire will do?"

"Not sure, but whatever it is, it won't be good."

Ryan's lips tightened into a bloodless line. "Don't worry. Wilshire will have to crawl over Gunner's bloated corpse to get close to a transport, and even then, there's no way my pilots will leave without us."

"But we still have to get out of here," Louis said, shifting through papers. "And since we have nothing that resembles a weapon, if the sekers come after us, all we can do is throw harsh words at them."

"That may be true," Ryan acknowledged. "But I've got the most stubborn fool in the solar system at the Alliance station, not to mention Europa's best engineer. We may be here a while, but our job is to figure out how to help them put together a plan that gets you and me back to Europa."

Plante cleared his throat.

"Right." Ryan nodded at the governor. "That gets *all* of us back to Europa."

# CHAPTER 24

*Study the past to divine the future.*

DAY 78, 1830 HOURS

Kasim ran into Archie outside Engineering. "Been looking all over for you," he panted. "Rani wants us to meet her in Ops."

Archie tensed like he suspected something amiss. "Anything I should know?"

The governor surveyed the concourse—a few people out for a stroll—before bending close. "She just received an update from Gunner. It's not good."

"What happened?"

Kasim kept his voice low. "They got attacked in the Federation station. Lucas and Compton are dead, and Braeder is missing. Gunner wants to launch a search-and-rescue attempt, but he's short on weapons and bodies."

"Shit. What's Rani going to do?"

Kasim grimaced. His thoughts drifted back to Braeder's Hail Mary attempt. "That's what scares me. It's not like she has a choice."

Archie's eyes widened. "By choice, I take it you mean the transport?"

The governor sighed. "The laser is still offline, the artifact is throwing bombs, and there's a real chance Ryan and the away team are not coming back. What would *you* do?"

Archie braced his arm against the wall, expression grim. "I don't like it, but I don't see another option. It's just, well, it's just a shitty position to be in. She won't want to pull the pin too early, but if she waits too long, the colonists will find out and she'll miss her chance."

Kasim's shoulders slumped. "I couldn't agree more, my friend. That's why she's the only one that can make this call."

Archie snorted. "Yeah, at least then it won't be our fault. And you can sleep at night when you leave the rest of us behind."

"You misunderstand me. Rani's making the call because Braeder trusted her to do it, but it won't affect me."

"You're not going to be on that transport?"

Kasim met and held his gaze. "I told her I'm staying on the moon. And to answer your next question, it's because I'm governor and it's my job."

"Goddamn." Archie patted him on the arm. "Then welcome aboard the *Titanic*."

He led Kasim down the concourse and into the Command Center. They found Rani in the briefing room, twirling the rings on her fingers.

Kasim slid into a chair opposite the ensign. He didn't say anything but Rani looked terrible, like she had aged ten years in the past week. New wrinkles had appeared on her forehead, and her hair appeared dull and lifeless.

She caught his eye. "Did you tell him?"

Kasim glanced sidelong at Archie and let out a breath. "Yeah, he knows."

"Gunner didn't give any details about what happened?" Archie asked. "Or what he was going to do?"

Rani shook her head. "To be truthful, I'm not sure if he knows. He sounded . . . distraught. The situation on Ceres is FUBAR."

"Damn," Kasim muttered. "That makes three dead and Ryan missing . . ."

Archie leaned back and folded his arms across his chest. "Europa was depending on those replacement parts."

Kasim's lips curved upward in disdain. "Forget us for a second. There's a little matter of our friend who's in trouble. The lieutenant? Remember him?"

Archie just smiled and kept his gaze on Rani. "Oh, I haven't forgotten, Governor. Nor has Rani. Am I right, Ensign?"

Rani didn't answer. She stared at the ceiling and continued to play with her rings.

Kasim's expression morphed into confusion. "Am I missing something?"

Archie inclined his head toward Rani. "Our new leader is trying to figure out what our old leader would do if he were in her shoes."

Rani's gaze zeroed in on the senior colonist. "Reading my mind now, Archie?"

"Only when I have to, missy."

She leaned forward and folded her hands on the table. "I think we all know what Braeder would do. He's done it before."

Kasim hesitated as the implication sank in. "You're going to take the transport, aren't you? Which means you're leaving me in charge." His hands began to shake.

"Archie will help you," Rani said. "And you have reservists."

Kasim almost barked a laugh. A few burly colonists taking a weekend course on crowd control was not going to turn the tide on his incompetence.

"When do you want to launch?" Archie asked.

"Tomorrow."

"Damn." Archie scratched his sideburns. "Is that enough time to prepare?"

"I spoke to Marcel, the pilot. He says Chan's program is downloaded and the ship is fueled. Besides, time is a commodity Gunner doesn't have. The sooner we leave, the better."

"What do you want me to do with the artifact?" Kasim asked.

"As little as possible," Rani said. "Let Vrabel study it but keep the reins tight until we get back."

Kasim gritted his teeth. "And if you don't come back?"

She shrugged. "Then do whatever the hell you want to, because you'll be the man in charge and we'll probably be dead."

Kasim leaned back, rubbed his face, and groaned.

Archie laid a reassuring hand on the governor's arm as he looked to Rani. "You got a plan how to make this happen?"

She hauled out her minicom and passed it across. "Yeah, Braeder had some ideas."

Archie glanced at the screen before chuckling. "How are your acting skills, Governor?"

*1719 Hours*

"It's a bloody maze over there," Gunner fumed as he changed the dressing on his forearm. It had been twenty-four hours since they scrambled back to the Alliance station, and his temper still simmered just beneath the surface. "The rats have infiltrated every inch of the nest."

Sasha paced in front of the portal in the observation room. Every few seconds, she stopped and fired a question at the veteran, "Are you sure they're still alive?" being the one repeated the most.

Gunner recalled the last time he saw the lieutenant. "He and the vet got through the barricade. I'm sure the sekers didn't see them. As long as they remain hidden, they should be safe."

Sasha resumed pacing. "But for how long? They don't have food or water." She hesitated as another thought struck her. "You said you tried coms, but there was no answer? Do you think . . ." Her voice trailed off when Gunner picked up his helmet.

"We had to suit up in Federation gear to get out, which means we had Federation coms. Even if Braeder found his helmet, the frequencies don't match. And we're too far away to try now." He fingered the thick fabric of the Federation suit. "The only way to get a message to him would be to reboot the coms system over there." He didn't comment on the odds of that happening. "Don't worry. The man's got more lives than a cat. He'll find a way to hide until we can pull them out."

Bennett walked in with Smith in tow. The reservist had a worn-looking sling over his left arm. "Did you just say you were going back to the Federation station?" she asked. "After barely escaping with your lives? Are you crazy?"

Gunner bared his teeth. "Where I come from, we don't leave a man behind."

"Look." Bennett sat beside him and spread her hands, palms up, on her knees, like a devotee praying before the altar of reason. "Even if they are alive, it won't be for long. The place is overrun with sekers."

"You don't know the man," Gunner snapped. "He's survived worse."

She shook her head. "Without weapons, you can't mount a rescue. The only logical thing left to do is load the transports and return to Europa. There's fifteen hundred living, breathing colonists waiting on you. There's nothing here but death."

Something akin to a growl spilled from Gunner's throat.

"We aren't leaving this rock without the lieutenant. So, don't mention that again."

Bennett tried to hold his gaze, but Gunner's stare didn't waver, and after several seconds, she looked away.

"We can't communicate with him," Sybil said, striding into the room. "So, how can we work out a plan?"

"We'll find a way," Gunner said. "Where you been?"

"Talking with the governor. He's pretty shook up about what transpired over there."

Gunner snorted. "Don't know why. He was as useful as tits on a bull. He even disappeared while we were searching Medical."

"Not everyone has your military training. Look at me." She held up one trembling hand. "It's been a full day since we got back, and I'm still shaking like a leaf. No way I want to venture out there with those monsters."

"Yeah, I can see you're worried sick about the lieutenant."

Her eyes narrowed. "I want to save him just as much as you." Her gaze flickered to Sasha. "But I'm not going to sacrifice my life doing it. So, unless and until you have a plan, we'll carry out his last orders."

Gunner scoffed. "That'll be a first."

Sasha blinked, confused. "What were his orders?"

"Bring replacement parts back to Europa."

Gunner had opened his mouth for a terse retort when his helmet com clicked on. "Chan to Gunner."

"Go ahead."

"I checked the communications terminal in Ops. It's toast. I don't know if it took damage when the EV doors were opened or it's something else, but the bottom line is that it needs a total rebuild. No way to contact the Federation station."

"Damn. What about the transport?"

"I ran some preliminary numbers. There's enough fuel for a short hop."

"Okay, meet me in Medical. Let's talk about options."

Bennett threw a puzzled look at the veteran. "So, you do have a plan?"

"Just kicking tires. You said it already: right now, we don't have weapons. We need to build those and figure a way into that station."

She tilted her head, like she wasn't sure how to respond. "That's going to take a while. Do you really think he can survive that long?"

"I do." Gunner got up and started for the door. Sasha moved to join him. "We'll be in Medical with Chan."

"What about loading the transports?" Sybil called. "Should we continue?"

Gunner stopped and turned in the doorway. "And who exactly is going to do the loading? You and Bennett? 'Cause Smith is down to one arm and we're out of reservists, and we already know how useful Plante is. So, no, the priority now is a rescue mission. Everything else can wait until hell freezes over."

*Day 79, 0740 Hours*

"On your mark, Ensign," Archie said, finger poised over the flashing yellow button on Gunner's console. "If you're sure you want to do this."

"Shut it," Rani snapped as she walked up to her old station and keyed the com. "We've been over this, and you don't get a vote." She ignored his snicker and leaned into the microphone. "Kasim, we're ready. Are you in position?"

There was a brief surge of static on the line before the governor responded. "Almost. Last pair of reservists leaving the airlock now. They'll join up with my group in front of the hangar."

Rani glanced out the nearest portal. A gaggle of EV-suited bodies mingled on the ice sheet. Jupiter was below the horizon, so it was easy to pick out a multitude of stars twinkling in the night sky. One of those faint yellow dots was Sol.

"That was a good trick, getting the right people outside," Archie murmured. "Lies and distraction. Braeder couldn't have done better."

Rani bit the inside of her lip. Archie was right. Deceiving the colonists was not something she was proud of, but medicine wasn't supposed to taste good.

"You know, you could have just asked for volunteers," Archie continued. "The colonists might have surprised you."

"I couldn't take that chance," Rani said. "A lot of people don't like him. And even those that do probably won't agree to leave their families and put their lives on the line. No, the smartest thing is to get them onboard and then explain the situation."

"If you say so."

Kasim returned after a minute. "We're ready."

Archie waited for Rani's nod before he pressed the button, and the familiar *whup-whup* of the klaxon echoed through the walls of the station. He opened the intercom. "Attention. We have detected an atmospheric leak in the concourse. Please evacuate to the hives. We will drop the emergency doors in two minutes. This is not a drill." He tapped a button and the warning repeated in an endless loop.

Stepping across to Marco's old terminal, he cut the power to the station's interior lights.

Rani gave him a strange look. They hadn't discussed this part.

He shrugged. "Thought it added a realistic touch."

Rani found herself liking it. She opened a channel to Kasim. "You're on."

Archie put the governor's com on speaker, and they could hear him talking to the small group of colonists outside the station. "I've just talked to Ops. They have the leak isolated, but it's going to take hours to fix. Since power to the airlock has been shut down, we need to get inside the hangar."

"Not sure that's the best plan," a man said. Rani didn't recognize the voice. "Our batteries are fully charged."

"He's right," a female said. "Best we stay here in case we have a narrow window to slip inside the station."

"Natives are proving difficult," Archie observed.

On the ice sheet, Kasim put his hand to his helmet like he was receiving a private message. "The Command Center says there's an ion storm brewing. We can't stay in the open."

Rani nodded approvingly. The governor was quite convincing.

Several people grumbled, but no one openly protested. Everyone knew what free radicals did to unprotected flesh. And with the station off-limits, the transport hangar was the safest place. Its thick outer walls acted like a bomb shelter.

They began to move toward the hangar.

"Do you think they'll get suspicious when they see a pilot in the cockpit?" Archie asked.

"His cover story is that he's doing routine maintenance," Rani replied. "That should hold for a while."

"And after you explain the situation? I'm not convinced they'll willingly step into the cryo-pods."

Rani stood. "Call me naïve, but I'm hoping they'll understand the situation: we need to save who we can and get those parts, including the wire."

"And for those that remain obstinate?"

She lifted her tunic to expose the handle of the revolver. "Even the diehards will see the writing on the wall."

Archie gave her a cynical look. "Even I know you'd never pull the trigger on an unarmed civilian."

Rani withdrew the weapon and pointed it at Archie's head. A cold smile formed, like the tip of an iceberg, and she flipped off the safety. "Are you sure? 'Cause if I exert another ounce of pressure on this trigger—"

"Damn, girl." He swallowed. "What the hell has Braeder taught you?"

Rani slid the gun back into her waistband. "He taught me shit. The bastard knew that once I saw the ugly side of human nature, I'd have to adapt if I was to manage the colony. And that includes shoving this gun in the face of any *obstinate* colonists." She exhaled. "Contact Kasim and tell him I'm on my way."

"He told me he wasn't going with you."

She snorted. "I should have guessed. That means I have one empty cryo-pod. Do you want to take his spot?"

Archie's gaze flickered to the bulge on her waist. "Nah, I figure my chances are better here."

Rani adjusted the gun on her hip. It felt heavy but not as heavy as the guilt weighing down her shoulders. The colonists had surprised her. Once she explained the Ceres situation, they quietly acquiesced to accompany her on the mission. Threats were not required.

She surveyed the sealed cryo-pods. Each one supported a colonist in a chemically induced coma, with metabolisms so low, they barely registered on overhead monitors. All indicators in the green. Her gaze landed on Solomon's pod. The big deuterium miner had flashed her a toothy grin before drifting into dreamland.

"Passing Io now," Marcel reported. The skinny mechanical engineer had trained alongside Stoll, "Still not sure the engines can handle this velocity for sustained periods."

"It's not like we have a choice." Rani slid into the copilot's seat and gave silent thanks to Chan. The pilot's computer program did ninety percent of the work. Rani's only issue: that the ship couldn't handle the stress from a prolonged hard burn. But there was no other way to shorten the duration of the flight. "Any word from the colony?"

Marcel stole a nervous look at her gun before shaking his head. "Frequencies quiet."

"Strange." Rani shifted the video feed to the rear camera. Europa was a shiny baseball receding in the distance. She figured the civilians would insist on Kasim sending a message to the transport, imploring them to return. Even after the governor explained the nature of their mission and why she had no choice.

She sank back into the cushioned chair as another thought percolated to the surface. After witnessing the actions of the individuals onboard, she wondered if she had underestimated the colonists. Maybe they were made of sterner stuff than she gave them credit for.

The pilot pushed a few buttons on the console. "Course laid in. Trajectory nominal. I think we can get into our pods, Ensign."

Rani exhaled as she realized her work was done. At least until they reached their destination. But she didn't want to think about that. Not yet.

Marcel hoisted himself out of his chair but paused when a yellow light flashed on his panel. "Incoming message."

Rani sighed. Some things were too much to hope for. "Let me guess. They want us to turn back?"

He pulled off his headset and frowned. "It was short. Just two words."

Rani twisted the rings on her finger. That didn't make sense. "What'd they say?"

The pilot met her gaze. "They said, 'Good luck.'"

# CHAPTER 25

*Better a diamond with a flaw than a pebble without.*

DAY 81, 1313 HOURS

You're running out of food and water," Ryan observed as he sucked the last drops from the glass. After several days of minimal calorie intake, he felt like he was back on Europa during the early days of rationing.

Plante tucked the long end of his belt into his waistband. The extra holes cut into the leather chronicled his weight loss. "We were on our last legs when you arrived, Lieutenant. Feeding two additional mouths has accelerated the dying process."

Ryan nodded. The extra rations the governor added to the kids' daily intake hadn't escaped his eye, but there was no way he was going to mention it. He glanced at the rows of growing vegetables under the heat lamps and the physician studying lab notes at the nearby counter. "Best guess, Doc. How long do we have?"

Louis leaned back and rubbed his eyes. "Based on our current consumption, a month, give or take. Since I'm the oldest, odds are something will hit me first. Probably renal failure or maybe an infection my immune system can't handle. The kids are already suffering from vitamin and mineral deficiencies. Next step is probably hair loss and dental problems, and then they'll really get sick."

"Such a wonderful bedside manner," Ryan said, giving Plante a wink.

The governor cracked a smile. "I bet you two got along swimmingly on Europa."

"Careful," Louis snorted. "That's treasonous talk, and the lieutenant might toss you into the brig and divvy up your calories."

"Smart-ass," Ryan muttered. With nothing much to do, they had plenty of time to bring the governor up to date on Europa. At the end, he was left shaking his head.

"I understand too well rationing and the gnawing pain at night," Plante said. "You guys did well to hold the colony together. Humans aren't made to survive out here, in the middle of nowhere." He pointed a finger at Louis. "So, you can bitch all you want, but in my mind, you get to take a victory lap."

"He does that a lot," Ryan admitted.

"What's that?" Plante asked. "Take a lap?"

"No, bitch." Ryan inclined his head at the doctor. "Haven't you discovered a cure yet?"

Louis started to put on his glasses but stopped in the act. He lifted up a single piece of paper and peered closer. "Funny you should say that, Ryan. I think I figured out what the Russians were doing, and it's absolutely wild."

Ryan put down his empty glass and walked over to the bench. Louis had immersed himself in the lab notes since they escaped the sekers, barely raising his head except to eat and use the facilities. This was the first mention of what he had found. "Don't keep me in suspense."

Louis folded his arms across his chest. It looked weird with just one hand sticking out. Plante came over to join them. "Remember when I said the reason scientists couldn't design an antibiotic was because the bacterium changed the proteins on its surface every few hours?"

Ryan scratched his chin. It had been a while. "That's what made the infection impossible to target, right? Not just for antibiotics but also vaccines."

"Exactly." Louis pointed his glasses at Ryan. "Which is why the bug was always one step ahead of us. Well, from what I'm reading, the Russians found some proteins on the surface that didn't change."

"I thought the bug was too virulent to contain in a lab," Ryan said. "Which meant no one could examine it."

"They figured out a containment process," Louis replied. "I think that was the big breakthrough. Once they stabilized the bacterium, they were able to map the surface. That's how they discovered these target proteins."

Ryan waited for his brain to catch up with the facts. "They could make antibiotics to kill the infection?"

"That's what they tried," Louis said, waving the paper in the air. "But they failed because the dose required proved too toxic for humans. It caused side effects like strokes and heart attacks."

"I wonder how many patients had to die to figure that out," Plante said.

Louis nodded. "Their disregard for life is appalling. Reminds me of Nazi death camps."

Ryan recalled the bodies in Medical. "I'm guessing they didn't stop there. What was their next step?"

"Just getting to that." Louis stood and walked over to a shelf that held a row of glass bottles. "They shifted their focus to designing a vaccine. If the artificially produced antibiotics were too toxic for humans, maybe they could induce the body to produce a cleaner version and avoid the side effects."

Ryan felt uncomfortable. They had gotten damn close to the corpses in Medical. "Uh, Doc, is it safe? Remember what we said about one bacterium worming its way into the station?"

"Fear not, Ryan." Louis picked up one of the dropper bottles. "The samples they experimented with were dead."

"You sound awful confident," Ryan asked. "How can you be sure?"

Louis pointed at Plante. "Because he's been living in the same room with them for months."

The governor paled and his gaze zeroed in on the row of bottles. "Well, shit."

*Day 96, 0630 Hours*

Rani almost reached the pail in time. Unfortunately, her legs failed just short of her objective, and she emptied her stomach on the deck. Between retches, she muttered an old Indian curse. The lieutenant would have left a bucket by his cryo-pod for when he was revived. She still didn't think far enough ahead.

The Zofran patches were stocked on a nearby locker, and she slapped one on her wrist. It took a few minutes, but her stomach eventually settled and she was able to sip some bottled water.

Someone had to be revived to check the status of the transport, and it was her turn. Leaning on the cryo-pods as a crutch, she made her way into the cockpit. A veil of darkness surrounded the transport with only a tiny smattering of distant stars to break the monotonous void. If she ignored the instruments, the ship could have been hanging motionless in vacuum, an invisible blemish on the fabric of the universe.

But the instruments didn't lie; the ship had travelled millions of kilometers. If she knew where to look, she could pick out good old Sol and maybe even Earth.

She sucked back another gulp of water and felt a measure of strength return. It took several minutes to verify the flight path and ship status: on course and all systems nominal. Nothing to fix or adjust.

Except for the flashing light on coms.

*More best wishes from Europa?*

She clicked on the recording and took a second to get over the shock of hearing Gunner's voice. The first part of the message was distorted by static—probably solar flares—but the last half came through clear.

". . . situation precarious. There's been no word from Braeder and Louis in over two weeks. Not sure what condition they're in, or even if they're still alive. Despite repeated attempts, I can't find a safe way into the Federation station. Our only option is to storm the building once Sasha and I finish building weapons. If you don't hear back from me, it means we've failed and to avoid Ceres on any future missions. Gunner signing off."

The channel closed, and Rani's head spun. What was happening on that asteroid? Frustrated, she smacked her hands together. Now she knew what the lieutenant meant during the uprising when he said he felt useless. She was in the middle of deep space and felt the same.

"Hang on, Gunner," she whispered.

Only a few lamps illuminated the concourse as Kasim wandered past the fountain, hands clasped behind his back as his thoughts drifted. The dirty boulevard reminded him of early years in the UN, visiting war-torn countries where devastated streets often generated similar feelings of bleakness and isolation. Where hope went to die.

He was on his own. His last connection to the insurrection and rationing had left on the transport. Ryan, Gunner, and now Rani. A small voice in his head suggested they were abandoning him and the colony, leaving them all to starve. He crushed the thought before it could put down roots.

The doors to Medical slid open. As with the concourse, the lights had been turned down and only the soft hiss of the IV pumps and the gentle ping of overhead monitors broke the early-morning silence.

"Something I can help you with, Governor?" the nurse asked.

Kasim startled. "Damn, Mabel. You're quieter than a mouse."

She smiled. "So, no more cardiac pain?"

He self-consciously rubbed his hand over his chest. "No, it's been good. The medications seem to be working."

"Don't push it," she warned, pursing her lips. "We still have to wait until the doctor returns to unblock those coronary arteries."

Kasim felt that familiar rush of anxiety. Gunner wasn't the only one who blanched at the thought of needles and medical procedures.

"If not chest pain, what are you doing up at this hour?"

"Couldn't sleep," he confessed. "Been thinking about the damn artifact."

She frowned. "With most of the scientists in the brig, I thought research had hit a wall. Vrabel can only do so much."

"Ain't that the truth," Kasim muttered. Vrabel continued to probe, but he wasn't getting anywhere. And they sure as hell weren't letting Rutherford out.

"So, if nothing has changed, why is it bothering you?"

"Because I feel like I'm missing something. Some button we're not pushing."

Mabel reached up and turned off a monitor over one of the empty beds. "I thought the ensign was going to touch the artifact before she left."

"She decided to give Ellen a shot at it first."

"And if Ellen fails?"

Kasim shrugged. He had intentionally not thought about that part.

Mabel studied his expression. "You really believe the aliens are benevolent?"

"Don't you?"

She shrugged. "Rutherford says otherwise, and so do his yes-men." She picked up a stethoscope and played with the diaphragm. "I want to believe it. I mean, don't we all? Maybe inherent good exists, not just in humanity but in the universe. And maybe the aliens are just waiting for us to extend a hand."

Kasim stared at her. Something nibbled on the fringe of consciousness. "What did you just say?"

"What? You mean about the universe?"

"No." Kasim waited until the thought emerged into the light. "About extending a hand."

"It was a figure of speech."

He reached out and pulled her into a hug. "No, it was more than that. Thank you."

Mabel was left with a bemused look on her face as he hurried out.

Standing in the middle of the ice lab, Kasim stared at the strange hieroglyphics on the surface of the artifact. They reminded him of his time in the Middle East, touring museums that housed some of humanity's oldest documents. He recalled the Kish tablet from the Sumerian civilization and the effect it had had on him. Like that ancient tablet, these swirling lines meshed and diverged like flocks of birds coming together before flying apart. They seemed random and meaningless, and yet something nagged at him.

"Not used to seeing you in here, Governor," Vrabel said, raising his eyes over the top of his monitor. "Is there something I should know?"

"That's my question for you." Kasim turned and stepped up to the engineer's desk. "Rani left over two weeks ago and we're no closer to an answer."

Vrabel folded his hands behind his head and leaned back in his chair. "I feel like an ant trying to understand how a computer works. Maybe we simply don't have the tools to take the next step. Hell, I'm not even sure, if it responded, what questions we would ask."

"You don't think humans are up to the task?"

"I'm coming around to that point of view," Vrabel admitted. "Any word from Ellen? How's her group doing translating the notes?"

"She says it's more complicated than they first thought, but they're making progress. She says the frequency and note modulation are completely off the scale. They're building instruments that produce sounds beyond the normal range of hearing."

Vrabel tilted his head, his skepticism shining through. "Are you really putting stock in her theory? It seems . . . out there."

"Music is just math, right?" Kasim spread his arms apart to indicate the surrounding machines. "And *your* math hasn't exactly paid dividends so far."

Vrabel's face reddened, exposing his embarrassment. "What about you? I haven't heard your opinion."

Kasim played with the cuffs of his thawb. He knew many colonists had given up on any kind of breakthrough, and communicating with an alien race was never going to happen. "I confess I was originally one of those Doubting Thomases, but one night while I was pacing in my quarters, I had a revelation."

Vrabel's eyebrows peaked. "And that would be?"

"We found the damn thing. I believe that was the hard part."

"And you think the rest should be easier?"

"Exactly. My guess is that the advanced species who planted it didn't intend to give us an IQ test to prove we were worthy. No, they just wanted to make contact. I think we're missing something simple."

"Well, I'd like to say that finding *something simple* would be easy for a roomful of scientists, but we don't have a roomful of scientists anymore."

Kasim didn't comment. Tossing Rutherford and his cronies into the brig wasn't just justice; it was a necessity. Leaving them free to spread their lies and conspiracy theories would only lead to more violence and bloodshed. And death. Every ship needed a resilient leader at the wheel, steering safe passage for those on board, not a rebellious group of hyenas snapping at their heels. Even if they were only days away from another random energy discharge.

What had Rani said? A two percent chance of hitting something vital?

The colonists were scared, and who could blame them? They were no closer to understanding the riddle of the artifact.

And Gunner's message was hardly reassuring. He wondered how Rani had reacted when she heard it.

Vrabel seemed to read his thoughts. "What do you think they ran into on Ceres?"

Kasim shrugged. "Maybe factions vying for resources and power, just like Europa last year."

"Too bad Braeder didn't have more guns."

That elicited a grunt from the governor. Kasim hated guns. Hated what they did to people on both sides of the trigger. Still, he couldn't argue with their effectiveness. And yes, he wished Braeder had taken more guns.

His thoughts returned to their earlier quandary. The talk with Mabel had left him with a conundrum. *Extending a hand?* His instincts insisted it was the humans' turn to respond to the alien artifact, but Ellen's musical reply was taking too damn long to finish. That left him with one option. "It only woke up after Rani touched it, right?"

Vrabel eyed him. "Yes, that's when the symbols began flashing, and soon after . . . the energy beams."

"And no one has touched it since?"

He shook his head. "On the ensign's orders. In case we made the situation worse."

Kasim approached the artifact. "How much worse can it get? We're either going to die when something mechanical fails or when the beam penetrates something vital like the extractor."

Vrabel raised his index finger, paused, then dropped it. "Good point."

Kasim slipped off his glove.

"What are you doing?"

"Taking a leap of faith." He focused on the strange symbols etched into the surface. Watched them pulse. Then, before his natural reservations could stop him, he bent over and touched it.

His first impression was how incredibly smooth it felt. And warm.

Then something rushed up his arm. His muscles spasmed, and a horde of pain fibers fired in protest. The sensation was so foreign, he couldn't begin to describe it: colors with taste, memories carried on a cinnamon smell . . . And underneath it all, in that millisecond of time, he sensed a presence lurking just beyond his reach. A cloud of curiosity saturated his being, making it hard to breathe. The pain surged into the back of his skull.

He jerked his hand away and staggered back.

Vrabel jumped up. "You okay?"

Kasim leaned forward and braced his arms against the closest chair. He took a deep breath and reeled in his thoughts. His skin ached as from a sunburn. "There's something inside that thing."

"Inside . . ." Vrabel took a step before a buzzer sounded. He glanced at his screen. "The hell?"

Kasim straightened. "What?"

"Something happened." Vrabel tapped his screen. "I'm reading multiple spikes in the quantum field."

Kasim threw a glance at the artifact. Did he just initiate another energy-beam attack? Possibly condemn the colony to a premature demise? He held his breath until Vrabel broke the silence.

"It's leveling out. The emissions have settled."

"Let me guess. No specific direction?"

"Correct. It's still a flood of particles going nowhere. But the good news is the countdown has stopped." He looked up and caught Kasim's eye. "Goddamned, Governor. I think you just disabled the bomb."

Kasim exhaled. In retrospect, it had been a stupid and desperate gamble. He recalled Braeder's actions during the crisis last year. *Was this how the lieutenant felt? Scared? Confused?*

He had an overpowering urge to take a shower and wash off any lingering guilt. Gambling with people's lives was not something he aspired to do. "I'm heading back to the station. Let me know if you detect any other changes."

"Will do. I'll update the next shift when they come in." He spread his long arms on his desk. "What's the plan? Just keep trying to find a pattern?"

Kasim paused in the midst of picking up his EV helmet. "For now. I'm going to see if Ellen is ready."

Vrabel hesitated. "You're bringing musicians into a science laboratory?"

"Why not? I think it's time we opened the field to more competition."

*Day 97, 1438 Hours*

Gunner found Plante and Sybil in the observation room. "Where the hell have you been?" he demanded. "Sasha and I spent the last two hours assembling the batteries for the new lasers, and you were supposed to help."

The pair exchanged a hooded look as they rose from their lounge chairs.

"Sorry," Sybil said. "I was on my way when the governor informed me they had an emergency last night."

Gunner focused on Plante. "What kind of emergency?"

"We lost power to the greenhouse," he said gravely. "It's a total loss."

Gunner's jaw dropped. This was not what he needed to hear right now. "What the hell happened?"

Plante shrugged. "Sam is down there now, trying to find out. It's probably mechanical, but it hardly matters. All we can do is pick what food is ready. There's no chance of replanting."

"It won't be much," Sybil said, wringing her hands. "Maybe buy us a few days, and the transports have minimal reserves. What will we do?"

Gunner felt his face redden. "Do? The same thing we've been planning from the beginning: finish the lasers so we can rescue Braeder."

"Come on," Plante scoffed. "You don't really think he's still alive? After this long? He has no access to food, and the sekers have the run of the station, including the decompression room. Which means he can't recharge his suit." He stared at Gunner, almost daring him to defy logic.

Gunner glared back. "Aren't you two peas in a pod? What would you have me do? Abandon him? Give him up for dead?"

"You've tried for two weeks to find a way to slip past the sekers and get inside the station," Sybil said. "You had zero luck with that. Now you want to build lasers to force your way in? Maybe it's time to face facts. The governor is right."

"I see you're all broken up about Braeder," Gunner sneered. "He should have spaced you after the uprising."

Sybil's eyes narrowed. "The fact that he didn't saved your ass. You forget: in the Federation station, I knew how to get back to the airlock. If I wasn't there, you'd be dead."

"You'll forgive me if I don't thank you." Gunner took a second to rein in his temper. Last thing he needed in the moment was more enemies. His gaze shifted to the back of the room when the door swished open and Chan walked in.

"I did the calculations," the pilot said. "There's enough fuel for a short hop to the Federation station. I just can't loiter there long."

Gunner nodded. "Sasha says she can have two lasers ready by tomorrow. I'll meet you in an hour and we'll work out the details."

"What details?" the governor asked, eyes darting to Bennett. "You're going to launch an all-out assault on the station? With two lasers?" He ran both hands over his scalp, smoothing down his scraggly hair. "It's time to take our winnings off the table."

Gunner felt his control slipping. Plante's arguments were eerily similar to his discussion with Bordeaux and Grimm before last year's uprising. "We're not leaving without the lieutenant and the doctor or"—he locked gazes with Sybil—"their bodies. So, the sooner you get off your collective arse and help Sasha, the sooner we *take our winnings off the table*."

"The governor could order you," she said. "This is his colony."

"And this is a military operation," Gunner growled. "Which means I have ultimate authority." He held her stare until she dropped it. "Now, I'm done talking. You can come and help, or hide until the work gets done. I don't give a shit." He stomped off before he decided it was time to throw her out the nearest airlock.

# CHAPTER 26

*Don't adjust the goals; change the plan.*

DAY 98, 1145 HOURS

They really were ruthless bastards," Louis said, stepping up to join Ryan at the portal.

Ryan stared at the pockmarked surface, ancient impact sites separated by hills of gray regolith. The blandness weighed down his mood, even more than being marooned in the Federation station. "I take it you're referring to the Federation scientists?"

"To a person. Total disregard for patients. From what I've read, the criminals they conscripted as test subjects were fooled into believing the vaccine was safe when, in reality, they were being injected with an unproven serum."

"Goddamn," Ryan muttered. "They were bastards."

"It's not just Europa where colonists reverted to their basic instincts."

Ryan glanced at the binders on the lab bench. The doctor had spent days examining the notes. And what he found disgusted him. Human beings used as guinea pigs. Then dissected to see where the vaccine went wrong. The Federation scientists valued progress over morality.

"I see them," Louis said.

Three stories below, two sekers left the main airlock. Their EV suits were soiled and dirt-stained. The fake governor had said they usually left around noon. The real Plante agreed and said they headed toward the other stations. Mostly, they returned empty-handed, but sometimes, they carried spare parts and supplies. And sometimes, dead bodies. Ryan shuddered. A whole new definition of the word *cannibal.*

Louis seemed to be on the same wavelength. "The vaccine may have spared some of their cognitive brain cells, but emotions like rage turned them into monsters."

Two more emerged from the airlock. "They look emaciated," Ryan said.

Louis cast a clinical eye over them. "Malnutrition is going to kill them soon, no matter how many desiccated corpses they consume. If we hid long enough, we could walk out the main doors after they all collapsed."

"Unfortunately, we don't have that luxury," Ryan said. Not knowing what was happening in the Alliance station was an itch he couldn't scratch. "I'm not sure what Wilshire is planning, but it can't be good. Plus, if we don't act soon, we'll be as weak as kittens, and that's not going to help any escape plan."

"You're not wrong," Louis admitted. "Our bodies didn't have much reserve to begin with."

"Tell me about the side effects of the vaccine," Ryan said as he watched the sekers group together and move across the surface.

"From what I can tell, there were three separate trials and three different results." Louis picked up a notepad and waved it in the air. "The first group of Russian criminals suffered the worst. Before they modified the vaccine, the concentration was too strong and the resulting host reaction killed the subjects outright. The bodies swelled up like blowfish, joint and muscle fibers stretching until they split . . ." The doctor looked like he wanted to throw up.

Ryan grimaced. "How fast?"

"Fast. Killed the subjects within days. Remember the bodies in Medical?"

Plante wandered over carrying empty plates. "The kids are fed. Are the sekers out yet?"

Ryan pointed. "Just left."

"They're still riled up after your intrusion. They'll probably loiter in the area for several weeks before falling back into their routine."

"Dr. Louis was telling me about the vaccine trials," Ryan said. "I can't believe Wilshire partnered with those scientists after what they did."

Plante shrugged. "People will do terrible things in the name of survival. The Russians pleaded with us to understand what was at stake. They convinced Wilshire all they needed was time to improve the vaccine."

"More time? Really?" Louis flipped to a dog-eared page in the journal. "I told Ryan how the first vaccine trial killed the convicts. The second attempt occurred several weeks later, after they removed the adjuvant and adjusted the concentration of the serum."

Ryan frowned. "Adjuvant?"

"A booster. Stimulates the immune system to react stronger than normal."

"I'm guessing the second attempt didn't go well either," Plante said.

Louis nodded. "That's where the sekers came from. Research notes indicate most subjects survived the vaccine but suffered damage to areas of the brain, specifically the limbic system."

"Which does what, exactly?" Plante asked.

"Controls our emotions. In common parlance, they became raging psychopaths."

"Christ," Ryan muttered. "That explains a lot. Can't see how they can manage basic maintenance."

"Besides their suits, it's not much," Plante said. "The station is falling apart. Power levels are below optimal, and the hives have depressurized."

"Doesn't surprise me," Louis said, "considering the amount of brain damage. And that leads me to the experiments on the third group."

"What happened to them?" Ryan asked.

"That's the big question." Louis lifted the notebook to display the last pages, all of them blank. "I knew they reformulated the vaccine, but there's no record of the results."

"What's your best medical guess?" Ryan said.

Louis turned to Plante. "I think the third group survived the vaccination process. I think that group included the scientists and what criminals remained. Those are the ones who stayed hidden while we conducted our salvage operation. The question is, how many are left?"

"It turned into a clusterfuck when the sekers were released," Plante said. "My initial impression was maybe a couple of dozen, but they were in pretty bad shape. Not sure how many are still breathing."

Ryan fumed. "I should have paid more attention to Sasha when she found those live circuits in the other Alliance station."

Plante carried the plates over to the sink. "So, what are our next steps?"

"For me?" Ryan turned his glare on the surface of the asteroid. "I've got to figure out an escape plan before we starve to death."

Louis glanced around the lab. "My next step is to figure out what exactly they injected into the third group and if it's the real deal."

Plante wiped his hands on a cloth. "And that's important why?"

"Because somewhere in this room, there might be a cure for the plague, and once Ryan figures out a miracle escape plan, I'm taking it with us."

"You can't be serious." Rutherford stared at Kasim through the narrow window in the brig door. "The antenna? You have no idea what could happen."

Kasim felt awkward speaking through the small opening, but he wasn't prepared to open the door and allow the scientist and the hulking deuterium miners access to the hangar.

"Maybe not," Kasim replied. "But touching the artifact a second time turned off the energy beams—"

"For now," Rutherford sniffed. "Who knows what else you may have initiated."

"—and it hasn't stopped emitting particles since," Kasim finished, letting out a slow breath. "The colony is in a safer place. Reattaching the antenna might allow us to make contact."

The scientist's eyes widened. "That's crazy. Letting it send a signal home would shine a spotlight on our location, effectively telling them how vulnerable we are."

"They're an advanced race," Kasim said, trying to hide his frustration. "Surely, they're beyond war and violence."

"And you know that how? Based on your experience with ruthless dictators in war-torn countries?" Rutherford's lips twisted into a sneer. "The UN was always a collection of hopeless idealists. Thank God the politicians kept your kind on a short leash."

"Yeah, those dictators did so much for their people," Kasim said before putting a lid on his emotions. "Look, I didn't come here for a fight. I came here to see if you'd agree to help Vrabel modulate frequencies on the computer while he tries to reattach it." Unfortunately, Europa didn't have a plethora of trained physicists.

"To help you shoot off a flare for the aliens? I don't think so." Rutherford folded his arms across his chest. "You're going to have to find someone else."

Kasim sighed. It had been worth a try. He picked up his helmet. "I'll let you know how it goes."

"Wait!" Rutherford stepped up to the door. "We've been stuck in here for days. I demand a trial. The colony is no longer under martial law, so you can't deny me due process."

Kasim stared at him. In a previous life, he would have capitulated on the spot. But something inside had changed. Some lever had been pulled. This man had tried to harm Rani and tear down what Ryan had so carefully constructed over the past year. Kasim recognized the spectra of hypocrisy when he saw it, and it turned his stomach. But it also shielded him from putting the colony at risk.

"Yeah, I'm working on that," he replied. "Damn paperwork keeps slowing me down."

Ryan stared out the portal and searched for the right spot on the horizon before pointing. "The Alliance station is this way?"

Plante stopped chewing on the remains of a carrot and followed his finger. "That's about right. Just two klicks with zero cover or hiding spots."

Ryan ignored the implication. The landscape was painfully tedious, with different shades of gray competing for attention. But if they were going to get out of there, they had to cross that desolate landscape. Unfortunately, after weeks of bouncing ideas off one another, they realized they couldn't accomplish that on their own. They needed help. "And there's no way to repair coms?"

"We'd have to get to Ops, and even then, there's no power in the terminal."

Ryan rubbed his chin thoughtfully. "I've been thinking. What about line-of-sight contact?"

Plante put down his food. "You mean like a flashlight? The only problem is, someone has to see it."

"Someone like Gunner?"

"Him or the sekers," Plante said. "The latter wouldn't be good."

"It wouldn't," Ryan agreed. "But if we need help to escape, and we do, we have to tell them where we are." He ran his gaze over the heat lamps. "How would you feel about me stealing some of your gear?"

Plante stared at his precious garden and frowned. "You'd hasten the ending? Not sure it's the best decision."

"On the contrary, it's our only option and a risk we have to take. If I can build a searchlight, we'll be able to signal anyone that comes in range."

Plante seemed to ruminate on the decision. After several seconds, he sighed. "Best we harvest what we can first. How strong can you make the beam?"

"Strong enough to reach the horizon."

The governor gave him a look suggesting he didn't know whether Ryan was joking. "How long?"

"Not long if we have the right pieces . . ." He stopped when a loud thud erupted from the fire door. It sounded like a shotgun blast.

"Shit." Another bang shook the frame. Plante started running. "Grab the metal box on the bench. The one wrapped in yellow tape."

Ryan hurried to the counter and picked up the box. He had a brief glimpse of Louis standing frozen, mouth agape.

"One of the sekers must have crawled through the fence," Plante huffed. He slid back a metal cover and put his eye to a spyhole. "Yes, there's one out there." He recoiled when the door shook again.

Ryan leaned over his shoulder. "What's he doing? Hitting it with something?"

"Sekers use their bodies as weapons. He's slamming himself against the frame. Either he breaks a bone and goes down, or the door cracks and we lose our last line of defense."

Ryan felt the embers of panic begin to burn. They had nowhere to retreat. "What do we do?"

Plante leaned over and pulled a knife from the box. He picked through the tools until he found a second one and passed it to Ryan. "Prepare yourself. We're only going to get one chance at this."

Ryan stared at the short blade. A butter knife might have been more dangerous. "We're going to attack him? With these?"

"You just told me our only option to escape involves tearing down my greenhouse," Plante said. "I'm telling you now our only option to stay alive is to do what I say." He pulled a long metal rod out of the box and attached it to a wire that dangled from the doorjamb.

"You built a cattle prod?"

"It only holds one charge," Plante said. "But it's all I got."

The door juddered again, and fine grains of sand drifted off the frame.

"Ready?" Plante asked.

Ryan nodded. His guts had twisted themselves into one large knot. No way he wanted to go face-to-face with one of those abominations again.

The governor slid open a second metal cover and inserted the bar. Then, keeping one hand on the handle, he looked through the tiny hole. "He's checking the area, searching for a weak spot."

Ryan held his breath. He felt a measure of guilt for making the hole in the fence, but looking back, he hadn't had a choice.

Plante's grip tightened on the bar. "He's coming back . . ."

He shoved the bar through the hole and a sizzling *zap* filled the air. The hair on Ryan's arms stiffened, and something akin to ozone tickled the back of his throat.

Plante threw open the door and charged. Ryan was one step behind him.

The seker lay twitching on the concrete landing. A male, probably in his late thirties, although it was hard to tell beneath all the dirt and blood. His unshaven face was covered in old bruises and scars. Plante descended on him before Ryan could react. The knife flashed once, twice, sending droplets of blood into the air.

Ryan dropped to his knees beside Plante, but the seker was already drawing his final breath, the governor's knife wedged between his ribs.

"Help me get him inside," Plante wheezed.

Ryan grabbed one arm, and together they dragged the body into the room. Louis had recovered enough to close the door behind them.

"Wait a second," the doctor said. "Let me have a look."

Ryan stopped, and after an indecisive few seconds, Plante also released his grip. Louis ran his scanner over the corpse as the governor pulled his knife free with a sucking sound. The kids peeked out from the closet, eyes wide.

"I'm reading multiple organ failure," Louis said, eyeing the small screen on his instrument. "But more important . . ." He held it over the skull, the dead man's unseeing eyes silently accusing. "There's significant cerebral damage. Looks like someone took an eggbeater to the frontal lobes."

"An eggbeater in the form of a vaccine?" Ryan said.

"Probably. But the only way to know for sure is to do an autopsy."

"What?" Plante stared at him. "Are you serious?"

"Sorry, but it'll confirm what I'm reading in the lab notes."

Ryan gritted his teeth and looked at Plante. "Would you mind?"

The governor glanced to where the kids huddled in the closet. He exhaled. "Do it in the back. I'll move some desks over to block the view."

Ryan didn't mention the smell. That would be impossible to hide.

They hauled the body across the floor and lifted him onto a table. Ryan took one last look at the scarred face, the wild eyes now glazed over, and the bloodstained fingers, and he shuddered. If the human race wasn't on its way to extinction, it was only because it had stopped for lunch in hell.

"Come with me." Plante picked up tools from the metal box. "We have to fix that hole in the fence before more of them crawl through."

Louis held the door as they slipped out.

Ryan caught his eye. "If we don't come back . . ."

"You will, Ryan. You always do."

A small breeze of confidence filled Ryan's sails. He followed Plante to the landing as the doctor closed the door behind them.

"Stay quiet," the governor whispered. "Sounds carry in the stairwell." He passed Ryan a wrench and extra wire before descending the stairs.

Ryan watched his footing. Broken glass and debris covered the concrete like dead cockroaches. A sudden screech of metal echoed up the stairwell, and Plante froze. He put a finger to his lips.

Ryan nodded and forced himself to breathe slow. Someone or something was moving down there.

They tiptoed to the second landing. The thick chain-link fencing was as Ryan remembered, although he didn't recall the rust that covered the mesh like a layer of paint. Plante pointed and a tide of guilt rose in Ryan's veins. The fencing had been pried further off the wall. Now the space was wide enough to jump through.

The governor didn't waste a second. He hurried to the defect and began pulling on the PVC-coated wire. Ryan joined him, careful not to rattle the twisted metal. They stopped twice when something moved in the stairwell below. After several minutes of tugging, Plante was able to loop one of the diamond-shaped pieces over a nail that had been embedded in the concrete wall. Once that side of the fencing was anchored, they attached the other links in short order.

Plante wiped his brow, and Ryan realized he too was sweating. It was humid in the stairwell and neither of them were in the best of shape. He gestured to the smashed door on the lower level, and Ryan's guilt meter rose another notch.

"I didn't realize you broke the door at the bottom of the stairs," Plante said, after they returned to the lab.

"Sorry about that," Ryan replied, watching Louis close and bolt the fire door. "We had about two seconds to find a hiding spot before we were discovered. It was the only exit in the hallway."

Plante shook his head. "Problem is, they now have access to the stairwell. Which means they will eventually stumble on the fence." His gaze drifted to the body in the back of the room.

"And your cattle prod?" Ryan asked.

"Takes two days to recharge. Once they get past the fence, they *will* get in."

Ryan mulled his options. The governor was right. Static defenses only worked for so long. "That settles it. We're on a timeline. When they hit the door, we have to be ready to run."

Plante's eyebrows rose and fused. "You have someplace in mind? Because I'm pretty sure we're in the penthouse. There's nowhere to go."

Ryan glanced at the large portal at the front of the room. "There are always places to go, Governor. Some are just more attractive than others."

# CHAPTER 27

*Do not impose on others what you yourself would not desire.*

DAY 99, 0800 HOURS

Jesus, old man. Are you sure this is a good idea?" Sasha said, her brow furrowing as she scanned the surface. "The sekers could be just over the horizon."

They knelt behind a low ridge. Sasha kept glancing back at the station barely visible in the distance. And the gator hidden behind a shallow swell.

"We need intel," Gunner said, using binoculars to scan the Federation station. "And this is the only way to get it."

Sasha grimaced. "We're sitting ducks out here. If we get spotted, no way we make it back before they catch us. Even with the gator."

"Then they better not spot us," Gunner said. "Keep your binoculars working. Two sekers went by an hour ago. A little warning is better than no warning."

Sasha swallowed and raised the glasses. "Sybil says no way they're still alive."

Gunner heard the governor say the same thing before he suited up. His first instinct was to smash his fist into the man's face. It wouldn't change Plante's mind, but he would feel a lot better. "Sybil and the governor are singing out of the same prayer book."

"She reminds me of Harriet Creaser," Sasha said. "We hated her as well."

Gunner turned his gaze on the young engineer. "'We'? From what I saw, she had the backing of many colonists."

"But not most. You heard and saw the vocal minority. The rest of us weren't fooled."

Gunner went back to scanning the Federation station. He and Braeder always suspected as much, but it was still nice to hear. It removed some of the guilt from his soul.

Something caught his eye. "What's that?"

Sasha tensed. "What's what?"

"I saw something flash on the station."

She rotated her binoculars. "Which side?"

"Window on the left corner. Third floor."

Gunner focused his glasses. Another flash. "There it is again."

"Wait a second." Sasha held up one finger as the light flickered. "Pass me the flashlight."

"What? No. The sekers might see it."

She punched his shoulder. "Look, you old fart, that's Morse code. Do you want me to answer?"

Gunner blinked. "Morse code? I haven't used that in years."

"Yeah, so, give me the damn flashlight and get ready to move your fat ass."

It was Gunner's turn to glance nervously at the gator before passing across the light. "What are you going to say?"

She narrowed the beam and aimed it at the window before sending out a pattern of long and short bursts. "Just an acknowledgement and a question."

Gunner scanned the surrounding regolith. Nothing moved. "A question?"

"I'm asking about a plan."

More flashes appeared. Sasha nodded and lowered the light. "Okay. Time to leave."

"What happened? What did they say?"

"Tell you on the way." Sasha got into a crouch and started for the gator. "Before the sekers show up and decide to ruin our day."

"What do you think?" Ryan asked, staring at the barren surface.

"It had to be Gunner," Louis said. "The Neanderthal wouldn't leave us for dead."

"They took off fast enough." The governor pulled his jacket tighter around his thin frame. "So, what happens next?"

Ryan leaned against the portal. "Now that they know we're alive, Gunner will put together a rescue plan. That means we have to be ready."

Plante frowned. "Not sure what we can do in that department. We're trapped on the third floor and there's no way to sneak the kids past those bloodthirsty monsters."

"Don't underestimate our lieutenant," Louis said, giving Ryan a sly smile. "Have you noticed how quiet he's been lately?"

Plante cocked an eyebrow. "That mean something?"

"Just that he's thinking about something. I'm guessing a plan. Is that right, Ryan?"

Ryan didn't answer. Their options were limited. He fingered the ripped fabric on his arms. "It's probably time we switched suits. Governor, you said you had extras?"

"That's correct." Plante stood and walked over to the locker. He hauled out two Federation EV suits. "They're not as comfortable as ours, but they'll work in a pinch."

Ryan took one set and passed the other to the doctor. "I'm not complaining. What about the kids?"

"They have their own. We can dress them when it's time."

Ryan turned to Louis. "How's the research coming?"

The doctor withdrew a notebook from his pocket and used his stump to steady it while he flipped to the right page. Ryan was reminded of how much losing a limb interfered with life. Everything took longer and was more deliberate.

"I've just about finished," Louis said. "Everything confirms there were three waves of experiments. The mutants are definitely from the second group, and the fact there's essentially no notes on the third group is interesting."

"*Interesting* is not a word I would have chosen," Ryan said.

Louis rolled his eyes. "I'm talking on a cellular level, Stupid Lieutenant. Instead of their bodies rejecting the vaccine like the first group, or suffering brain damage like the second, they must have survived. Which means the vaccine didn't damage the prefrontal cortex."

Ryan pursed his lips. "But does it kill the bacterium?"

"Can't tell." The doctor waved his hand. "Yet." He picked a hard drive off one of the shelves and placed it on the table. "This is the one I found in Medical. I thought I lost it in the mad dash to survive, but it was stuck in my EV suit."

Ryan glanced at the charred edges. "Looks like it was in a fire."

"Wilshire started several fires when they made their break," Plante said, studying the burnt slate. "I remember the one in Medical."

"Yeah." Louis said, an undertone of regret in his voice. "This could answer our questions. I'm guessing it includes details on the vaccine and the third test group. Now it's toast unless someone like Sasha has a go at it."

Ryan plucked it out of Louis's hand and held it up for inspection. "Maybe I'm paranoid, but if someone wanted to deliberately conceal the results of experiments, burning the evidence would be a good way to start."

Plante frowned, like he hadn't considered that angle. "That makes sense. Something criminals would do to cover their tracks."

Ryan sat down and tried to organize his thoughts. He felt like time was slipping through his fingers. "It's been weeks. I'd like to know what Wilshire is waiting for."

"An opportunity," Plante said. "I know the man. He's like a lion waiting to pounce. When it happens, it'll happen quick."

Louis took his last spoonful of tomato soup and paused to savor the taste. "Since I'm a little short-handed at the moment, I require your services." He offered Ryan a self-deprecating smile and nodded toward the corpse at the back of the room.

Ryan rubbed the stubble on his face. "Not sure what I can do. My medical career never got off the ground."

"Follow me." The doctor led Ryan toward the seker.

Ryan nearly choked on the smell. It was like meat left out in the sun too long. The doctor had removed a large flap of skin on the side of the scalp, and something white peeked through a thin layer of muscle.

"I need you to cut through." Louis outlined the area with his finger. "I don't have a bone saw, so you're going to have to use this." He passed Ryan a hammer and a chisel.

Ryan stared at the primitive implements. "You're not serious."

Louis tilted the seker's head to better expose the surgical site. "This was done thousands of years ago by individuals with less training than you. Besides, he's already dead. How much more damage can you do?"

Ryan felt the acid pool in his stomach. "You really need this?"

"I need to confirm the lab notes. If what they say is true, I should see the characteristic signs. Now hurry up. We don't have all day."

Gritting his teeth, Ryan placed the edge of the chisel against the bone. He struck it once with the hammer, and a piece flew off and landed in the sink. It felt like he was carving a frozen turkey.

"Harder," Louis said, inspecting the site. "Along the muscle."

Ryan grimaced but lined up the chisel. Another whack, stronger this time, and he felt something *give* under the blade. His stomach heaved, and he hurriedly looked away. He hit it again and the bone sank an inch.

"Good," Louis said. "Now extend the line."

Viscous fluid leaked around the edges of the fracture, forcing Ryan to breathe through clenched teeth. He extended the cut and then turned the chisel ninety degrees. More whacks with the hammer. Liquid squirted out, covering his shirt. He retched in his mouth.

Louis eyed him critically. "You need a break?"

Ryan nodded and ran to the nearest garbage bin. Even the smell of his own vomit didn't compare to the miasma drifting over the corpse. It took a few minutes before his legs signaled they could safely bear his weight. Louis handed him the tools.

"Complete the cut on the other side."

Reluctantly, Ryan struck the chisel with the hammer, careful to tilt his face away from the impact site. When the cuts lined up, Louis stepped in and gripped the edge of the bone with a thick pair of pliers. Ever so slowly, he peeled it back with a wet, sucking sound. Strings of fleshy tissue hung off like wet spaghetti. He placed the bone on the lab counter.

"Isn't that interesting?" The doctor peered inside the skull, his nose almost touching the gray, amorphous mass that bulged out like a greasy balloon.

Curiosity outdueling his revulsion, Ryan stepped up. "What am I looking at?"

Louis touched the brain with the tip of the pliers. "See these black stripes? They're dead portions of the cerebrum. It's like someone applied a soldering iron to the prefrontal cortex. That's why they're running around like madmen. They have zero control of their limbic system."

"Can they reason?"

"When they're not stimulated. As soon as the brain receives a rush of endorphins or a burst of nerve impulses, they lose control."

Ryan lifted his arm to breathe through his sleeve. This close to the corpse, the smell was overwhelming. "You found what you were looking for?"

Louis grunted and used his sleeve to wipe his forehead. "Yeah, if the vaccine did this . . . they never had a chance. It's like their brains rotted from the inside."

"So, we can get rid of the body now?" Even to his own ears, Ryan sounded desperate.

"Ah, sure." Louis seemed distracted, and Ryan could visualize the wheels spinning behind those glasses. "You realize what we're seeing?"

"A human being who was used as a rat in some misguided experiment?"

"Not exactly." Louis touched the corpse with his pliers. "This is humanity's first salvo in the fight against the plague. An early version of a vaccine that tried to marshal the resources of our immune system. Yes, there was significant collateral damage." He tapped the gray tissue. "But the person survived."

"Excuse me, but it sounds like you agree with what the Russians did to these people."

Louis's eyes narrowed. "Don't get all high and mighty on me, Ryan. Your soul isn't exactly pristine after what happened on Europa."

Ryan felt the tips of his ears redden. He started to protest when Louis waved him silent.

"Of course, what they did was unconscionable, and I can say with absolute certainty I would never have taken these steps. But we're talking past tense. This seker is evidence of a partial cure."

Ryan kept his mouth shut as the doctor's words sank in. His gaze strayed to the portal at the front of the room. The darkness of the void seemed to parallel humanity's descent into oblivion. Even the survivors on Ceres were living on borrowed time.

Plante walked over, interrupting Ryan's pernicious thoughts. He took one look at the exposed brain and shuddered. "I hope you got what you needed, Doctor, because frankly, you're scaring me. What's next?"

"We need to find out what happened to the third group. The fact the Russians tried to burn the evidence tells me they feel guilty as hell about the atrocities they committed."

Plante shook his head. "Wilshire's bunch may feel guilty, but it's not enough to dissuade them from further action. They're completely without morals."

"I should have been more suspicious," Ryan said, kicking himself.

Louis put a hand on his arm. "Not your fault. We all missed the signs."

Ryan fumed. How could he have been so blind? Another threat to humanity that never appeared on his radar, just like the civilian insurrection and the senator's marines.

"Are we done here?" Plante asked.

Louis put down the pliers. "We're done."

Plante found a plastic sheet tucked in the corner. He handed one end to Ryan. "Wrap it in this."

Ryan draped his end over the corpse. "Stairwell still quiet?"

"Yes, although I can't escape the feeling we're living on borrowed time."

No one argued. They all felt the same.

"What's your friend Gunner going to do?" Plante asked.

"He'll be back in the morning. I expect some sort of plan."

"What if the sekers see him?"

Ryan's expression hardened. "Then I hope he can run."

"You expect me to believe that?" Standing in front of the portal in the observation room, the governor showered Gunner with an incredulous look. "Random flashes of light coming off the station?"

"They weren't random," Gunner repeated, exasperation creeping into his tone. He nursed a bottle of water at the bar. "It's Morse code. Braeder and Louis are alive and they've got four survivors with them."

"Or it could be reflections off the metal corners of the station," Bennett countered, pacing in front of Plante.

"It was repeated twice," Gunter said.

"How do you know it was Braeder?" Sybil asked.

"Because the lieutenant is resourceful. He would have figured out a way to communicate."

The governor threw up his hands. "You said only the doctor and the lieutenant got separated. Where did the other four come from?"

Gunner shrugged. "Who knows."

Bennett looked down her nose at him, making Gunner want to slap that haughty expression off her face. Sybil seemed to waver, like she was balancing on a fence.

"We're down to a handful of bodies, and you want to risk everything in some crazy rescue attempt?" Bennett said. "The smart move is to get off this rock before the sekers kill us."

"That's the third time you said it in the last ten minutes," Gunner growled. "And I'm tired of hearing it."

"All right." Sybil slid into a chair opposite the veteran. "Let's say they're alive. How do you propose to get them out? Considering they're trapped on the top floor and there's no way we can fight our way in. Not with two lasers."

"Chan and I are working on that. For now, we need to send a message. Let him know we're coming."

Plante raised both hands, like a soldier surrendering in battle. "I'm not going out there. Not after what happened last time."

Gunner stared at the man. His character was shining through, and it wasn't noble or virtuous. "Don't you worry, snowflake; I'll be the one taking the risk."

Plante glared.

"You're going by yourself?" Sybil asked.

"The gator should be recharged by morning, and Sasha's agreed to come." Gunner looked the governor up and down. "At least she has the balls."

# CHAPTER 28

*Never contract friendship with a man who is not better than thyself.*

DAY 100, 0740 HOURS

A cascade of stars flickered overhead as Gunner crept across the asteroid's surface as a cascade of stars flickered overhead. The ranger dictum of "moving slow and staying low" was impossible to follow when the asteroid's weak gravity refused to cooperate. He felt like a target at the end of a shooting range, waiting for the first shots to ring out. His feet sank several inches into the regolith, which made him yearn for past battlefields: hard-packed dirt or valleys filled with bone-dry brush.

He stopped and glanced over his shoulder. The gator sat half-hidden behind a low ridge, exposed black rock through gray powder. Perhaps five minutes away if the sekers spotted him.

The Federation station loomed in the distance, a collection of blocky modules assembled on site. It screamed utilitarian, a reflection of the political system, and contrasted with the smooth lines of the Alliance colonies. The dirty white color blended into the background.

He crouched down and pulled out his binoculars. The window on the top level reflected feeble starlight, preventing him from seeing inside. He removed the flashlight from his satchel and settled into a small depression.

It had been a last-minute decision to leave Sasha in the station. She wasn't happy, but he remembered his promise to Braeder about keeping her safe. At least this way, she had time to complete her work on the other weapon.

Taking a deep breath, he hit the button. Long, short, long, long, short . . .

*Rear entrance. Three days.*

His pulse picked up as seconds ticked by. How long did he have? He scanned the surface. Nothing. He was ready to repeat the message when a light flashed and his heart skipped a beat.

"Damn, Ace," he muttered. "What have you got for me now?"

The reply was short and blunt, and Gunner's jaw clenched. *He can't be serious.*

Movement on the ice focused his attention: dirty EV suits leaving the hive. It was time to get out of Dodge. He hurried back, his suit fans picking up speed as they dealt with increased heat production.

The gator waited for him like a close friend. He clambered into the driver's seat, hit the power button, and slammed his foot on the accelerator. A quick glance over his shoulder confirmed mutants closing in from both sides.

"Gunner to Sasha. Message sent. Inbound now."

Sasha came back immediately. "What about the sekers?"

"On my ass, but I should be okay."

"You think the lieutenant got the message?"

Gunner smirked. "Oh, he got it and changed it."

"What?"

"Rescue timetable has been moved up."

"Moved up?" She sounded incredulous. "To when? I still need time to build—"

"Tomorrow. Oh nine hundred hours."

The pause on the other end was all Gunner needed to hear.

It took longer for Rani to empty her stomach this time. Despite not consuming meals during cryo-sleep, the human gut continued to secrete digestive juices that accumulated as the rest of the GI system remained in a paralytic ileus. Some people tolerated it better than others.

"Sorry to wake you, Cap'n," Solomon said. "But I just received a message from Gunner."

Rani took a small towel and wiped driblets off her chin. She could only imagine how bad her breath smelled. Not that she really cared, since the rest of her body felt worse. Her brain took several seconds to corral her thoughts. "How did you get the message?"

"It was my turn to perform diagnostics. Here." The big miner passed her a bottle of water, and Rani forced herself to take a sip and then another. The aches and pains slowly faded, and one question popped out of the others.

"What did it say?"

"It's encrypted. For your eyes only."

"All right." Rani took a final drink from the bottle before putting it down and swinging her legs over the edge of the cryo-pod. Solomon reached out and steadied her as she took a few tentative steps. Her legs trembled like a newborn colt.

It was an effort to maneuver herself into the pilot's chair. The com light flashed expectantly as she punched in her code, and the speaker came to life.

"This is Gunner on Ceres. Rani, if you're receiving this, I have bad news. We're launching a rescue mission for Braeder tomorrow, and I'm having a hard time convincing the locals to support the effort." Rani thought she detected an undertone of anger. "If you don't hear from me in the next forty-eight hours, consider yourself the new boss. Good luck with that."

The message ended, forcing Rani to rein in her emotions. Who was Gunner kidding? If they lost the lieutenant, they were as good as dead. No one else could run the colony. She played with the rings on her finger, the nervous habit returning in times of stress. The gold band was her last memory of Marco.

"What are we going to do?" Solomon asked.

"Nothing we can do," she said, rubbing her temples as a headache loomed. They were pushing the engines too hard already. "Gunner is on his own."

*Day 101, 0635 Hours*

A single *whack* on the door focused their attention. Plante's head spun toward the sound, and Louis's eyes widened until Ryan thought they were going to roll back in his skull.

"Shit!" the governor blurted. Ryan caught his expression before he sprinted toward the door. The man looked scared.

Ryan grabbed the knives and followed.

Plante bent over the spyhole. "Three of them. Milling around on the landing."

"It's too early," Louis whispered. "Gunner won't be here for another two hours."

Ryan nodded grimly. The sekers had found a way past their makeshift repair job on the fence. Their honeymoon period had just ended. "Get the kids into their suits, Doc."

Louis hurried over to the closet where three anxious faces peered out.

Plante straightened as a second blow shook the frame. "It'll only hold for so long."

Ryan passed him a knife. "Just in case."

"We're trapped." The governor rubbed his arms, and his gaze darted around the room. "There's no way out."

"Not necessarily." Ryan watched Louis help the kids into small EV suits. "We just have to make another exit."

"The sekers are blocking the only . . ." Plante stopped as Ryan's words sunk in. "You have a plan, don't you?"

Ryan reached into the doctor's bag and hauled out the last IED.

Plante's eyes widened. "You're not serious. We're three stories up and you want to detonate a bomb next to the portal? The glass is reinforced to handle micrometeoroid strikes. The IED won't even scratch the surface."

"I'm not going for the portal," Ryan said. Just like on Europa, the internal supports were the weakest points, the most exposed. He recalled when the rebels had tried to cut through the floor of Europa's hangar in an attempt to steal food. They almost made it. What they lacked was the power of an explosive device.

Something slammed against the door, vibrating metal. The kids whimpered, and Louis pulled them together in a hug.

Ryan hurried up to the portal. Endless fields of gray stared back at him. No movement on the surface. As he zipped up his Federation suit, he checked the IED's detonator before clicking on the power source. The battery was small but would last long enough to do the trick. He linked it to his minicom and a tiny light turned green. The TNT packet lay flat against the metal frame, secured with strips of duct tape.

Louis finished getting the kids into their suits. "What do you want me to do, Ryan?"

"Move them somewhere safe. The explosion may not be an issue, but sudden decompression will suck everything out." Visions of the young ones being hurled into space made him shudder.

Louis clenched his teeth. "There you go again, hitting every problem with a hammer."

Ryan forced a grin. "If surviving was easy, Doc, everyone would do it."

Shaking his head, Louis picked up his helmet and herded the kids to the back of the room. Beside the corpse. To their credit, none of the young ones cried out.

Ryan searched for a seam in the wall. It was almost impossible while wearing gloves, so he peeled them off. After a minute, his fingers fell into a narrow depression. He repositioned his hands and hauled on the layer of plastek. It peeled back like wallpaper, exposing an empty space beneath the portal. He wrapped a hand on the wire running below the ledge and hauled out several feet.

Plante approached and examined the makeshift bomb. "I sure hope you know what you're doing. This is going to sound like a dinner bell to the sekers."

The governor's words triggered an image that made Ryan cringe. "Gunner is going to arrive in about ninety minutes. That means the IED must be in place and the kids ready to move."

Plante frowned. "Even if it blows a hole large enough, it'll take time to drift down to the surface."

"Which is why we're going to use this to pull ourselves down." Ryan handed the governor the wire he had hauled out of the wall. "Anchor it to something strong and pray it survives the explosion."

Plante glanced at the kids as if assessing Ryan's plan. "We'll each have to carry one down. I'll take the boy. What happens when we get to the bottom?"

"That part will be up to Gunner. I'm trusting he's got something planned."

Plante wiped his brow, and Ryan realized the governor was sweating profusely. The pressure of the moment. "Damn, Lieutenant, you're asking me to put a lot of trust in a man I don't know. If he screws up—"

"Sorry, Governor," Ryan grunted as he hauled another wire from the wall. "But I'm not asking anything."

Plante raised his eyebrows. "No?"

"Asking is only relevant if there's choice involved."

As if to accentuate the point, another *whack* echoed across the room. Plante's gaze swiveled to the sound and then back at Ryan. "Okay, point taken."

Ryan didn't like it either, but this was no time to play nice.

Louis joined them and tried to help Ryan haul out wire with his one hand. Plante seemed to come out of his stupor and joined in. When he figured they had enough, Ryan cut one end and tied it around an exposed plumbing conduit.

"I suppose you want three separate lines?" Louis asked.

"You read my mind, Doc." One for each of them. Any delay in getting to the surface was not something they could afford.

Two blows on the door in rapid succession sent Ryan's pulse pounding.

"They're getting antsy," Plante muttered. "That's usually a sign something's got their attention."

Ryan looked at his watch. Eighty minutes until Gunner arrived. He took the bomb and inserted it between the plastek beams under the portal. Whether this was going to work was anyone's guess.

Plante wound up a section of wire. "Not sure there's enough to reach the surface."

"Doesn't matter," Ryan said. "We can float down the final few meters." He reviewed the details in his mind. Unlike Europa, Ceres presented him with a new set of physics.

A heavy *bang* and the kids ran up to hug Louis. He looked at Ryan. "I'll stay with them. You good here?"

Ryan nodded. "Double-check their suits and helmets. We may have to detonate sooner than planned."

Louis picked up the boy. "We'll be ready." With that, he hurried over and settled all three under the counter. Both girls jumped into his lap.

Plante glanced out the window as the door shook again. "This is a shitty plan."

Ryan smiled in spite of himself and pulled on his helmet. "Gunner would say I have a history of shitty plans." He attached both ends of the detonating wire to the bomb and stretched it across the floor, careful to keep the two ends separated. Plante smoothed out any kinks.

"Better put your helmet on, Governor," Ryan said, running his hand along the struts in the wall. "When the time comes, there won't be any warning."

Plante grimaced but pulled the helmet over his head. Ryan heard the click of the internal com. "If anyone is sucked out during decompression, they'll probably reach escape velocity."

Ryan shivered. Shot into space like a rocket was not something he wanted to experience. The look Plante gave him told Ryan he was thinking the same thing.

Seventy-five minutes.

The surface was a static picture of regolith and impact craters. And, more importantly, no sekers. Thankfully, the mutants had to retreat into the hive to recharge theirs suits. And rest, if they did that sort of thing. Gunner crept up behind the low ridge and raised his binoculars. Nothing about the station had changed since yesterday.

Braeder had something planned; of that, Gunner had no doubt. What it was exactly, he hadn't a clue, so he decided to be ready for anything. And he had planned accordingly. If Braeder exited the front airlock, which was highly unlikely, he would use the gator to scoop him up and hightail it out of there. If he chose the rear airlock, Smith waited with a second gator. And then there was his backup plan using the transports. Just in case the sekers took out the gators. And their drivers.

His heads-up display said he was thirty minutes early. He surveyed the third-floor window, but nothing stood out. The thick, alloy-infused windows that reflected starlight were impregnable to the naked eye.

Whatever the lieutenant had planned would happen when the man was ready. He had learned to trust Braeder. Over the course of a hellish year, the young, naïve lieutenant had transformed into a true leader.

A *click* in his ear stole his attention.

"Gunner, Chan here. Powering up engines on the transports now. Waiting on the governor and Bennett, and we'll be ready for liftoff. Which means I need coordinates."

"Understood," Gunner replied. "For now, just get them in the air." Even as he uttered the words, he realized how foolish they sounded. As if Earth metaphors applied here. But humanity hadn't developed enough verbiage to cover the new physics of space exploration. He listened to Chan's two clicks as she signed off.

His gaze returned to the building. The mutants weren't usually active this early, but that could change on a dime, just like when they attacked Gonzalez. He had wracked his brain all night trying to figure out Braeder's plan, but there were too many unknowns, so he shut down his thoughts and managed a few hours' sleep. He was scanning the station through his binoculars when the com opened.

"Gunner, we got a problem."

The veteran forgot about Braeder. "Talk to me, Chan."

"Engine started throwing up red lights. I sent Sybil out to take readings."

Gunner's pulse skipped a beat. "Something wrong with the engines?"

"Don't know. Bennett went with her. Hopefully, it's nothing serious, but I wanted you to know we'll be delayed."

Shit. Gunner checked his watch. If they needed those transports . . . "All right, Chan. Just get airborne ASAP."

He scanned the surface. Experience had taught him that when one part of a plan goes awry, the rest usually follows.

The blows on the door had become stronger and more persistent. The sounds echoed through the room and gnawed at them like fingernails across slate.

The frame shook, and dust wafted off the ceiling. Ryan half-expected it to give way any second.

"It's not going to hold much longer," Plante warned. He gripped the underside of the lab bench with both hands but kept his gaze firmly on the door. "The room was designed to be airtight, not a bank vault."

Ryan didn't reply. His gaze landed on the doctor, who had his arm spread around the kids like a mother hen. They were still twenty minutes ahead of schedule. God knew if Gunner was ready.

Another heavy *thud*, and this time a *crack* echoed across the room. A jagged fissure appeared in the middle of the door.

"Shit!" Plante exclaimed. "It's going . . ."

Ryan didn't bother replying. He had anchored himself to the base of the sink, one hand wrapped around the metal drain and one hand holding the detonator.

Louis's low voice played over the com as he tried to calm three panicked children.

Ryan said a silent prayer. For any of them to live, they had to survive the blast, hope the explosion blew out the portal, climb down thirty feet of wire, and make a mad dash across the surface. Before the sekers ripped them apart.

He felt like he was back in Europa's concourse, trying to stop the rebel advance.

A loud crash and the door split in half.

"Lieutenant . . ." Plante warned.

Ryan had a momentary vision of two sekers squeezing through the narrow entrance, faces scarred, hands bloody from assaulting the door.

"Braeder!"

After five painful minutes waiting on Chan to report, Gunner gave up and opened a channel. "Chan, what the hell is going on? It's almost time."

The voice that answered turned Gunner's blood cold.

"Sorry," Sybil said. "The governor and I discussed your plan last night, and we're not prepared to take the risk. There's a good chance we could all die here, and then what happens to the human race?"

Gunner forced himself to take a breath. "What are you doing, Lecky? Where's Chan?"

"She's here," the governor answered. "She just can't talk because she's got a knife at her throat. Ms. Lecky is correct. We're not prepared to assume more risk, not after the year we've been through."

"What are you talking about?" Gunner felt like someone had just pulled out the reality rug from under his feet. "Braeder was taking you back to Europa. You and the others were safe."

"That's where you're wrong," Plante said, his voice rising an octave. "No one is safe on the colonies. They're not made to exist by themselves. The only way to ensure long-term survival is to return to Earth."

"You're crazy. The bacterium would kill you just like the other eight billion humans."

"It might have," Plante acknowledged. "Except that we're armed with something those eight billion people didn't have. A vaccine."

Gunner's thoughts swirled. The man had a vaccine? He checked the timer on his heads-up display. Fifteen minutes. "Governor, I need those transports to rescue Braeder."

"And we need them to get off this rock."

Gunner slammed his fist on the steering wheel of the gator. "Sybil, tell him! Without those transports, you're hanging me out to dry."

"Sorry, Gunner." She actually sounded apologetic, remorseful. "I . . . didn't want it to come to this."

"We're taking both ships," Plante said, his voice disgustingly sweet. "So, enjoy the asteroid. I hear the water volcanos are out of this world." He snickered at his own joke.

Gunner balled his fists. "You can't take the transports to Earth. We didn't prep them for a long journey."

"Unfortunately, you are correct," Plante said. "Which means we have to head back to Europa first and prepare the ships."

"Rani will never let you land." Even as he said it, Gunner knew his words were bullshit.

"The ensign will make a deal." Sybil sounded confident, like she was negotiating from a position of power. "She knows how desperate the colony is for replacement parts. We'll agree to surrender the parts and she'll allow us to land."

Gunner seethed. "You're condemning Braeder to death."

There was the briefest hesitation before she replied. "I'm sorry about that, too, Gunner, but like I said, I really don't believe he's alive. Not with sekers controlling the station. Not after this long."

"You don't know that!" Gunner hissed. "We have a chance to bring everybody home and you're pissing it away."

"No, Gunner, I'm trying to save what's left." With that, the channel closed.

Gunner jumped off the gator and spun to face the Alliance station, a dark smudge on the horizon. He kicked a black rock out of his path, throwing up a plume of gray dust.

*What the hell was he supposed to do now?*

His thoughts were in a state of chaos when something exploded in the Federation station.

# CHAPTER 29

*To see the right and not to do it is cowardice.*

DAY 101, 0815 HOURS

Ryan hooked his arm around the metal drain and touched the exposed ends of the wires together. Flames burst out of the wall, followed by a cloud of black smoke that poured into the room. In the doorway, the sekers stopped moving, their jaws dropping in shock. Ryan felt the beginnings of panic—the portal was still intact—until a large crack appeared in the center. It branched into a dozen smaller fissures that tracked to the edges. And then smoke rose to cover everything.

Louis's voice in his helmet. "Ryan, what . . ."

A tremor shook the room. Something akin to an earthquake he'd felt on the American West Coast when he was young. Except this one died as rapidly as it appeared, and sucked the smoke away. He had a momentary visual of a gaping hole where the portal used to be before sudden decompression created a gale-force wind lifting him off the floor.

Plante cursed and gripped the counter with both hands as his legs were pulled over his head. Ryan prayed the doctor had secured the kids. Everything loose was sucked out in a storm of debris, a massive vacuum cleaner with the setting on infinite. Chairs, clothes, Louis's lab books, even the corpse wrapped inside the sheet. In the span of several heartbeats, the room emptied, and two sekers were carried away on the leading edge of a tsunami. Other mutants, wedged in the doorway, held on until the freezing tentacles of space froze their lungs and the nitrogen in their arteries ripped their damaged brains apart. They sank glassy-eyed to the floor, fingers twitching as the last nerve fibers died.

Ryan released his grip on the metal pipe and stood. What was left of the portal had been twisted into a shattered mirror, each splintered fragment reflecting a different image. Pieces of paper and ripped fabric floated in vacuum, caught on jagged plastic edges or twisted around metal conduits.

Ryan automatically checked his heads-up display: oxygen, temperature, and other vitals in the green. "Doctor?"

"Here, Ryan. Kids are good."

"Plante?"

"Bruised but intact."

"Okay, Governor, grab the first line."

Plante pulled himself to a standing position and took a breath. "On it, Lieutenant."

Ryan withdrew two of the cables he had secured around the bulkheads and leaned over the broken ledge, careful to avoid razor-sharp plastek slivers. The smallest puncture spelled a death sentence. Thirty feet below, the surface of the asteroid waited. It took a second to switch his brain to the new physics. If he jumped that distance on Earth, it'd spell broken bones or worse. Here, it meant a ponderously slow descent and a waste of valuable time. He tossed both cables over the side and watched them fall in slow motion.

Louis slipped past him with the kids in tow, each one holding on to the other's suit. Plante grabbed the boy and started rappelling down, while one of the girls wrapped her arms around the doctor's neck before they began to descend. Ryan scanned the horizon. Gunner wasn't supposed to arrive for another ten minutes . . .

"Surface looks clear." Plante said. He had already descended twenty feet.

"Head away from the entrance," Ryan ordered. "Don't wait for us."

"Copy that."

Ryan felt like a clumsy teenager as he cradled the third child and secured the guidewire. It took precious seconds to get a rhythm going, and by the time his feet sank into regolith, both Louis and the governor had a thirty-foot head start. Plante cradled the boy in his arms while Louis held the hand of the girl and pulled her along.

Ryan chanced a glance at the main airlock. He exhaled when he realized it remained closed, the indicator light over the entrance black. Ryan whipped his gaze back to the surface and started running before he tempted fate. The fans in his environmental unit ramped up to compensate for increased heat production, and the sound of his breathing rang hollow in his ears. They moved as fast as the kids could manage. Fifty feet. One hundred.

"Ryan!" Louis's panicked voice. "They're coming!"

Ryan looked over his shoulder. The indicator light had switched to red, which meant the hatch was depressurizing. Someone was preparing to exit.

*Damn. Where was Gunner?*

The light over the airlock flashed green.

"Hurry!" Ryan shouted.

The doctor scooped up the kid in his arm and lengthened his stride. Plante increased his pace. Ryan marveled at the governor's abilities on the surface. Years on the asteroid had taught him how to move in low gravity.

The metal door cycled open and a mutant stepped onto the surface. Its helmet swiveled back and forth as though confused by multiple targets. Finally, it focused on Louis and began to move. Ryan felt sick. It was too fast. One look confirmed the rate of closure at less than a minute. The airlock door shut and the light shifted to amber as it began to cycle. That meant more were coming.

Ryan angled toward the doctor. If he could intercept the seker, Louis could keep going with both kids. Before they were overwhelmed by bloodthirsty mutants charging out of the hive.

Something flashed in his peripheral vision.

"There!" Ryan shouted. It had to be Gunner. "Aim for the light."

The seker closed inhumanly fast. Its EV suit was smeared with dirt and dark stains, and frayed bits of cloth fluttered on its legs. A predator closing on its prey.

Ryan released his grip and pushed the kid forward. "Keep going!" Then he shifted his weight and changed his angle. The gap narrowed and, at the last possible moment, he launched himself off the surface. "Doc, get down!"

Louis doubled over, arm draping across the kid like a protective parent. The seker's arms flailed, sentenced by its momentum to sail past. It swiveled in midair and landed on its feet, wild eyes fixed on its prize.

That's when Ryan hit him. Three percent gravity reduced Ryan's two-hundred-pound weight to six, but the impact was still solid enough to knock the creature sprawling.

Ryan pounced, reaching for the oxygen seal behind the damaged helmet. He had a blurred image of a scarred face, patchy beard, and black-rimmed eyes. Dirty gloves scraped across his faceplate. A foot kicked out, narrowly missing his neck. Ryan let go when the seal refused to budge and slammed his fist against the helmet. The faceplate cracked. A second uppercut missed badly, the low gravity playing hell with his coordination.

The seker wrenched his arm back and hurled him off. Ryan twisted away from a fist that whiffed in front of his helmet, but he couldn't avoid the body tackle as the mutant drove him to the ground. The regolith wasn't hard, but the creature falling on top set off warning bells. He recalled the marine landing on him outside Europa station, cracking his ribs, before Chan ran him over with the gator. This time, the mutant whaled on him with its fists. Ryan managed to block a score of blows, but then one got through and whacked his helmet. He saw stars. Another fist struck his shoulder, and pain like an electrical buzz shot up his neck.

A small voice in his head said he couldn't survive this, so he swiveled his hips and thrust the creature off. It fell away in slow motion, and Ryan cursed the asteroid's physics.

A channel in his com crackled open. "Lad, need some space!"

Ryan didn't take his eyes off the seker as it hauled itself to its feet. It rotated to face him, flexed its legs, and jumped. Ryan dove to the side, landing awkwardly, and thrashed like a turtle on its back.

Gunner's laser flashed.

The seker twisted in midair, no doubt confused by suit alarms going off. The fabric melted and split, and an exodus of air allowed the suit to constrict like vacuum wrap. Red splotches dotted the whites of the seker's eyes before it collapsed.

"Ace!" Gunner hollered. "There's more of 'em coming."

Ryan hauled himself to his feet. A quick glance at the station confirmed four sekers pouring out of the airlock. The veteran had one kid in his arms already while Plante clambered aboard the gator with his human payload. Louis was fifteen feet away.

"Shit! Gunner, what's the plan?"

"Load everyone on the gator and hightail it out of here. So, move your ass!"

Twenty yards. Ryan's legs were already in motion, and he closed the distance fast. Gunner pivoted the gator and hit the accelerator as soon as Ryan got a hand on the siderail.

Louis reached out and hauled him over the side. Through his faceplate, he looked terrified. "They're faster than we are."

Ryan glanced over his shoulder. The four sekers were coming hard. "Where's the laser?"

"By my feet, Ace, but it'll do you no good." The veteran didn't take his eyes off the surface as the gator bounced across ancient impact sites. "Battery was only good for one charge."

*Damn.* If they were going to make it back to the Alliance hive, they needed to buy time, and there was only one way to do that. He dropped his legs over the side of the gator . . .

A hand squeezed his shoulder. "Don't be thinkin' of any hero shit." Gunner's gruff words in his ear. "I got something else in mind."

Ryan relaxed as the veteran let him go and gripped the steering wheel. The vehicle was going at top speed, and it still wasn't fast enough. He swung the gator hard to the right to avoid a gaping fissure.

"They're closing . . ."

"Be patient, Ace," Gunner said. "Need another minute."

Ryan was about to ask what the hell he was talking about when something appeared on the horizon or, more accurately, above the horizon. He blinked. "What's that?"

Gunner looked back and grinned. "Just a little surprise Sasha dreamed up."

Ryan peered closer. "A drone?"

"Not just a drone. A drone with teeth."

Ryan heard a com channel open and Gunner's voice. "Sasha, we're entering the target zone. Be ready."

"I see you," she said. "Damn, old man, they're right on your ass."

The sekers were closing the distance in chunks. Gunner had a minute at most before they'd be near enough to shake hands.

"I need space between you and them," she warned. "This is not an exact science, and I really don't want to kill the lieutenant."

Ryan noted the drone dropping into an attack run. "Just do it, Sasha. I promise I won't blame you. No matter what happens." The obvious retort—that if Ryan died, there wouldn't be a blame game anyway—was left unsaid.

The sekers were twenty feet away and closing. The kids' sobbing sounded in his ear.

"Ten seconds," Sasha said, her voice shaky. "Hang on."

Starlight reflected off metal wings as the drone leveled out.

Plante wrapped his arms around the kids and crouched down inside the vehicle.

At the last second, Gunner angled the gator behind a small ridge of surface rock.

Ryan had a brief impression of the drone impacting the surface smack-dab in the middle of the four sekers. He closed his eyes as a giant hand slapped the gator and the vehicle skidded sideways, slewing through half a foot of gray powder. The engine emitted a high-pitched squeal and gave out with a final shudder.

"You okay, Ace?"

Ryan felt a hand on his arm. "Yeah, everyone else?"

Plante and Louis answered in the affirmative.

"Kids are good," the doctor said.

Ryan turned and stared into a cloud of gray powder, and four bodies lying motionless on the surface. "Hell of a shot, Sasha."

"Thanks, Lieutenant," she said, "but it was more luck than skill. We didn't have time to fine-tune the control unit."

Another gator approached from the direction of the Federation station.

"That's Smith," Gunner replied to Ryan's unasked question. "In case you went out the back exit."

They unloaded the kids from the dead gator and filled the second vehicle. Gunner picked up the laser and waved at Sasha, who was running from her hiding spot on the surface.

Something about Gunner's expression bothered Ryan. He had seen it before when things went sideways on Europa. "What's wrong?"

Gunner grunted. "Your girlfriend and the governor decided they don't want to play with us anymore. They've hijacked our transports."

"What? When?"

"I found out minutes ago."

"How did they get into both ships? The codes for the hatch—"

"Lecky," Gunner said. "She knew the codes."

Plante leaned in. "Did I hear you talk about *the governor*?"

Ryan pointed a finger. "Gunner, this is Max Plante."

Plante extended his hand and, after a pause, Gunner reached out and they shook. "So, who's the imposter?"

"Name's Wilshire," Plante replied. "One of my former Board members who bought into the old saying of every man for himself. Figured once they got the vaccine, they could head back to Earth."

Gunner frowned as Sasha climbed into the gator. "So, they do have a vaccine?"

"Explanations will have to wait," Ryan said. "Where are the transports now?"

"They were prepping for launch when they contacted me," Gunner said, lifting his gaze to scan the heavens. "Don't know if they left yet."

Ryan squinted into the darkness, but all he saw was a blanket of distant stars. He opened a channel. "Braeder to Sybil. Come in."

There was a brief delay before the line connected. She sounded surprised. "Ryan? You're alive?"

"At least for the moment." Ryan stole a glance over his shoulder. A seker was trying to pick itself off the surface, but one leg was bent at an unnatural angle. "Gunner tells me you've decided to plot a different course. Again."

"They have a vaccine, Ryan. We can return to Earth."

Ryan looked at the doctor, who had a strained expression. He shook his head.

"If that's true, Sybil, let's sit down and discuss it. We don't have to make rash decisions."

"Sorry, Ryan, but I know you're not going to abandon Europa. Wilshire and I agree that the only way to survive is to go somewhere that has unlimited resources, and that doesn't include any of the colonies."

"We found out about the vaccine," Ryan said, exchanging a look with Gunner. The man's expression had turned feral. "We also learned that Wilshire had marooned the real governor over here. Along with some surviving kids."

By the pause on the other end, Ryan figured Wilshire had omitted telling Sybil certain details. "Sybil, you there?"

"I'm sorry, Lieutenant," Wilshire said. "But she's done talking."

Ryan's anger ballooned. "She's done, or you won't let her?"

Wilshire chuckled. The sound sent a chill down Ryan's spine. "Doesn't matter. We have control of your ships and are getting ready to launch."

"Why don't you wait until we return to the station, and we can discuss this."

"I don't think that's in our best interest, Lieutenant."

"The pilots will never take your orders."

This time Wilshire's laugh seemed genuine. "Actually, you'd be surprised what pain can do to a person's motivation. Stoll came around quickly. Chan, on the other hand, took more convincing. Plus, we happened to have some sodium thiopental. That always helps."

Louis's eyes widened, and he mimicked injecting a needle into his neck.

Ryan closed his eyes. *Truth serum.* "You hurt my crew and I'll kill you."

"Well, Lieutenant, you're going to need awful long arms, because in a few minutes, we'll be gone, and you're going to starve."

"Where are you going?" Ryan already knew, but he wanted it confirmed.

"Since the transports aren't equipped for a long journey, we have to make a pit stop to prep them before we head in-system."

Ryan felt like his chest was about to explode. Never in his life had he wanted to hurt someone so bad. Wilshire was stealing his crew and his ships, and snuffing out hope of leaving this rock. And he was going to land on Europa and take over *his* colony.

"I have fifteen hundred people on that moon. Ask Sybil. They're depending on me to keep them alive."

"Don't worry, Lieutenant; I'll be sure and leave them a few scraps."

Ryan willed himself to stay calm. "With a vaccine, we can work together. Our doctor can manufacture more. We can save everyone and return to Earth." He tried to keep the pleading out of his tone. By the look on Louis's face, he wasn't entirely successful.

"After the last year, I no longer believe in altruism," Wilshire replied, his voice suddenly as hard as ice. "And you wouldn't either if you saw what happened here. Bottom line, I'm not buying what you're selling. So, goodbye, Lieutenant. Have a good life, as short as it may be."

Ryan gripped the side of the broken gator. "I'll find you," he snarled. "There is no place in the solar system you can hide. I will find you, and you will pay."

Wilshire laughed. "Sure, Lieutenant. Whatever you say."

The line went dead.

"Should never have brought that viper here," Gunner growled.

"It's not all her," Plante said, meeting Gunner's stare. "Wilshire may be a bastard, but he's smart. I'm guessing he found out what makes her tick and pressed the right buttons."

Ryan couldn't trust himself to speak. He took the laser from Gunner and walked up to the surviving seker. The mutant was still trying to right itself on one leg.

"There's no charge in the battery," Gunner reminded him.

Ryan didn't answer. He gripped the barrel with both hands and swung at the helmet. The faceplate shattered. Space sucked the air and the life from the seker. The body seized for ten seconds before going limp.

He walked back to Smith's gator and sat down in the front passenger seat.

Sasha stared at him wide-eyed.

"How long to the hive?" he asked.

"Twenty minutes," Gunner replied.

Louis pointed. "There go the transports."

Ryan tilted his helmet. Two ships rose over the distant Alliance station. They banked overhead before altering course and ascending into the void. "Don't worry," he murmured. "Fate has a way of evening the score."

Even before they removed their EV suits in the decompression chamber, Sasha ran up and gave Gunner a massive hug. "I thought you were dead, you old fart. Those sekers got damn close."

Gunner's face turned beet-red. "It'll take more than a pack of zombies to put me down."

She turned to Ryan. "It's good to see you and the doctor again, sir. You gave us quite a scare."

Louis helped the kids out of their EV suits. "*Scared* is a good word, Sasha, but *terrified* might be a better description. The sekers broke into our hiding spot, and the lieutenant had to detonate the bomb early. They almost caught me on the surface." He nodded at Ryan. "Thanks for jumping in when you did."

"No problem." Ryan gestured toward Plante. "Sasha, let me introduce you to the real governor of Ceres, Max Plante."

Sasha's eyes widened. "The other guy—"

"Was a fake," Plante said, zipping down the top half of his suit. "A Board member who turned traitor and joined the Russians."

"Son of a bitch," Gunner murmured.

"It gets worse," Ryan said. "There were a bunch of Wilshire's accomplices hiding in the station the whole time. Waiting for this opportunity. I should have listened to Sasha and checked out those electrical circuits."

"I'm guessing they took the replacement parts with them." Louis looked to Gunner for confirmation.

The veteran nodded. "Stabbed us in the back."

"I see they left in a rush," Plante observed. "Didn't bother to stick around."

"Probably because they knew the lieutenant was coming for them," Louis said. "Another twenty minutes—"

"Could have been twenty or two hundred," Ryan spat. "They still got away."

Louis helped the young boy step out of his suit. "They didn't just *get away*. They took our ride and probably every morsel of food. At this moment, we're looking at six adults and three kids. Nine mouths to feed."

"No food?" Sasha asked and focused on the kids. "And they are . . ."

"The last survivors from the Federation station," Plante replied, rubbing the boy's hair. "I found them in the upstairs lab."

"What happened to their parents?"

When Plante didn't respond, she paled.

# CHAPTER 30

*Ability will never catch up to the demand for it.*

DAY 108, 0558 HOURS

Gunner fell into one of the chairs around the small plastek table in the observation room and rubbed his weary eyes. "You're good, Ace, but you're not that good."

Ryan didn't answer. He sat at the head of the table, gaze fixed on the ceiling. It had been a week since Wilshire had hijacked the transports and marooned them on the asteroid. A week of scrounging for food and a way off this rock. A week of futility.

"He took every scrap from the greenhouse," Gunner continued. "As well as the vet's vitamins. Don't know why he'd want those."

Louis stopped watching the kids long enough to stab Gunner with a scathing look.

The veteran ignored him and turned his attention to Plante. "The food you brought from the Federation station is nearly gone and the cupboards are empty."

"What about other stations?" the doctor asked. "Any chance they left something behind when they opened their EV doors?"

"Unfortunately, no." Plante folded his hands on his hollowed stomach. "We made runs to the other colonies after we came out of hiding. A mouse couldn't survive on what was left."

Sasha slid her chair back from the table and wandered up to the portal. "I can't believe we're going to starve to death. After all we've been through?"

"I'm sorry, little lady," Gunner said. "I don't see a way out of this. Wilshire fixed us good. There's no way off this rock."

"What about other ships on the asteroid?" she asked, her voice trembling as the implication sank in. "We need to check their landing strips."

Plante shook his head. "When Fleet grounded the transports, there was only one ship on Ceres. It was at the Caliphate station, and it left two days before they opened their EV door."

"What about the Russian transport that delivered the plague sample?" Gunner asked. "And the ship with the food that diverted from Mars? Are they still here?"

"No," Plante replied. "They launched months ago. Before the Federation station opened its EV door."

Ryan leaned forward. "Let me guess. Some higher-ups decided to make a run for it when the food supply dwindled."

Plante shrugged.

"Another shining example of human nature," Gunner muttered.

Sasha placed her hands on either side of the portal. "I hate this place. It's so dreary and . . . boring. I don't want to die here."

Smith silently nodded his agreement.

Gunner looked at Ryan. "Like I said, Ace. You're not that good. Houdini couldn't find a way out of this mess."

Ryan didn't answer. He had played every card in his hand and lost. How did he not see this coming? The live circuits Sasha detected should have hinted at others hiding in the station. Wilshire's lies about not using the EV suits should have triggered his sixth sense. Even the suspicious fire in Medical should have rung a bell. Individually, each item seemed random and inconsequential but together formed a conspiracy that would cost them their lives. And, worse, doom his colony.

He slammed his fist on the table. The kids jumped. One squealed in alarm.

"Ryan," Louis cautioned, reaching down to soothe the frightened child.

"Sorry." He forced himself to sit back. Relaxing was a bridge too far. He couldn't abide failure. Not after having gone through so much. After losing friends and family. After surviving famine and insurrection. To fail now because of a stupid oversight . . . to a bunch of criminals and traitors . . . He bit his tongue so hard, he tasted blood.

"Excuse me," Sasha said in a voice that made her sound like a little girl.

Gunner, mired in his own depressive thoughts, looked over. "Yeah?"

"They took both transports, right?"

Louis stopped soothing the kids. "Wilshire? Ah, of course."

Sasha frowned but didn't say anything.

"Is something wrong?" Plante asked. "You seem . . . preoccupied."

She tapped her finger against her lower lip. "If the transports are gone, and there's no other vessels on this asteroid, why am I seeing a ship coming in for a landing?"

There was a race to the portal.

The com units in the EV helmets had limited range, which is why it took ten minutes for Sasha to find a frequency that worked. "Got one!" she announced.

Ryan stopped pacing and raced over to grab the helmet. He held it up so everyone could hear. "Ceres Station to approaching transport. Do you read?"

The squelch of static filled the line. Sasha reached over and adjusted several controls before Ryan tried again. "This is Ceres—"

"Ceres Station," a male voice broke in. "We read you. This is Alliance transport *Justice*. Who's in command down there?"

Ryan stared at Gunner. *Justice*? "This is Lieutenant Braeder."

"Understood, sir. Wait one."

There was a brief pause until a familiar voice filled the airway. "Lieutenant! Thank God you're alive."

Ryan sagged against the portal. "Damn, Rani, it's good to hear your voice. How in hell did you end up here?"

"Figured you might need a hand, sir. The messages were getting bleaker every day."

A smile slowly formed on Louis's face. Even Gunner grinned.

"Damn, Ensign. We're glad you decided to visit."

"What happened to the other transports?"

"It's a long story, Rani. What say you land and we'll bring you up to speed?"

There was a brief pause, and Ryan heard a muted discussion in the background. Then Rani was back. "It might take us a few minutes, Lieutenant. My pilot is very green, and he wants to review the landing protocols one more time."

Ryan recalled Chan coaching Stoll as he landed *Serenity* on the asteroid. "No hurry, Ensign. We're not going anywhere."

Rani chuckled. "I guess you need a lift?"

"You got that right." Ryan paused, and his expression tightened. "One last thing. When you do land, do not open the hatches. I repeat, do not open the hatches."

"You want us to stay onboard, sir?"

"I want you to stay alive. There are survivors wandering the surface that you do not want to meet."

Ryan didn't know who was more surprised: Gunner, after Rani ran out of the airlock and wrapped her arms around him, or Plante, standing by the door, watching the overt display of emotion. After a pregnant pause, Rani stepped back and took off her helmet. "Good to see you alive. After that last message, we feared the worst."

"Aye, it wasn't looking good."

Rani turned and walked over to shake Ryan's hand. "Sounds like you had quite the scare, Lieutenant. We saw the suits on the surface as we made our final approach. Didn't figure them for bloodthirsty savages."

"They're that and worse, Ensign." For some reason, Ryan felt a small void form in his gut. He glanced at the two people Rani brought with her from the transport. "Pilot Marcel, right?"

He shook his hand. "That's correct, Lieutenant. We met during Chan's training sessions."

Ryan recognized the third face. He had left the miner with instructions to assist Rani in running the colony. "Solomon. Welcome to Ceres. I wish it were under better circumstances."

Solomon nodded at Rani. "Cap'n hinted you might need our help."

"She wasn't wrong." Ryan pointed at Plante. "This is Max Plante, governor of Ceres."

Plante raised a hand in greeting.

"Rani, how many people did you bring?" Ryan asked.

"Eight, sir. The three of us and five reservists."

"When did you leave Europa?"

"About thirty days ago." A hint of a smile appeared at Ryan's sudden consternation. "We pushed the engines, sir."

"And the cryo-pods handled the extreme velocity changes?"

She held up her hands. "No strokes or heart attacks."

Ryan grimaced. "You were lucky. And Chan will still have your head for taxing the engines."

"She will, sir, but I figured time was a factor."

Ryan paused, unsure if this was the moment to bring it up. "I understand there's been an unprecedented discovery on the moon. Just so you know, I only told Chan and Gunner. No one else."

Sasha's ears perked up. "What discovery?"

Ryan held up his hand. "In a minute. First, Rani, did you detect the transports leaving Ceres?"

Rani's brow knotted. "We did."

"Did you get a chance to confirm their trajectory?"

She let out a breath. "Europa."

"Any way we can catch them?"

"Not unless you have a warp drive in your pocket. They have too much of a head start."

Ryan's jaw tightened. That made his decision easier.

"What discovery?" Sasha repeated, pumping her arms.

Rani started to answer before Ryan cut her off. "I think everyone needs an update of what's happened, both here and on Europa. Before we do that, I have two questions."

Rani tilted her head. "Sir?"

"How is the colony faring?"

Rani put down her helmet and unzipped the top of her suit. "Not great. The laser keeps shorting, and I've had a little problem with some scientists and miners."

Ryan's eyebrows peaked. "Problem?"

"We had an . . . incident, and I had to throw some of them into the brig."

By her hesitation, Ryan sensed this was a topic they should discuss in private. "Okay, how many lasers did you bring?"

"Ah . . . ten all told, and twice as many batteries."

"You got a plan to use them, Ace?" Gunner asked.

"We need that wire in the Federation station."

"There's still sekers on the surface," Louis reminded them.

"Can't be that many left," Ryan said. "And the cavalry just showed up. It's time we end the war on Ceres and leave this damn rock."

"We're going back to Europa?" Rani asked.

"As soon as possible," Ryan said. "And this time, it'll be us attacking the colony."

Gunner snorted. "Then I hope we do better than our old friend Senator Lecky."

*1650 Hours*

Alone in the briefing room, Kasim paced back and forth beside the plastek table. He would have compared himself to a caged tiger, except that the carnivore moved with lethal intent. Not much of a resemblance to his nervous stride and the waves of angst that rolled through his gut. Even now he felt like throwing up. He was never good at handling the emotions that came with conflict: anxiety, trepidation, and intimidation. Braeder was better at that stuff. Well, maybe not in the beginning. He wondered if, at some point, he would acquire the skill set required to become as cold-hearted as the lieutenant.

*Nah, it's impossible to change this late in life.*

He stopped pacing long enough to pick up his lemon-infused drink. It was lukewarm now and barely palatable, but it was all they had, so he dared not waste it.

The door swished open and Vrabel walked in. "Sorry I'm late, but we're still working on the laser."

Kasim grimaced. The reason for the meeting. "Where's Archie?"

"On his way." Vrabel walked over and drew a cup of hot water from the dispenser. He sipped on it before taking a seat at the table. "Any word from Rani or the lieutenant?"

Kasim shook his head. "I stopped by Ops on my way here. No messages."

"Who's on duty?"

"Mobin. He knows to alert us if the com starts flashing."

Vrabel arched his eyebrows. "I hope he knows to alert us if *any* button starts flashing."

Kasim settled in a seat opposite the engineer and let out a long sigh. "True, that. At least he was a computer programmer before turning colonist." Too many of the civilians covering shifts were teachers or maintenance workers. Great attitude. No experience.

Archie almost fell into the room. "Sorry," he grumbled, prompting Kasim to wonder if the last thing to fail in the colony would be manners. It seemed everyone was sorry for something these days.

"The pump is fried," Archie said as he slumped into a seat next to Vrabel and wiped sweat from his brow. "That's the second time this week. There's a short somewhere in the laser. We need someone who knows what they're doing to find it."

Kasim recognized the indent on Archie's forehead from his EV helmet. After assessing the damage, he had rushed back to the station to deliver the bad news. "Can you get it back online?"

"Not until we replace the pump."

"I'll get a crew working to remove the old one," Vrabel said. "I figure maybe three hours. The problem is, where do we get a replacement? And even if we find one, there's a good chance it will fail in the not-too-distant future."

"How often do asteroids threaten the colony?" Kasim asked.

"Around once a month," Vrabel said, running a mitt-sized hand through his hair. "Although some months are worse than others. Which is why parts eventually fail."

"Like every other mechanical piece on this moon," Archie grunted.

"We could just leave it," Vrabel said.

"What? Leave the laser offline?" Kasim looked at him as if he had two heads. "We'd be defenseless."

"Only until Braeder gets back. He's supposed to bring extra pumps."

"We're still talking weeks," Archie said.

Kasim ran his palms over the table as two pairs of eyes fell on him. He felt the intensity in their glare. "Last time, we took one of the two pumps from Beta Hive. It's time to take the other one."

"What about the colonists?" Archie asked. "The water pressure will fall to useless within an hour."

"I'll put the word on the colony net. Everyone in Beta has to pack up and move to Alpha Hive. They have two hours before we turn off the power." He left unsaid that families would have to share domiciles. The colonists wouldn't be happy, and they'd be sure to let him know.

"What happens if that one shorts out too?" Vrabel asked. "You can't take any from Alpha Hive, not with the entire population of civilians depending on the plumbing."

"No, but at least it'll buy us time," Kasim said. "Every day with a laser shield is a blessing."

Archie stood. "I'll send a work crew to the hive and start removing the pump."

"Never mind," Vrabel said, waving a hand. "I'll handle that part. You grab a bite and maybe a short nap. You've been at this all night."

Kasim peered close. Archie's color was off, and the lines on his face seemed deeper than normal. Vrabel was right: the man was running on fumes. His own cardiac condition notwithstanding, they all were.

Archie started to protest when Kasim cut him off. "No bullshit. I'm ordering you to get some sleep. I'll wake you in four hours." He held the man's glare until Archie looked away. The geologist grumbled something about incompetent politicians before stomping out.

Vrabel chuckled. "I don't think the old man likes you throwing your weight around. He had better luck when Rani was boss."

Kasim saw red. How dare he infer Rani could be manipulated? "What the hell are you still sitting here for? You're the one telling me we don't have a lot of time."

Vrabel gave him a strange look as he took one last sip and headed out the door.

Kasim leaned back in his seat and waited for the expected guilt to bubble up. After all, Vrabel was a good lad and didn't deserve to get yelled at. But as the seconds passed, all he felt was a lingering frustration.

*Interesting*, he thought. Maybe it wasn't too late to change.

Everyone had gone to bed when Rani slipped into Ryan's quarters. Ryan stood at the portal, staring at the fields of regolith. "God, I hate this place. It's like spending your life in a sensory deprivation tank. It's—"

"A feeling of doom," Rani said, stepping up beside him. "I felt it the moment we landed."

Ryan smiled sadly and turned around. "I'm glad it's not just me. Take a seat."

She dropped into the only chair in the room while Ryan sat on the edge of the bed.

"I'm guessing you're here to tell me more about the artifact."

Before she could answer, the door hissed open and Gunner walked in. "Not going to start without me, are ya?"

Rani blinked. "You knew I was coming?"

Gunner smirked. "I suspected. You spent a lot of time playing with your rings when you told the others about the alien 'egg.' You only do that when you're nervous."

Rani's face took on a crimson tint, and she shoved her hands into her pockets. "Sorry, I haven't been able to break the habit since Marco . . ."

Ryan laid a hand on her shoulder. "It's all right. Why don't you tell us about the station first? You left Kasim in charge?"

She nodded. "I used your idea to slip my group into the transport without the colonists finding out. The only people that knew in advance were Archie and Kasim."

"I don't imagine they were happy," Gunner said.

"They were disappointed with my decision but they didn't argue," Rani said. "I think they had learned to trust me."

Ryan smiled. "Welcome to leadership. Anything else?"

"Like I mentioned, the colony is hanging on by a thread. The laser is temperamental, but the greenhouses are functional. I asked Archie to haul *Churchill* and *Atlantis* into the hangar after we left."

"And the scientists and miners?" Ryan prompted.

Rani related the events of the conflict with Rutherford's group, including the fight in the hive and the resulting incarceration.

"How did the colonists take it?" Ryan asked.

"As well as can be expected. Truth be told, everyone's mood has been subdued. The artifact is a big unknown."

"That's probably an understatement," Gunner said. "You found it in the ice?"

"Next to the extractor," she confirmed. "It's exothermic. That's what caused the cave to form." She went on to tell them about the deadly result when they tried to remove it.

"Anything you want to add to what you told the group?" Ryan said.

She grimaced. "After all we've been through, I feel stupid bringing it up."

"Try us," Ryan said as Gunner got comfortable leaning against the wall. "It's not like we haven't done stupid before."

A small grin broke through and she exhaled. "I told you how our scientists worked on it for weeks and ended up with exactly nothing. Which is why I decided to touch it."

"And initiated those energy beams," Ryan said.

"What I didn't tell anyone was what I felt."

Gunner straightened off the wall. "You *felt* something?"

"A presence. An immense and powerful consciousness. The moment I made contact with it, it made contact with me."

"Damn, missy. Did you talk to it?"

"No, in the moment, I was overwhelmed. It surged into my brain, a series of emotions that were so foreign and powerful, I almost passed out."

Ryan noted she had started playing with her rings again. "Did you get any information from it? Any underlying motive or purpose?"

She shook her head. "It was weird. The feeling was so all-encompassing, I thought I was going to drown, so I jerked my hand away. The emotions and sensations were something I can't even describe." She paused, gaze focused on the past. "Except for one."

Gunner tilted his head. "And that would be?"

"Curiosity. The artifact was just as inquisitive as we were."

The veteran frowned. "And you didn't follow up?"

She leveled her gaze. "I turned on a process that almost destroyed the colony, and you expected me to touch it again?"

Ryan got up and started to pace. "An alien artifact buried in the ice for thousands of years. And it's conscious?"

"No question in my mind, Lieutenant."

"Wilshire can't find out about this," Gunner said. "No idea what he would do."

"Agreed." Ryan stopped in front of Rani. "We'll send a message to Kasim to keep it a secret."

Gunner raised his index finger. "Ah, Ace. *Phoenix* can intercept our signals. If you tell the governor not to say anything about the artifact, Wilshire will learn about the artifact."

Ryan puffed out his cheeks. "Not to mention the message itself will confirm we're coming."

"Do you want to keep quiet?" Gunner asked.

"No," Ryan said. "Kasim needs to be forewarned. We can't have Wilshire showing up unannounced."

Gunner's jaw muscles tightened. "Then what do we do? Everything we say will be intel for the enemy."

"Not if we talk in code. Remember how we passed messages during the insurrection?"

"Right." Gunner relaxed. "When are you going to tell him?"

"About the artifact, or about Wilshire's plan to take over the colony?"

"Both."

"As soon as we're ready to leave. I want Kasim to know exactly how long he has to hold out before we get there."

"And the artifact?" Rani asked. "What are you going to do when we return to the colony?"

Ryan sank back down on the bed. It was the question he had asked himself since the meeting. "I'm going to talk to it," he decided. "I just hope I get the chance before Wilshire does something reckless."

# CHAPTER 31

*Virtue is not left to stand alone. He who practices it will have neighbors.*

DAY 108, 2130 HOURS

What do you think?" Kasim asked, hands clasped behind his back as he stared at the alien object. This late in the day, only Vrabel worked the sensors and computers, the other scientists having gone home to be with their families after another fruitless day.

Vrabel looked up from his monitor. "Not much to say that's not already been said. It's still sending out those weird antimatter particles at regular intervals, but no damaging emissions since you touched it."

Kasim savored a feeling of pride. In Rani's absence, it was his job to protect the colony. And stopping life-threating energy beams fell into that category. He watched Vrabel tap commands into his keyboard, biting his tongue before he commented on the engineer's gray complexion. The man had been up for twenty-four hours, helping Archie in Ops and then performing his regular work. He'd said he only wanted to check the computers before hitting the sack, but he seemed to be doing more than that.

"Isn't it time you got some sleep?"

"Couple more minutes. Just want to be sure nothing's changed."

Kasim offered a tired smile. "Like maybe it started broadcasting a welcome message in Swahili?"

Vrabel chuckled and threw up his hands. "All right. You win. I'm heading back to the station. You coming?"

"In a few minutes. I want to enjoy a few moments of quiet before I go back and face more angry colonists. The ones I evicted from Beta Hive want to space me."

Vrabel's smile dissolved. "It's been a tough week: no word from Rani and the loss of the laser pump." He paused, adjusting the settings on his computer. "Don't figure many people will blame you for shutting down a hive, not when it's a matter of life and death."

Kasim shrugged. "Something I learned from Braeder. People will assign blame just because they can, and it usually falls on the closest target. Most you can convince with logic and by pointing out the greater good. The rest will fall victim to their emotions."

"And those are the ones that spark trouble." Vrabel stared at the artifact.

"They're scared," Kasim said. "And everyone on this moon has good reason."

"Before she left, Rani said we were living on borrowed time."

Kasim paused, considering. "Can't argue with that. Our best chance is for Braeder to come good with replacement parts."

Vrabel shifted his gaze back to Kasim. "What do you think?"

"I think if Rani had anything good to report, she'd send a message."

Vrabel zipped up his EV suit and picked his helmet off the hook. "Don't stay too long, Governor. Tomorrow will be another busy day."

Kasim nodded. Archie had said as much before crashing for the night. He walked over to the artifact. The strange hieroglyphics flashed violet and gold. The antenna sat on a nearby table, looking lost without a grip on its big brother.

Vrabel cinched up his wrist straps and paused with his helmet over his head. "See you in the morning?"

"Yeah." Kasim watched the scientist step into the airlock before turning back to the empty lab.

The alien situation didn't make sense. When he introduced himself to representatives of a foreign country for the first time, he made it easy for new friends to reply to his greeting. There were no secret codes or handshakes or a Rubik's cube puzzle to solve. It was a simple black-and-white response. Which meant they were missing something.

Rani had plastered every bit of information about the artifact on the colony net. *Let everyone see and play with it,* she said. Was there a pattern in the strange etchings? Perhaps a formula or hidden message? The responses that came back were as varied as the colonists who submitted them.

Ellen said she and her bandmates were putting the final touches on a musical response. All that remained was for the engineers to finish building the instruments that could emit notes beyond normal human hearing.

*An artsy response to a science question?*

It kind of made sense: a melding of math and emotion, logic and passion. Something an advanced civilization would have achieved? Maybe.

There had been other colonist suggestions: insert universal constants inside ultraviolet light, sketch the human body out of gamma rays, bury it in the ice and ignore it.

One comment from a thirteen-year-old girl had stuck in his brain. “Touch it again,” she said. “The aliens are confused; help them.”

He might have taken the suggestion seriously except after the first human touched it, it initiated energy beams that nearly destroyed the colony. They only stopped after he put his hand on it a second time. Did he dare risk it again?

When he first read the suggestion, he dismissed it out of hand. It seemed crazy at the time. Now, with the colony one mechanical failure away from extinction, it held a certain appeal.

His feet were moving before the idea reached consciousness. The swirling colors seemed to beckon him, like a carnival Ferris wheel to a child.

Did he dare? Braeder had once told him they all had jobs to do on the moon, all had decisions to make that affected their collective future. Was this his moment?

He picked up the antenna. Many people had handled the light piece of metal, including Rutherford and his goons, so he knew it was safe. Without thinking, he aligned it with the end of the artifact. The two pieces fit snugly together like a washer over a bolt.

Taking a deep breath, and before his cowardly personality could exert itself, he touched the broken end of the artifact. For a second, nothing happened. It felt soft and viscous at the same time, as though his fingers could sink into a layer of slimy foam. Except they didn’t.

The surface markings momentarily blazed and went out.

Kasim jerked his hand away. What just happened? He was conscious of how quiet it was inside the lab. Right before all hell broke loose.

Buzzers erupted from surrounding scanners, and sirens blared from computers and wall-mounted speakers. The hieroglyphics blazed blood-red, and Kasim felt a wave of heat radiating off the surface. The structure of the artifact seemed to blur before settling back into reality, and the remains of the scissor truck compacted another inch. Ice in the floor cracked.

Vrabel came flying down the stairs. He slammed his palm on the airlock button and jumped in. Thirty seconds later, he ran into the room and ripped off his helmet. "What the hell happened?"

Kasim cheeks burned as he backed away. "I touched it."

"Goddamn." Vrabel stared at the pulsating red insignias. "The markings have changed."

"Changed? How?" Kasim stopped retreating. It was true: the etchings had transformed into straight lines. Some short, some long. Some bisected each other while others ran around the circumference of the artifact. "It's . . . different."

Vrabel stepped closer. "It's like some type of mathematical formula. No, multiple formulas. Look." He pointed to one section that encompassed rows of small vertical lines. "It's the prime numbers; one, two, three, five, seven . . ."

"Any emissions?"

The engineer hurried over to his terminal. "Nothing. Whatever you did is confined to this room or, rather, the artifact." He scratched his head. "What do you think it means?"

Kasim felt a smile coming on. "Get Ellen in here. I think we just started a dialogue."

*Day 109, 0900 Hours*

He had to rap his knuckles on the plastek surface to get them to calm down. Conversation around the table slowly ceased, and one by one, all heads swiveled in his direction.

Kasim pulled the sleeves of his thawb over his hands and leaned back. "Thank you. We're not going to accomplish anything if we keep bickering." He pointed at Vrabel. "You said you detected a positron emission?"

The engineer spun his handheld around so the other three scientists could see. "Started exactly ninety-seven minutes after you touched it, Governor. A single emission. The rate is similar to last time except it doesn't seem to be counting down. Almost like it's waiting for something."

Rutherford snorted. "Just when we deactivated the bomb, you went ahead and did something rash. How long until it starts firing energy beams?"

Kasim glared at him. It helped conceal the guilt that bubbled just under the skin. "I believe I *deactivated the bomb*. But put that aside for the moment because what we need now is a strategy. If you don't want to help, the reservists can escort you back to the brig." His gaze flickered to the pair of big-boned men cradling lasers by the door.

The scientist's eyes narrowed, but he didn't respond.

"You really think this is part of a *conversation*?" Vrabel asked.

Kasim nodded. His pronouncement was what had ignited Rutherford's ire in the first place. "I've been involved in hundreds of these types of introductions. There's always back-and-forth to establish credibility. I believe we're entering a feeling-out process."

The scientist beside Rutherford leaned over to get a better look at Vrabel's screen. "If that's the case, why did they fire lethal beams in the beginning? That seems more like a punishment than a handshake."

"I believe those quantum discharges were intended to send a message home," Kasim replied. "Because the antenna is not able to focus the message, we ended up with random discharges of antimatter. What we're seeing now is a dampening-down of that energy, and I believe it's intended to start a dialogue."

"You sound awful confident," Rutherford said. "What if you're wrong? What if it's like we said, the aliens are hostile and intend to subjugate us, and you're in the process of selling us out?"

Kasim gave him a look. "Somehow, I don't think a technologically advanced race would waste their time on a single energy weapon when they could show up with an armada and blast us to oblivion." His gaze swept the table: four scientists, including Rutherford. All of them retrieved from the brig in order to pick their brains. At the moment, they looked dubious. "I'll repeat my question. How do we respond?"

"I thought you were going to send the musicians in." The scientist on the other side of Rutherford sneered. He had a white keloid on his right cheek, a lingering scar from last year's insurrection. He claimed it was a random burst from a rebel laser. Gunner and Braeder had been dubious, but without witnesses, there was no proof.

"Ellen thinks they're ready," Kasim confirmed. "They're going to play a musical response."

Rutherford snorted. "And then we'll all sit around the campfire and sing 'Kumbaya.'"

His colleagues snickered.

Kasim glared until their smiles evaporated. "If that happens, the results will be exactly the same as yours, except you took weeks to reach that conclusion."

Rutherford didn't make eye contact.

The governor nodded at the pair of reservists standing by the door. "Take them back to the brig. They've been a tremendous help."

It took Ryan ten minutes to walk from the station to the transport, trudging through a thick layer of dirt. His mind dredged up an old memory of running up sand dunes in New Mexico on a family vacation. The sensation felt the same.

He passed six crispy EV suits half-buried in the regolith. After *Justice* landed, sekers had swarmed the transport. A few tried to scale the landing gear but, thankfully, the vessel was locked down, and nothing short of a laser cutter could penetrate the hull. Marcel, the pilot, briefly ignited the engines and ended the threat.

He ripped his eyes off the burned carcasses. Now was not the time to immerse himself in depressive thoughts. Reality was bad enough. The transport's ramp lay open like a dragon's maw waiting for a meal. Louis and Plante stood guard, lasers dangling from straps slung over their shoulders. The sekers never appeared this early, but Ryan had learned not to take chances.

The doctor acknowledged him with a curt nod. "Did you send the message to Kasim?"

"No. I decided to wait until we launch." He had wrestled with the decision all night. They had to warn the colony that Wilshire had hijacked the transports and that he and his criminal goons were en route, but at the same time keep the message brief and in code. Sybil and Wilshire were able to eavesdrop on every communication that entered the void, including the one Kasim sent to Rani telling her the colony was on the last laser pump, and there was a good chance it would fail in the near future.

Of course, that information was liquid gold for Wilshire. One less obstacle for them to overcome, not that Kasim was likely to shoot down the transports. Not with Chan and Stoll aboard.

"Do you think Kasim will reply?" Louis asked.

"I'll tell him not to. The less strategy that gets discussed over the airwaves, the better."

"I didn't know we had a strategy," the doctor deadpanned.

Ryan bit his cheek before he said something that didn't play well over the open frequency. Still, Louis was right; there was no strategy other than get back to Europa as fast as possible and try to intercept Wilshire before he destroyed the colony.

"What do you think Kasim will do?" the doctor continued, seemingly unfazed by Ryan's silence.

"I'm going to tell him to defend the station," Ryan said, stepping over one of the seker corpses. "For as long as he can."

Louis's expression hardened. Plante said Wilshire had escaped from the Federation station with about twenty survivors. The odds of Kasim and a few poorly trained reservists holding back a group of determined criminals hovered somewhere around zero.

Ryan changed channels. "Gunner, are you in position?"

"One minute, Ace."

Ryan checked his watch. "When you're ready, begin your sweep."

"Copy that," Gunner replied. "Solomon, Rani, keep it tight over there."

Ryan heard two clicks in response. He battled the urge to jump in the nearest gator and join Gunner's group. They had ten lasers and twenty batteries among them. The veteran had insisted he stay back with the noncombatants.

As he fumed, Louis caught his attention. He had a sparkle in his eye. "Didn't Captain Tracy once say leaders don't have to lead from the front?"

"Shut up," Ryan snapped. "I'm trying to listen."

"Right." Louis turned to Sasha and winked. "Of course you are."

Sasha joined Ryan as he stomped away from the transport. The fact that she only came up to his shoulder reminded Ryan of how small she was. Barely taller than Chan.

Ryan's attention remained focused on the com. The sooner Gunner dispatched the remaining sekers, the sooner they began stripping wire from the Federation station, and the sooner they lifted off for Europa.

"I see them," Rani said. "Solomon, keep your head down."

"Copy that, Cap'n."

"Easy," Gunner replied in a steady voice. "Let them get close. Solomon, on your mark."

"Understood."

Ryan recalled how the sekers had looked as they swarmed the gator last time. He shivered.

"Almost in range," Solomon said. "Four sekers. Ready . . . Fire!"

Ryan fisted his hands as he waited.

Finally, Rani's voice. "Four sekers down. Moving skirmish line forward. What's your status, Gunner?"

"Seeing two coming out the back entrance. They're moving to engage."

"Watch for stragglers," Ryan warned.

"Smith has it covered, Ace. Ready, lads . . . Now!"

This time, Rani heard the high-pitched whine of Gunner's weapon through the com.

"Targets down. Move forward. Rani, join up with my line."

"I see you. Coming across now."

Ryan exhaled. His crew could handle it. In a way, it was nice not to be needed. He walked back to Sasha. "Are you ready?"

The young engineer brandished a crowbar in one hand. "Just tell me how many feet of wire you want packed, Lieutenant."

Ryan looked up into the infinite void. Step one, sekers, done. Step two, get the wire. Step three, haul ass back to Europa. And hope the colony was still in one piece when he got there.

# CHAPTER 32

*Faced with what is right, leaving it undone shows lack of courage.*

DAY 109, 1327 HOURS

"Are you sure about this?" Archie asked. "Because last time Rani did something similar, it started chucking bombs around."

Kasim planted his fists on his bony hips and stared at the artifact. The weird markings hadn't changed since he touched it. For someone who had spent his life negotiating with warring factions, this felt familiar; both sides were waiting on a dialogue to begin and searching for the right process.

"I'm sure. We've been taking the wrong path with our science and machines. This response goes beyond math and reveals what we are as a species."

Archie gave him a look. "A species that keeps killing each other?"

Kasim grimaced. "You know what I mean." He stepped over to where Ellen and two colleagues were setting up their instruments. "Just about ready?"

The engineer put down her guitar and gave him a nervous smile. "I hope so. It's been a long haul." She inclined her head toward the drums and keyboard each with a box-like unit taped to the side. "We modified every instrument to play notes well above the normal range."

"I hope my touching the artifact and changing the markings didn't throw you off."

"Actually, it helped. The new patterns turned out to be a different representation of the same universal constants. We translated each weird-looking scribble into a note and combined them into a musical response."

"Well, whenever you're ready." He joined Vrabel at his computer. "Here's waiting for lightning to strike."

Vrabel grinned. "Can't be worse than the scientists, Governor. We set a low bar."

The musicians took their seats on stools they had carried from Alpha Hive. Kasim had offered them chairs, but they said musicians always played better when perched on a stool. Ellen warmed up her guitar while the two men—Kasim recognized them as teachers—practiced on their instruments. After a minute, Ellen stopped and gave them a nod, and they began to play.

The song was a slow, mournful piece, reminding Kasim of something that might be played in the background at a wake or a funeral. The underlying beat was established by the man on drums as he tapped softly with his sticks, while Ellen's guitar notes seemed to linger in the air. The young man on the piano played a melancholy form of a canto that was slightly out of rhythm.

After several minutes, Kasim threw an inquisitive look at Vrabel. The scientist checked his screen and shook his head. Nothing.

He waited another minute, until the musicians finished and the last notes faded, before walking up to Ellen. "It was a good try. Too bad . . ." He stopped when the markings on the artifact abruptly flashed and disappeared.

And a recessed door opened at the base.

"It'll take another day to load the transport," Ryan said, his hands buried inside the bulkhead. The corpses remained stacked against the back wall of the Federation medical room, and he did his best to ignore them as he worked to remove long sections of wire. "I want you to be ready to leave the minute we close the hatch."

Marcel's Adam's apple bobbed like a yo-yo as he pulled off the next piece of external casing. The newbie pilot didn't say it, but he looked nervous as hell about the prospect of getting back in the pilot's chair. "If you say so, sir."

"You got this. Chan's program does most of the work, right?"

"Ah, yeah." Marcel swallowed. "I wish there was some way to catch the other transports."

"Me too, but Rani says in order for that to happen, we need to figure a way to bend the laws of physics."

Gunner led Sasha into the room. She kept her gaze averted from the bodies.

"We found a few more sekers in the station," the veteran said. "Solomon locked them in one of the storage rooms."

Sasha gave him a look. "What's going to happen to them?"

"They're going to die," a new voice said. Ryan turned as the doctor walked in. "Without access to food . . . of any kind, they're not long for this world." He slumped into a chair. "When I examined one of the mutant bodies in the lab, I found widespread organ damage. It's just a matter of time."

"Best guess?" Gunner asked.

Louis shrugged. "Days. Maybe a week."

Sasha shook her head. "First a vaccine turned them into psychopaths, then they were abandoned. And we thought we had bad luck."

Ryan shared a look with the doctor. He couldn't argue.

Plante walked in, carrying an armful of processors. "Solomon found these in the hives. Looks like one of Wilshire's people was collecting them and got ambushed by the sekers. There was blood everywhere."

Sasha gasped, and Plante bit his lip. "Sorry."

"Not your fault." She waved a hand and composed herself. "It just seems wherever we go, we're surrounded by death."

"It's been tough," Ryan said, trying to ease her angst. "Not exactly what you signed up for when you joined the colonies."

"It could have been worse," she said in a quiet voice.

"How's that?"

"I could have stayed on Earth."

Gunner wrapped an arm around her shoulders and gave her a squeeze. "We'll be back on Europa soon enough. Think of all the repair jobs ahead of us. Just me and you and our closest engineering friends, all working to keep those non-engineers alive."

She pushed his arm away. "This time, you're going to give me my own work crew, right? I don't want to be stuck listening to your old war stories again."

Gunner feigned a look of shock. "Now, that hurts my feelings. After all the help I've—"

"Help?" She jabbed a finger into his chest. "You're the one who doesn't know the business end of a multitool or what gauge to use in the bulkheads. Hell, I make you look good."

Gunner's mouth opened, but no words emerged. He looked to Ryan for support, but the lieutenant threw up his hands and stepped back. He wanted no part of this.

"I think she's got you pegged," Louis smirked. "She's smarter than you by half."

Gunner's eyes narrowed. "That from a vet whose IQ is written on the bottom of his shoe."

The doctor's face reddened, and he looked about to snap back when Ryan intervened. "Enough. Time to gather your gear. Tomorrow is a big day. I want everyone rested and"—he stared at each of them—"cooperative. So, get packing."

Still muttering under his breath, Gunner headed toward the exit. Louis was right behind him.

"I think they like each other," Sasha said.

"Really?" Ryan's eyebrows rose in unison. "How can you tell?"

Sasha's gaze fell on the dead bodies. "Because they haven't killed each other yet."

*Day 110, 0500 Hours*

Sasha loitered to see if there'd be any fireworks, but this time, the doctor didn't argue about getting into his cryo-pod. Gunner seemed disappointed.

Ryan didn't comment. Every minute wasted was an opportunity for Wilshire to take the station.

"Thirty-five days," the pilot reported. "I rechecked our trajectory and ran the numbers, and that's what the computer says."

Sasha stopped undressing and looked at Gunner. "Five weeks?"

"Aye, missy. And we're still pushing the engines." He turned to Ryan. "Did you send the message, Ace?"

"I did. Kasim should be receiving it right about now."

"That's sure to ruin his day."

"It will when he learns Wilshire's going to land before us."

"Yeah," Gunner grunted. "And you know he's gonna try to repair the laser and blow us out of space."

Sasha shivered. "Will he do that?"

"He's already responsible for hundreds of deaths on the asteroid," Gunner said. "What's a few more?"

"It's not like we have a choice," Ryan said. "There's nowhere else for us to go. Our only chance is to get back before they repair it. Good thing for us Wilshire doesn't have a transport full of engineers."

Louis crawled into his pod and allowed Rani to attach the electrical leads. His pale complexion belied his underlying angst, and Ryan pretended not to notice when Rani slipped him a sedative.

"Ready to go?" Ryan asked as he stepped into the cockpit.

Marcel gripped the yoke with both hands and took a deep breath. "On your order, sir."

Ryan glanced at the gray regolith that extended to the horizon. Even if he died trying to reach Europa, it'd be worth it to leave this place.

"Get us the hell out of here," he muttered.

*Day 111, 0625 Hours*

"What are you going to do?" Archie asked, pacing back and forth at the front of the starboard portal in Ops.

"About the artifact or about Wilshire?" Kasim sat hunched over in the command chair and fiddled with the sleeves of his thawb. He hated being in this position. Hated being forced to make life-and-death decisions. He silently cursed Braeder and Rani for letting it happen.

"Start with the artifact. Vrabel's scans have revealed nothing about the interior. He wants to bombard it with exotic particles to see if they will produce a reaction."

Kasim snorted. The artifact had opened a port, but a fuzzy blue haze obscured everything inside, like a curtain drawn across a stage. He had given Vrabel time to analyze the change, but that had proved a total waste. Kasim was building his courage to lay his hand on it when Ryan's warning arrived.

"It's not like you have a lot of time," Archie continued. "We need a plan."

"How long until they arrive?"

Archie scratched his temple. "That's the strange part. Both transports are thirty days out but only because the ships are on some weird trajectory. It's adding days to their trip."

"You think Chan's got something to do with that?"

"Has to be," Kasim said. "I don't figure Sybil or that Wilshire asshole know much about orbital trajectories."

The governor looked up. In his mind, a ray of hope appeared in the darkness. "She's trying to delay their arrival?"

Archie set his jaw. "It's possible. But Braeder still can't catch them before they get here. We're on our own."

The ray of hope vanished, leaving Kasim morose.

"At least he sent us a warning," Archie said. "Glad you were able to figure out the code."

"Yeah," Kasim mumbled. "A lot of help that was." Short and sweet, "Twenty survivors—criminals and scientists—hijacked transports. Chan and Stoll hostage. Sybil switched sides. Don't let them inside the station. And don't mention the artifact." Kasim would have liked to have the laser as an option, even to threaten them, but the last pump had shorted out a week before. They needed someone like Sasha or Gunner to fix the damn thing.

"What would Braeder do?"

Archie turned around. "For one, he'd take stock of our assets: six reservists and plenty of lasers. Not to mention two real guns."

"Yeah," Kasim snorted. "But only a handful of bullets."

"Then there's the station itself," Archie continued. "It's not constructed to be a fortress, but we could seal the airlocks. Make it difficult for them to break in. I'm thinking it might be better to hit them when they're the most vulnerable, when they land."

"You mean like crater the runway the same way Braeder did?" Kasim asked. "But that might kill everyone aboard, including Chan and Stoll."

Archie shook his head. "No, Ryan used all the explosive we had in stores. Not sure I trust any of the colonists to make more. Remember when the rebels tried and blew themselves up?"

Kasim nodded. He recalled the condition of the bodies when he arrived on the scene.

"I meant a quick attack with the reservists right after they touch down," Archie continued. "Pin them inside the ships so they can't get out."

"That sounds like our only option," Kasim said glumly. But even his non-military mind recognized the weakness of that plan: Wilshire would have days to sneak his men out before Braeder arrived. "What about the artifact? Braeder doesn't want them finding out about it."

"We can disguise the cave entrance," Archie said. "Have the reservists move the ice around and hide it from view."

"Good idea, but Rutherford will probably tell them as soon as they let him out."

"Then it's our job to make sure they don't find out about him and the others," Archie said. "Cut the video feed from the brig."

"What about food? If we don't bring in meals . . ."

"We'll leave some supplies with them, but we don't want Sybil or Wilshire seeing anyone go into the hangar."

Kasim rubbed his hands together. Not feeding prisoners went against the Geneva Convention. "That seems kind of . . ."

"Necessary?"

Kasim frowned. "Cruel. It's an ugly way to fight a war."

Archie flashed him a cold smile. "Well, bring your makeup, Governor, 'cause things are about to get real ugly around here."

# CHAPTER 33

*The firm, the enduring, the simple, and the modest are near to virtue.*

DAY 141, 1247 HOURS

Archie checked the digital clock in Ops. "Two hours until they enter laser range, Governor. Four hours until they land."

"Why mention the laser?" Vrabel asked. He had appropriated Chan's chair and typed in commands until a hologram of near space appeared at the front of the room: a dozen of Jupiter's moons and two fuzzy transports on an approach vector. "It's still offline."

Kasim's upper lip curled in disgust. Even if they could repair the colony's only defensive weapon, he doubted he could order the death of everyone on those ships. Especially Chan and Stoll. Braeder could, but he didn't have the guts.

Archie swiveled his chair to catch the governor's eye. "He's right. They're going to land no matter what we do. Any magical thoughts on revising the plan?"

Kasim's brain fumbled and came up empty. "No, let's go with what we got. Any word from Braeder?"

"Nothing since the original message," Vrabel said.

"The reservists are suited up and ready," Archie said. "On our mark, they'll surround the transport and keep Wilshire and Sybil bottled up."

"I wish we knew what kinds of weapons they have," Vrabel said.

Kasim groaned and buried his face in his hands. Braeder was still four days out. In the moment, he hated and needed the man. "I'm worried they will find a way to get past our lines."

"We talked about that," Archie said. "If that happens, we fall back inside the station and seal the hatches."

"And the temporary entrance to Delta Hive?" Vrabel asked. "We blocked it best we could, but there's no way to fully seal that one. We'd have to station guards there, which is not exactly a great plan if they have weapons."

Sweat beaded on Kasim's brow. This was turning into his worst nightmare. Visions of last year's battle in the concourse flooded his mind with anxiety. He recalled the rebels pushing their homemade tank up the wide corridor, and lasers and bullets flying overhead. He dropped his hands and looked at Archie. "I checked that barrier earlier. It doesn't look very sturdy."

Archie shrugged. "All static defenses can be overcome eventually . . ."

Vrabel gave him a look. "I never thought, but you're right. If they have a laser saw, they could cut their way through the external hull. It's not that thick."

"We have cameras," Kasim said. "We can watch them." Gunner's idea to put eyes on the surface had sounded like a wasted effort last year. Now he was glad Ryan overruled his protests.

"If they get out of the transports, the cameras won't last long," Archie said. "And once they're destroyed, Wilshire can pick the location and time of his choosing."

Kasim felt like his head was going to explode. Too many options. Too many variables. He watched a distant moon sail past in high orbit, unaffected by his internal angst. "I'm out of my depth here. What do you recommend?"

Archie folded his arms across his chest. "What I said when we first put this plan together. We have a few bullets left in the revolver and half a magazine for the machine gun. Once the transports land, we can copy what Braeder did with the senator's transport: take out the cockpit windows."

"What about Chan and Stoll? It'd just be like cratering the runway."

"I'm guessing if Chan or Stoll saw me standing outside the cockpit with a machine gun, the first thing they'd do is reach for their helmets."

"Yeah," Vrabel said. "They would know what's coming."

Kasim forced himself to lean back in his chair. He had initially refused to consider that option, but with reality bearing down on him, he was having second thoughts. "What if it doesn't work and Wilshire gets inside the station?"

"You already briefed the civilians," Archie said. "They may not like Braeder, but they're pissed that these bastards tried to kill him. If they get inside, even if they have weapons, there will be a mob willing to take revenge. I say, good luck handling fifteen hundred enraged colonists."

"And we still have our reservists with lasers," Vrabel said. "They will not be able to take the colony by force."

"Okay." For the first time in weeks, Kasim felt a modicum of hope. Europa had survived threats in the form of asteroids, power failures, and armed insurrectionists. He didn't want to be the captain of the ship when it finally went down. "All right, you convinced me. Archie, suit up and join the reservists. As soon as the ships land, surround them."

"And if it looks like Wilshire is going to make a break for it?"

"Shoot out the windows. Just make sure Chan and Stoll can see the gun and have time to react."

"Copy that," Archie said, standing.

"I'll go with you," Vrabel said.

"That's a negative," Kasim replied. "I need you here to coordinate . . ." He stopped when a yellow light flashed on Rani's old terminal. "Vrabel?"

The scientist leaned over, brow furrowed. "Incoming message, Governor."

Kasim's insides relaxed. "From Braeder?"

"Negative." Vrabel touched a few keys on the console. "It's from one of the approaching transports."

"Shit," Archie muttered, hurrying back to his chair. "What do they want?"

Kasim forced himself to remain calm. "Open a channel."

The speakers crackled before a familiar voice came through.

". . . Europa, this is incoming transport *Phoenix*, requesting permission to land," Sybil said. "Do you read?"

Archie's eyes narrowed. "What game are they playing?"

Kasim shook his head until he remembered this was the daughter of a politician. "This is Governor Aziz. Please state your intentions or we will blow you out of the sky."

There was a slight hesitation on the other end, and Kasim heard muted voices in the background. Then Sybil was back, and her tone carried a hefty amount of sarcasm. "I suspect you've never played poker, Kasim. You're not a good bluffer. We intercepted your message to Braeder. We know the laser is offline, and you don't have the capacity to repair it, which means you can't 'blow us out of the sky.'"

Kasim squeezed the edge of the terminal until the anger dissipated. "I thought you had changed, Sybil. I foolishly forgave you for your past actions, and now I see how wrong I was. You don't have the capacity to become a better person."

Static briefly invaded the frequency. "Sorry, Kasim, but my comrades are asking if you're part of the UN because the rhetoric sounds very familiar. Fancy words. Little action."

"We survived this long by working together, Sybil. Following Braeder's lead. Now you want to complete what your father started and drag us into the abyss?"

"Ryan kept us alive," Sybil agreed. It sounded like she was spitting the words through clenched teeth. "But the end is coming. We can all see it. You haven't got a laser, for Christ's sake. How long can the colony survive without that? No, it's time we employed a different strategy."

Kasim laughed in spite of himself. "You want to take over the moon? Is this déjà vu all over again? Sorry, but the colonists will not accept another wannabe dictator. You're not welcome here."

"Even if I come bearing gifts?" she asked. "I have two transports full of replacement parts, including pumps for the laser. Items the colony desperately needs."

Kasim hesitated. Could he turn down valuable equipment? As much as he wanted to extend his hand, he'd be inviting a viper into the nest. "The parts are important, but you're not getting into the station until Braeder returns."

Archie raised an eyebrow. "I didn't know we were negotiating."

Kasim held up his hand. If he was right, there was no way she could wait until the lieutenant arrived. Her answer would reveal her true colors.

"You need those parts now, Kasim. It's not safe for the colony to delay any longer. Ryan doesn't have a magic wand."

Kasim nodded at Archie. If there was any doubt about her true motive, she had just quashed it. "I recall another person offering to protect us if we surrendered the reins of power. It didn't work out so well for him."

"Last time, only a portion of the populace wanted a leadership change. This time, it'll be different."

Kasim settled back in his chair. What game was she playing? "You tried to kill Braeder and maroon the rest of the away team. Good luck getting the colonists to buy in."

Sybil chuckled. "I was raised by a politician, Kasim. I don't need for them to buy in. I only have to present options and allow them to pick the least unpleasant."

The channel closed.

"What the hell is she on about?" Vrabel asked.

"I don't know, but I don't like it." Archie checked the hologram. "Their trajectory hasn't changed."

"Wait." Vrabel checked his instruments. "They switched channels. Looks like she's broadcasting to the colony."

Kasim jumped up. "Can we block her?"

Vrabel threw up his hands. "Rani probably could, but I don't know how."

Archie made a frustrated noise in his throat. None of them had the skills to run Ops the way Rani and Braeder did. "Put it on speaker."

Vrabel flicked a button.

". . . is Sybil Lecky on *Phoenix* approaching Europa. You may have heard stories of what happened on Ceres. Some may be accurate, and some"—she chuckled lightly—"have no doubt been embellished. I offered to sit down and tell my side of the story to your governor, but he's not interested. Nor is he willing to negotiate."

She paused, and Kasim was forced to admit she had a gift for theatrics.

"We will be landing in approximately four hours," she continued. "If you want us to offload our supplies—medications for the sick, pumps for the laser and the hives, and even extra food—I suggest you let the governor know. We'll be waiting on your response."

"Son of a bitch," Archie muttered. "She just lit the fuse."

Lines formed on Vrabel's forehead. "What fuse?"

"The fuse of discontent," Kasim said, folding his thin arms across his chest. "The idea will fester inside the colonists until they can't resist any longer. Parents will hug their sick kids. Repair crews will rub their hands in front of empty supply sheds, and everyone will stare at the malfunctioning laser until they can't take it anymore."

Archie started for the door.

"Where you going?" Kasim asked.

"To get the machine gun," Archie replied. "I believe we still have a plan, and damned if I'm going to let that bitch stop us."

Ryan checked the clock on the instrument panel before kneading the arm of the copilot's seat in frustration. The minutes seemed to be passing in slow motion. Four days out and he had no idea what was happening on the moon. Part of him was desperate to contact Ops, but anything said over the open frequency was intel for the enemy. Wilshire's transports were about to land and there was nothing he could do about it.

The question was, when they landed, would they get into the station? If that happened, Wilshire would break radio silence and brag about his victory while at the same time repairing the laser in order to blow them out of the sky.

Kasim had weapons but little in the way of trained personnel. Any direct assault on the transport would probably degenerate into a bar fight. It wouldn't be pretty.

"Can we increase speed?"

Marcel gave him a sidelong look. "Ah, we're currently decelerating toward the moon."

"Well, can we decelerate less fast?"

"Maybe," he replied, straight-faced. "But that would disengage Chan's computer program, and crash landings are one thing I haven't trained for."

Ryan ground his teeth together. He couldn't change the rules of physics, no matter how many lives were at stake or how delicately his species tiptoed toward extinction.

Louis leaned into the cockpit. "I just used my last anti-nausea injection on Sasha. How long until we touch down?"

"Too long," Ryan said.

The doctor stared at the gas giant loitering in the distance. Europa was just one of many tiny dots surrounding the planet. "What do you think we're going to find?"

"Not sure." Ryan leaned forward, elbows on knees. "Last time, Bordeaux and the Board had a plan. I'm sure Sybil and Wilshire wouldn't have come all this way without one. As for what it is, I've wracked my brain, but it's a waste of time until we reach the surface."

"They can't take over the colony with twenty people."

"No, but there are different ways to maneuver the levers of power. If I was smart enough, I'd figure it out."

Louis patted his shoulder. "No one has accused you of being very bright, but you've done pretty good so far."

As Louis left the cockpit, the pilot gave him a smile. "I'm with the doctor, Lieutenant. No matter what Lecky does, my money's on you." His gaze returned to the instruments, and suddenly, he was all business again.

Ryan blinked. He hadn't expected the support and yet it was sorely needed. He leaned back in his seat and checked the clock. Another five minutes had passed.

"Bastards," Archie muttered as he peeled off the upper section of his EV suit.

"What the hell happened?" Kasim stood in the center of the decompression chamber with his hands on his hips. The geologist's startled cry on the surface and his rapid retreat to the station had prompted Kasim to come running.

"They were waiting for me," Archie snarled. "They deliberately landed the transports at the far end of the runway. By the time I got close, several of them had left the ship. They had lasers, and one beam grazed me." He lifted his leg to show the scorched fabric.

"You couldn't shoot out the cockpit window?"

"The transports are pointed away from the station. If I tried to sneak around, they'd have had a clear shot. At that range, they wouldn't miss."

Kasim remembered Braeder's battle on the ice sheets. The lieutenant had used his military training and his knowledge of the surface to outflank the senator's marines. "Maybe we can sneak out of the Delta Hive entrance."

Archie snorted. "In case you hadn't noticed, I'm not exactly a young man anymore, and I sure as hell don't have the training."

Kasim planted his legs and stared out the nearest portal. "Where are the reservists?"

The geologist jerked a thumb toward the hatch. "I gave them my gun. There's no cover on the landing strip, so if any of Wilshire's group try and approach the station, our guys should be able to take them down."

"Damn. It's a standoff. They can't get in and we can't get close to the ship."

"For now. Until they find a way around us."

Kasim felt like he was painting himself into a corner. With every move Sybil made, he had fewer and fewer options. "Organize a rotation with the reservists. Tell them not to fire that gun unless they absolutely have a target." They only had so many bullets.

Archie pulled off the lower half of the suit, exposing a pair of thin white legs and knobby knees. "What are you going to do?"

"For now, meet with the colonists and try to reassure them. And, more importantly, convince them to hold on until Braeder's transport arrives."

Archie whistled. "You think a group of weak-willed civilians can hold out for four days?"

Kasim didn't answer as he walked out of the room. The hard part wasn't convincing the civilians; it was convincing himself they could actually win.

*Day 143, 1530 Hours*

"Can't we make a deal?" the woman pleaded. She had short, spiked hair and a lazy eye that twitched when she spoke.

Seated at the head of the briefing table, Kasim pushed his water bottle away with the back of his hand. It had been two days since the transport landed, and not a peep from Sybil. Archie and the reservists maintained watch, but so far, it had been quiet.

"We tried that, Mary. They want full access, which translates into taking over the station."

The man seated beside Mary wrung his hands. "But they have parts for the laser, the extractor, and just about everything else. Can't you do something?"

Kasim puffed out his cheeks. They had sucked him into their circular thinking, and he felt like a dog chasing its tail. The two representatives had been chosen by the colonists when Braeder ended martial law, but Kasim had never officially reconstituted the Board. Still, the reason he had called them to this meeting was to help calm the rest of the colonists who were on the verge of outright panic.

He folded his hands on the table. "The fact of the matter is, they're not going to surrender and allow us to march them into the brig, and I'm not going to acquiesce to their demands. We have to forge a united front until the lieutenant returns. He'll know what to do."

Mary and her friend exchanged a look. Neither appeared mollified, but Kasim didn't need them to be happy, just compliant.

"Two days?" Mary asked.

"Two days," Kasim confirmed. "We need to trust that the lieutenant can do it again."

He sat for several long minutes after they left, thinking through his next steps. The good news was, the two colonists would spread the word. There would be griping and complaining, but everyone would hold the line for now. How long they could defend the station was something else entirely. They didn't like Braeder, but they trusted him. He had gotten them this far.

Kasim tapped the com on the wall. "Kasim to Archie. Any change?"

"Negative. I replaced the reservists an hour ago. The transports look quiet, and there's no one on the surface."

"All right. We've got forty-eight hours to maintain the status quo. Watch for any tricks." He clicked off the com and walked back to Ops. The hologram at the front of the room showed near space: Jupiter and a slew of moons, and a tiny silver speck drawing closer.

"I hope you have a plan, Ryan," Kasim murmured. "Because I'm drawing dead."

# CHAPTER 34

*When anger rises, think of the consequences.*

DAY 144, 0813 HOURS

Kasim stood on the surface and stared at the transports parked on the far edge of the runway. With Jupiter blazing overhead, the ice reflected golden hues, and hoarfrost glistened like strings of diamonds. He checked his heads-up display: vitals fine except for a mildly elevated heart rate. Battery and oxygen levels both read ninety percent.

Vrabel put down the revolver on a block of ice and rubbed his gloved hands together. "Been quiet all morning. Anything on the com?"

Kasim shook his head. Lecky had maintained radio silence for three days, no doubt purposely letting the tension build. Waiting for some emergency that would tilt the scales and pull the colonists to her side. And there had certainly been discontent. He had several additional meetings with the reps, trying to reassure them. If it wasn't for the fact Braeder's transport was almost within visual range, he was sure the colonists would capitulate and accept Wilshire's offer of replacement parts in exchange for amnesty.

"They can't just sit there," Vrabel continued. "They're running out of time."

"That's what worries me," Kasim replied. "I know Sybil, and she only plays a hand when the cards are strong."

Vrabel didn't comment. Not being involved in the insurrection last year, he didn't know the woman like Kasim did.

The governor opened a channel. "Kasim to Ops. Everything okay on your end?"

"No warning lights are flashing, if that's what you mean," Archie replied with just the right amount of sarcasm.

Kasim pictured the geologist rolling his eyes. "Well, keep—" He stopped when his display announced an incoming call. "Wait one." He switched channels. "Governor Aziz."

"This is Sybil. Have you decided to agree to our terms?"

Kasim almost felt giddy delivering the bad news. "Sorry, Sybil, we won't negotiate with terrorists or murderers. The answer is still no."

"That's too bad," Sybil said, her words sounding almost nonchalant. "But since it's not unexpected, we took matters into our own hands."

Kasim's heart skipped a beat. "What are you talking about?"

"We made a trek to the thermal extractor and attached an explosive device to the transfer coils. If you don't change your mind in the next thirty minutes, we'll blow the sucker up."

A wave of panic engulfed Kasim. She would cut power? He never considered . . . "You'll kill everyone on the moon? Are you insane?"

"Not insane. Just desperate. And we won't kill everyone. As we have plenty of power, those of us on the transport will be perfectly safe."

Kasim exchanged a panicked look with Vrabel when he realized they were speaking on a common frequency. Everyone inside the station would be hearing the message.

"How do I know you're not bluffing?"

Sybil chuckled. "I knew you were going to ask me that, so we planned a little demonstration."

Kasim heard her speak to someone in the background.

"In exactly one minute, we're going to shut down the extractor. Don't worry; it'll be a brief stoppage, and no damage will be done. This time. But your thirty minutes begins now."

The channel closed.

Kasim fumbled before switching back to Ops. "Archie, did you—"

"I heard," he replied, tone grim. "What do you want me to do?"

"Tell the colonists to return to the hive and shut down all nonessential systems. Check the batteries to make sure they're ready to take the load, especially for the greenhouses. With any luck, she's bluffing." But deep in his heart, he knew Lecky didn't bluff.

He hadn't considered the extractor, didn't figure it for the weak link in their defense.

"I could put together a small group to sneak past the transport and maybe defuse the bomb," Vrabel suggested, picking up the gun. "We know the ice out there. They don't."

Kasim shook his head. It was an effort to battle the rising frustration. Lecky had outmaneuvered him. "Not enough time. Besides, there'd be plenty of casualties, and I'm not putting that on my conscience."

Vrabel's expression hardened. Kasim figured he was experiencing a similar frustration.

When Archie spoke next, Kasim heard the resignation in his tone. "Power's out. Batteries have kicked in." He paused. "She wasn't bluffing."

Vrabel slammed his fist against a block of ice. It cracked down the middle.

Kasim opened a channel. "You made your point, Sybil. What do you want?"

The woman chuckled. "You know what we want. Control of the station. And your weapons. Put them down on the ice and go back inside. And . . ." She hesitated. "Please leave the hatch unlocked."

Kasim had to bite his lip to control his anger. He didn't see another option. "You said you'd turn the power back on."

"Change of plan. It's off until you agree to our terms."

"You mean until we surrender."

"I prefer to think of it as a transition of power."

"You're a selfish bitch, Sybil." The words fell out of his mouth before his brain could filter them. "You don't care about anyone else. What did Braeder ever see in you?"

"Take your time, Governor," Sybil said sweetly. "We'll be waiting on your decision. Oh, one last thing. If you try something desperate like swarming the transport or sending a group to defuse the explosive, we will blow up the extractor. Talk soon."

"*Bitch* is an understatement," Vrabel muttered on a private channel. "She's holding fifteen hundred people hostage. Are you sure we can't do something? I'm thinking the reservists will want a go at that ship."

Kasim fisted his hands inside his gloves. Despite wanting so badly to let the reservists off the leash, he knew it was a losing proposition. Without military oversight, any assault would most certainly turn into an unmitigated disaster.

Archie's voice in his ear. "I'm being inundated with panicked calls from colonists."

"They heard the exchange?"

"Every word. They want us to give in to their demands."

"What do you think?"

"It's better than the alternative."

Kasim stared across the ice plates. Jupiter was beginning its descent, and already the surface ice was taking on darker tones, reflecting greens and blues. Small dust devils lived and died between slabs of million-year-old ice.

"Drop your weapon, Vrabel," Kasim said.

The engineer's face was a mask of deep lines. "Are you sure?"

"My duty is to the colonists. To keep them safe and, more importantly, alive. I can't do that without a thermal extractor."

The reservist slowly deposited the gun on the nearest block of ice. "What now?"

Kasim sighed. "Now we go inside and wait for Caligula to arrive."

*1030 Hours*

The governor paced in front of the terminals in Operations, stopping every few minutes to stare out the portside portal at the massive Fleet transports on the runway. When they first landed, black, tarry smoke oozed from the engines, and exhaust manifolds blazed red as they radiated heat into the infinite coldness of space. After three days, the exothermic process had concluded, and the last joules of heat had been siphoned from the hull.

With the extractor offline and the temperature in the station falling, he had intended to stop in his quarters to add another layer of clothes. That was before his brain became mired in depressive thoughts. Now, as he stared at his white fingers, he realized how cold it was.

The gas giant stared down at them, as though trying to discern the purpose of the new arrivals on one of its inner moons. Surrounding storms in the planet's upper atmosphere flared and merged with the Great Red Spot.

*Where were they?*

Kasim wrung his hands as he surveyed the frozen tectonic plates. He had succumbed to their ultimatum an hour before, and there had been no word since. The hologram at the front of the room showed a schematic of the planet and surrounding moons.

He felt like a prisoner waiting on the gallows for the executioner to appear. And there was no cavalry in the wings to ride in on white horses. Ryan's transport was still a day out, and there was nothing Kasim could do to stop the inevitable.

The door hissed open and Sybil walked in. Kasim's sense of relief at seeing a familiar face disintegrated as a group of gaunt-looking men and women filed in behind her. Something seemed off until he realized each of them wore a different cut of EV suit, rough and blocky, without the smooth lines of the Alliance equivalent. They were also charcoal-gray and covered in dark stains.

"Governor." Sybil marched up and planted her hands on her hips. In her Federation attire, she looked different, like a carbon copy of herself. But then Kasim peered closer and noted the gray hair and new lines on her face.

"Sybil." He inclined his head but didn't take his eyes off the group spreading across the room: four men, two women. Each held a helmet in one hand and a laser in the other. Their hair was thin and wispy, and each person seemed to be walking with some type of limp. Ulcers and sores revealed the condition of their skin.

Sybil gestured to one of the men. "This is Wilshire, a former board member from Ceres. He's in charge."

The emaciated man with a sparse silver beard and bad teeth stepped forward to extend a hand. "Pleased to meet you, Governor."

Kasim looked at the offering but didn't take it. He wasn't about to shake hands with a devil. "You threatened the lives of every person on this moon. What do you want?"

Wilshire shrugged and dropped his hand. "What do *we* want?" His gaze touched on his comrades, and he received answering smiles and grunts. "For starters, we want your food. As you can tell"—he gestured to the weeping lesions on his face—"our diet has gone to hell over the past year, and we could really use some calories, not to mention the vitamins and minerals your doctor told us about."

"You could have asked. We would have shared."

Wilshire broke into a smile. He pointed a finger. "You're the UN guy. Sybil told us about you. Always willing to compromise. I like that."

Kasim's anger, lurking just beneath the surface, started to boil. "Do you realize what you're doing? This is the last refuge of human civilization. You're pushing us over the edge of extinction."

Wilshire made a disparaging noise in his throat. "Please. You sound like the lieutenant, and I'm tired of hearing the same refrain."

"Braeder said you killed innocent colonists on Ceres." His words came out sounding more like an accusation, but Kasim didn't regret saying it.

Wilshire, however, jerked back as if struck. "We did what we had to. Your lieutenant did worse on this moon. I'm told he murdered over five hundred people."

"This colony survived because of him," Kasim snapped, shooting a hard look at Sybil. "If you knew . . ." He stopped when several of Wilshire's men edged forward menacingly.

"We can get into details later," Wilshire continued, sounding bored. "For now, please give my assistant, Bennett, the codes for the dispensary." A tall female stepped forward. "And we'll get started on equipping the transports."

Kasim couldn't believe his ears. "You're going to take our food? But there's only a handful of you."

Wilshire continued as if he hadn't heard. "After that, I'll give you a list of the mechanical parts we'll need for the trip to Earth."

Kasim's brain clicked over to a new concern. "You have Chan on board? And Stoll? Can I see them?"

"Sorry, Governor. They're indisposed at the moment. Long trip and all." He leaned forward and patted Kasim on the shoulder. "I'm sure you understand."

Kasim battled the urge to bat the hand away. "What about the plague? Aren't you afraid of catching it?"

Wilshire snickered. "Let's just say we have an insurance policy."

Kasim's eyes widened. "You have a vaccine?"

"We do." Wilshire nodded toward a man standing beside Gunner's terminal. "Let me introduce you to Dr. Pavel of the Russian Federation. He and his fellow scientists did the heavy lifting on perfecting the serum."

Kasim did a double take. The man reminded him of Vrabel, well over six feet tall and thin as a scarecrow. At the moment, he stared at Kasim impassively.

Kasim eyes narrowed. Revulsion fueled his defiance. "You killed those colonists?"

"Need test subjects," Pavel said, his deep Russian baritone filling the room. "Like cake need broken eggs."

"Not sure how that's going to sound to future generations."

Wilshire chuckled. "Haven't you heard, Governor? History is written by the winners."

One of Wilshire's men abruptly sagged, and his comrades grabbed his arms before he face-planted. They helped him to a sitting position on the floor.

"Damn gravity," Bennett said. "We've been taking anabolic steroids for the past two days, but that's only temporary. We need to get off this rock before our muscles really start cramping up."

"Never mind." Wilshire waved at Bennett to be quiet. "That's none of your business, Governor. What you have to focus on is keeping your people alive, and to do that, you need to cooperate."

Kasim struggled to rein in his emotions. "How long will you be staying?"

"He said it was none of your business." A thick, heavyset man walked up to stand uncomfortably close to Kasim. Despite having no neck, the man loomed over him like a storm cloud. The heavy reek of BO wafted in the air, and Kasim held his breath so he didn't retch. The man poked him in the chest, hard. "Do what you're told, and nobody gets dead."

Wilshire sighed as Kasim rubbed his chest and stepped back. "Sorry about Andrei. Like many of my crew, they've spent too much time behind bars and are dying for payback. I'd advise staying on his good side."

Kasim looked at Sybil. "I can't believe you're part of this, pillaging the colony and leaving us here to die."

"Your lieutenant was doing the same to Ceres," Andrei said.

Kasim fisted his hands. "That's hardly a fair comparison. We were told the asteroid colonies were empty, and I'm sure Braeder offered you a home here."

Andrei spread his arms wide to include all the people in the room. "Why would we want to live in this shithole?"

"Just do what they say," Sybil said, focusing Kasim's attention. "A couple days, a week at most, and we'll be gone."

Kasim took a deep breath. It did little to lessen the angst that flooded his veins. "I actually forgave you, Sybil. For your actions during the uprising. This is ten times worse."

"I guess you're a lousy judge of character." Andrei snorted.

Kasim ignored him, directing his words at Sybil. "And how will we survive? Braeder went to Ceres because Europa was on life support. You think leaving us alive is doing us a favor?"

"Consider the alternative," Wilshire said. "We turn off the power and then walk over your corpses to steal everything we want."

"The man is right," Andrei said, giving Kasim a hard look. "We can do it the easy way or the hard way. Your choice." He stepped back and folded thick arms across his chest.

Kasim vacillated. He really didn't have a choice. The bastard just wanted the governor to admit it. Basically handing over the keys to the colony.

Kasim set his jaw and refused to answer.

Andrei leaned forward and slapped him on the back. "That's the spirit."

Bennett pulled a paper from her pocket. "I have a list of supplies for the transports. The gravity on Europa is twenty times stronger than we're used to, so we'll need colonists to do the grunt work. Can I leave that in your hands, Governor?"

Kasim managed a single nod. He was afraid to read the paper.

"Excellent." Wilshire rubbed his hands together like an excited kid. "Now, how do we fire the laser?"

"What?" Kasim blinked, confused. "What do you mean?"

Andrei poked him in the chest. Kasim grunted.

"He means what he said, shithead. Show us where the laser controls are."

Kasim backed up until his hips brushed Gunner's terminal. "The laser is offline. You know that. There's a short in the system that keeps melting the pumps."

"Let me guess," Andrei said. "Braeder was going to bring new ones."

Wilshire picked at a scab on his cheek. "Do we have them on the transport?"

"I'm thinking yes, but we'll have to look."

Wilshire gestured, and one of the men hurried out of Ops.

Sybil walked up to the hologram that displayed the gas giant and surrounding moons. And the single ship approaching the planetary system. "He's only a day out."

Kasim startled. "You want to shoot down the lieutenant's transport?"

Sybil grimaced, and she cast a nervous glance at Wilshire. "We'll try to disable it, right?"

Wilshire smiled. "That's the plan."

"You're crazy," Kasim said. "The laser is not a surgical tool. It's a blunt instrument designed to destroy asteroids."

Wilshire shrugged. "We'll see, but first, we have to tie off some loose ends."

Alarm bells sounded in the back of Kasim's skull. "What are you talking about?"

The door swished open, and Vrabel was shoved into the room by two disheveled men wearing Federation suits. Both carried lasers.

"'Bout time," Andrei murmured.

"Took a while to find him," one of the men said, pointing his laser at Vrabel. "He was hiding in Engineering."

Kasim tensed. "What the hell is going on?"

"Nothing much." Wilshire gave Vrabel a once-over. "Sybil said Braeder depended on loyal colonists during the uprising, reservists and such. I figured it's probably best if we rounded them up and removed the threat before we started prepping the transports."

At the concerned look on Vrabel's face, Kasim's gut tightened. What were they planning to do? He stepped in front of the engineer. "He's not going anywhere."

"Relax." Sybil waved her hand. "It's nothing terrible. We just need to stick them somewhere until we leave. I was thinking of my old cell in the brig."

Kasim wrung his hands. He didn't want them anywhere near the transport hangar, not with Rutherford and his cronies incarcerated inside. "We can't use the brig."

Sybil hesitated. "Why not?"

"We had . . . a gas leak two weeks ago. It's fixed, but ammonia levels are still high." He clamped his mouth shut and willed his heart to slow down.

She stared at him for several long seconds. "All right, we'll stick them in the hive."

Kasim seized the moment, before someone changed their mind. "Just don't hurt anyone."

"Not your decision, Governor," Andrei said. His fingers twitched like he wanted to wrap them around a throat.

Sybil stepped up, drawing Wilshire's attention. "We talked about this."

Wilshire grimaced and gave Andrei a hard look. "Do it. It's part of our deal."

Andrei looked ready to challenge Wilshire before he abruptly relaxed.

"Damn." One of the men holding a laser turned it over in his hand. "I'm dying to fire this thing."

"It's okay." Vrabel put a hand on Kasim's shoulder and gently pushed him back.

Two Ceres men pinned his arms and hustled him out.

Sybil lifted her helmet to her ear. "Lecky to transport."

A female voice answered. "Go ahead."

"Station is secure. You can turn off the timer on the bomb."

"Copy that. Transport out."

Kasim's eyes widened. "You really were going to destroy the extractor?"

"If you tried to pull something," Wilshire said. "Happy now?"

"What about the replacement parts?"

"Once the concourse heats up, you can organize a work crew to start unloading," Bennett said. "I'll make sure there's plenty of oversight."

Kasim bit back a snide comment. Wilshire's group was going to play Big Brother. "I don't know how you can sleep at night, Sybil. You used to be one of us."

Sybil slipped into Rani's old chair, making Kasim wonder if she was delivering a message. "Don't play stupid with me. We all know the colony is on its last legs. That's why Ryan went to the asteroids. The problem is, he didn't find the right wire, which doesn't change your outlook."

"At least he's trying," Kasim said. "You think this vaccine is going to work? That's a huge gamble."

"A gamble many colonists will be willing to take," Wilshire said.

It took Kasim a second to catch the underlying meaning. "You're taking our people with you?"

"We're going to install the cryo-pods the lieutenant removed," Wilshire said. "Which means we can fit about forty units total. Counting my crew of twenty, that leaves roughly twenty seats in each transport that we can put up for auction."

"Auction?" Kasim looked at Sybil, but she wouldn't meet his gaze. "What the hell are you talking about?"

"I'll let you figure it out." Wilshire's eyes sparkled. "Don't worry; you'll have fewer mouths to feed when we leave."

"I was wrong," Kasim said, disgusted. "You're not a bastard; you're a monster. When is this *selection process* supposed to happen?"

"As soon as possible. It won't take long."

"I'm guessing you're going to pick people with little in the way of morals?"

Wilshire frowned. "Colonists need to be flexible in their thinking. Can't have people holding grudges, you know."

Kasim felt sick to his stomach. They were going to rebuild the human race using stock scraped off the bottom of the barrel. That wouldn't bode well for the future.

"Why not just let Braeder land and lock him up, Sybil? After all, he let you live when many in this station wanted to space you."

"He's too much of a symbol," Sybil replied, eyes downcast. "Colonists might make the wrong choice."

"You mean a *better* choice?"

Andrei snorted. "Sarcasm is not your forte, UN man. Stick with negotiations."

"Yeah." Wilshire stared into the hologram. "He's come three hundred million kilometers to seek revenge. No way I'm giving him the chance."

# CHAPTER 35

*Only the wisest and stupidest of men never change.*

DAY 144, 1442 HOURS

You want me to move all the stretchers into Beta Hive?" Kasim couldn't disguise the incredulousness in his tone. On the surface, the ask was crazy. What made him more uneasy was the underlying meaning . . .

Wilshire shook his head. "Not all of them. Just a half dozen. Dr. Pavel needs space to inject the colonists who will be joining us on the transports."

Kasim's gaze flickered to the row of stretchers in Medical, each one attached to the wall by a plethora of wires and cables. All were empty except one. Ellen was helping Mabel apply a dressing to a colonist who had suffered a second-degree burn while fixing a circuit board in Engineering. "Why not just vaccinate the colonists here? This is Medical, after all."

Wilshire exchanged a look with Bennett. Kasim sensed information being shared, but he had no idea what that could be.

"Look, once in a while, there's unintended side effects," Bennett confessed. She held up her hand before Kasim could interject. "It's rare. Pavel says it's like one in a thousand, but it's not something we want people to see. It might give them the wrong idea."

"The wrong idea? What kind of side effects?" Another thought struck Kasim. "Did people die?"

Mabel stopped dressing the burn and stared.

"It was rare," Wilshire repeated.

"Goddamn," Kasim whispered. They weren't telling him everything. Where was Louis when he needed him?

Wilshire leaned into his personal space. "We weren't asking, Governor. Round up some colonists and move the stretchers. Now."

Kasim didn't budge. "You think people are going to volunteer to go with you? You're crazy."

Sybil walked in. "Who's crazy, Governor? Those who join us and get to enjoy a full life, or those who refuse and end up starving to death on the moon?"

"Are you going to tell the colonists about the side effects?" Mabel asked.

Sybil threw her a desultory look. "They'll be told what they need to know."

Kasim folded his arms across his chest. "So, the plan is to sell them a bill of goods."

"I'll interview them," Wilshire said. "If they want to come, they have to get vaccinated. Have those stretchers out of here by the time I get back." He turned to Sybil. "You said you had some news for me."

"I do." She sat on one of the stretchers. "I was checking the camera feeds, and guess what I found? Prisoners in the brig! Apparently, our governor here was less than truthful about the so-called leak in the transport hangar. I recognized scientists and miners in my old cell." She looked at Kasim. "What happened, a little civil discontent while we were gone?"

Kasim didn't trust himself to answer. The artifact secret was about to come out. He could only hope the delay made a difference.

"Where are they now?" Wilshire asked.

"Andrei said he'll let them out after he takes a load of supplies to *Serenity*. I'll talk to them. Have to verify why they were incarcerated, but I'm guessing they'll join our side easy enough."

"Good, because our people could use a break. Damn gravity is taking a toll." He threw a nasty look at Kasim. "And since the governor flouted our good faith, I think he deserves to lose his freedom. Secure him in Ops when you're done."

"What about the prisoners we've been holding in the hive?" Bennett asked. "Maybe move them to the brig?"

"Good idea," Wilshire said. "Have Andrei transfer them."

Bennett flashed Kasim a cold smile as she followed Wilshire out of Medical.

After the door hissed shut, Kasim turned to Sybil. "Did you get vaccinated?"

She nodded, rubbing her shoulder. "Before I went into cryo. It wasn't a pleasant experience."

"How long does it take to work?" Ellen asked, passing Mabel some gauze.

The colonist grimaced as the nurse peeled off dead skin.

"Pavel says it takes about two weeks for the immune system to produce antibodies."

"What about the side effects?"

"Apparently, some subjects reacted to the vaccine on Ceres . . ." Her voice trailed off, making Kasim even more curious.

"You're not going to tell me?"

"Not my place to say anything."

"But you're now immune to the plague?"

"That's what the doctors said."

"The Russian doctors?" Kasim made a show of surveying Medical. "And where exactly are they now? They don't seem to be around."

"Pavel's the last one. The rest died of starvation before we arrived on the asteroid."

Kasim's eyebrows rose, conveying his disbelief. "Sorry, the dots don't line up, Sybil."

She shrugged. "I don't know what else to say. They based the vaccine on an actual sample of the plague, so it should work."

Kasim took a deep breath. "You're going to hell. You're condemning fifteen hundred men, women, and children to death, just to save yourself and your psychopathic friends. How does that make you feel?"

Sybil glared without blinking. "Wilshire is leaving no matter what. It boils down to a simple choice, and I choose survival."

"Sounds like pure selfishness to me."

"This is not a case of misplaced altruism, Governor. Our ancestors made similar choices, which is why we're here talking today."

"That part is true," Kasim acknowledged. "Just like the guards at Auschwitz did what was best for them."

Sybil gritted her teeth. "I can see the UN in you. How long have you been practicing those lines?"

Kasim refused to take the bait. "Ryan and Louis were your friends. They went to bat for you, protected you, and this is how you repay them?"

Sybil shook her head. "I . . . I tried to convince Ryan on Ceres. Sometimes, it's better to cut your losses."

"The lieutenant won't leave a man behind, Sybil. You know that." Sensing a weakening in her defenses, Kasim leaned in. "It's not too late."

She snorted. "It is for me. You already said it: I'm going to hell. I sold my soul to the devil twice. First my father and now Wilshire. All to prolong my existence. What's an apology going to do?"

"Maybe Ryan needs more than an apology," Kasim said. "Maybe he needs a helping hand in a moment of crisis." He waited, and the silence stretched almost a minute before Sybil jumped off the stretcher.

"Why are those people in the brig, Kasim? You might as well tell me now, before Wilshire loses patience with you. He will take out his anger on your colonists if you push him."

Kasim debated briefly before giving up. He sighed. "We found something by the extractor. An alien artifact."

Sybil's jaw dropped, and it took a second for her poker face to slide back into place. "No shit? A real alien object." She hesitated. "What happened with the scientists? I'm guessing some sort of disagreement?"

"They want to bury it in the ice and forget it," Kasim said, casting a wary eye on Ellen. Now was not the time for the engineer to say anything. She gave him a barely perceptible nod.

"Sounds like I'm going to have a little talk with these scientists," Sybil said as one of the Ceres men walked in with a laser. "You better hope Wilshire isn't pissed when I finish. Christ knows what he'll do to you."

Kasim felt a definite chill in the air as she stomped out.

Seated in the copilot's chair, Ryan glanced at the instrument panel and scratched at his nascent beard. "What's wrong with our vector?"

Marcel stopped typing commands into the nav computer. "Contingency planning, Lieutenant. You said the laser is down, but I thought it'd be safer if I used the moons as cover for as long as possible. Just in case?"

Ryan blinked. He hadn't thought of that, but then again, he wasn't a pilot. "Sounds good."

"You really think they'd try to shoot us down?" Rani asked, sticking her head into the cockpit.

"No question," Ryan replied. "He killed dozens on Ceres. What's a few more?"

Rani stared at the gas giant in the distance. "If they did get the laser working, at least it's not Marco at the controls."

Her comments gave Ryan pause. Marco could hit a baseball with that laser. Wilshire and his goons would be doing the aiming and the firing, and they weren't exactly familiar with the controls. "Eventually, they will have a clean shot."

"I know," Rani acknowledged, her expression grim.

Ryan leaned forward, elbows on knees. He didn't relish the thought of playing duck-and-cover with the transport, but he liked the idea of getting killed even less. "What's our ETA?"

Marcel pointed at his screen. "The new trajectory will add a couple of hours. Best guesstimate is oh seven hundred tomorrow."

Ryan sighed. Even if they reached the moon, it would only get harder. Wilshire had the advantage in every respect, including the number of lasers. "We have to be ready to disembark as soon as we land. Before Wilshire attacks."

"Understood, Lieutenant. I'm hoping they don't do something to the landing strip."

A chill ran up Ryan's spine. Would Sybil think of that? She had been stuck in the hive last year when he ordered Decker and Chan to crater the runway. But if she did . . . well, shit, there was nothing they could do about it. No way the transport could make it back to Ceres. Not enough supplies. Not enough fuel.

He got up and headed into the cargo hold. "Gunner, we need to talk."

The veteran paused in the middle of his meal. "Let me guess. You're changing the plan."

Ryan grunted. "I like it when you read my mind."

*Day 145, 0530 Hours*

Hands bound behind his back by a leather strap, Kasim squirmed in Rani's chair while Pavel punched commands into Marco's old terminal using the hunt-and-peck method with his index fingers. It was painful to watch.

"Damn, Pavel!" Wilshire blurted from the command chair. "Can you go any slower? I should have let Andrei handle this part."

"Terminal complicated," the scientist growled. "Federation computers . . . simpler."

"A computer is a computer," Wilshire snapped. "Find the targeting controls and let the AI do the rest."

"Not easy. Alliance setup different. Like new language."

Kasim shifted his weight in a futile attempt to get comfortable. His hands and wrists were aching since Andrei—Mr. No Neck—tightened his restraints. Wilshire had sent the burly Russian to supervise the insertion of the new laser pump while Pavel worked on the targeting computer.

At the front of the room, the hologram showed a closeup of the Jovian system: a dozen moons dominated by the gas giant. And on the edge of resolution, a small silver vessel.

"I told you the system won't work," Kasim said. "Every pump we inserted shorted out within hours. Somebody who knows what they're doing needs to run a diagnostic."

Wilshire flashed him a furious look. "Shut your pie hole, Governor. Your little secret about the artifact torpedoed any trust we had in you."

"But—"

"Man said shut it." Pavel pulled a switchblade from his pocket and mimicked drawing it across his throat. "Speak again and I cut deep smile."

Wilshire's expression softened. "When we finish here, I think Pavel and I will take a walk out to this ice cave of yours and see what this alien hardware is all about."

The idea of Wilshire playing with the artifact gave Kasim chills and, more than that, incentive to keep working his restraints. His skin under the leather was red and raw, but after pulling and twisting the restraints for an hour, he detected a lessening of the tension. He focused on the Russian scientist. "If you don't follow proper procedure, the battery will overcharge and explode."

"And if chickens could swim, they'd be called fish," Wilshire said. He got up and walked to the front portal. "Looks like they're nearly finished inserting the new pump, Pavel. I want that laser operational."

"Will be."

"I don't know why you're wasting your time," Kasim persisted. "Even if you fixed it, some other part will fail. It's a box of bolts at this point."

Wilshire flashed him an evil grin. "You'd like that, wouldn't you? Give your boy a chance to land safely. All I need is enough charge to fire a single burst. Then you can melt the laser into tin hats for all I care."

Kasim bit his tongue. Provoking Wilshire further wouldn't help. He tried to sow doubt, but it obviously wasn't working.

"Got it!" Pavel exclaimed. "Laser online."

Wilshire hurried back to his chair. "It'll take a while to charge the system. Just like on Ceres. Try and get a fix on him while we wait."

"Sending commands." Pavel's index fingers resumed their awkward journey. "Computer searching."

Kasim glanced out the portal. On an elevated ice sheet, the laser began to swivel. He recalled how Marco used to make the weapon dance.

"Can you lock on?" Wilshire's fingers tapped impatiently on the arms of the chair.

The door swished open and Sybil walked in. "What's the status of his transport?"

"Passing outer moons," Pavel reported. "Trying to get lock."

"Sybil, you can't let them do this," Kasim said. He twisted his wrists and the leather separated another fraction. "This is murder."

Sybil's lips tightened into a fine line. She looked at Wilshire, but the man's hard expression didn't waver. "The laser will probably just disable it," she said, her tone hopeful.

"We can't let him land on the runway," Wilshire growled. "If he can set down away from the station . . ."

"Murder," Kasim repeated.

The ship in the hologram grew larger with each passing second. Minutes away from final approach. His pulse quickened. He had told Braeder the laser was inoperative. If something happened, he would have to shoulder the blame. A small voice in his brain whispered this wasn't happening. Braeder couldn't die. Not after all that they'd been through.

"Locked on!" Pavel announced, raising his arms like he had just scored the overtime goal. "Laser charged."

"Then fire!" Wilshire exclaimed.

The scientist lowered his arms. He searched the console until he found the correct button.

Kasim closed his eyes as Pavel pressed Execute.

Nothing happened.

Wilshire searched the hologram. "Did the laser fire? Where's the ship?"

Sybil's eyes darted between Kasim and Wilshire. "I don't see it."

Pavel's brow furrowed. "Computer aborted because . . . target disappeared. Went behind moon."

"Try to reacquire."

Pavel raised his finger . . . and dropped it. "Using moon as shield."

Kasim exhaled. The leather knot slid over his thumb.

Wilshire stepped up to Pavel's shoulder. "Show me the plot."

A graph appeared on the lower half of the screen. "Laser no good. Path interrupted."

Wilshire cursed. "There's only so many moons. He's going to run out of protection right about . . . here." He tapped the screen. "Be ready."

Pavel nodded and inputted the commands.

Panic threatened to derail Kasim's thoughts. It didn't matter how good the pilot was; nobody could ignore the rules of physics. Braeder, Gunner, and Louis were going down unless . . .

"Twenty seconds," Pavel said, finger poised over the button. "Fifteen."

Wilshire settled back in his seat and rubbed his hands together like a kid waiting for his birthday cake. He flashed a smile at Sybil.

"Five, four, three . . ."

Kasim launched himself at Pavel. The scientist took the impact square on his chest and was catapulted backward over the chair. His head slammed against the duroalloy floor with a dull thud. Without breaking stride, Kasim slammed the palm of his hand on the kill switch at the same moment something flashed outside the portal. The terminal seized and went dark. He looked up in time to see Wilshire's fist connect with his face.

"Jesus! That was close," the pilot blurted. "They just missed us."

Ryan was still trying to process what happened. There was a flash outside the window, and then several lights started blinking in the cockpit. "The laser?"

Marcel nodded. "They must have gotten the laser working. Don't know how they missed."

Ryan tried to swallow the lump in his throat. He recalled what the laser had done to the Russian ship that tried to land last year. And even a glancing blow sent one of the senator's transports into an ice fissure. He didn't want to go out like that. "Get us down as fast as you can."

"Trying, Lieutenant."

Gunner stuck his head into the cockpit. "Everything all right?"

"Wilshire took a shot at us with the laser," Ryan said.

The veteran's eyes widened. "They missed?"

"Not exactly," the pilot said testing his instruments. "Portside thrusters are throwing up errors. I think they're damaged."

Ryan and Gunner exchanged a look. They were at the mercy of a newbie pilot, and there was absolutely nothing they could do about it. Ryan hoped Fate had a sense of humor.

"Get everyone in their suits, Gunner. This may not be a smooth landing."

"Copy that, Ace." He reached out and touched Ryan's shoulder. "And if something happens, it was good knowing you."

The ceiling spun just like the merry-go-round at the annual fair. It had the same bright lights, the same strobing effect, the same rushing wind . . . except this time, there was no music. Just some guy yelling expletives in the background. And one massive headache.

Kasim tried to focus, but his vision remained blurry, and his stomach threatened to rebel.

"Get the damn terminal back up!" Wilshire barked. "They're almost out of range."

"I'm trying, damn it," a familiar voice said. He should know that voice, but his brain refused to work. He rolled onto his back and groaned. His shoulder brushed against the terminal.

"Targeting up," Sybil announced. "Laser recharging. Computer trying to get a lock . . ."

"At least they ran out of moons to hide behind," Wilshire spat. He hovered over the terminal like a tiger about to pounce.

It took a supreme effort for Kasim to focus as the room drifted in and out like a mirage. Pavel lay unconscious on the floor beside him, the scientist's contented snores in contrast to the blood dribbling out his nose. His open switchblade lay under his sleeve. Ever so slowly, Kasim stretched out his arm and grasped the knife.

"There!" Wilshire stabbed the screen. "He has a narrow approach vector. Get ready."

Kasim's face felt like a swollen grapefruit and he couldn't breathe out of the right side of his nose. Ever so slowly, he reached his arm around the terminal, fingers falling into the recess at the back where the electrical wires exited.

"They're on final approach," Sybil said.

"Got you now, you Fleet bastard," Wilshire hissed, finger poised over the trigger.

Kasim heard the telltale click of the laser activating, followed by the dimming of the overhead lights as gigawatts of power were sucked from the grid. He regripped the knife and sawed through the wires. A warning buzzer sounded just as the laser fired.

"Shit!" Wilshire blurted.

"What?" Sybil straightened. "Did we hit him?"

"I think so, but power dropped at the last second."

"Why would . . ." Wilshire glanced down and seized the governor by the scruff of the neck. The knife flew from his grasp.

"Transport is veering off course," Sybil reported.

Wilshire leaned in until his face was inches away from Kasim's. "Think you accomplished something? Well, you're wrong." He pointed at the hologram. "Have a look. Its trajectory is off. Even if it somehow reached the moon, at that speed it'll hit the ice so hard, Humpty Dumpty wouldn't recognize it." He punched Kasim in the stomach and grinned as the governor retched.

"Have Andrei take him to the brig," Wilshire ordered. "And if he causes a problem, cut a hole in his suit and leave him on the runway."

Warning lights and sirens filled the cockpit. Marcel reeled back as sparks arced out of the instrument panel. "Goddamn! We're hit."

Ryan braced his arms against the bulkhead as the copilot's chair and everything not nailed down shook like a child's rattle. "The laser?"

"Yes." The pilot pushed several buttons, and the high-pitched whine mercifully ended. But ozone still leached out of the ship's internals. "Circuits overloading."

Ryan squeezed the sides of his chair. Visions of the transport spiraling off into the void or down Jupiter's gravity well sent chills up his spine. "Can you get us back on our vector?"

"Trying," Marcel grunted. "It's like a boxcar on wheels." Another red light pulsed just before something exploded in the ceiling. Flames belched between bulkhead seams.

Ryan grabbed the portable canister and sprayed white foam until the fire receded into black smoke.

"Sh . . . shunting emergency power," the pilot stuttered, his hands shaking like an addict in need of a fix. "Starboard thrusters unresponsive." He paused and stared at Ryan. "I think they're gone."

"Easy does it." Ryan intentionally kept his voice calm, his words measured. He sensed the pilot losing control, and now was not the time. "You got this. Remember Chan's lessons."

Something flashed past the cockpit window. Marcel gasped. "Parts of the external hull. Laser fried some of the plating."

"What do we do?"

The pilot froze. Ryan was about to take over when Marcel reached forward and stabbed several buttons on the instrument panel. "Chan says to use momentum to keep the ship on its vector." He pulled on a lever between the seats and hauled on the yoke with both hands. The transport shuddered, and the sound of screeching metal filled the cockpit.

"Is she responding?" Ryan shouted over the cacophony of discordant buzzers and sirens.

Marcel grimaced. "Barely. Even if we reach the moon, it's not going to be pretty. Odds are we're going to wrap ourselves around a hunk of ice or plunge into one of the fissures."

"How long?"

"Ten minutes."

"That's not good," Ryan muttered, staring at the gas giant growing larger by the second. Their target, the moon, was a small dot in the distance. He staggered into the hold as the ship shook from side to side. The rear section of the transport was a mess, with supplies and metal containers scattered across the floor.

Gunner had everyone strapped in with their suits buttoned up, and all the cryo-pods had been closed and locked. Ryan recognized the scared looks behind each faceplate. Louis and Plante had the children nestled between them, and Rani's hands trembled in her lap.

Something shorted beside Sasha's cryo-pod, and blue-tinged flames licked the air.

"Put that fire out!" Gunner shouted.

"On it!" She unhooked her restraint and dashed over to the electrical conduit before pulling down the power bar. The flames died.

"Brace for a hard landing," Ryan called. "Five minutes to impact."

Gunner gave him a tight-lipped nod, and Ryan hauled himself back into the cockpit. The ship shook like it was in the middle of a hurricane, and he had to brace himself before he could fasten his restraining harness. Outside the cockpit window, the moon was coming up fast. He could see the sheets of ice, the swells of frozen surface that formed tectonic plates.

"Three minutes," Marcel said, before whispering a quiet prayer.

Ryan didn't comment. He'd take all the help he could get.

"You should get back in the hold, Lieutenant," Marcel said. "The cockpit is the most exposed part of the ship."

Ryan forced a smile. “I have confidence in you. Now find a clear section of ice.”

“A clear section?” Marcel paused with his finger hovering over the console. “Goddamn, that’s it! The senator’s transport landed north of the station. Chan took us there during training.”

Ryan felt a faint hope stir in his breast. “Can we reach it?”

“Don’t know, but I’m sure as hell going to try.” He hauled on the yoke and the nose lifted a few degrees.

As the transport approached the moon, Ryan felt the weight of gravity pushing him into his seat. The station was a gray smudge in the distance with two transports parked on the runway. The rows of crosses remained unchanged. He wondered if they would be adding to the numbers shortly.

The ice came up fast. Ryan tightened his restraining harness. When the Russian transport had struck the surface, there’d been nothing left but a field of debris. And a child’s toy.

Jupiter gazed down on them, a bitter, ancient god bent on revenge.

“Hang on,” the pilot grunted. “I’m going to pull her nose up or she’ll come apart like a piñata. Need to bleed off momentum.”

“All right,” Ryan muttered, gripping the sides of his chair. “Not sure exactly what you mean, but all right.” He had a brief image of blue and green swirling on the surface, and frozen ice sentinels forming an honor guard as the ship went down.

They hit hard . . . and bounced. Ryan was thrown against his restraints, the straps cutting into his shoulders and thighs. His head whipped back as they struck the ice a second time. Titanium welds screamed in protest, and a high-pitched whine invaded the cockpit as the ship scraped across the frozen surface. The wings shredded the ice like a barber’s razor, throwing up a rooster tail of frozen spray. Something crashed in the cargo bay, and Ryan had a mental image of cryo-pods being torn off their bases, metal warping and glass coverings shattering.

Ryan saw it first: a thirty-foot wall of ice shaped like a dam. “Can we slow down?” he hollered over tearing plastek.

“Nothing I can do,” the pilot shouted, throwing up his hands.

“Shit,” Ryan whispered. It was instinctive; he closed his eyes. The rest was up to Fate.

He heard a loud crash, and everything went dark.

# CHAPTER 36

*It does not matter how slowly you go as long as you do not stop.*

DAY 145, 0715 HOURS

The station trembled like a tin hut in a windstorm as the transport thundered past. Kasim initially thought the ship was going to crash into the hangar, but then its nose rose a few degrees and it flew over *Serenity*, heading for the ice fields.

Standing beside him in the decompression chamber, Andrei gawked as the ship sailed only meters above the station. The whites of his eyes doubled in size. "Holy shit."

They watched the transport until it disappeared from view.

"Get dressed!" Andrei shoved Kasim toward the suit rack. "You heard the man: if you give me a problem, I'll feed you into the airlock without a helmet."

"Braeder reached the moon," Kasim whispered.

Andrei snorted. "For all the good it did. Do you think he's going to survive a landing on the ice sheets? In a wrecked ship?"

Kasim didn't reply. He knew the odds.

The speaker on the wall crackled to life. "Wilshire to Andrei."

"Go ahead."

"Where are you?"

"In the decompression chamber, getting suited up. About to take the governor to the brig."

"Forget that. I'm sending someone else to escort the governor. Your job is to find out what happened to that transport."

Andrei scratched an ulcer on his face. "You think they're alive?"

"Not likely. Rutherford says the ice sheets beyond the landing strip are full of fissures and crevasses, but I want to be sure. I'll send some help, so suit up and wait for them outside. Need you to confirm they're all dead." The channel closed.

Sybil burst into the room. "What the hell was that? I heard a loud roar."

"Ryan's transport survived your laser attack," Kasim replied, a touch of spite in his tone.

"It's headed for a crash landing," Andrei said, grabbing Kasim by the arm and shoving him toward the suit rack.

"Where's it going down?" she asked.

"Wilshire says somewhere beyond the landing strip."

Ignoring Kasim, Sybil stepped up to the portal. A dust devil spun across the surface. "You going to check?"

"As soon as reinforcements arrive." He grinned coldly at Kasim. "And I'll be bringing lasers. Just in case."

Sybil's expression cracked, enough for Kasim to see past the facade. Did she still have feelings for Ryan? It was time to find out.

"Must be tough to sell your soul like this, Sybil," Kasim said matter-of-factly. "Or do you consider it a trade? Your life for Ryan's?"

Sybil's jaw worked, but no words emerged. Kasim filed that away.

Andrei grinned. "Emphasis on the word *life*, Governor. Anything less doesn't count."

"And the rest of the colonists?" Kasim asked. "What do you say to those left behind?"

"Nothing." Andrei shrugged. "You UN types are good at the talking stuff."

Kasim spared Sybil a look before he stepped into the airlock. She didn't appear happy.

Consciousness was slow in returning, like morning fog dissipating in a sun-induced haze.

Ryan felt himself being dragged across the ice. Someone had one hand under each shoulder and was unceremoniously hauling him over the ruts and divots that littered the moon's surface. Chunks of ice snagged the fabric of his EV suit, pulling and stretching but not tearing, thank God.

His mind kicked into gear, and he remembered the transport and the seconds before they slammed into that wall of ice. He opened his eyes and noted the flashing yellow icons on his heads-up display. Battery at fifteen percent, vitals not even close to normal. That's when the pain hit: a gnawing ache in his shoulder that raced up his neck. He groaned.

The hands released him. "You awake, Lieutenant?"

Ryan blinked his eyes into focus. Smith hovered over him, a worried look behind his face shield. Black burn marks covered his EV suit like streaks of mascara. "What happened?"

Smith looked over his shoulder. "Transport's busted up pretty good. There was a fire in the cargo hold we couldn't put out, so the doctor and I started hauling people clear."

Ryan's brain remained cloudy. *Louis pulling people out of the wreckage?* "Where is it?"

Smith pointed. "Landing gear sheared off when we hit, and the bulk of the ship is fetched up against the ice."

Ryan turned and . . . shuddered. It looked like the fuselage had been squeezed in a vise. Ribbed lines of compaction extended in a circular pattern, and cracks radiated through the portals on the starboard side. The main hatch, dangling on one hinge, was barely visible through a pall of dark smoke.

"Did you get everyone out?"

The lines on Smith's forehead deepened. "Working on it. We grabbed the first bodies we found and started hauling. There's the doc."

Ryan rolled on his side. The pain in his shoulder was beginning to fade, and his arm started working again. Across the ice ravine, Louis hauled a prone Gunner with one hand.

"I'm good," Ryan said, pulling himself up to his knees. "Get the rest out." The transport looked like it could explode at any minute, especially if internal flames touched something vital.

"On it." The big man hurried back to the ship.

"Louis, you read me?"

Twenty feet away, the doctor released Gunner. "Copy that," he panted. "You okay, Ryan? The cockpit was crushed. You and Marcel were pinned under the front section of the ship. We had to pry you out with a metal beam."

"How's Marcel?"

"Dead. Internal bleeding. Nothing I could do."

Ryan gritted his teeth. Marcel, despite his nerves and inexperience, had put them down in one piece. More or less. "I'm coming to help—"

He recoiled when a laser whizzed over the doctor's head. "Get down!"

But Louis looked around, confused.

"Now, dammit!" Ryan shouted as Smith came stumbling back. "Find cover!"

Louis finally seemed to gather his senses. He ducked behind a thick block of ice.

"Three approaching from the station side," Smith wheezed. "By the suits, I'd say two from Ceres and one from Europa."

*One of our own colonists?* Ryan had a problem digesting the concept. "Are you sure it's not a Ceres survivor in one of our suits?"

"No, two are walking funny, like they're trying to figure out gravity."

Ryan grimaced. Smith didn't have to explain further. The Ceres crew had just transitioned from three to sixty percent gravity. Their bodies would be fighting every step. "Did you grab any weapons?"

Smith ducked as another laser flashed. "Sorry, I was focused on getting everyone out of the ship."

Ryan surveyed the nearby ice. It was hard to blame Smith, but that meant they couldn't stay. "Doc, wake up Gunner, I don't care how, and back away from the ship. We'll link up on the other side of the crevasse."

Louis gave him a quick thumbs-up.

"What about the others?" Smith glanced anxiously at the wrecked transport. "The fire was spreading."

"We'll have to come back." In his head, Ryan knew that was a forlorn hope. But staying put and facing three men armed with lasers spelled a quick death.

He slid sideways down an ice sheet until it transitioned into a fissure that ran parallel to the station. Raising his head over the berm, he was able to locate the enemy. Smith was right; two of them were moving like drunk teenagers.

Another beam of light flashed overhead.

"Th-they know where we are," Smith stammered.

"Yes, but they don't know the icefields like we do." Or at least two of them didn't. Plus, Ryan was betting they would stop and check the transport, gifting him time.

He slid down the fissure into an ice ravine, where Louis and Gunner waited. "Okay?"

"Fine." The veteran grunted, leaning on the doctor for support.

"Took a pretty good knock to the head," Louis explained, catching Ryan's eye. "Helmet is dented, and he's got a deep laceration on his scalp."

Ryan noted the blood dripping down Gunner's cheek and the glazed look in his eyes. "Need help?"

"I got him." Louis wrapped his good arm around the veteran's shoulders. "Let's move before they find us."

They needed a plan, but right now, it boiled down to *run and stay alive*. Ryan spun toward the ice sheet that tilted away from the station. "Smith, take point. Follow the fissure." About two hundred meters ahead, the surface splintered into a maze of ice blocks. Where he'd lost the senator's marines last year.

"On it." Smith kept his head low as he started off.

Three figures circled the crashed ship before firing off several laser blasts. Ryan ducked around a low ridge just before one beam stabbed into the surface.

He caught up to Louis and Gunner and grasped the veteran's free arm. "They're right behind me." They half-carried, half-dragged Gunner along the surface as laser beams split the darkness.

Five minutes later, an exhausted foursome stumbled into the familiar maze of ice blocks. Parts of the old Russian ship, the one Ryan had shot down a year earlier, were still visible, frozen in the ice. Jupiter blazed overhead, storms swirling deep in its atmosphere.

"Keep moving," Ryan panted over the hum of the fans in his suit. They ducked behind a column of ice pillars that ran deep into the maze. Only after they made it into the heart of the icy labyrinth did Ryan allow them time to take a break. While they huddled in shadow, Ryan scanned the far side of the ridge. It wasn't a minute later that three EV suits popped into view. Two were visibly laboring, hands on knees, lasers hanging loose off wrists.

He could only imagine the animated discussion between the Ceres survivors and whoever was in the Alliance suit. Gravity had to be exacting a punishing toll on the new arrivals, and the thought of descending into the maze would seem like a hellish punishment. After frantic gesturing, all three turned and headed toward the station.

Ryan fell back against a six-foot pillar. "They're leaving."

"Good thing," Louis wheezed. "My battery is down to ten percent."

"Mine's at twelve," Smith said.

"Gunner?"

"Fifteen."

Ryan peered closer. The veteran didn't look good, but at least the blood had stopped dripping down his face.

"We'll recharge at the extractor," Ryan decided. They were halfway there anyway.

"And after that?" Louis asked. "They control the station and we don't have so much as a peashooter."

Ryan wracked his brain but came up empty. "One problem at a time. First step is to recharge the suits and take care of Gunner."

"I'm fine," the veteran grunted, even as he swayed unsteadily on his feet.

"Yeah," Louis said. "You and your concussion are doing great."

Gunner looked ready to snap back when the com clicked on. Somebody was broadcasting on all frequencies.

"Lieutenant, are you out there?"

Ryan recognized Wilshire's voice. He raised a finger as if to his lips.

"If you can hear me, you should know I've taken everyone from your transport prisoner. Those that survived, anyway. Some of them are hurt bad and may not live if they don't receive medical attention soon."

Louis's eyes widened, but Ryan shook his head.

"I'll give you ten minutes to answer, and thirty to appear at the main airlock," Wilshire continued. "After that, I'll start spacing colonists every fifteen minutes. Maybe I'll start with the one named Rani. We just pulled her off that wrecked transport. Sybil says she's pretty important around here. Her blood will be on your hands."

Ryan waited. He sensed the tension in the group and used his hands to calm them.

"Think about it, Braeder," Wilshire said. "How many friendlies do you have out there? Two? Three? Probably injured from the crash and running low on battery power? Do yourself a favor and surrender. Sybil promises you'll be treated humanely."

Ryan had heard enough. He held up one finger.

"Damn, Ryan," Louis said on channel one. "He's going to start killing colonists."

"He won't," Ryan replied. "He doesn't know if his message got through, and even a bastard like him won't waste lives unless it gives him an advantage."

The doctor tilted his head as if considering the thought. "That makes sense. But he's right about our situation."

"Vet's full of shit," Gunner muttered. "Wilshire's wrong."

"Something I'm missing?"

"Yeah." Gunner grabbed Louis for support but directed his grin at Ryan. "He doesn't realize this is our backyard, and the last person who tried to take it got his ass kicked."

As they approached the extractor, Ryan checked their six for the umpteenth time. He breathed easier when he realized no one was following. The surface was barren, with only a few dust devils wandering over ice that glowed orange and gold under Jupiter's watchful eye.

Louis threw him a concerned look as he helped Gunner. "Still clear?"

"Yeah, I think they went back to the station."

"I hope Sasha and Rani are okay."

Smith edged over a small rise. "Lieutenant, take a look at this."

Puzzled, Ryan joined him. The extractor was a few hundred meters ahead. Except it looked different. "What the heck is that?"

"Looks like the entrance to some sort of cave," Smith said.

In Ryan's mind, the dots lined up. "That's where Rani said they found the alien artifact. Take us there."

"What about our suits?" Louis asked. "My battery is down to five percent."

"Rani said they set up a lab, which means there's a power supply. And maybe we can find something to use as a weapon."

Smith led them down a set of ice stairs into a large cave. An airlock greeted them at the bottom, and the group quickly cycled into the makeshift lab. Ryan's feeling of relief at finally getting out of the boxy suits was tempered by what he saw inside: a well-equipped workshop with computers, desks, and chairs, and monitors hanging from plastek walls. All surrounding an egg-shaped object sitting in the center. White hieroglyphics pulsed softly on the surface.

"I'll be damned," Louis muttered. "An alien object. Something I never thought I'd see."

Ryan stepped closer and peered at a surface that resembled fine resin. A thin foil—the antenna, according to Rani's report— sat on a small table at one end, and parts of the scissor truck peeked out from underneath. He unsealed his helmet and pulled it off. "Let's get our batteries charged. Smith, find an outlet."

"That's not going to be a problem, Lieutenant," the reservist said, walking up to a circuit box. "Looks like the whole place is layered with power cables." He cleared a space in front of one of the outlets.

"Rani was a busy beaver," Louis observed, unzipping the top half of his suit. He filled several glasses of water from a nearby dispenser and passed them around.

Ryan nodded his thanks. He didn't realize how thirsty he was until he sucked back the entire contents. "Smith, see if you can find the com or any direct line to Ops. We need to know what the hell is going on in the station."

"On it." The reservist started at one end of the lab and began checking terminals.

Ryan walked over to Louis, who was helping Gunner get out of his suit. "How is he?"

"I'm fine," the veteran growled. "Just a scratch."

"He's got a concussion," Louis said, giving Gunner a sidelong look. "If I can find some supplies, I'll sew up that cut on his scalp."

"How bad is it?"

Louis planted his hands on his hips. "His vision is blurry and he's ataxic."

Ryan frowned. "Ataxic?"

"Hard time walking because his coordination is shot. In an ideal world, I'd restrict him to bed."

"Unfortunately, that's not an option," Ryan said, studying the veteran. "Gunner, I need to know if you can function. Or do I leave you here?"

Gunner leaned his head against the plastek wall and closed his eyes. "I'll be fine, Ace. Just need a few minutes."

Ryan raised his eyebrows at Louis.

"As much time as you can give us," the doctor said. "I'll get some fluids into him and see if that helps."

Ryan rubbed his whiskers. "Wilshire will probably use our own colonists to search the surface, which includes this cave. We have to be gone when they get here."

Louis rubbed the end of his stump. "You think our people will follow him? After they learn what he did?"

"*Our people* will hold their nose when they vote if it means a chance to survive," Ryan replied. "Don't forget about the scientists and miners Rani said she tossed into the brig. I'm guessing they're not favorably inclined toward our cause."

Deep furrows formed on the doctor's brow. "You have a plan?"

"Working on it." He gestured to Smith. "Right now, the priority is intel."

Louis inclined his head toward the artifact. "I can't believe I'm in the same room with something constructed by an alien race." He shook his head. "Like Rani said, our first contact with ET, and we can't talk to it."

Ryan's lips tightened into a white line. "There'll be time for that later, maybe. Get Gunner settled and I'll start looking for a weapon." Not that he expected to find anything useful in a science lab.

The reservist straightened over a monitor. "Sir, I found the com."

Ryan hurried over. "Looks like a direct line to Ops." He slid into the seat and entered instructions into the closest computer.

"What are you doing?" Louis asked.

"Using the circuit to dive into the main server." Ryan didn't take his eyes off the screen as he plugged away. "If I use my command codes to access internal systems, I might find out what we're up against."

"Won't they spot it?"

"They're civilians like you. Did you think of it?"

"Uh, no."

"Then they shouldn't either." Ryan tapped a few more keys and hit the Execute button. "Okay, I'm in. Time to see what's going on."

A window in the bottom corner of the screen opened, and suddenly they were looking at the inside of Ops. Ryan recognized Bennett pacing back and forth in front of the command chair, and seated at Gunner's terminal, a morose-looking Rani staring out the starboard portal. Two other men he didn't recognize sat slumped against the servers at the back of the room.

He reached over and turned on audio.

"*. . . don't care,*" Bennett snarled. "*Send your men out with lasers and find them. I can't resume prepping the transports until I know the surface is clear.*"

*"Should we give them a chance to surrender?"* a male voice asked. *"If they're on the surface, their batteries will eventually run low, and they'll have to come in."*

Ryan panned the camera left. A tall, thin man stood next to Rani, rubbing his hands together anxiously.

"I recognize him," Louis said, stepping closer. "That's Rutherford, one of the scientists. Kasim put him on one of the cleanup crews last year. Arrogant SOB."

Bennett cast a furious glance at Rutherford. *"Did Ensign Singh give you a chance before she shoved you into the brig? After she killed three of your comrades? What do you think* Braeder *will do to you if he regains control of the station?"*

Ryan blinked. He had forgotten Rani had killed people, a fact she glossed over in the retelling when they were still on Ceres.

Rutherford looked like he was struggling for something to say. Finally, he threw up his hands. *"All right. Tell Wilshire I'll send out three miners to help search."*

*"Make sure they have lasers,"* Bennett barked.

Rutherford's lips curved upward in a snarl. *"You don't want to go with them?"*

The brunette didn't answer. Instead, she walked over and passed some water to the men at the back of Ops.

"Gravity is taking a toll," Louis observed quietly. "The longer they're here, the harder it will be on their bodies."

Ryan nodded. That made sense. "Which means Wilshire must be in a hurry to get off this moon. Before all his men and women turn into quivering piles of Jell-O."

"Where's Wilshire now?" Smith asked.

"Probably getting the ships ready for launch," Ryan replied, watching an anxious-looking Rutherford hurry out of Ops. "Like Doc said, time is a factor."

Louis taped a bandage over Gunner's cut. "You think he's going to Earth?"

"Not initially," Ryan said. "If sixty percent gravity is torture, one hundred percent Earth gravity will kill them. I'm thinking they land on Luna and acclimatize until they can build up their muscles and bones. It'll take months."

"And then home?"

"Why not? He's got a vaccine. And it's the only place in the solar system with enough oxygen, food, and water."

"Except for one problem," Louis said. "There's no guarantee the vaccine works."

"What are you talking about? The Russian scientists had a sample of the bug and made something to kill it."

"That's not exactly correct." Louis pushed his glasses up the bridge of his nose. "They injected pieces of dead bacteria into a host and waited for an immune response. No one tested the results against the real thing."

Gunner stirred and opened his eyes. His color was whiter than usual. "Are you saying it might not work?"

"I'm saying medicine is littered with cases of positive lab trials that never translated into real-world success. The way the Russian scientists ran roughshod over protocol, I sure as hell wouldn't volunteer for the test group."

Ryan exchanged a look with Gunner. "That's interesting."

Smith walked over. "Nothing here, Lieutenant. No weapons or gear we can use."

Gunner sat up and leaned against the counter.

"How you feeling?" Louis asked.

"Better. Legs coming back and vision is clear. Help me up."

Louis's eyes narrowed, but he didn't object. "Take it slow."

Gunner groaned as his legs absorbed the weight. Louis found a cloth and wiped the blood off his face.

"If we can't find weapons—" Ryan stopped when Gunner pointed at the screen.

"Rani knows we're here. Look."

They crowded around the monitor. The ensign had dropped one hand and subtly tapped three fingers against her thigh.

"She wants us to use channel three," Ryan said.

Lines formed on Louis's brow. "How does she know?"

"Because she can work her terminal blindfolded," Ryan said, recalling how good she and Marco were at their workstations. "Something must have alerted her."

"She's got babysitters, Ace, and we can't wait around for a chance to talk," Gunner warned. "Not if they're sending out a hunting party. I figure twenty minutes."

Ryan got up and checked the batteries. Forty percent. Better but not great. "They need more time to recharge."

"Where are we going, Lieutenant?" Smith asked.

"We'll circle around the extractor and approach the station from the second greenhouse," Ryan decided. "The temporary airlock to Delta Hive is still there. I'm betting Wilshire won't know enough to cover that entrance."

Gunner gave him a look but didn't say anything. He didn't have to. Last time they had launched an attack through that entrance, a lot of people got dead. Including Marco.

This time, without weapons, the odds were worse.

# CHAPTER 37

*What you do not wish upon yourself, extend not to others.*

DAY 145, 0905 HOURS

When the yellow indicator on her board stopped flashing—and no one noticed—Rani was finally able to breathe again. She'd nearly had a heart attack when it activated, and she was lucky Bennett was occupied coordinating launch preparations. Rani would have tried to blame it on a subsystem failure, but an inner voice suggested her captors were the paranoid type and wouldn't believe her.

Someone had accessed the internal security system, including the cameras. But from where? And who?

Whoever it was should have seen her signal, so she subtly shifted one of her com channels to number three and left it on mute. She'd be ready whenever that person could talk.

The fact that someone was out there, someone on her side, infused her with a sense of hope. To this point, her tenure as leader of Europa had been an abject failure. She had rescued the group on Ceres but lost the colony in the interim and then gotten captured. Braeder would have done things differently. Somehow, he would have found a third option, even though she still didn't see a way through the problem.

Wilshire hurried into Ops, Sybil and Bennett right behind him. "Show me the hangar, Singh," he snapped. "I want to see the prisoners."

Rani stole a look at Sybil as she slipped into Marco's old terminal. The senator's daughter had stuck close to Wilshire since they landed, almost like she feared if she strayed too far, the Ceres survivors would leave without her. Rani briefly considered refusing his orders, but the last time she had tried to resist, Wilshire put Solomon in the airlock without a helmet and threatened to push the button. His casual disregard for life shocked her.

She begrudgingly typed in commands, and a view of the transport-hangar interior appeared on her monitor.

Wilshire struggled to catch his breath, and Rani savored his discomfort. Every Ceres survivor was suffering, their muscles and joints no doubt screaming as tissues stretched under the weight of gravity. He leaned over the back of her chair. "Focus on the brig."

Rani dutifully zoomed in on the locked room at the far end of the building. Eight people were packed into its narrow confines. She recognized Sasha and Archie rubbing their hands together in temperatures barely above freezing. Solomon had his back to the camera and blocked part of the view, but Plante, Vrabel, and the surviving reservists were in there somewhere, jammed in so tight, it must have felt like a tomb. Thankfully, the kids had survived the crash and had been sent to the hive, and the pilots were in the transports, prepping them for the long flight into the inner system. The goons who marched her friends into the brig had unplugged half the portable heaters just for the hell of it. On the transport back to Europa, Braeder had told her most of them were criminals, and by their actions, it was easy to believe.

Wilshire opened the com. "Andrei, everything good?"

"Status quo. Although it's damn cold in here."

"All right, turn on some of the heaters, but tell them if they try something stupid, I'm going to shut them off for good."

Rani's jaw tightened. Archie's attempt to break out of the hangar hadn't gotten far, not after they discovered Wilshire had taken their EV suits back to the decompression chamber. Now Andrei and another goon stood guard with the heater controls at their fingertips.

Wilshire stood and rubbed his legs, wincing slightly. "Sam, keep an eye on Singh until we get back."

"Where are you going?"

"It's time Sybil and I began the interview process. See who wants off this moon. I'll send someone to spell you when we're finished."

Bennett jerked a thumb toward the men slumped in front of the servers. "What about Boris and Dimitri?"

"Wake them," Wilshire said, and passed Sybil his laser. "I need two men in the decompression chamber to stand guard. It's almost time to leave this moon and I don't want any screw-ups."

Rani shivered as Wilshire walked out the door. She felt the sands of time slipping between her fingers.

*1000 Hours*

Rani's heart jumped into her throat when the com flashed once and went out. She tried to cover it with her hand, but her lack of coordination showed as she banged it off the side of the terminal. Insides tightening, she stole a look at Bennett in the command chair . . . and said a silent thank-you after realizing the woman had closed her eyes again. She was worn out, gravity sinking deep into her flesh, draining her strength.

The yellow light flashed again. This time, she caught the words on the screen before they disappeared.

*Update. Crew.*

She took a slow, deep breath to calm her nerves and typed in a response.

*Locked down. Brig.*

Several long seconds dragged by. What was happening? She wanted to scream.

*Access system. Sasha.*

Her brow knotted in confusion. With everything falling apart, it felt like she was in a madhouse. Nothing made sense. As if on cue, Bennett startled herself awake.

"What are you doing?" she demanded, aiming the laser at Rani's head.

Rani summoned the courage to regard the other woman coolly. "I'm doing nothing. You're the one talking in your sleep and waking yourself up."

Bennett's eyes narrowed. "You're lying."

Rani shrugged. "Suit yourself, but look at my board. It hasn't changed since you drifted into dreamland." She spread her hands over the control panel as if to display the evidence.

Bennett lowered the laser and pulled the blanket tighter around her thin frame. "Better not try anything," she muttered.

Rani leaned back and played with her rings. Even if Bennett fell asleep, it wouldn't help. Somebody was reaching out and she desperately wanted it to be Braeder. Wilshire said they found casualties on the crashed transport, but he never specified if the lieutenant was among them. And he sure as hell would say something if his nemesis had up and died.

Sasha? She was a great engineer, but even she couldn't do anything from the brig. Rani had taken Sybil's meals to that cell for almost a year. The inside was as familiar as the back of her hand: the bed, desk, computer . . . She stopped. *The computer*. It had never been a threat because the senator's daughter didn't have a clue how to hack the system. Sasha, on the other hand . . . Rani began typing.

Bennett resumed snoring as Rani sent an encrypted message to the brig.

Kasim felt the frustration build until he thought his brain was going to burst. He was stuck in the brig, barely able to move, while Wilshire and his goons ransacked his colony. He had started thinking of it as *his* colony weeks before, after Ryan lifted martial law. His colony. His responsibility. And now the bastards were raiding the cupboards and stealing the valuable bits.

He unconsciously started to pace before he realized there wasn't enough room. Not with Archie taking the cot—he needed it after two Ceres goons worked him over after the aborted escape attempt—and Solomon and the others standing in front of the door. And Sasha hammering away at the computer.

"Anything?" he asked, instantly regretting the impatience in his tone.

The young engineer didn't look up. "Rani dropped the firewall. I'm trying to link up with the servers and access the mainframe."

"Don't you need command codes to do that?"

She made a face. "I stole them from the old fart a long time ago. He doesn't even know. It saves a ton of time when we make repairs."

Kasim blinked. He wasn't sure if he was shocked more at her breach of protocol or her casual disregard for doing it. He went with the latter. "Gunner won't be happy when he finds out."

"What's he going to do, fire me?"

Kasim's mouth opened before he realized he had no words. She had a point. "If you get in, what's our next step?"

Solomon squeezed past his comrades to stand behind her. "How about activating the internal cameras so we can see how many of the bastards we're dealing with."

"That was first on my list," Sasha said, as if explaining the importance of vegetables to a preteen.

Solomon turned red.

"What about getting us out of here?" Vrabel asked. "We're as useless as a bag of hammers."

"Yeah," Solomon grunted. "Love to get my hands on them Ceres bastards when they don't have a laser pointed at me."

Sasha looked up at Kasim. "I need ideas. What do we do after I gain control?"

Frustration continued to flow through Kasim's veins, this time directed at his own incompetence. She was asking about some type of military response. He was a lowly administrator. This was out of his depth.

Archie stirred on the bed and groaned. The senior geologist looked like a car had run over his face: two swollen eyes, a broken nose, and multicolored bruises that were starting to come into their own.

Kasim laid a hand on his shoulder. "Easy, my friend. You need rest."

Archie opened one eye. "And you need a plan before Wilshire blasts off in our transports."

Kasim wrung his hands. "What can we do? They control the station."

"Think outside the box, Governor. You worked with admin types. What would slow them down?"

Novel thoughts jumbled inside Kasim's head. *Throw a wrench into the works?*

He turned to Sasha. "Can you access secondary systems?"

She stopped typing commands. "Ah, yeah, but why?"

Kasim bared his teeth. "Because we're about to become a major pain in the ass."

"Our people got the message," Ryan said, leaning back in his chair.

Louis stepped over to his shoulder and blew out a cloud of gray mist. It was cold in the ice cave. "How do you know?"

Ryan pointed to a section of the screen that had gone dark. "The concourse lights just went out."

"And how does that help us?"

"Slows down Wilshire, for one. The longer we delay his launch, the more opportunities we'll have. How are the suit batteries?"

"About eighty percent," Smith replied.

"We better get ready," Ryan decided, sensing the endgame approaching. "Wilshire's goons won't be long."

Gunner pulled on the lower half of his suit. Louis had found some medical supplies in a cabinet and had given him a shot. The veteran's color looked almost normal.

Ryan started to reach for his own when something about the artifact caught his attention. He walked over until he was an arm's length away. Dark, squiggly lines had appeared on the surface.

"What are you doing, Ace?"

Ryan hadn't noticed it until now. "Don't you see it? The markings changed after we arrived, almost like it sensed us."

Gunner stopped getting dressed and peered closer. "I hadn't noticed. What do you think it means?"

Ryan rubbed his jaw thoughtfully. "Rani said it reacted to external stimuli."

"You're not figuring to do something rash, are ya, Ace?" Gunner asked. "'Cause she also mentioned something about lobbing bombs. You willing to accept the risk? When the colony is balancing on a knife's edge?"

"Not sure I agree, Gunner." Ryan walked around the artifact. The lines pulsed white, then cycled through shades of blue. Silently beckoning him. . . He stopped. "Did you see this?"

Louis was the first to join him. "What?"

Ryan pointed. A recessed port sat open near the base, revealing two narrow openings.

"You're scaring me, Ace," Gunner said, voice low. "When did that happen?"

"I think it's been there the whole time. We just didn't see it."

"So, what now?" Louis asked.

Ryan stared at the artifact. The open panel felt like an invitation.

Taking a deep breath, he reached inside the artifact. He was about to leap over a cliff blindfolded and didn't know if he was going to hit water . . . or a pile of rocks.

His skin touched something solid, and a warmth spread up his fingers and into his arm. The color of the markings deepened to a dark violet, and a soft hum filled the air. The heat sank deep into his bones before expanding to fill his entire being, like steam released into a room. His brain struggled to describe a myriad of strange sensations, but it was like assigning color to a taste, or shape to the wind. There was no reference point. And lurking in the background . . .

"We gotta move, Ace!" Gunner barked. He grabbed Ryan and yanked him away. "They're in the tunnel." He made a beeline to the second airlock at the back of the lab.

"What?" It took Ryan a full second to focus. The lab. The tunnel? Light beams splitting the darkness. "Shit!" He hauled on his helmet and ran after Gunner. Louis and Smith were already in the airlock.

"Go!" Gunner shoved him inside and hit the button on the control panel. The hatch started to close but not before they got a look at bodies running down the stairs.

"Deuterium miners," Ryan observed as the thump of air being pumped out vibrated his bones. "I recognize them."

"Traitors," Gunner muttered. "And we still have nothing to fight with. If this cave turns into a dead end, they'll be shooting fish in a barrel."

Ryan didn't answer. Those were *his* colonists who had switched sides. Just like last year. Maybe he was the common denominator.

The green light flashed, and they spilled out of the hatch and ran deeper into the cave. Suit lamps revealed towering walls of ice, glistening surfaces that hadn't been disturbed in eons. Smith took point, his suit light bobbing in the darkness.

"Mind your step." Gunner grimaced when Ryan almost slipped. "You won't be much good to me if you break a bone."

"Not sure how much *good* we can do against lasers anyway," Ryan panted, the whine of his fans making it hard to hear. "And I'm pretty sure they're not taking prisoners."

"True, that," Louis huffed, and abruptly held up.

Ryan came to a sliding stop. "What's wrong?"

The doctor pointed. "I see light."

"Goddamn." Ryan didn't want to jinx what looked to be a miracle as he hurried over. A ten-by-ten-foot-square section of ice had been cut out of the ceiling, revealing a smattering of stars.

Gunner examined one of what appeared to be several guidewires hanging from the ledge. "They must have used this opening to lower the scissor truck." He stared at Louis. "Can you climb?"

The doctor glanced behind. "Do I have a choice?"

"I'll help," Smith said, grabbing a wire. "I'll climb below you and take the weight. You keep your hand on the wire and your feet on my shoulders."

Ryan was dubious, but the deuterium miner erased any doubt as he helped the doctor up the line. Europa's gravity was only sixty percent of Earth's, and yet they all had a healthy sweat going by the time they reached the top.

Ryan was struggling on the lip when Gunner shouted, "Look out!" and hauled him over the edge just as a laser blasted out of the tunnel and melted several inches of hard-packed ice. They tumbled backward together.

Smith pushed Louis over the top and quickly followed before two beams flashed past his helmet. He fell face down on the surface, puffing hard.

"Thanks," Ryan wheezed. "That was close."

Gunner patted him on the chest. "You can buy me a bottle of the vet's rotgut when we get out of this mess. Right now, cut those lines before the turncoats climb up."

Ryan forced himself to his knees. A wave of grayness momentarily stole his vision, reminding him of the artifact. *What the hell did I feel?*

He pulled out a knife from his toolbelt and helped Gunner cut the guide wires that had been secured to bolts hammered into the ice. The last one gave way with a jolt, and Ryan figured at least one of the bastards had a good fall.

"Let's go," he said, getting his bearings.

"Which way?" Gunner asked. "If we head away from the station, we can lose them in the icefields."

Ryan pondered his options. Gunner was right; it was the best chance to survive. But that wouldn't help them regain control of the station or free his crew.

"No, Wilshire and his band of criminals are preparing to leave the moon. If we don't stop them, we might as well open our EV door, because there'll be no way to save the colonists."

Gunner frowned. "You want to head to the station? Don't mind saying it's a hell of a risk. If one of Wilshire's patrols finds us . . . well, we got lucky last time."

"I hate to say it, but the Neanderthal is right," Louis said. "Now that they know we're alive, they'll scour the surface."

"They will," Ryan acknowledged. It was a stupid decision, but he was at peace with it. Even if it got him killed. "I'm not giving up this colony without a fight. Not to Bordeaux or the senator, and certainly not to Wilshire." He paused. "You don't have to come."

Gunner gave him a wide grin. "'Course we're coming, Ace. I've never been one to shy away from a good fight, and I'm sure as hell not starting now. The vet will be useless, but Smith wants to crack a few heads."

The big miner grinned while Louis shot daggers at Gunner.

"That's it, then." Ryan stared into the distance, to where vast ice sheets dominated, and started walking. "Let's finish this thing."

The doctor caught up to him as they started across the ice field. "What happened with the artifact? You looked like you went into a trance."

"I think it's alive."

Louis turned his gaze on him. For a second, Ryan thought the doctor was going to burst out laughing. "Did it zap you in the head or something? It's not organic, and Rani said it's been in the ice for thousands of years."

Ryan ignored his derisive tone. "Maybe some type of AI intelligence, but there's definitely a cognitive entity inside. I felt a . . . presence."

"'A presence' doesn't help."

"Sorry." Ryan threw up his gloved hands. "It's not something I can explain. There was a curiosity, maybe even sadness . . . until Gunner hauled me away."

"It's my fault?" Gunner's eyebrows merged into a single fuzzy line behind his shield. "I was keeping you alive."

"It's always your fault," Louis muttered as they skirted a row of ice columns that were almost as tall as an Alliance transport. Then, to Ryan: "How far?"

"About half a klick. Keep your head down. The landing strip is over that ridge, but they could still see us." He scanned the surrounding ice sheets. With Jupiter moving across the sky, bright colors were giving way to blue and purple shades. Unlike Ceres with its monochrome palette, Europa's stunning display imparted a soothing feeling.

"You thinking about the Delta Hive entrance, Ace?"

"It's probably not on Wilshire's radar. Think you can bypass the lock?"

The veteran's eyes narrowed. "Pretty sure. After Marco disabled the control panel last year, we never repaired it. Never thought it would be necessary. Figure all we need to do is open the box and splice a couple of wires."

"If they have no one watching that entrance," Louis cautioned.

Ryan didn't comment. He was taking a big gamble. If Wilshire had someone with a laser stationed by the airlock, the result wouldn't be pretty.

Gunner took them on a circuitous route to the station and then slid around the side to the makeshift entrance. Heat spilling out of the uninsulated airlock had melted the top millimeters of ice, leaving a sheen that resembled a skating rink.

As if on cue, Smith uttered a warning. "Mind your step. It's slippery as hell."

"Keep your eyes peeled," Ryan said. "Gunner, bypass the lock."

"What about me?" Louis asked, breathing heavy.

"Stay on Gunner's hip. The moment the hatch cycles open, jump inside."

The doctor slid up beside Gunner, who already had the metal flap peeled off the panel. His gloved fingers shifted through the wires before finding the right pair.

"One second, Ace," he murmured. "Just need to connect these two."

The hatch began to rise on hydraulic motors. Louis squeezed inside.

"Gunner, follow . . ."

Something flashed overhead.

It took a millisecond for Ryan to connect the dots: a bright light, a new smudge on the exterior hull . . . "Get down!" he shouted. "Laser!"

Smith was a second too slow reacting. Ryan had a close look at his confused expression when a beam struck his helmet, and his faceplate actually glowed red before he screamed and doubled over. A second beam hit his regulator seal, melting the soft joint into burned cinder. Ryan lunged forward even as part of his brain pleaded against the inevitable. Air belched from the hole, and the white fabric shriveled like vacuum wrap. A final yelp sounded over the com before Smith's eyes rolled back and his body began to seize.

A strong hand gripped Ryan's shoulder, whipping him around. "He's dead, Ace, and we're gonna join him if we don't get out of here."

Ryan started toward the open airlock but jumped back when a laser singed the hull by his hand. He dived away from the hatch.

"What are you doing?" Gunner demanded, dropping into a crouch.

"If we enter the airlock, they'll pin us inside. We need to draw them away from Louis." Ryan hurdled an oblong chunk of ice and took a route at right angles to the station. He thought he heard the veteran curse, but when he looked over his shoulder, Gunner was right behind him.

# CHAPTER 38

*Attack the evil that is within you, rather than the evil that is in others.*

DAY 145, 1100 HOURS

Louis huddled inside the airlock as the outer door whirred closed. Outside the portal, streaks of light hunted Ryan and Gunner—predators stalking their prey. The com relayed their shock and panic as the hunters closed in. Terse words. Orders from Ryan, and Gunner's muted response. He couldn't see them dart between the tall pillars, but by the flow of laser fire, they were retreating deeper into the maze of icebergs and fissures.

"On your left, Gunner! Stay low."

"See 'em, Ace. Coming around you now . . ."

"Follow the fissure—"

"Watch it!" Gunner barked. "Third one on the plateau."

"Bastard," Ryan hissed. "They're trying to flush us out. You good?"

"Laser winged me," Gunner panted, and Louis's hand instinctively went to his damaged arm. Nightmares of a bullet punching a hole in his suit.

"Any damage?"

"'S okay, Ace. Keep moving."

Louis exhaled. How long could they keep running? Static cut into the frequency as Jupiter's radiation blanketed the airways.

Ryan's voice. "Crevice coming . . . up . . ."

"Shooter . . ."

The voices faded into static, and Louis pounded the side of the airlock in frustration. His friends were dying, and all he could do was listen.

Twin beams split the darkness. Ryan stayed low, using the ice ridge as a shield as they alternately crawled and sprinted deeper into the desolation. A hunk of ice melted by Gunner's boot, and he jerked his leg back before radiant heat burned a hole in his suit. Ryan jumped a wide crevice and panicked when the ice started to crumble under his boots. It was a hundred-foot fall to the bottom. Gunner leaped past and reached back to haul him off the ledge.

They slid down a steep slope of hoarfrost, their boots catching on tiny edges as they tried to control their skid. Jupiter blazed on the horizon, the gas giant spewing radiation and rage. Massive storm clouds swirled in a vortex of power and destruction.

The bottom arrived too fast, and Ryan tumbled over before he got his footing. Gunner was already moving toward a maze of ice chunks that were strewn across the surface like discarded LEGO pieces. A laser beam pierced the crenelated top of one, splitting it in half.

"They're trying to flank us," Ryan wheezed. "Need to slip past before they close the net."

"Over here!" Gunner beckoned him with a sharp wave, and Ryan plunged between two car-sized blocks before landing on his stomach.

"Where are they?"

Gunner peered over the edge. "On top of that ice wall. I'm guessing they're arguing about coming down."

"How many?"

"I'm counting four. Three Europa suits, one Federation."

Ryan took a breath. "Ready to move?"

"No need, Ace. I don't think they're all that invested."

"What? How can you be sure?"

Gunner tightened the straps over his thighs, which had loosened in their mad dash across the ice. "Because it's risk versus reward. Their risk, Wilshire's reward."

Ryan hesitated as the veteran's words resonated on a deeper level. "They're leaving with Wilshire?"

"Exactly. And they won't risk their skin chasing us if the end goal is to be on those transports." Gunner's expression mirrored Ryan's disgust. "Selfish nits."

Ryan eyed the ridge. The man was right; the pursuit had fizzled out. "What's our next move?"

Gunner shrugged. "Wait till they leave before exposing ourselves. After that, it's on you, Ace. You're in charge."

Ryan stared across the frozen surface. For a moment, while Gunner was demonstrating his insight, the weight of command had lessened. Now it was back, and his shoulders felt as tight as a fisherman's knot. He had zero in terms of assets, no weapons and no leverage.

Gunner checked the burn mark on his suit. "Do you think the vet is okay?"

Ryan grimaced. Had the goons seen him enter the airlock? "I'm thinking yes. They came after us."

Gunner nodded, accepting the rationale. "But that doesn't help. We can't go back to the ice cave, and there'll be patrols around the station."

"You're right," Ryan replied, as a plan came together in his mind. "That's why we have to go someplace Wilshire won't expect."

Louis raised his helmet above the lip of the portal and stared into the concourse. Muted lighting splayed over the wide boulevard and hive entrances. It was empty of civilians, and refuse covered the dirty polymer tiles. Then he spied them: two men slumped against the wall outside Engineering. Wilshire's men, judging by the blocky EV suits. Their helmets sat on the floor, and both looked ready to keel over at any moment. With gravity twenty times what they were used to, it was easy to understand why. Even one-handed, he could almost take them. Except for the lasers they cradled in their arms.

Should he make a run for it? Where would he go?

The hives seemed the natural refuge. He could hide among the civilians until . . . He paused. Until what? Until Braeder performed a miracle and saved the day? No, that wasn't the answer. To save the colony, he had to disrupt Wilshire's plans, and to do that meant taking risks.

His gaze landed on the entrance to Medical. No way he could make it without being spotted.

The lights suddenly went out, and the concourse was plunged into darkness.

"What the hell?" He slammed the palm-shaped button, and the internal airlock door began to rise. He had no clue what had just happened, but this was his chance. Navigating the concourse was second nature. Eyes open or shut, he knew how many steps to Medical, and he had to get there before emergency lights powered up.

He heard the Ceres men curse and mutter to each other as he held his breath and tiptoed past them, praying he didn't run into something on the floor. His hand brushed the glass entrance and the handle on one side. He cracked the door and slid inside just as the emergency lights flickered to life.

The waiting room was empty, but he heard voices inside, somewhere close to the stretchers. A male voice, angry and strident, and a female trying to placate him. He recognized her voice, and the tension in his shoulders lessened a fraction.

"See, the lights are coming on," Mabel said, her attempt at reassurance ringing hollow in the doctor's ear. "We get disruptions all the time."

"I don't believe in coincidences," the male retorted, suspicious. "Something's wrong with the power."

"Maybe we should contact Ops," the nurse suggested.

"Like I want to bother them when they're in the middle of prepping the transports," the man sneered. "I don't know why I'm supposed to be watching you or why they put you here and not in the brig."

"Because every person from Ceres will need medical attention soon enough," Mabel snapped. "Sybil wants me to set up IVs when your 'buddies' start collapsing."

"Like you're going to help us."

"I'm a nurse, Fletcher. That's my job."

Louis stretched his neck around the corner. A tall, skinny man in black Ceres coveralls and a dirty bandana sat in his chair, feet on the doctor's desk. Louis felt instant resentment. How dare he treat his desk with such disdain?

Mabel stood facing him, arms folded across her chest like a teacher silently admonishing a student. Except the student had a laser. She inclined her head toward the supply room. "Wilshire has stolen most of our medical supplies." She didn't try to mask the accusation in her tone. "Which means when you leave, we're going to be left with nothing."

Fletcher shrugged. "What's the old saying, the strong shall inherit the Earth?"

"Actually, it's 'The meek—'"

"Whatever." He waved away her words.

"Wilshire moved some colonists to the transports," Mabel said, her gaze flickering toward the exit. "How many are you taking?"

"Enough." He flashed a dirty grin before reaching for a mug of water. "Bet he'd make room for a nurse if you asked nice."

"No, thank you. I'm okay to die with a clean conscience."

He shrugged. "Then sucks to be you."

While Fletcher gulped down his drink, Louis reached out and wiggled a finger. Mabel froze before her brain clicked into gear.

"You know, it's time I checked the SPET scanner," she said, stepping into an adjoining room. "Whenever the power oscillates, there's a chance the magnetic coils might activate, and that could cause a reaction."

"Wait!" Fletcher lurched to his feet and lifted the muzzle of his laser. "Stay where I can see you."

"Relax." She stopped in the doorway and brushed hair out of her eyes. "It'll just take a minute and it's better than an explosion."

He frowned. "What do you mean, 'explosion'?"

She beckoned with her hand. "Don't you know anything about magnetic coils? Static charges are dangerous when they build up."

Lines formed on his brow as he hobbled after her.

Louis hurried across the room. The medicine-cabinet doors were spread open, and most everything was gone. Looted by Wilshire's refugees. He spied a glass vial on the floor. Fentanyl. A box of syringes and needles sat untouched on the bottom shelf. The sight of the needles triggered a wave of concern. Gunner hated needles. Had he and Ryan escaped?

He loaded the syringe with the clear fluid. Enough to anesthetize an elephant.

The conversation in the next room grew animated, and Louis sensed the man's rising frustration. He slid behind the door. With only one hand, he had no room for error.

"You're lying!" Fletcher snarled, and Mabel was propelled out of the room, landing hard on her back. "Wilshire won't mind if I remove another splinter from our skin."

Louis waited for boots to emerge in the doorway, a dirty Ceres logo imprinted over the steel toecap. The barrel of the laser lined up with Mabel's head.

The nurse froze.

Louis stepped around the corner and plunged the needle into the man's neck. Fletcher's eyes nearly jumped out of his skull as he tried to reconcile the doctor's sudden appearance with his lethal intention. A second later, his brain must have prioritized the threat, because the laser swiveled toward Louis.

The doctor released the needle and clutched the barrel of the laser. Rough metal edges cut into his skin, sending shock waves up his arm. He could only hold the muzzle away from his face for a few seconds, his single limb no match for Fletcher's strength. But it was long enough.

Fletcher faltered, his muscles failing as foreign molecules raced through his blood, paralyzing serotonin and glutamate receptors in his central nervous system. His eyes glazed over, and Louis was able to rip the laser from his grasp.

Mabel grimaced as the colonist landed face-first on the floor and something cracked. She noted the empty vial. "Fentanyl? Won't he asphyxiate?"

Louis's first instinct was to brush off her concern; Fletcher had been ready to kill Mabel. Then the tension left his bones, and he bent down to roll the man over. Blood poured out of his nose, forming small red bubbles when he breathed. "Help me put him on a stretcher."

Together, they dragged him onto one of the empty beds, and Louis strapped a portable ventilator to his face. He tensed when Mabel unexpectedly hugged him. "Thank God. He was getting more and more riled. Where did you come from?"

"Ryan and Gunner snuck me in through the Delta Hive entrance."

She moved back but kept her arms on his. "The lieutenant? He's alive?"

Louis swallowed and bent down to pick up the laser. "Hope so. Last thing I saw was some deuterium miners chasing them across the ice field."

Mabel's jaw tightened. She glanced warily toward the entrance. "What are we going to do? They're almost done loading the transports. How soon until they launch?"

Louis's gaze strayed over the unconscious patient. His respirations were shallow but regular. "First thing is tie this bastard up. If we're not going to let him die, he's going to wake up sometime."

"And then?" She looked at him with a curious expression. "We can't hold off Wilshire's goons with only one laser."

"No." Louis checked the battery. The green light indicated a full charge. "I think it's time we went on the offensive."

Wilshire ran into Ops, his gaze landing on Sybil sitting in the command chair. "What the hell happened? Power's out in the concourse. We had to stop loading the transports." A blood vessel pulsed on his temple like an aneurysm about to burst.

Bennett hurried in behind him and shot an angry glare at Rani. "Is she involved?"

Sybil shook her head vigorously. "She's been quiet since I got here. I've been scrolling through the camera feeds but haven't seen anyone messing with the terminals."

Wilshire opened a channel on coms. "Andrei, did you track down the problem?"

"Negative. Whoever is doing it is covering their tracks. Only way to fix it is reboot the system from Engineering."

"Then get in here and do it!" Wilshire slammed his fist on the side of Sybil's chair. "And when you're finished, talk to Jorge about the patrols. Braeder is out there somewhere." He fell into Gunner's chair, seething. "First the airlock, then the battery packs, and now the lights. Someone is fucking with us. Every time we fix a system, another one is sabotaged."

Rani hid a smile. Sasha was good. Shutting down the airlocks and disconnecting the battery chargers had disrupted Wilshire's schedule. Now, with the lights offline, the Russians had to track down a bunch of flashlights. The hours were ticking by, and the Ceres group was looking worse by the minute.

"Could it be the civilians?" Sybil asked.

Wilshire threw up his hands. "I checked. The hive is locked down and we disconnected the colony net. They don't have access."

"What about terminals along the concourse?"

"I have men out there." He focused on Bennett. "You stay here and disable the laser. When we launch, I don't want anyone taking potshots at us."

Bennett slumped into Gunner's chair. Rani noted her color was off, and beads of sweat ran down her temples. "I can't wait to get off this moon."

"The sooner, the better." Wilshire fumed. "Show me the brig."

Rani shifted the feed, and an image of the room appeared. Solomon stood front and center, blocking any view of the cell behind him. He smiled and waved at the lens.

"Somebody's doing it," Bennett muttered. "And I bet they know who it is."

"They're locked in the hangar," Rani said, trying to inject the right amount of disbelief into her tone. "They're freezing and isolated. What could they know?"

"Don't care." Wilshire straightened. "Sybil, suit up and get out to the hangar. Grab the governor and put him in the airlock. Stream the feed to the hive. If someone doesn't point a finger in fifteen minutes, open the outer hatch."

Rani's heart leapt into her throat. "You're going to kill an innocent man?"

"No." Wilshire grinned. "I'm going to encourage the colonists to give up the culprit."

"That's still murder."

"That's what happens when you screw with me." He got up and jabbed Rani in the back. "Now make it happen. Stream the camera feed."

Rani thought about refusing, but Wilshire would just toss her ass in the brig with the others, and that would spell the end of the resistance. As Sybil marched out of Ops, Rani tapped in commands to stream the video to the colonists. Then she sent a cryptic message on channel three.

And waited.

# CHAPTER 39

*The man who moves a mountain begins by carrying away small stones.*

DAY 145, 1240 HOURS

Sybil and Wilshire were only gone five minutes when Rani heard a faint beeping on the com.

*What the hell?*

She let her hand fall to the channel knob. Bennett was dozing, but every few minutes, she opened her eyes and glared, as if she was expecting to catch Rani in the act. Then again, Wilshire's girl probably couldn't stay asleep with all the muscle and joint pain. She had managed to disable the laser as per Wilshire's orders, but that appeared to be the limit of her tolerance, and she fell back in the seat after that.

Rani's fingers touched the familiar grooved knob on the edge of her terminal and slowly rotated the frequency. She heard an answering click and stopped.

A familiar voice in her ear made her pulse jump.

"Got your message," the doctor whispered. "Focus her attention."

For a second, Rani didn't move.

*Louis was alive?*

She chanced a glance over her shoulder. The door to Ops was closed.

There was no time to waste. She flicked a switch on her console and stood. "Hey! Got a warning light on one of the subsystems. Have to check it out."

Bennett roused herself and rubbed a set of bleary eyes. "Which one?"

Rani pointed to a server on the back wall. "Environmental. Temperature's dropping in Alpha Hive. Need to find out what the problem is."

She took a step toward the machines humming against the bulkhead but stopped when Bennett raised her laser. "I don't care about environmental," she hissed. "We'll be off this moon before anything crashes."

Rani placed both fists on her hips. "You may, but the rest of us will be stuck here, and I'm not going to freeze into a human popsicle just because you're too lazy to get off your ass and let me check the circuits."

The muzzle of the laser rose another inch, and Rani worried she may have pushed too hard. But then Bennett grunted and waved the gun toward the servers. It was an effort to stand and take unsteady steps. "Don't try nothing funny. I'm watching you."

Rani bit her tongue before anything incriminating slipped out. She knelt down in front of the environmental server, pulled out her powered screwdriver, and peeled off the outer casing. Every indicator was in the green. Shoving her hands inside the wires, she shifted on her haunches to block the view.

"What game you playing, bitch," Bennett muttered, looking over Rani's shoulder. "I don't see anything wrong. I should shoot you now . . ."

The door hissed open, stealing her attention. "That you, Wilshire?"

"Sorry, he's a little busy," Louis said, walking into the room. "How about a house call?"

"You!" Bennett's eyes narrowed, and she scrambled to bring her weapon up.

Mabel stepped around the corner, laser leveled, and pulled the trigger. There was a flash of scarlet light. Bennett screamed and fell back, a black line appearing on her suit. She fired a wild blast that blistered the bulkhead beside the doctor.

Louis gasped and dove behind the command chair.

Mabel returned fire but missed badly.

Bennett crawled to her knees, one hand on her injured side. The barrel of her laser fell across the open server and swiveled toward Mabel.

Standing in the center of Ops, the nurse seemed paralyzed.

Rani launched herself at Bennett and stabbed her in the neck with the screwdriver. The brunette howled and twisted away, the laser beam going wide. Louis jumped up and punched her square in the face. She staggered but didn't go down. Rani grabbed the end of the power tool and drove it deeper. Something stretched and popped. Bennett recoiled and walloped her across the face. Her vision blurred, and her legs gave out.

"Move!" a voice shouted.

Rani was too dazed to understand. She pushed herself up on her elbows.

"Bitch," Bennett hissed. "You're dead . . ."

Something hot, like a branding torch, singed Rani's scalp. She yelped and covered her head with both arms.

Seconds later, a strong hand hauled her into a sitting position.

"You all right?" Louis asked, his hand palpating her scalp. "That shot nearly parted your hair."

Rani groaned when he hit a tender spot. His hand came back covered in blood and charred fuzz.

"Sorry." Mabel stood behind the doctor, the laser dangling in her grasp. "She was going to kill you. I almost . . . I didn't mean . . ."

Rani glanced at Bennett's corpse and shuddered. One eye was gone and the opposite cheek pulled back like a broken chicken wing. The laser remained tight in her grasp.

"Thank you." She sucked in a breath. "I'm not complaining."

Mabel smiled, relieved. She looked at Louis. "What now?"

The doctor shrugged. "Our job was to get an ally, preferably a military one. Check that box." He inclined his head toward Rani. "Your turn."

Rani tried to ignore the throbbing in her scalp. "You realize I'm a specialist, right? Basic training is as good as it gets."

"That's more than we have," Mabel said, staring at the flashing indicator on Gunner's terminal.

"Shit," Rani said. "That's probably Wilshire checking in."

"What do we do?" Louis had a worried look in his eye. "Ops is a dead end."

Rani pried open Bennett's dead hands and took the laser. "Come on. When he doesn't get an answer, he'll send people to check."

They hurried out of Ops and down the narrow corridor that led to the concourse. The doctor was starting for the exit when Rani put a hand on his arm. She glanced at the 3-D monitor hanging over the door—the one Gunner had installed before the uprising—and checked the battery in her laser.

"What are you doing?" Louis asked. "Shouldn't we make a run for it?"

Rani shook her head. "No time. Wilshire will send his closest minions, which means they'd spot us in the concourse."

"You're right." Mabel pointed at the monitor that showed two men leaving Engineering.

The doctor's jaw tightened. "Damn. Good call. What do we do?"

Rani moved to the blind side of the door. "Doc, behind me. Mabel, around the corner. Don't come out until you hear my voice."

The nurse's hands trembled like she was going to drop the weapon, but she managed a nod and backed out of sight.

Rani felt the doctor's presence behind her as she crouched against the wall. A final look at the monitor confirmed both Ceres men approaching the door. A small voice in her head—one she recognized as the old Rani—begged her to offer an ultimatum before she opened fire. Then she remembered the panic she felt when Rutherford's goons pinned her in the hive. No, she wasn't going to take chances.

The door screeched open, and she took a hurried step back when she realized she stood too close. Her heart thudded in her chest like a drum solo. She could barely hold the laser steady. Two figures walked in. She recognized the cheap ink-based tattoos on the back of their necks. The muzzle of her laser rose seemingly of its own accord. Her finger tightened on the trigger until the weapon jerked and a yellow beam erupted, striking one of the men in the back of the head. He had enough time to utter a surprised yelp before his hair burst into flame and the back of his skull ceased to exist. He crumpled like a puppet after the strings were cut.

His comrade reacted faster than Rani thought possible, diving to one side and rolling into a firing position. His laser appeared in one hand, and the beam took the color off her uniform. She cried out as something akin to a branding iron pierced her side. He fired again, and she jerked back when the blast scarred the wall inches in front of her face.

"You're dead!" he shouted, sparing the briefest look at his dead companion before adjusting his aim. A head shot.

A narrow beam took him square in the back. His look of hatred morphed into confusion and shock as the laser cut through skin, fat, and muscle. Ligaments and tendons were cauterized as it burned through to the vital organs.

His eyes rolled back, and he sagged to the floor. Smoke oozed from the massive wound.

Mabel dropped her laser and ran over to help Louis pull Rani to her feet.

"Jesus!" Louis breathed. "You're hurt."

Rani didn't have to be told. Waves of red agony rolled up her side. She tried to use his arm for leverage but her legs barely took her weight.

"Must get to decompression . . . before Wilshire sends more goons."

"Wait." Louis examined her wound and pulled a small canister from his pocket. "This should numb the area." He sprayed white foam over blistering skin.

Rani recoiled from the freezing sensation, but seconds later, the pain faded into the background. She unclenched her teeth. "Thanks, Doc."

Mabel picked up the lasers before slipping one arm under her shoulder, prompting the doctor to follow suit. A cool breeze hit them as they left the Command Center, and Rani exhaled when she saw the concourse was empty.

"What's the plan?" Louis asked as they passed Medical.

Rani didn't answer. It took every joule of energy to keep her legs moving. The pain had been muted, but it wasn't gone. For a brief moment, she felt like she was going to pass out. Her handlers seemed to sense it as well, and their grip tightened.

A familiar door appeared: a repaired steel shell that barely functioned after an explosion had ripped it apart a year earlier.

"Stop here," Rani grunted.

Lines formed on Mabel's brow. "The storage room? What's in there?"

"Something we need."

The doctor noted Mabel's puzzled expression and shrugged.

The door wasn't locked. Louis edged in first and kept his grip on Rani as she and Mabel sidestepped through the tight entrance. Rani let go and fell back against one wall of the storage compartment. Aluminum shelves lined the walls, holding numerous tools and implements. She recalled the day the rebels blew the lock on the door, killing two of their own when the bomb went off prematurely. By the disgust on Louis's face, he was recalling that time as well. A third rebel had died on the operating table.

Mabel hauled the door shut. "All right, Rani, you got us here. Before Wilshire sends more people to scour the concourse, you better tell us why."

Rani took a second to catch her breath. The pain had settled into a constant burning, like a toothache spreading across her chest. She pointed to the end of the room. "Braeder stored them here after the explosion. Just in case another bomb depressurized the concourse."

Louis scratched his stump which had started to ooze a dark fluid since their fight in Ops. "Stored what . . ." He stopped when his gaze fell on the row of EV suits hanging in the corner. "Son of a gun."

"Yeah." Rani felt a smile emerging through the pain. "Time to get dressed and find our friends."

Kasim rubbed his cheek, carefully avoiding the golf-ball-sized lump beneath his left eye. Jorge had exacted a modicum of revenge by putting a beating on him before Sybil marched him to *Serenity*. The big miner wanted payback for the time they had retrieved the antenna from Rutherford's domicile.

"Move your ass, Governor," Jorge spat as he stacked another metal crate between the cryo-pods. "Or I'll put my fists back to work."

Kasim stepped back. The man wasn't bluffing, and Kasim didn't want to give him an excuse. He tried to blend into the background as Jorge ambled to the ship's airlock. Wilshire's threat—to space him if they didn't find who was sabotaging the station—still rang loudly in his ears. Thank God, Sybil had convinced the Ceres leader he was still of value, that he held sway with the colonists. Just in case, he kept his helmet gripped tight in one hand and his EV suit zipped up.

After packing dozens of storage containers and installing extra cryo-pods, space in the cargo hold of the transport was at a premium. That being said, no one suggested reducing the number of pods. Everyone in the ship was looking for a ticket off the moon, including Rutherford's scientists, Jorge's miners, and even the colonists Wilshire had selected.

"You're looking a little nervous, Governor," Rutherford quipped. He sat on one of the open pods beside his colleagues, his thin legs dangling over the side like two wet noodles. "Something bothering you?"

Kasim's eyes narrowed. "You mean something other than you stealing our food and leaving us here to starve?"

"Hey." The scientist spread his arms to indicate the colonists stripping down in preparation to enter the pods. "We had to beat off volunteers with a stick. Everyone knows this sinking ship has to go down at some point. It's just a matter of time."

A sliver of guilt wormed its way into Kasim's breast. After Wilshire sent out the invitation, the response had been overwhelming, and he had his choice of recruits, most of which included a preponderance of young females. Colonists chose survival over morality. "Fate has a way of rewarding people like you."

Rutherford chuckled. "You're upset. Can't say I blame you, but life sucks. We didn't survive a hellish year to play nice. It's time to take our ball and go home."

"You really think you'll make it to Earth?"

Rutherford shrugged. "That's up to Wilshire. Mars is an option, or maybe one of the orbital satellites off Luna. We'll see."

"You're sure about the vaccine?"

"It'll work," Rutherford said, although his words didn't quite carry the right amount of conviction. "Pavel said as much."

"The same Pavel who experimented on unsuspecting colonists." Kasim couldn't hold back the sarcasm.

Rutherford found something on the ceiling to stare at. "They didn't know what early versions of the vaccine would do."

Kasim shook his head. Wilshire and Pavel were psychopaths. They could twist events as much as they liked, but it didn't change the fact that the Russian had been complicit in the death of hundreds of innocents. And now they were packaging their guilt and doing it again.

Rutherford's expression twisted into a malicious smile. "Are you sure you don't want to beg me for a pod? I might be able to put in a good word for you with Wilshire."

Kasim's gaze flickered to the cryo-pods. The man was baiting him. There was nothing he could offer that would see the Ceres group take him instead of one of their own or a willing Europa colonist. But even if he had something valuable to trade, the stain on his soul would forever haunt him. No, better to suffer and die with friends than live a life of fraud among deranged narcissists.

As if on cue, Sybil exited the airlock by the cockpit. She pulled off her helmet and focused on Jorge. "Andrei reported in. He says they chased Braeder out of the ice cave."

"How long ago?" Rutherford asked.

"He didn't say."

"Wilshire promised he'd pack the cave with explosives and blow it before we left."

"What?" Kasim couldn't believe his ears. "Are you that paranoid about the aliens?"

Rutherford looked down his nose at the governor. "I told you weeks ago not to trust the thing. You think I'd leave you here with it? Who knows what you would do?"

"Don't worry," Sybil said. "Andrei is setting the explosives now."

The scientist nodded and picked up his electrical leads.

Jorge finished stacking his container and walked back. "You just came from Wilshire? What did he say?"

"He wants you to send out more patrols," Sybil said. "Braeder's out there somewhere."

Jorge made a face. "Everyone from Ceres is on their last legs, and I only have a handful of miners."

Sybil hung her helmet on a hook, her tight expression telling Kasim what she thought of Wilshire's plan. "They only have a couple of places where they can charge their batteries. Andrei's got the ice cave and extractor covered."

Kasim straightened, remembering Wilshire's threat. "You still have a bomb in the extractor. If that detonates, we're dead."

Sybil exchanged a look with Jorge. "Wilshire is not going to destroy the extractor. He promised me that."

"Yeah," Kasim muttered. "He's so good at keeping promises."

One of the Ceres men walked out of the cockpit and pointed at Jorge. "Just received new orders. Bennett and the guys in the station are not answering the com. Wilshire wants you to check it out."

"That's weird." Jorge chose one of the helmets from the shelf. "What about the patrols?"

"He says he'll organize them. Just find out what's going on."

"All right. Lecky, watch the governor."

"What about the supplies?"

"Almost finished. I'll grab some colonists to replace the miners heading out on patrol." He pulled on his helmet and cycled open the airlock.

When the hatch closed, Kasim turned on Sybil. "It's starting to fall apart."

Sybil snorted. "He can't save you this time, Governor. Wilshire is almost ready to launch, and once we're wheels-up, Christ himself can't touch us. One of Bennett's jobs was to disable the laser so shooting us down is not an option."

"Unlike your Ceres friends, we're not murderers."

She gave him a look. "I seem to remember a certain lieutenant shooting down a Federation transport, and a governor using a laser on a helpless mother."

Kasim felt his cheeks redden. "There's a difference between self-preservation and murder."

"So, it's all a matter of perception? Sounds like something a UN representative would say."

"I misread you, Sybil." His eyes searched hers. "After the insurrection, I actually took pity on you." He paused as his introspection turned over new rocks, and he faced his failure. How had he been so wrong in his judgement? "My job in the UN was based on unabashed optimism, that people and nations could change. That human nature was intrinsically good."

Sybil winced, like the words themselves were tiny knives. "My father taught me that life's journey is basically self-promotion. Everything people do is in their own best interests, especially when it includes secondary gain. The trick is to prioritize what you want and hook your wagon to those people with the best chance of success. All relationships are transactional."

"That's a sad way to view human beings. Especially your friends. The ones that stood up for you."

She laughed, a strangely hollow sound. "I already thanked you for persuading Ryan not to space me. But that's water under the bridge. It's the 'now' part you should be concerned with. Like, how are you going to keep breathing when Wilshire decides you're no longer of use?"

Kasim's lips tightened. His thoughts had already traveled down that road, and he didn't like what they'd found. Still, it hadn't upset him as much as he would have predicted. Too long living under the sword of Damocles had that effect.

"Ryan wouldn't have spaced you," he said. "He hated you for what you did and, more than that, for betraying him. But he wouldn't have done what Gunner and half the colonists wanted him to do."

Sybil blinked, her expression guarded. "What makes you so sure? Even Rani needed closure. I saw it in her eyes every day when she dropped off my meals."

"She wanted closure for the loss of Marco, true, but not in the way you think. Most of us are not like you. We don't believe in *transactional* relationships. We don't keep a running tab of favors doled out. Deep inside, we're fighting not for ourselves but for something bigger."

"Really?" she scoffed. "You expect me to believe that? After what happened on Earth? On Ceres? Mankind's depravity knows no bounds."

"Collectively, maybe," Kasim admitted. "But individually, we trust one another. The big picture does not reflect the individual parts, which can be so much better."

She stared at him for several long seconds. "You really believe he wouldn't do it?"

"I'd bet my life on it. He's not like that." Kasim wanted to say more when Wilshire's voice shot out of the radio.

"Sybil, get in here. Bennett is dead."

She fumbled with her helmet before finding the right button. "She's dead? What happened?"

"Someone shot her with a laser. Boris and Dimitri as well. Had to be Singh, and she's missing."

"What do we do?"

"Jorge is going to shift the patrols into a tighter search pattern. If she's around the station, we'll find her. Tell Chan and Stoll to begin their preflight checklist. Chan might need more *encouragement*."

Sybil checked her watch. "You're moving up the timeline?"

"That's right. Not sure what the hell is going on, but I'm not waiting around to find out."

Sybil stole a look past Kasim to where Rutherford and his cronies were attaching electrical leads and hooking up IV lines. "We're almost ready here."

"If they don't find Braeder," Wilshire continued, "I'm going to establish a perimeter around the transports until we launch. And I haven't forgotten about the governor. If he tries anything, space him." The channel closed.

"I told you," Kasim said. "It's falling apart."

"If I were you, I'd worry about my own skin," Sybil snapped. "Sounds like Wilshire is not in the mood for taking prisoners."

Kasim leaned back and folded his arms across his chest. Oh, yeah, it was falling apart.

# CHAPTER 40

*I dreamt life is beauty, I woke to find that life was duty.*

DAY 145, 1356 HOURS

Gunner took point and led Ryan along fissured ice sheets and towering cliffs of speckled hoarfrost. Ganymede soared overhead, a dirty rock world spinning in the void.

After fifteen minutes at a harried pace, Gunner stopped to get his bearings. "Looks like you were right, Ace. No sign of Wilshire's patrols. They must have figured we wouldn't come back to the Delta airlock. We're close, so keep your eyes peeled."

"Copy that." Ryan leaned against an ice pinnacle that harbored a vague resemblance to the Statue of Liberty. It had been a gamble, but Wilshire was not military-trained. It wouldn't be second nature for him to protect his flanks.

Both men dropped into a crouch as they moved. Gunner used chunks of ice as cover, scurrying from one piece to the next before surveying the area and waving Ryan forward.

Rounding a deep crevasse, he abruptly raised one fist in the air. Ryan froze. Gunner signaled: three figures straight ahead. He looked back, silently inquiring as to the plan.

Ryan vacillated. Two against three, and the enemy probably had weapons. The alternative was to abandon the attempt and hand Wilshire victory. No. That option sputtered in the face of his innate stubbornness. If he was going to lose, he was going to go down swinging. He gestured to Gunner. *Take right flank. I'll go left.*

And pray it was the right decision.

His training kicked in as soon as he took his first step: vision focused, pulse steady, respiration slow and regular. He crept behind several oblong blocks of ice until he was parallel to where the three figures huddled together. Taking a quick breath, he gripped the lip of the largest block and propelled himself over the top. He landed on his feet, knees bunched. His eyes recorded the scene in microseconds: three Europa suits, two figures reaching for lasers dangling from cords around their necks. Bending low, he swept his leg out, tripping the closest target. The person landed hard on their back, and the laser went skidding across the ice. He turned and was aiming a fist at a second helmet when something caught his eye. He managed to pull his punch just as Gunner hurdled over the ice and body-slammed the third person.

"Hold, Gunner! They're friendlies."

"What?" Gunner hesitated, his hand wrapped around the regulator, ready to tear it off the helmet. "Are you sure?"

Ryan strode over and lifted Gunner off his victim before helping a stunned-looking Louis to his feet. Blood leaked out of his nose. "Sorry, Doc. We didn't know it was you."

Louis speared him with a furious look. "Damn, Ryan, you could have asked."

Gunner's jaw nearly dislocated. "Son of a bitch. I nearly killed you."

Ryan checked on the person sprawled on the ice. "Are you—"

"I'm fine," Rani groaned. "Thanks for asking." She stopped rubbing her side and stared. Then realization kicked in, and she reached up and embraced him in a hug. "Ryan! Thank God you're alive!"

Ryan was caught off guard but, after a moment, relaxed and wrapped his arms around her before helping her up. He recognized Mabel behind the third faceplate.

"How did you get past the patrols?" Rani asked. "Wilshire has Andrei and Jorge organizing hunting parties."

"Aye," Gunner grunted, wiping dirt off the doctor's suit before Louis angrily pushed him away. "They nearly cornered us in the ice cave. Lucky to have escaped. How did you get out?"

"Mabel and I handled the guard in Medical before freeing Rani," Louis said. "Took out three of the Ceres bastards, including Bennett."

"We can't go back inside," Rani said, glancing at the Delta airlock. "Wilshire's goons are searching the station. We were trying to find somewhere to hide."

"Hiding's not going to take back the colony," Gunner said. "We need another option."

All eyes landed on Ryan, and he felt the weight of their expectations. His crew had gotten lucky before. Could they do it again? He walked over and picked up Rani's laser. "Time to play a little game called misdirection."

Gunner grinned. "About time."

The veteran peered over the ridge of ice. "I figure we got about ten minutes before one of those patrols spots us. Time to shit or get off the pot, Ace."

Ryan paused to survey the landing strip. *Phoenix* sat at the end of the runway alongside *Serenity*. Three miners stood guard at the base of the stairs that led to the front hatches. Every few minutes, two colonists left the station's airlock, carrying containers for the transports.

"I heard Wilshire earlier," Rani said, lying on her stomach next to Ryan. "They're almost finished loading."

Ryan's lips tightened into a thin line. They were running out of time. Which meant he had to act now. "Gunner, find a secure spot on the other side of the transport." He gestured to the laser the veteran cradled in his lap. "On my signal, draw their attention. Back off when you have to."

Gunner flashed him a look. "You're not trying to take the transport with one laser?"

"No, that would be suicide. We need to build up our assets."

"If by *assets* you mean *more guns and bodies*, I'm good with that," Mabel said, watching the colonists carry heavy metal bins up the boarding stairs.

"Amen to that," Rani muttered.

"The rest of you are with me." Ryan straightened. "We're going to sneak around to the hangar. Gunner, when you see us approach the airlock—"

"I'll give them something to think about. Don't know how long I can keep them occupied, so be fast."

"That's my intent." Ryan patted the veteran on the shoulder as he slid past.

The route he chose around the transport was the quickest, but it was also the most dangerous. If Wilshire's goons spied them, the results wouldn't be good. Thankfully, the ice in this area had rolled up on itself like a breaking wave and provided protection from prying eyes. Ryan stopped several times and scanned the surface. No signs of pursuit, but he knew they had to keep moving.

They ended up on the far side of the hangar and carefully edged around to the front. Ryan relaxed when he saw the airlock was unguarded. But then, why would Wilshire waste men there? It wasn't like the prisoners were going to break out and run to the station.

Not without suits.

"Get ready," he said, and waited until Louis and Mabel moved up next to the airlock before leaning over the ice ridge and flicking his helmet lamps. The goons at the base of the transport were facing the other way, but Gunner would be in position to see it.

A laser flash split the darkness, and one of the guards under the nose of *Serenity* crumpled. The other returned fire, and three figures in Europa suits spilled from the transport's front hatch.

"Get out of there, Gunner," Ryan muttered.

Mabel activated the airlock, and they fell inside before the hatch fully opened. Louis palmed the flashing green button to close the door and initialize repressurization.

Ryan debated pulling off his helmet, but even though the hangar had atmosphere, the temperature would be close to freezing. He kept it on.

"Stay behind me," he ordered, motioning with his hand. "As soon as the inner hatch opens, keep low and find something to hide behind." He figured he had the element of surprise, but that would only last until somebody discharged a weapon.

The airflow ceased with a final thump, and the inner door cycled open. Ryan sprinted inside. Only half the boxcar-sized lamps in the ceiling were lit, bathing the cavernous space in twilight. He activated his lamps in case someone loitered in the shadows, and found himself staring at two massive Fleet transports, *Churchill* and *Atlantis*. He stopped for a split second until he remembered what Rani had said: that Kasim had used the gator to haul them into the hangar after she left the colony. Numerous refueling trucks and repair vehicles lay scattered across the floor. Louis, Rani, and Mabel slipped in behind him. When nothing threatening appeared, the doctor started to stand before Ryan roughly hauled him down.

A laser filled the space the doctor's head had just vacated.

"Don't make yourself a target," Ryan hissed. He instinctively shut down his lamps and dove to one side, behind a pile of coiled hoses and empty pallets. Two more blasts split the cool air of the hangar, and Ryan was able to locate the source: the Ceres guard hiding behind the front wheels of a rust-covered forklift.

He fired a single beam to let the bastard know he was armed and then slid to his right, under the wing of *Churchill.* He gestured for the others to stay down. Last thing he needed to worry about was their safety. A vision of the marines hunting him last year briefly stole his thoughts, but this combatant was no marine. Ryan fired a second blast, making the guard think he was moving to the other side of the transport. Then he shifted behind one of the gators.

Two laser discharges from the guard, both in the wrong direction. The man was trying to shake the tree. Make him give away his position. Ryan waited for his scotomas to fade before shifting around the enemy's flank. He had a partial view of a helmet peeking over the forklift's front tires. Ten feet of open space separated him from his prey.

He keyed the com. "Doc, make some noise."

A single click answered, followed by a loud *bang* as an aluminum shelf came crashing down. Inside the hangar, it sounded like an explosion.

"Damn," Ryan murmured. Louis didn't mess around.

The guard craned his helmet over the side of the forklift. It wasn't much, but it was enough. Ryan hit him with a single beam. It burned through the flimsy fabric and deep into flesh. A shrill scream rang out, and the man sank from view.

Ryan hurried over, gun leveled, but the guard's eyes had already started to glaze over. Smoke oozed off the scorched suit, right over the heart.

Rani followed and wordlessly scooped up the laser.

Ryan hurried to the brig door. Last time he had visited this place was to say goodbye to Sybil. That was months past.

Louis joined him. "Problem eliminated?"

"Yeah." Ryan lifted the deadbolt. "That was some distraction."

The doctor shrugged. "You asked."

Ryan examined the lock that hung open on the hasp. Apparently, the guard didn't think it necessary to use both a padlock and a deadbolt. He tossed it to one side, hauled the door open, and found himself staring into the bruised and bloodied face of . . .

"Archie?"

"Lieutenant?" The man's face registered shock. "You're alive?"

Ryan hesitated. Why did everyone keep asking him that? "Apparently. Who's in there with you?"

"Eight of us including Sasha," Archie said.

Max Plante walked up and extended a hand. "Good to see you again, Lieutenant. Wish it was under better circumstances."

"Agreed, Governor. You okay?"

He pointed to some bruises on his face. "Wilshire wasn't happy to learn I was on the transport. He exacted a measure of revenge before throwing me in here."

Solomon approached with Vrabel and three reservists, and Ryan breathed easier knowing his "army" had just increased in size. "Where's Kasim?"

"Don't know," Archie said. "Wilshire's men pulled him out a while ago."

"Damn." That created another problem: if the governor was on one of the transports, it wouldn't be easy to rescue him. "Okay, time to leave before Wilshire figures out what's happening. Do you have suits?"

Archie shook his head. "The goons took them back to the station."

Ryan set his jaw. He had expected that. However, Wilshire wouldn't know what was in the hanger. "Check this transport. There should be emergency suits stored in the back. Doc, go with them and use your medical codes to override the lock on the hatch."

Louis followed Archie and the reservists up the ramp that led to the cockpit. Solomon and Vrabel joined them. Sasha paused in the doorway and beamed a smile at Ryan. "I knew you'd come for us, Lieutenant." She looked around. "Where's Gunner?"

"On the surface. I needed someone to distract the bad guys."

Concern clouded her features. "He's okay?"

Ryan grinned. "On the ice plates? I pity anyone who tries to hunt him on his home turf. Now, grab a suit. Quick."

She nodded and ran after the others.

Ryan sagged back against the forklift and wiped the sweat from his forehead.

Mabel joined him. "So, what do we do now?"

Ryan closed his eyes for a moment. "Not sure. Haven't thought that far ahead."

"Last chance for redemption, people," Kasim said. The cargo hold wasn't big, especially with half the space filled with supplies and pods, but he still raised his voice so everyone could hear. "Don't know how you're going to live with yourselves after the fact."

The civilians stopped undressing and glanced nervously at one another. None of them met Kasim's stare. Except for Rutherford, who scrunched his eyebrows together. "Don't blame them, Governor. This is your fault."

Kasim nearly choked. "How is it my fault? You're the ones selling your souls to a bunch of criminals and abandoning the colony. And stealing us blind."

Rutherford remained unfazed. "You killed two of my people who were trying to protect the colony. You allowed the ensign to interact with the artifact, which unleashed those energy beams. We"—he spread his arms to indicate his colleagues and the colonists—"advised you on a safer course, but you ignored us."

Kasim recognized rationalization when he heard it. "You can lie to yourself, but that won't wash the blood from your hands. You're sacrificing the lives of every person on this moon to save your own. You're pathetic."

Rutherford shrugged and taped the IV to his wrist. "We'll say a prayer for you when we land. If you're still breathing, we might even send you an update."

Kasim fought a rising tide of anger. "You're putting a lot of faith into an untested vaccine."

"Seemed to work pretty well for them." Rutherford inclined his head toward the two Ceres men standing guard outside the cockpit. "They didn't get infected. They survived."

"The only thing they survived was the vaccine!" Kasim exclaimed, louder than he intended, and the guards gave him a warning look. He lowered his voice. "They weren't exposed to the plague."

Rutherford shifted his weight from one skinny leg to the other. "Doesn't matter. They used the real bacterium to develop the vaccine. The immunological response should be the same."

"And you call yourself a scientist," Kasim scoffed. "Even I know lab results have to be verified in human studies. And since that didn't happen, you're throwing the dice on this one. Your friends should understand that." He sensed the scientists beside Rutherford wavering, but before he could continue, Wilshire burst out of the cockpit.

"They're attacking!" he shouted. "Outside. Now!"

Both Ceres men grabbed their helmets and hurried into the airlock. Wilshire pointed at Kasim. "Get ready, Governor. Almost time for you to play a part."

Kasim hesitated. “I thought I was a hostage, not a human shield.”

Wilshire barked a laugh. “You’re whatever we need at the moment.”

“Have a nice life,” Rutherford said, squeezing his long frame into the cryo-unit. “I don’t think we’ll be seeing each other again.”

“No,” Kasim muttered as he picked up his helmet. “I don’t imagine we will.”

# CHAPTER 41

*A superior man is modest in his speech but exceeds in his actions.*

DAY 145, 1509 HOURS

How are we going to do this?" Solomon asked as the inner airlock rotated open. He was a good six inches taller than Ryan and towered over him like a redwood.

Ryan stared out the narrow portal. The fact that Wilshire hadn't tried to break into the hangar bothered him. They sure as hell had scoured the station and found the bodies by now. Since the guard in the hangar was no longer responding, Wilshire would know he had lost control of the building. The smart thing to do was pin Ryan's group inside until the loading process was finished. The fact that he didn't left Ryan with only one option.

"We have to make a break for the station," he said. "If we can seize Ops, we can take control of the laser, and that transport won't be going anywhere."

"Bennett disabled the laser," Rani said. "If we get into Ops, our first job is to repair it. But they still have a dozen armed men guarding the transports, half of whom are disgruntled miners who want to get off this moon bad."

"Cap'n's right," Solomon said, nodding at Rani as he slipped a big arm around Archie. The geologist's complexion had turned pasty white, and his legs seemed on the verge of buckling. "They'll fight tooth and nail to launch the transports."

"I was there when Wilshire released them from the brig," Mabel said as Plante stepped up to take Archie's other arm. "Most of them supported the old Board, which means they've never been enamored with you. They see this as their one and only chance to get even."

Ryan checked the battery on his laser. None of that was good news, and yet, it was not entirely unexpected. Few colonists made an effort to get to know him after the insurrection. He thought it was mostly shock at what had happened, but as the weeks passed, he realized the feelings went deeper. Something about him, or the way he governed, rubbed colonists the wrong way. It wasn't something he could explain.

"How many did Wilshire bring from Ceres?"

Rani gritted her teeth against the pain in her side. The doctor's treatment was wearing off. "From what I saw, no more than twenty. Including Sybil."

"They can't be in any shape to fight," Louis said. "Doesn't matter how much steroids or supplements they've consumed; their muscles and joints must be screaming by now."

"Point taken," Ryan said. Which meant he had to push them harder. But with only two lasers, the odds weren't good. "How's the batteries?"

Solomon released Archie, and the geologist sagged back against Plante. The bruises on his face made it look like he was wearing a mask. "Fully charged," the miner said. He gestured at Rani. "Cap'n says they should be good for three or four discharges."

Ryan performed a quick head count: twelve bodies but only two with military training, him and Rani. Even the reservists would be hard pressed to hold their own when energy beams started whizzing past their ears. Gunner was out there somewhere hiding in the ice fields, on the far side of the transports. Unfortunately, the veteran wasn't in a position to help them at the moment.

He leaned over and gave Solomon and Vrabel orders, and the two hurried off.

"Okay, listen up. We have one shot at this. As soon as we step out of the airlock, we'll be visible, which means Wilshire's people will start shooting. Our job is to make them think we're going to attack, so they'll pull back to the transports."

Louis gave him a quizzical look. "It's open ice out there. No protection."

"Which is why we're not going to get close. Fire off a few shots and stay low."

"I take it this is a diversion?" Plante asked.

"It is." Ryan's gaze landed on Sasha. "As soon as we start firing, make a beeline to the main airlock. It may be locked, so you may have to hack it. I'm giving you sixty seconds."

Her eyes widened.

"Doc, you and Mabel are our medics. Anyone gets hit, cover the wound and drag them toward the hatch."

"Understood." Louis passed the nurse some dressings he had taken from the transport. He pulled out the small canister and reapplied the ointment to Rani's side. The ensign seemed to relax slightly.

Ryan took one laser and gave the other to Rani.

"You sure you're up for this?" he asked a woozy-looking Archie.

Archie grinned. "If I'm not, Gunner will have my hide."

"Okay, check suits. We leave in one minute."

No words were spoken as seals and straps were tested and oxygen levels checked.

Rani edged up to Ryan. "What if we run into Wilshire's goons inside the station?"

"They're not military," Ryan replied, cinching up his wrist straps. "If we hit them hard and fast, they should break."

"And on the surface? Despite what you told Louis, we're still fish in a barrel."

Ryan laid a hand on her shoulder. "Don't worry. I didn't make a supply run to the asteroids just to get everyone killed."

Rani blinked. "Then what—"

"The gators and loaders," Ryan said, pointing to Solomon and Vrabel climbing into the cabs of the parked vehicles.

Her jaw dropped. "You're going to use them as shields?"

"Exactly. I figure we'll be able to advance fifty meters up the landing strip and maintain cover. That should buy Sasha enough time to hack the airlock."

"Son of a bitch," she muttered. "That could work."

"I'm glad you approve." He gave her a wry smile before sealing his helmet. "But I have one question."

"Sir?"

"Why did Solomon call you *Cap'n*?"

She fumbled for something to say, and Ryan's smile widened. He changed channels. "Vrabel, Solomon. Crank them up and let's move. The rest of you, fan out behind them."

"You got the main hangar door, Lieutenant?" Vrabel asked over the com.

"Copy that. Ready?"

A chorus of ayes answered as Ryan stepped up to the control panel by the entrance. He keyed in his code and a yellow light in the ceiling began flashing, followed by a high-pitched wail as the huge, rolling door started rising on hydraulic motors.

Ryan held on to the support beam as air was sucked out of the building. Vrabel and Solomon started up the gators, black smoke belching out of the exhaust vents, and steered them to the front.

"Slow and steady," Ryan ordered. "Rani, don't worry about hitting anything. We're just distracting them."

Solomon's gator led them out onto the icy surface. Jupiter was rising over the horizon, a conflagration of storms filling the sky. Two laser beams whizzed overhead as Ryan peered down the runway. It looked like somebody had stepped on an anthill; people ran up and down the transport's stairs, some ferrying boxes of supplies, others firing wild laser blasts.

Ryan kept his voice calm and measured as he moved up and discharged his laser over the hood of Vrabel's loader. "Stay low. Just the occasional shot." The battery charges were finite.

The machines advanced at a snail's pace, metal grilles and panels deflecting the high-energy beams. In the driver's seats, Vrabel and Solomon made themselves as small as possible.

"Sasha, go!" Out of the corner of his eye he watched the engineer sprint toward the station's airlock. A countdown began in his head. "One minute, people."

More lasers flashed overhead as Wilshire's crew seemed to have gotten themselves organized. Four shooters hid behind the boarding stairs. Their shots were mostly wide, but quantity had a quality all its own. One of the reservists was hit in the shoulder and spun like a marionette. Louis was on him before Ryan got the warning out, slapping a patch over the rip and starting CPR. Mabel fell to her knees beside him, and they worked on the man together. Seconds later, the doctor leaned back. His gaze found Ryan and he shook his head.

*Damn.* Ryan's mental clock clicked on zero. "Vrabel, your side first. Solomon, shift your gator left to provide cover."

A single laser burned a hole in the driver's chair two seconds after Vrabel vacated the seat. He tripped, and the doctor hauled him up and helped him limp toward the station's airlock.

"On my mark, Solomon, turn it sideways and get out. Plante, haul ass behind him. Ready . . . Now!" The big miner swung the vehicle hard, tires skidding across ice. Ryan fired two long blasts at the enemy, and Wilshire's men dove for cover. Rani attempted one last shot but nothing happened. Her cursing was audible over the com.

"Run!" Ryan shouted, and retreated in a low crouch, using the vehicles as cover.

The airlock was open and waiting when he reached the side of the station, and Sasha stood poised with her hand over the green button.

"Everyone in?"

"All accounted for," Louis said.

Ryan sucked in a breath. "Go."

Sasha slammed the button and the hatch cycled closed.

"Rani with me at the front. Gun up."

"I'm out," she said, squeezing her laser. "Battery is dead."

Damn. One weapon left.

Air was pumped in, and the inner hatch began to rise with a steady *chug-chug*.

Ryan relaxed when he realized the decompression chamber was empty. But that wouldn't last long.

"Solomon, with me." He hurried past the row of lockers before stopping on one side of the door leading into the concourse. A small voice in the back of his head welcomed him home. It had been weeks, and the sight of the familiar suit rack and helmets lent a comforting feel.

The door hissed open and two people clad in Federation suits stumbled in: a short bald man and a taller, scraggly woman. His gaze landed on the lasers in their grasp a nanosecond before his finger mashed the trigger of his own weapon. The beam burned through her left eye and straight into her brain. She made a weird croaking sound before pitching face-first onto the floor. Blood pooled around her head.

Ryan fired again and missed, the beam burning a hole in the plastek wall. Before the man could return fire, Solomon reached out and wrapped his hands around his neck. He twisted and squeezed, and there was an audible *crack*. The miner released his grip, and the body sagged boneless across the bench.

*Damn.* Ryan picked up the lasers and peered into the concourse. "It's clear. Rani, take Sasha and Vrabel into Ops. Get the laser online."

Rani nodded before sprinting down the concourse, Sasha and the lanky scientist on her heels.

"You two." Ryan pointed at the reservists and passed over one of the lasers. "Sweep Medical and Engineering. Make sure none of Wilshire's group are hiding in there. Doc, Mabel, seal this airlock. We don't need anyone sneaking up behind us. The rest of you are with me." He didn't wait for an acknowledgement as he hurried out of the room. Time was the enemy. If Wilshire panicked and launched, there was nothing he could do.

"Where are we going?" Plante wheezed. Archie and Solomon struggled to keep up.

Ryan skidded to a stop in front of the supply room and swung the door open. "Grab extra batteries. As many as you can carry."

"You told the doctor to seal the airlock," Plante said, opening the door. "How are we going to reach the transports?"

"There's another exit at the end of the concourse."

The governor's brow wrinkled. "By the hives? Wilshire doesn't know about that one?"

"He does, which is why we have to hit it fast." Ryan hesitated when his breath came out as gray fog. The air was cold. "What's wrong with the temperature?"

Archie began shoving batteries into his pockets. "Wilshire hooked up some kind of kill switch. The Ceres group is able to control power transmission." He took a second to catch his breath. "And, in case you don't know, they also wired a bomb inside the extractor."

A knot formed in Ryan's gut. "Son of a bitch." If he harbored any doubt about Wilshire's intentions, it had just gotten vaporized. "Solomon, on point with me. Archie, Plante, watch our flanks. There shouldn't be any of Wilshire's men left in the station, but stay alert."

"We're going for the transports?" Solomon asked, a nervous hitch in his tone.

"No choice. By now, Wilshire knows he's lost the station. All he's got left are the ships. And the sooner he puts them out of reach, the better for him." Ryan chose one last battery and wedged it into a hip pocket. It rubbed against his leg when he moved, but he'd suffer the discomfort as long as he had a functioning weapon.

As they passed the boarded-up shops on the concourse, Ryan abruptly held up. Something was wrong. Then it registered—an emergency bulkhead had dropped in front of Alpha Hive. He peered closer: someone had manually opened the entrance behind it.

Archie noted his puzzled expression. "Kasim placed the hive off limits after removing both pumps. Figured it was best to seal the entrance."

Ryan ignored a growing sense of futility. The colony was going to shit.

The sound of running feet riveted his attention as Louis and Mabel ran down the concourse. The doctor carried a laser in his hand. "Main airlock offline," he panted, giving Ryan the weapon. "And Mabel found this next to the EV suit rack. What are you looking at?"

Ryan took the laser and gave it to Archie. Now they had three functioning weapons. "If Alpha Hive is supposed to be sealed, why is the door ajar?"

"Because that's where Wilshire vaccinated the colonists," Mabel replied. "He said there were side effects he didn't want other colonists to see."

At that moment, two bodies stumbled out of the entrance. Their clothes were shredded and dried blood caked their faces.

Archie's eyes widened. "What in the name of Christ . . ."

"Sekers," Solomon grunted, leveling his laser.

"Damn, Ryan," Louis whispered. "I thought we left this nightmare back on Ceres."

Ryan could barely contain his anger. If mutants found a way into Beta Hive . . . "Take them down, Solomon."

Twin beams punched holes in both sekers, burning through the chest wall straight into the myocardium. Neither creature had time to scream before crumpling to the floor.

"Doctor, seal that hive," Ryan ordered. "Just in case there's more in there."

As the medico hurried to the hive entrance, Ryan reined in his emotions and sprinted to the end of the concourse. He breathed easy when he saw the Delta airlock remained empty. Wilshire was too slow reacting, which meant Ryan had to keep the pressure on.

"Suits buttoned up. Solomon, Archie, get in."

Plante looked over, confused. "What about me?"

"The airlock is a natural chokepoint," Ryan replied. "Wilshire may be slow but he's not stupid. I'm thinking his people are waiting outside. Too many bodies would make for an easy target." He shepherded Archie and Solomon into the small chamber before anyone could ask the next logical question: what happens if they got pinned?

Archie slapped the button. The metal hatch rotated shut, and air was pumped out of the chamber.

"Stay low," Ryan said, dropping into a crouch. "And get ready to move."

Archie snuggled against the metal wall and raised his laser. Solomon's eyes darted nervously behind his face shield.

The overhead light flashed green and the hatch cycled open.

Two laser beams struck the back of the airlock.

"Go!" Ryan shouted. He fired a random burst and sprinted outside. Some part of his subconscious was aware of Archie dashing at a right angle and Solomon diving behind a low ice ridge.

"No! Don't stop; keep moving."

Solomon flattened himself against the ice as repeated laser strikes melted holes in his cover. Ryan caught a glimpse of movement—the familiar Federation EV suit—and he squeezed the trigger. The beam went wide, but the attacker panicked and missed Ryan. A second beam punched a hole in the ice by his feet, forcing Ryan to change direction. He leapt over a surface fissure and rolled into a shooting position. A shape separated itself from the closest ice pillar. Ryan settled his pulse, aimed, and fired.

The beam, colored gold and scarlet in the thin atmosphere, hit the person square in the chest. Unlike a bullet, there was no punch to the impact but rather a small puff of smoke as the energy burned through the flimsy fabric into vulnerable flesh. Ryan had a brief impression of a panicked expression on a female face before she dropped out of sight.

Something flashed over his head, and he dove to the side, his feet losing purchase as he slid down a steep slope. His arms flailed, and the bottom came up fast. He barely twisted his body around before he struck, helmet first. The impact rattled his teeth.

He hit the com. "Archie, Solomon, can you read?"

At first, only static. Then Archie's voice. "Two on my ass! Trying to create space, but I think they're some of ours. They know how to move on the ice."

*Shit.* Ryan tried to clamber up the slope, but his EV boots couldn't find purchase. After a second failure, he gave up, skirted around the side, and scaled a crumbling ice wall that resembled a rockslide back on Earth. The Great Red Spot stared down at him, a storm that had raged for centuries. Nothing he did in the next few minutes would affect that behemoth. He crept around a series of ice boulders until he approached the airlock. Solomon had crawled against the station and was exchanging fire with two assailants who had him flanked. Ryan remembered what happened to Louis and Peters when Lecky's marines flanked them outside the main airlock. That firefight lasted all of two minutes.

He jumped up and ran straight at the closest shooter. Twenty feet. His laser seemed to aim and fire on its own, the beam passing inches in front of the enemy's faceplate. The assailant reeled back, and his helmet swiveled toward the new threat.

Ten feet. The enemy laser came around. Ryan crouched lower, letting his momentum carry him the last few steps, praying the bastard didn't get lucky.

The beam flashed wide, but he still felt it as joules of energy heated the fabric over his arm. He tucked and braced before his shoulder plowed into a body twice as thick as his own. Both men went over in a tangle of arms and legs, and both lasers skidded across the surface.

He threw a wild punch that glanced off the other face shield. A second overhand right missed completely. The man threw him off. Ryan recognized the broad face of a deuterium miner, Jorge.

Ryan regained his feet and launched himself at the turncoat. A left jab connected with the man's shoulder, but a counterpunch caught Ryan in the chest. The air went out of him in a single *whoosh*, and pain shot up his neck. He stepped back as a fist whizzed past his helmet.

Behind his faceplate, Jorge's eyes narrowed and he flashed Ryan a malicious smile. He was bigger and stronger, and he knew it. Ryan scanned the surface in a desperate gamble to find something to even the score, but the ice remained impervious to his needs.

The big man charged and tackled Ryan around the stomach. Ryan hammered the back of the helmet with zero effect, stopping only when his back slammed against the surface. A solid thump to the side of his helmet rocked him, and he instinctively pulled his arms in to ward off the next blow. It still sent shock waves through to his bones. Another heavy punch put his teeth through his tongue. He tasted blood.

The man continued to land blows, and Ryan felt panic swell inside. He couldn't win this. Jorge was a street fighter and was going to finish him. One fist got through and struck his shield, and Ryan momentarily lost consciousness. He couldn't focus. It looked like there were three assailants straddling him, raining down punches. Reality began to fade, and he could barely keep his arms up.

Jorge hesitated long enough to grab a huge chunk of ice. He raised it over Ryan's helmet and mouthed something Ryan didn't want to hear.

Some inner voice screamed at Ryan to defend himself, but his limbs refused to respond.

The ice started its descent just as a laser beam struck the miner's helmet. Jorge recoiled. Even in the thin atmosphere of the moon, Ryan heard him scream. The ice fell from his limp hands and bounced off Ryan's chest.

Ryan lay stunned for several seconds, his brain trying to analyze what just happened.

A shadow bent over him. "You okay, Ace?"

*Gunner?* It took a second to focus. Something wet and sticky ran down the side of his face. Hands reached under his arms and helped him into a sitting position. He stared into the familiar face of the doctor. "You're not Gunner."

"Thank God for small miracles," Louis grunted, but his look of concern didn't diminish. "We were watching through the airlock when the big guy jumped you. I notified Gunner and he got here just in time. How you feeling?"

Ryan rotated his head, and a mass of pain fibers registered their discontent. "Like I just got run over by a steamroller."

"Sorry, Ace." Gunner stepped into his field of vision. "I was busy with the buggers chasing Archie when the vet called. Took me a few minutes to get back." He peered at Ryan's face. "My fault."

Ryan waved a hand and then realized it was blood running down his cheek.

Louis took his arm. "I should get you to Medical."

"No time." Ryan started to shake his head before throbbing muscles warned him off. "Wilshire is about to launch." He scanned the surface. "Is everyone okay?"

"Solomon was winged on the arm, but I patched it before he lost his air. Archie is alive thanks to the Neanderthal."

Gunner snorted.

Plante walked over. "Three hightailed it back to the transports, which means Wilshire knows we're coming."

Ryan felt a measure of strength return and allowed Louis and Plante to help him stand. After a few seconds, his legs agreed to take the weight, and he exhaled. "No choice. We're close, but it means nothing if we can't take those ships. Any word from Rani?"

"All quiet on the com, Ace. I didn't want to break radio silence and give away our position."

Solomon appeared, carrying Ryan's laser. He had a blue sealing patch over one arm and a resigned look on his face. "Sorry about panicking when we opened the airlock, Lieutenant. It won't happen again."

"Forget it." Like most of the reservists, the miner had little military training. Ryan pointed to an elevated slab of ice. "I need someone on high ground to pin down Wilshire's men."

"Keeping them pinned won't stop the ships from launching," Gunner said.

"No, but it will keep them busy. Maybe even pick off a few." Ryan's gaze fell on Solomon and Plante. "Think you can do that?"

They nodded.

"I'll stay with them," Louis said, withdrawing a patch kit from his suit pocket. "Just in case."

"Focus their attention," Ryan repeated. "The fewer people shooting at us, the closer we can get to the ships."

Gunner balanced on the balls of his feet. "I'm figuring Wilshire for a defensive perimeter by now. Attacking static defenses with two men is crazy. Even for you."

Ryan tapped Gunner on the chest. "First of all, it's not you and me. It's two military-trained officers against a mob of unruly civilians. They don't understand concepts like tactics or cover fire. We should be able to cut a path to the transports. You good with that?"

Gunner made a show of checking his battery. "I've come this far with you, Ace. No way I'm quitting now."

# CHAPTER 42

*He who learns but does not think is lost. He who thinks but does not learn is in great danger.*

DAY 145, 1645 HOURS

Rani removed the last recessed screw and hauled the external casing off the terminal. The metal clanged against the duro-ally floor. Ops felt empty. Despite her and Sasha hunkered over the terminal, it seemed something or someone was missing. Then it came to her: Braeder and Gunner were risking their lives trying to save the colony, and Marco and Captain Tracy were dead. She was the last original crew member left. She wanted to cry or maybe close her eyes and pray for this nightmare to end.

Sasha reached into the guts of the terminal and pulled out a fist-sized processor. "Let's start here," she said. "If we can send a trace signal down the line, we might be able to find the corrupted circuit."

It took a moment for Rani to pull her thoughts together. She resisted the urge to walk up to the portal and see if both transports were still parked at the end of the runway. Of course, they were. On the other side of the landing strip, the laser sat atop a slab of rockcrete next to the hangar.

"Rani?" Sasha had a concerned look in her eye.

"Yeah, right." Rani took the processor from Sasha and laid it on top of the terminal before plugging in a portable diagnostic unit. A small indicator light on the side turned green. "Program running."

Sasha hauled out a section of cable and laid it on the floor before separating the strands into red and yellow.

"What are you doing?" Rani asked.

"Preparing another circuit to charge the laser," she said, sitting down next to the cable and pulling a power tool off her belt. "If diagnostics finds a short in the main line, we have to be able to load up on amps. I'm going to set up a secondary electrical line so we can bypass the problem and still charge the system."

Rani blinked. "Damn, girl. You sure you're not related to Marco?"

Sasha's cheeks bunched. "I don't—"

"Never mind. How can I help?"

She pointed. "Find where this line terminates. We'll have to splice it to a working subsystem to complete the circuit. Pick something we won't need. I'm thinking concourse lighting."

"That's a negative." Rani bent over the exposed innards of the terminal. "The greenhouses are on the same circuit, and we can't lose them. Our best bet is environmental for the Command Module."

Sasha frowned. "That doesn't sound good."

"It'll get cold in here," Rani acknowledged. "But the hives and greenhouses won't be affected. It'll also play hell with the still Gunner and Louis set up in Captain Tracy's old quarters, but they can bitch at me later."

Sasha paused with her hands wrapped around the wire. "A still? To make moonshine?"

Rani searched through the mass of circuits until she found the right one. "Where do you think the doctor's rotgut comes from? They've been brewing that crap since the pubs ran out of the real stuff. Hasn't Gunner ever offered you a drink?"

Sasha cocked her head to one side. "Gunner says it's not good for me. Says it'll kill brain cells."

Rani laughed. "He really protects you. I had someone like that once."

"Gunner told me." Sasha looked up and caught her eye. "I'm really sorry."

Rani's expression fell, and her gaze landed on Marco's old seat. "Yeah, well, let's get this laser working and take that bastard down."

Ryan knew this section of surface ice like the back of his hand. They crossed it every time they made a trek to the extractor. Deep fields of splintered ice, fissures, and ridges that blended into the massive tectonic plates and flowed in ultra-slow motion under the influence of Jupiter's immense gravity.

They moved in tandem toward the transports, a well-practiced choreographic dance between trained professionals. The lead person advanced, crouched down, and covered the second man as he rushed to the next point. Eyes in constant motion, searching. Economy of movement, controlled lethality.

Gunner halted behind a ridge covered with hoarfrost and used hand signals. *Two enemy combatants. Nine o'clock.*

Ryan surveyed the slope and made several rapid gestures. Gunner would wait sixty seconds and then draw their fire, allowing Ryan to flank them. He slid down and followed the ridge to where it dropped into a hundred-foot crevice. Flipping the laser over his shoulder, he jumped across open space and hugged sharp chunks on the other side. The laser dangled on the strap as he climbed up the icy slope.

A single discharge burned into the ice fifty feet away. Gunner poking the bear.

Ryan waited until a pair of answering beams carved a hole in the moon's thin atmosphere before running at a diagonal away from the fight. Fifty feet in, he changed direction and pulled the laser off his shoulder. Stepping around a block of ice, he aimed and fired two blasts in rapid succession. The first melted the oxygen regulator on the back of a Federation suit; the second burned a hole in the fabric of his partner's Alliance outfit. Both spun in shock and then flailed like wounded animals as nitrogen in their blood exploded out of solution.

He stood up and waved. Gunner joined him seconds later.

"No problem?"

Ryan glanced at the bodies. One of them looked familiar. "All good. Let's find our next lucky couple."

Kasim didn't know which was the biggest threat: whoever was about to emerge from the transport's airlock or the gun leveled at his face by a nervous colonist. With hands tied behind his back, he could do nothing about either. The light over the hatch flashed green, and two people in Federation suits hurried out.

"What the hell is going on out there?" Wilshire screamed from the cockpit. "They only had a couple of lasers when they attacked the transports."

Andrei pulled off his helmet and grimaced. "That attack was a ruse. They busted into the station and took out the guards we left in the concourse."

Wilshire fumbled for something to say. "They took the station? Then why am I seeing laser fire outside the cockpit?"

Pavel sagged against the hull. "Braeder found more weapons. Launch attack from other side."

"He's desperate," Andrei said. "He knows if he doesn't take the ships soon, he's lost. How long until we're ready?"

Wilshire cast a furious glance at the metal containers stacked between pods in the cargo hold. The narrow confines made it a tight squeeze for the men and women preparing for cryo-sleep. "Another ten minutes for the pilots to complete preflight checklists."

Andrei cast a suspicious eye at the cockpit. Kasim couldn't see Stoll at the helm, but he'd heard his screams earlier when Wilshire made a visit to ensure the pilot's compliance.

"You sure he won't sabotage our launch?" Andrei asked.

Wilshire smirked, and his gaze fell on Kasim. "Between my subtle encouragement and some chemical inducement, we'll be fine."

"And the pilot on the other ship?" Andrei persisted. "What's her name, Chan?"

Wilshire waved a hand. "Don't worry; I'll take care of her. Can you hold Braeder off?"

"I've formed a perimeter around the ships," Andrei said. "No way he gets through."

"How many lasers do we have left?" Wilshire asked.

"Plenty," Pavel replied. "But only three miners."

"What about our Ceres group?"

"Eight," he said. "But can barely move. Must leave soon."

Kasim peered closer. The Russian doctor looked terrible. He wondered how the man was still standing. After days suffering the effects of Europa's gravity, their bodies were calling it quits. And all the drugs in the solar system weren't going to change that.

"Ten minutes," Wilshire repeated. "Then we'll be gone and Braeder can die of starvation or asphyxiation. I don't care."

"I want to kill him myself," Andrei said, eyes narrowing. "Along with that bitch, Singh."

"Stand in line," Wilshire grunted. "But sometimes, we have to take our winnings off the table. Now get out and do your job."

Andrei wiped his forehead with the back of his sleeve before pulling the helmet back on. Pavel stared at his with a mixture of apprehension and disgust before following suit. They stepped back into the airlock and the hatch closed behind them.

Wilshire paced like an agitated animal. He returned to the cockpit, and Kasim watched him exchange words with Stoll. He couldn't hear what was said, but the wicked smile on Wilshire's face didn't bode well. After a minute, he walked out and pointed a bony finger. "Governor, it's time for you to play your part."

"Kind of difficult at the moment." He turned to show his bound hands.

Wilshire gestured, and the colonist guarding him bent down to untie them.

"Follow me," Wilshire ordered as he picked up his helmet and stepped toward the airlock.

Kasim tried to edge up to the cockpit and get a look at Stoll, but the colonist shoved him roughly in the back. "Keep moving."

"We going somewhere?" Kasim asked.

Wilshire smirked. "I kept you alive in case I needed a hostage, and I hate wasting assets."

Kasim raised his eyebrows as he waited for the man to finish.

"I'm going to put you in front of the transports. If Braeder wants to attack, you're going to be in the line of fire."

Kasim gave him a sidelong look. "You're a real piece of work, aren't you?"

Wilshire snarled and yanked him into the airlock before gesturing to the colonist. "Stay here and pass out the lasers. And watch the pilot."

Kasim pulled on his helmet and tightened the seal as air was pumped out. The exit hatch opened, and Wilshire pushed him toward the boarding stairs. "You try something stupid and I'll shoot you myself. Now get down there and stand on the landing strip. I want Braeder to be able to see you."

Kasim inched down the stairs ahead of Wilshire. He noted the row of armed colonists and Ceres survivors arrayed in front of the transports. About a dozen huddling behind gators and fuel-supply trucks. The scene reminded him of ancient vids of American settlers circling the wagons.

"I seem to remember you had more people when you arrived."

Wilshire jabbed him in the back with his laser. "Doesn't matter. I've enough volunteers on both ships to fill the holes."

Kasim glanced up at *Serenity*. Whispers of smoke leaked out of the engines as the pilot brought systems online. It wouldn't be long now.

Something flashed behind them, and one of Wilshire's men crumpled. The rest turned and fired into the darkness.

"Keep going." Wilshire shoved him when he paused to see what was happening. "He's not getting close before we launch."

Kasim stepped onto the ice and stared up at the gas giant blazing in the void.

"Hurry up, Ryan," he whispered.

"On your left, Ace. Behind the ridge."

Over the com, Gunner's voice sounded nonchalant, like they were choosing what salad dressing for supper. But after thirty minutes hunting the enemy, it was almost routine. Ryan checked his battery—enough for one shot—before setting his sights on a low ridge of ice that grew out of the surface like a serpentine monster. He exhaled slowly and wrapped his finger around the trigger. Five seconds later, a helmet appeared, and Ryan nailed it. He had a brief image of a black scorch mark before the figure disappeared.

"Target down. Will confirm. Ready?"

"Got you covered," Gunner said. "Stay low."

"Copy that." Ryan hunched over and crab-walked to the ridge. The body lay sprawled face-down on the ice. "Confirmed, Gunner, but I don't see his partner." Wilshire's goons never patrolled alone.

"I got him already. He was hunkered behind one of the pillars."

Ryan exhaled. One less worry. That made eight enemy down. He changed channels and glanced toward the elevated ice ridge. "Plante, any more in the area?"

"Negative, Lieutenant. They've pulled the rest in tight around the transports."

"Can you get a shot?"

"We did until they used your idea and brought out vehicles from the hangar to hide behind. Now all we can do is keep their heads down."

"That's better than nothing. Let us know if anything changes." Ryan heard two clicks before switching frequencies. "Rani, what's the status on the laser?"

"Sabotage wasn't that bad, Lieutenant. We fixed it. Sasha also located the short circuit that had been frying the pumps. We're bypassing it now."

"Fast as you can."

"Understood." The channel closed.

Ryan leaned back and was grabbing the last battery from his belt when Plante's voice startled him. "Lieutenant, the transport's engine lights came on. I think Wilshire is preparing to launch."

"Shit!" Ryan shoved the new battery into the slot. "Gunner, on me. We have to hit them now."

"On my way. Thirty seconds."

"Ryan." Louis's voice in his ear. "There's somebody standing in the middle of the landing strip! I think it's Kasim. What's going on?"

Anger flooded Ryan's veins. "Wilshire's sending a message. If we threaten his ships, he'll kill the governor."

"Why, that piece of—"

"Never mind!" Ryan snapped. In his mind, the decision was already made. "Solomon, Plante, move up and attack the transport. We're going in."

Ryan slumped to a sitting position, his back wedged against a flat ice slab as he stole precious seconds to catch his breath. Sweat dripped down the side of his face despite the EV suit's environmental system working overtime. Jupiter remained overhead, beating down on them like a midday sun.

Gunner almost tripped over the Federation body before dropping beside Ryan.

"Ready, Ace?"

"Yeah." Ryan's gaze landed on the dead colonist, one of Wilshire's converts. The man had been hiding between blocks of ice when Ryan spied him and kept him pinned until Gunner had a clear shot. "How's your laser?"

"Half a charge. You?"

"Just switched in my last battery." Ryan took a deep breath. "One last push?"

The veteran grinned. "Time for payback. Can't wait to get my hands on that bastard."

"All right. Let's do this." Ryan swiveled his body around until his laser rested on top of the ridge. The two transports sat on the landing strip, their exhaust vents emitting white smoke as the engines heated up.

They had thinned out Wilshire's lines, and it was time to go for the kill. Ryan mapped their approach before crawling over the ledge. He didn't have to check; Gunner would move up and defend his flank. His first targets hid behind a raised crease of ice that circled the edge of the runway behind *Serenity*. They had a good defensive position except that Ryan had taken out their comrades who had been protecting the other side of the strip. Now their side was exposed, and Ryan seized the moment to exploit that weakness.

Two laser blasts struck the ice on their right: Louis and Plante keeping the defenders' heads down.

He sensed Gunner's presence behind him as he crested the ridge. Both EV suits were facing the other direction. He motioned and lined up the one on the left. The laser struck just below the thin plastek tube that controlled oxygen flow, and the man jerked as if stung. Gunner's laser blast was a second behind and burned a hole in his partner's suit just above the hip. The result was the same. In seconds, both lay seizing on the ice.

"Go!" Ryan shouted. They had opened a path to the transports.

"Plante. Hit them from your side. Keep the pressure on before they can regroup." He thanked Fate none of those sons of bitches had any training.

Gunner pulled up and shot a Federation-clad defender under the nose of *Serenity*. He went down, clutching his stomach. A helmet appeared over a block of ice by *Phoenix*, and Ryan sent a beam of energy straight into the faceplate.

"Which one?" Gunner panted, and Ryan realized a decision loomed: which transport to hit first. They could only attack one at a time. His eyes landed on the figure in the middle of the runway. Kasim. The governor was gesturing frantically toward *Phoenix*.

"This way!" Ryan sprinted toward the nearest transport. If Kasim was pointing, their targets must be onboard.

Two figures tried to scramble up the boarding stairs. Gunner shot one in the back and Ryan winged the second. Both tumbled over the side. The battery in Ryan's laser flashed yellow. Low-charge warning.

"The hatch is closing," Gunner warned as they vaulted the stairs.

A laser blast whizzed past his helmet, and Ryan gritted his teeth. Perched on top of the ladder, both of them were exposed, but there was nothing they could do.

Gunner shoved the barrel of his laser in the opening before the hatch could close. It tried to seal twice before the hydraulic motors gave up and, like a set of elevator doors, slid open.

Ryan palmed the button and they jumped in.

"They'll be waiting as soon as the inner hatch opens, Ace."

"They're civilians, Gunner. They don't think outside the box."

Behind his faceplate, the veteran's eyes narrowed. "You're thinkin' the deck?"

Ryan dropped into a prone position. "They won't expect it." In times of crisis, people reverted to habit, and most civilians were only accustomed to standing in airlocks.

The inner hatch slid open and two laser beams struck the back wall. Both shooters hesitated, seemingly confused about the empty space. That's when Ryan's and Gunner's lasers struck them point-blank, burning through skin and bone and butchering facial muscles into slabs of cooked meat. They collapsed, screaming, as blood poured from partially cauterized blood vessels. Ryan was up and moving before they hit the deck. A skeletal-looking male stepped out of the cockpit. Ryan's beam took him in the throat. Another person, a girl in the cargo bay, dropped her weapon and hurriedly raised her hands.

Ryan took in the scene in a millisecond: ten individuals, three holding lasers, open cryo-pods, and stacks of supplies against the sides.

Gunner appeared at Ryan's side, helmet off. "Anyone else with a weapon has two seconds to drop it," he bellowed, his voice carrying through the ship.

Lasers fell and rattled against the floor.

"Lieutenant."

Ryan spun around, weapon raised, finger tight on the trigger.

Chan smiled weakly, one arm braced against the cockpit doorway. "Thanks for coming."

Ryan peered close. The pilot had a glassy look in her eyes and what looked to be cigarette burns on her face.

"Shit. You okay?"

Her response was buried in static as Ryan's com activated.

Kasim's voice. "Ryan, you better get out here. *Serenity* is moving."

Gunner's eyes widened.

"Here." Ryan shoved his laser into Chan's arms. "Shoot anyone who moves." He hurried into the airlock. Gunner was still sealing his helmet as the air was pumped out.

"Wilshire must be on the other ship," the veteran said. "Why did Kasim send us here?"

Ryan had already asked himself that question. But he knew the answer. The governor prioritized saving a life over killing one, and Chan was on *Phoenix*.

But if Wilshire made it out alive because of Kasim's decision, he'd have a hard time not shooting the governor.

Louis silently cursed Fate. Being down one arm meant his balance was always off. He hustled from one block of ice to the next, all the while praying one of those laser beams didn't have his name on it. His only consolation: Plante was worse. Like Wilshire's men, he was suffering the effects of Europa's gravity.

The Ceres governor was doing his best to keep up with Solomon, but his color was off and he was visibly laboring. Louis felt his front pocket to confirm he had nitro and adrenaline available if something happened.

Solomon leaned over a ridge of hoarfrost and exchanged laser fire with two individuals hiding behind one of the refueling trucks from the hangar. Plante almost tripped over him but managed to bring his laser up and fire a wild beam that had zero chance of hitting anything smaller than the moon itself.

Ryan and Gunner had stormed *Phoenix* less than a minute before, and Louis would have given his remaining arm to know what was happening inside that ship. He edged up behind a thick plate of ice. His group was maybe fifty meters from *Serenity*, close enough to identify the type of EV suits on the stairs. Close enough to see a mad scramble as people rushed to board the ship. A lineup formed in front of the airlock. Solomon fired, and one person tumbled over the side. Louis cringed as he slammed into the verdigris ice. The remaining people on the steps began hammering on the hatch with their fists. Solomon fired again, and another body went down.

"Have to keep moving," Louis warned.

Plante took a deep breath. His skin had inherited an unhealthy gray tinge. "Copy that. I'll go left. Solomon, you go right."

"On you," the big man said.

The governor took one step around the pillar and walked right into a laser beam. Louis heard an abbreviated scream before the man went down.

"Plante!" He sprinted to the governor's side. A smoking hole in his suit announced the impact site, right over his heart.

Louis slapped a patch over the tear and pressed down tight to seal the edges. His sixth sense screamed at him to examine the wound closer, and his gut tightened. The beam hadn't been absorbed by the suit or even the chest wall. It had burned deep into cardiac muscle.

He met the governor's panicked look, the wide eyes, the mouth trying to form words as blood flow to his brain ebbed and stopped. It was second nature to grab Plante's hand before his eyes rolled back, and his lungs reached for that last breath of air before going still.

"Goddamn," he whispered, staring at the planetary monster bearing down on them. "Are you happy now?"

Ryan activated the com as the hatch cycled closed. "Plante, what's your status?"

"Plante's dead," Louis said. "Solomon just took out the last Ceres guard on the steps, but they already closed the hatch. The ship is lining up for takeoff."

"Shit!" The outer airlock opened and Ryan launched himself down the boarding stairs. The massive transport was moving. He recognized Solomon and the doctor running up the ice strip.

"Aim for the landing gear!" he shouted.

Gunner hurdled the last steps and sprinted after the ship. His first shot went wide. The second left a scorch mark on the underside of the hull.

Without a weapon, Ryan was useless. He tracked the speed of the transport. Solomon would never reach it in time. Gunner was their only hope. The veteran got within twenty feet before leveling his weapon. The beam struck one of the rear tires. Gunner held it steady and, after several seconds, it came apart, rubber bands splintering off the rim.

But any hope of stopping the launch evaporated as the transport continued to pick up speed. Gunner was left behind, his last desperate shots useless. Thirty seconds later, the ship lifted off the ice and headed into the void.

"Goddamn!" Ryan fell back on the boarding steps. He wanted to throw up. Wilshire had made good his escape. And what had he taken with him? How many people? How many vital supplies?

Kasim joined Gunner on the runway and stared at the departing transport. Solomon and Louis hurried over, both panting. The big miner braced himself against the landing gear.

"Damn, Ryan," Louis wheezed. "What do we do now?"

*What now?* Ryan had a déjà vu moment of entering his family home after the fire and sifting through the debris. He pointed at the doctor. "Chan's inside *Phoenix* and needs your help. Wilshire tortured her."

"Son of a bitch." Louis started up the stairs.

"Solomon, put the rest of them in the brig," Ryan continued before changing channels. "Rani, I need an update."

"Almost finished, Lieutenant. Laser should be operational in a few minutes."

Gunner and Kasim met him under the nose of *Phoenix*. "Sorry, Ace. Getting slow in my old age."

"Not your fault, Gunner. I should have figured out a better plan."

Kasim snorted. "Yeah, right. And for your next trick, I have some water that's looking to become wine."

Ryan stopped and stared at Kasim. The governor's face didn't look good. "You okay?"

Kasim waved away his concern. "Just bruises. Sorry about the station."

"Not your fault either. Your job was to keep the colonists alive. You did that."

Kasim's gaze swept the runway, pausing over the bodies. "I can't believe it's come to this. Have we not learned anything?"

Ryan began striding toward the station's airlock. "Hold that thought. We're not done yet."

# CHAPTER 43

*I'd rather die for speaking out than to live and be silent.*

DAY 145, 1810 HOURS

"Almost finished, sir," Rani said the moment Ryan rushed into Ops. "Sasha's soldering the last wires now."

"What happened?" Ryan asked. The terminal looked like an eviscerated animal carcass with its insides splayed open and wires covering the floor. Sasha sat cross-legged in front while Rani fed her pieces from a pile on Marco's old terminal.

"Bennett tried to sabotage the circuits," Sasha said. "Took a while to repair and replace the damaged ones, but we found them all."

"And the pumps? Kasim said they kept burning out."

"There was a short in one of the maintenance circuits," Rani said. "We swapped in a secondary line. It should function normally now."

Ryan hesitated. "But we still need a new pump to make it work."

"I sent Vrabel outside with a new one, Lieutenant," Rani said. "He should be just about finished installing it."

Gunner, Solomon, and Kasim entered the room as Ryan slid into his chair. It felt comfortable, like a favorite coat rescued from the refuse bin. Solomon walked up beside Rani's terminal.

Ryan opened a channel. "Europa to *Serenity*. Come in."

It took several seconds, but a familiar voice answered. "You really are a pain in the ass," Wilshire said. "I'm sorry we weren't able to conclude our discussions."

"Well, we *concluded* a lot of your people. Their bodies are all over my runway."

"Their loss," Wilshire said, and Ryan detected more anger than remorse in his tone. "They should have been quicker to board when the order was given."

"Yeah." Ryan felt a smirk coming on. "Like they could have moved faster with their bodies wilting under Europa's gravity and dodging laser blasts. How many do you have left, Wilshire? Ten, fifteen people? And you want to restart humanity?"

"Doesn't matter how many I have on board," Wilshire snarled. "It'll be more than you soon enough. Your colony is on its last legs. Even Lecky knows that."

Sybil? Ryan hesitated. She had made it onboard? "I wouldn't count on it, Wilshire. In fact, I'm going to do you one better. If you don't turn that ship around, I'm going to melt it into something the size of a shoebox. Good luck reaching Earth in that."

"Nice bluff, Braeder, but the laser is inoperative."

"Not bluffing. My engineers have completed repairs. I'm going to give you ten minutes to talk it over with your friends. Then I'm going to blow you out of the sky."

Wilshire barked a laugh. "You wouldn't dare. I have your pilot, Stoll, onboard. You wouldn't kill one of your own."

Ryan leaned over the arm of his chair and lowered his voice. "Ask Sybil about the Russian transport, or better yet, ask her if she thinks I have the guts to pull the trigger. I'll be waiting on your reply." He snapped off the channel and found himself meeting Rani's stare.

"Stoll is one of ours," she said quietly.

Ryan leaned back. They had been through this a year before when the rebels took the concourse and, together, they'd made that fateful decision to open the EV door.

"How many do you figure are onboard, Gunner?" he asked. "Fifteen?"

The veteran ran a hand through his beard. "The way the rats boarded in a hurry . . . yes, Ace, about that."

"They experimented on dozens of innocents on Ceres, Rani," Ryan said. "And murdered even more. Not to mention what they tried to do here. Wipe out the colony."

Bits of moisture formed in the corners of her eyes. "But do we have to keep killing? Why seek revenge when we have the colony back?"

She hesitated when Louis walked into the room.

"Chan's going to be all right," he said. "Mabel's treating her in Medical." He seemed to sense the tension and glanced at Rani. "What is it?"

She wiped her eyes. "The lieutenant wants to shoot down the transport."

Louis stepped over to Sasha. "The laser?"

The young engineer put down her multitool. "Rebooting now."

"The killing has to stop," Rani said. "There must be another way."

Louis seemed to shrink in place. "I'm sorry, Rani. I saw what they did to the colonists on Ceres. Some people don't deserve redemption."

Ryan tapped the com button on the arm of his chair. "Vrabel, what's your status?"

"Screwing down the external casing, Lieutenant. Panel here reads green across the board."

"Thank you." He closed the channel and looked at Rani. "Do you want me to do it?"

She sucked in a deep breath and wiped away a tear that had escaped down her cheek. "No, Lieutenant. That's my job." She took her seat at the terminal, her deliberate movements eerily similar to last year.

Ryan hit the com. "Wilshire, your time is up. What's your decision?" He secretly prayed for a refusal. The images of Compton, Smith, Gonzalez, and the others flashed in his mind. He owed the bastard so much.

"Sorry, Braeder, but I've got a date with the inner system, and you're not going to wreck my plans."

"Well, then, you just sealed your fate." He glanced at Rani and the ensign gave him a solemn nod.

"No, Braeder, you just sealed yours. I might have been tempted to let sleeping dogs lie, maybe let you slowly starve to death. Believe me, I know the feeling. But now my decision is simple. You're all going to die, most likely in the next few hours."

"What are you talking about?"

"Oh?" Wilshire's voice sounded sickly sweet. "Didn't anyone tell you about the bomb? Goodbye, Braeder."

Kasim's eyes went wide. "Ryan, the extractor!"

A sudden glow appeared outside the portal, like the sun momentarily breaking through a layer of cloud. It was gone just as fast.

"Rani, fire!" Ryan yelled.

She stabbed the laser button, but it was too late. All hell broke loose inside the station.

The lights went out, and the *whup-whup* of the emergency klaxon vibrated the walls. Red and yellow warning lights appeared on every terminal accompanied by the buzz and whine of servers in distress. In the darkness, they sounded especially bleak.

Gunner scanned his readouts. "Power out across the station."

"The bomb in the extractor," Kasim said, wringing his hands. "That's how he blackmailed his way inside."

Half the lights in Ops sputtered to life.

"On batteries," Gunner announced.

"How long will they last?" Ryan asked.

"Twelve hours," Sasha whispered. "If we don't fix the extractor by then, Wilshire's right: we're all dead."

Ryan stood beside Gunner and stared silently at the ruined extractor. No words needed to be said. All the work that had gone into maintaining it, to repairing it . . . It was all for naught. There was nothing left to fix. The technologically advanced power unit that siphoned joules of energy from the innards of the moon and allowed humans to live in such an inhospitable environment no longer existed. There were shards of metals, frayed pieces of wiring, and even burned circuit boards littering the surface, but nothing that resembled an extractor.

Gunner bent down and picked up what looked to be the cover of an electrical panel. "Sasha sure makes a heck of a bomb."

Walking up beside them, Louis growled. "You tell her, I'll kill you myself."

Ryan's stare didn't waver. Gunner surmised that Wilshire had taken the explosives from Ceres, from the batch Sasha helped manufacture to use on the sekers. But no one was going to tell the young engineer it was her creation that led to the colony's demise.

He glanced over his shoulder at the doctor. The man seemed to be in shock, staring at the debris field. That he'd wanted to come surprised Ryan. It was as though he'd suspected something evil lurked on the surface and he had to see it for himself.

Ryan opened a channel. "Braeder to Rani. Tell the work crew not to bother suiting up."

"Lieutenant?"

"I'm sorry. There's nothing they can do." He paused when he realized he still had a duty to perform. "Rani, patch me into the PA system."

"You want to speak to the colonists?" Rani sounded defeated, and Ryan could picture her sagging into her seat.

"I don't want to, Rani," he said quietly. "I have to."

There was a slight pause. "Go ahead, sir."

Ryan sucked in a breath. "This is Lieutenant Braeder. I have bad news. Wilshire wasn't bluffing about the bomb. The extractor is a total loss. There is no way to repair it." He noted a hardening of Gunner's expression while Louis remained focused on the debris field. "I know all of you have suffered, all of you have sacrificed to get this far. And, to be clear, we've lasted longer than any other colony, or Earth, for that matter. If anything, that's something to be proud of. For what it's worth, I'm sorry I couldn't drag us across the finish line. For that, I hope you'll forgive me. This is Braeder signing off."

He closed the com. Jupiter blazed silently overhead, a judge delivering the ultimate verdict.

"Any final thoughts, gentlemen? We had a good run."

"The artifact," Louis said. "If we're going to die in the next twelve hours, I want one last look. Maybe see how close humanity came to joining the big leagues."

Ryan glanced toward the cave entrance, which remained mostly hidden behind large blocks of ice. "Well, Gunner, what say we show the doc mankind's greatest discovery."

Gunner gave the doctor a sidelong look. "That's what I want to do, spend my last minutes showing the vet what real science looks like."

Ryan ignored the bickering and started down the gentle slope. He checked his heads-up display: ten hours of station battery left. Probably less, considering the shape they were in. Backup batteries were not designed to be turned off and on like a light switch, and the past year had seen them repeatedly abused.

He palmed open the airlock at the bottom of the stairs and waited for the other two to join him. No one said a word as the chamber repressurized, making Ryan wonder if this was how a condemned man acted in his last hours. Silent and pensive.

The inner hatch cycled open, and Ryan shed his helmet and gloves. He would have unzipped his suit, but the temperature hung just above freezing. A sign of things to come.

Louis plopped himself on one of the scientists' chairs and massaged his stump while Gunner paced back and forth in front of the artifact.

"There you go, Doc," Ryan said. "A symbol of what humanity might have reached. If they didn't kill themselves off along the way."

The other two didn't answer, and the silence stretched into minutes.

"I could really use a drink," Louis muttered, watching Gunner pace. "Should have brought a bottle with us."

"You call that rotgut a drink?" Gunner grumbled. "It tastes worse than those damned vitamins, and that's saying something."

The doctor's eyes narrowed, and he took a second to push his glasses back up his nose. "Now he complains. After he's been sneaking in to steal bottles when I'm not around."

Gunner spun around. "Who said I was stealing?"

"Mabel." Louis pointed an accusatory finger. "And don't deny it. She saw you herself."

Gunner's cheeks reddened, and he looked about to protest when he abruptly grinned. "And me being as quiet as a mouse."

"Admit it." Louis turned his finger into a gun and mimed pulling the trigger. "You like my Jovian Spirits. In fact, say it out loud. It's the best alcohol around."

Gunner threw up his hands. "It's the best rotgut within eight hundred thousand klicks."

"There." Louis lifted his finger and blew away imaginary smoke. "Was that so hard?"

Ryan wanted to inform them they were both crazy when a light flashed on the wall. He stabbed the button. "Braeder here."

"Lieutenant." Rani's voice. "I just finished speaking with the colonists. They're asking us to power up the concourse."

"What?" Ryan exchanged looks with Louis. "That would increase the drain on the batteries."

"The batteries will go dry in a matter of hours anyway, sir. They want a place where they can spend their last minutes with family and friends. Even if it shortens the time we have left."

Ryan sagged back against the side of the airlock as reality closed in. The endgame was approaching. The colonists knew it. It was up to him to accept it.

"Go ahead, Rani. And any food we have left."

"Understood." There was a brief pause. "Sir, are you coming back to the station? Kasim and I want to know what your plans are."

Ryan felt a tear form in the corner of his eye. He had one family ripped from his grasp when he was young. Now he was about to lose another. Fate was the ultimate bastard.

"We're coming to you," he said. "How much time?"

"Vrabel says the batteries should last about three hours once we heat the concourse."

Ryan looked at Gunner and the man nodded. "We'll be back shortly." He turned off the com.

"It's the right thing to do," Louis said, his voice low. "People need a place to grieve, somewhere to support one another."

"Are you thinking about the EV door?" Gunner asked.

Ryan shuddered. Back on Ceres, he had told himself he would never do such a thing. That he would never give up. Now the world took on a different shade.

"Freezing to death is a painful way to go," Louis said.

Ryan tried to answer, but his mouth refused to cooperate. Something inside rejected the notion outright. Despite overwhelming odds, he would not surrender. There was no way he could order the death of his people. Of his colony.

Louis stared at him, like he knew what was going through his mind. The doctor smiled and pointed at the artifact. "Man, I'd really like to know where this thing came from."

"Well, you're going to go to your grave disappointed," Gunner grunted. "Because Rani said the scientists learned nothing."

Ryan swallowed the lump in his throat as the weight of his pending decision weighed down his shoulders. "According to Kasim, it was a set of musical notes that caused the port to open."

"And there's been nothing since?" Gunner asked.

"Kasim said they were starting to establish a dialogue," Ryan said. "But then Wilshire landed, and they never got a chance to finish. Not that it will make a difference now."

Louis stood and approached the artifact. "A dialogue implies a back-and-forth between two parties. If the door opened last, wouldn't that mean it's our turn?"

"Our turn for what?" Gunner asked.

"Interesting thought, Doc." Ryan walked up between the two men. He recalled the conversation with Rani about a lurking consciousness and how her description mirrored his own confusion after touching it. Foreign sensations that were impossible to explain. Maybe they were leaving a stone unturned. "Do you think it's time to find out?"

The veteran grimaced. "You want to touch it? Didn't that turn out badly last time?"

Ryan almost laughed at the irony. "What's it going to do? Destroy the colony? I think we're past that." He rubbed his hands together. "It's getting colder. When we get back to the station, Doc, how about slipping into Medical for a drink? Just to warm up."

"That depends." Louis offered a sad smile. "Do you have a reservation?"

Ryan walked around the artifact. When it had first fallen out of the ice, Rani reported strange hieroglyphics on the exterior that could pulse and change color. Kasim said a whole new set of markers appeared after he touched it, and that that was when the port opened. Now it was uniformly gray, except for a blue haze that obscured the opening.

He looked at Louis. "Would you agree there's nothing left to lose?"

The doctor's hesitation was enough for Ryan. He reached out and slid his hand inside the open port.

For a second, nothing happened. Then a sensation like an electrical impulse surged up his arm, a force invading his skin and muscles and bones, migrating up his neck and into his brain. It was the same feeling as before, but exponentially stronger. Some type of cognitive entity that seemed hesitant and yet curious. A mixture of logic and emotion that blended into a brazen request for more data. Tentacles crept into his mind, slithering through his gray matter like a pack of eels, tasting his memories and quantifying his knowledge. Primal instincts screamed at him to flee, like prey caught in the open. It took every inch of courage to hold his ground and let the entity catalogue his mind.

It hovered there, like the sun behind a band of clouds. Except it didn't feel real but more like a projection. A hologram built around the memory of a life. A fabricated, mechanical doppelganger of an entity that lived and died a long time before. And within that artificial presence he sensed understanding and then anger as recent images flashed in his mind; the marines shooting Louis on the surface, Bordeaux and Creaser leading an insurrection in the concourse, mutilated bodies tied down in the Federation Medical. The emotion swelled until his head threatened to explode, and he jerked his hand back.

Gunner gawked. "What did you do, Ace?"

Ryan blinked his vision back into focus. It took a moment for his mind to register what his eyes were seeing; the artifact had changed. It pulsed with a stunningly bright white glow, like a magnesium flame burning in the dark.

"I . . . I don't know. It was weird. But I think Rani was right; there's a consciousness at the core of this."

Gunner fingered the cut on his forehead. "You mean some type of advanced AI?"

"Yes. Maybe." Ryan shrugged. "Or something else. Whatever it is, it took a stroll through my memories. I think it's angry."

"Well, that's icing on the cake," Louis deadpanned. "We're all going to die in the next few hours and you just pissed off the aliens. Congratulations."

"No." Ryan shook his head. "It's not mad at me; it's . . ."

Louis waited. "It's what?"

"I'm not sure."

Gunner stepped back and glanced at a monitor. "Whatever else you did, Ace, you just turned it on. Lab temperature has jumped five degrees. Monitors are reading a surge in EM emissions."

Ryan's thoughts tripped over a memory. Something Rani had said back on Ceres. "Isn't the artifact exothermic? Over millennia, it melted the ice and formed this cave?"

Gunner stopped playing with his cut and dropped his hand. "Ah, yeah. So?"

Louis walked over beside Gunner to check the sensors. "Damn, there's a lot of power in that thing."

Divergent thoughts merged in Ryan's brain. "Power?" He stared at the open port as a novel idea took root. Could it work? He stepped over to one of the desks and picked up a portable lamp.

Louis rubbed his stump nervously. "What are you doing?"

"Probably something crazy." He walked up to the open panel on the side of the artifact.

"Don't exactly see a place to plug in," Gunner said, giving Ryan an odd look. "Not sure what you expect to accomplish, Ace."

Ryan felt a tad embarrassed, standing over the alien object with a lamp in one hand and a power cord in the other. Like a caveman brandishing his spear when the flying saucer landed.

*What was he doing?*

Before self-doubt got in the way, he bent down and inserted the plug inside the port.

The light brightened.

"Jesus!" Louis whispered. "What just happened?"

Gunner had to pick his jaw off the floor. "Ace?" he asked quietly. "Why is that light on?"

"I think it understands," Ryan said. "I think Kasim was right about starting a dialogue. It listened and now it's offering to help."

"Not sure how a table lamp is going to save the colony," Louis said.

"Didn't you just tell me there's a lot of power inside that thing?" Ryan said. He watched the doctor's eyes widen as realization took hold.

"Well, I'll be damned." A broad smile emerged before Louis grabbed Gunner around the neck and pulled him into a hug. "We're not dead."

The veteran tried to act mad and push him away, but his expression betrayed him. "Son of a bitch. What do we do now?"

Ryan summoned the courage to pull the cord out—the light went out—before putting it back. The light turned on, brighter this time.

A huge weight rolled off his soul, and he felt like crying. "Call Rani and tell her we won't be coming back to the station. Ask her if she'd be kind enough to join us and bring several hundred feet of that transmission wire we brought from Ceres."

# EPILOGUE

*Words are the voice of the heart.*

DAY 200, 1600 HOURS

At least the ceremony was brief.

Any longer listening to Gunner and Louis's quiet bickering and Ryan would retrieve one of the lasers and shoot them both. The two grumbled like an old married couple: about the waste of time, about the poor job engineers did setting up the new wire, about each other. Ryan only heard it because they were on a private frequency. Standing beside him, Rani remained mute despite being exposed to the same nonstop verbal barrage.

Truth be told, Ryan only felt bad for Kasim. By virtue of his position, the governor had been forced to officiate the ceremony. He stood on a makeshift plastek dais on the moon's surface, facing rows of crosses, and tried to drum up words of sympathy and regret.

Despite every one of the bodies they'd buried in the ice being a selfish, murdering son of a bitch.

The innocent civilians killed during Wilshire's short tenure on the moon had been buried weeks before, and the entire population of Europa had turned out for that service. Now, almost two months after the firefight, they had gotten around to burying the Ceres survivors who had perished and the Europa traitors who had aided them. Ryan had refused to waste time on the second group until priority jobs had been completed: planting new seeds in the greenhouses, repairing secondary engineering systems, and building a new electrical grid to handle power from the artifact.

And even then, Gunner's work crew had dug only a single hole in the ice. A mass grave.

"If Wilshire wants something better, he can come back and bloody well dig it himself," the veteran grumbled when Rani pushed too hard one night at supper. "I don't think the bastard will shed any tears for his *friends*."

Rani had turned to Ryan for support, but he didn't have it in him to offer a sliver of sympathy for the dead. They'd chosen their path, and they'd paid for it.

So, Kasim was left rummaging for positive things to say, and the small crowd of colonists waited patiently for the ceremony to end so they could return to the station and the rest of their lives.

Rani had placed one large cross on the small rise that marked the top of the grave, in contrast to the hundreds of smaller crosses from last year's insurrection. Gunner hadn't fought her on that one.

Ryan's gaze landed on the thick cable running alongside the runway. The colony's new lifeline. He didn't understand, but he was grateful anyway. Besides, after all the shit they had been through, he figured they were due for a break from a higher power.

He changed channels. "Sasha, everything okay in Ops?"

"All systems reading nominal, Lieutenant. Rani checked in ten minutes ago and said she wants to run diagnostics on the greenhouses. Something about checking the progress of the new seeds."

Ryan chanced a look at Rani. She had her eyes closed, making him wonder if she had finally found peace within herself. Or if she was still struggling with residual guilt after agreeing to shoot down a transport full of people. And Stoll.

She hadn't spoken to Ryan about the incident, instead resuming her duties as though the entire Ceres incident had never happened.

"I thought she ran diagnostics last week."

"She did. She wants to do it again."

Ryan sighed. Another one of his crew trying to bury themselves in work. The seeds they'd carried back from Ceres were a godsend, just like the wire and all the items they took off *Phoenix*. Thank God it never launched.

"All right. I'll check in later. How's Ellen doing?"

Sasha's chuckle sounded mechanical on the com. "Her band is analyzing the new markings on the artifact's surface. She thinks she can put together another response in a few days."

Ryan snorted. Rani said the first musical response had taken Ellen and her fellow band members weeks to put together. "Braeder out."

Kasim stepped off the podium, and civilians started to disperse.

"You need me for anything, Lieutenant?" Rani asked.

The way she looked at him, the slight tilt of her neck, suggested she wanted to say something more.

"Ah, no, Ensign. We're good."

She waited a few seconds before nodding and walking away, and Ryan sensed he had missed an opportunity. For what, he wasn't sure.

Louis stepped up. "If you don't need Kasim, I'd like to take him to Medical and run another stress test on his heart. His color is off."

"He's all yours, Doc." Ryan watched the governor exchange platitudes with several colonists. "And if he gives you any hassle, sic Mabel on him."

The doctor chuckled. In their fight with Wilshire, the nurse had turned out to be their new secret weapon.

Kasim walked over to join them. "Well, that was painful. Tell me we won't be doing that again."

"Don't know about that." Gunner gave him a look. "We seem to attract a lot of attention out here in the back-ass of nowhere."

"Nothing new on the artifact?" Kasim asked.

"Vrabel is still putting the lab back together," Gunner replied. "Shock waves from the extractor explosion turned the room into a shaken martini. It'll take a while to fix the computers and sensors."

"As if they'll make a difference," Kasim said. "The artifact never reacted to our science experiments." He waited for a nod from Ryan before continuing. "Which begs the question: are you going to touch it again or wait until Ellen is ready?"

"Nobody's touching anything until we get this colony squared away," Ryan said. "Doc, you have to finish those caloric calculations, and Sasha is still surveying secondary systems. That's enough on our plate at the moment."

"And later?" Gunner asked, eyebrows rising.

"That's a bridge we'll cross when we get there," Ryan replied, his tone sharper than he intended. "So, how about—"

"Ops to Braeder." Sasha's urgent voice in his ear.

Ryan's sixth sense woke up. "Go ahead."

"Picking up an incoming message, Lieutenant."

Ryan exchanged a look with Gunner. "Origin."

"There's no fingerprint on it, sir, but the computers were able to identify the origin. It came from Mars."

"Mars?" Louis frowned. "Governor Wilson's last message said the plague was about to wipe out the colony, and that was over a year ago."

"We're coming in, Sasha," Ryan said, a feeling of foreboding filling his veins. "Download it and wait for us."

"Copy that."

No one spoke as Ryan led them into the station. They didn't stop to undress in the decompression chamber, simply leaving their gloves and helmets on the shelf.

Chan met them in front of Medical. The recent skin grafts on her face remained fiery red, and her cheeks and lips were still swollen. "Sasha called me," the pilot said. "Who do you think it is?"

"I think we're about to find out." Ryan quashed the irritation before it crept into his tone. They all knew who it was.

"How you feeling, Chan?" Rani asked.

The pilot self-consciously touched the dressings on her face. Wilshire's torture sessions had played hell with her looks, but the doctor had worked hard to remove the larger scars.

"Day by day. Thanks."

Rani reached over and gave her hand a squeeze.

Sasha surrendered the command chair to Ryan when he entered Ops. Gunner, Chan, and Rani took positions at their old terminals while Louis and Kasim stood at Ryan's shoulder.

"Message downloaded," Sasha said.

"Play it."

A hologram of a familiar face appeared at the front of the room. It took a second for the audio to catch up with the visual display.

". . . not sure you're still alive, Ryan," Sybil said. "But I wanted . . . no, I needed to send you this message. Just in case."

The image panned out to reveal a small room complete with table, two chairs, and a bed shoved into the corner. A small portal occupied the near wall.

"Events here have taken an . . . unfortunate turn," she continued. "We landed one week ago. Stoll got us down in one piece. Kudos to Chan for her training courses."

Chan squeezed the sides of her chair. Rani laid a hand on her shoulder.

"Everything was fine until the third day. We were stocking supplies when Wilshire discovered the bodies. Hundreds of them stacked inside one of the hives. The next day, he started throwing up. It spread through the crew like wildfire. Everyone bolted for the doors. I found this domicile in one of the outlying farms and have been holed up here for the past three days." She stood and walked over to stare out the portal. "I know for a fact most everyone on the transport is either infected or dead." She giggled, her voice straying an octave too high.

Ryan felt a clammy hand in his gut. Something was off with Sybil, like her mental defenses were collapsing.

"Dr. Louis was right about the vaccine," she continued, clearing her throat as she composed herself. "Pavel and his comrades may have been a little too confident. If it's any consolation, the last time I saw Andrei and the Federation doctor, they were vomiting blood in one of the engineering bays."

Ryan stole a glance at Louis. The medico maintained a poker face but his color had turned beet-red.

"I made the wrong decision, Ryan. Going with Wilshire was my mistake. I want you to know that. In fact, my entire life seems to be a collection of mistakes. Well, except for one." She smiled, and Ryan felt the tips of his ears burn. "So, I wanted to tell you and the others I'm sorry. Especially Kasim. Tell him what he said to me in the transport was spot-on. He should know that as well." She turned back to the camera and took a deep breath. "A few of us haven't shown any signs of infection yet. Not sure what that means. Take care, Ryan. I'll miss you."

On some level, he was sure the artifact was baiting him, and that pissed him off.

Ryan folded his arms across his chest and stared at the egg-shaped alien construct in the center of the lab. The golden hieroglyphics on its surface pulsed with the regularity of a heartbeat. Sasha had been the first to notice subtle changes in the markings—sometimes on a daily basis—and it was slowly driving him crazy. Neither Rani nor Ellen could answer the question why. The only reassuring part: that the thick black cables connecting the artifact to the colony still flowed with enough power to keep his people alive.

And then there were the goddamned dreams.

A subtle throat clearing drew his attention away from the alien egg.

"Begging the lieutenant's pardon, but it's after midnight," Archie said. "And we should be getting back."

Ryan turned. "Haven't I told you that you don't have to come?"

"Every time," the geologist nodded. He had appropriated Vrabel's seat behind one of the monitors and had his hands clasped behind his head, his feet resting on the closest desk.

"And yet you still walk to the lab with me?"

"Every night, as per Gunner's instructions."

Ryan frowned. "You realize I could make that an order."

"Absolutely. You are in charge of the colony."

"So, you would stay in the station, right"

"Of course." Archie's poker expression didn't waver. "Except when you take your midnight strolls, sir."

Something inside Ryan wanted to scream. He was in charge of all aspects of the colony . . . except when he wasn't.

Archie waited until Ryan exhaled before standing and passing him his EV helmet. "Any scintillating insights tonight, lieutenant?"

Ryan took one last forlorn look at the artifact. "Nothing, Archie. Just like every other night. Vrabel's given up on his scans, and Emma's musicians have packed away their instruments. I don't think we're meant to talk to it."

"It's still supplying power," Archie said, leading Ryan into the airlock.

"Small miracles," Ryan muttered, and listened to the chug of air being pumped out before the outer hatch cycled open.

"I guess that leaves only one option."

Ryan felt the familiar angst roll through his veins. "I already told Gunner and Rani, and everyone else: I'm not doing it. I'm not gambling with fifteen hundred lives just to satisfy our curiosity."

Archie half-turned and graced him with a smile. "Truer words were never spoken."

Ryan's eyes narrowed. "Why do I sense you're being facetious?"

The colonist took the lead as they headed back toward the station. "Could be because you're paranoid, Lieutenant. I hear all leaders get that way eventually."

"Archie, you're an asshole."

"Could be, Lieutenant. I hear colonists get that way sometimes. Fortunately, it doesn't last long."

Ryan's ears perked up. "No? Why not?"

"Because the leader usually spaces them."

"Asshole," Ryan repeated.

Twenty minutes later, they cycled through the station's main airlock and changed back into their civvies in the decompression room.

"You might want to check out the Event Horizon, Lieutenant," Archie said. "Colony scuttlebutt hinted at something happening tonight."

Ryan buttoned up his tunic. "In the pub? What for? There's no booze."

Archie nodded solemnly. "You're right, sir. It's probably nothing. Well, have a good night, Lieutenant." He headed off toward his hive.

Ryan hung up his EV suit and started back to his quarters before realizing Archie's words nagged at him like an itch under the skin. He turned around and made a beeline for the pub. To his surprise, the lights were on and several people sat around a table in front of the bar. The rest of the tables and chairs had been stacked against the back wall.

"What the heck is going on?" he demanded before recognizing faces; Gunner, Louis, Rani, Kasim, and Solomon. "Aren't you guys supposed to be in bed?"

Gunner grinned. "We were, Ace, except for one thing. It's the vet's birthday. Bugger was hiding it until Rani found out."

Ryan finally noticed the glasses in front of each person and the half-empty bottle in the center of the table. "Ah, well, Happy birthday, Doc."

Louis raised his glass in a mock salute.

"Now maybe we can get back to our quarters," Ryan continued. "We're supposed to haul *Phoenix* out of the crevice early tomorrow."

"That's the plan," Kasim said. "Except there's a little matter of a certain message to Mars."

Something caught in Ryan's throat. "How do you know about that?"

Solomon slid back his chair and stood. "I better get back, Cap'n." He squeezed Rani's hand. "See you later."

Ryan blinked. He had no idea . . .

Rani patted Solomon's now-vacant chair. "Have a seat, sir. Sasha happened to come across it when she was doing diagnostics."

Ryan bit his tongue before he called bullshit. "It was in my personal file."

She shrugged. "Then maybe she discovered it by accident. Doesn't matter. We're wondering if you're going to send it."

"What the hell is it any business of yours?" He distributed his glare evenly along the table. "If I want to send a message to Mars to find out about their situation—about other humans alive in the solar system—that's my decision."

"Except when it's really not about other humans," Louis said, swirling his drink, "but just one in particular."

Ryan felt his rage start to boil. "This is a command decision. It's up to me—"

"She tried to kill you, Ace," Gunner said quietly. "And me, and everyone at this table."

"And she's probably dead already," Ryan growled.

Gunner met his gaze and held it. "Karma's a bitch."

Louis put his drink down and waited until he had Ryan's attention. "Fact is, we don't give a shit whether she's alive or dead. What we care about is you."

Kasim put his hand on Ryan's arm. "Let her go, my friend. Time to move—"

He stopped when the door screeched open and Chan walked in wearing nothing more than pajama bottoms and an oversized sweatshirt. She nodded at Ryan before turning to Kasim. "I thought you said this was going to be a short meeting."

Kasim turned a shade red. "Sorry." He nudged his glass. "The doctor just rolled out a keg of Jovian Spirits—"

"A new batch?" She reached over and picked up his glass, studying it in the light. "Gunner, what say you? Any better than the last?"

"Maybe a little. Hate to admit it, but the vet's improving."

"Okay." She tossed back the entire contents. Kasim blanched but Chan seemed to savor the taste. "Not bad." She pushed the empty glass to Gunner and sat on the governor's knee. "Refill, please."

Ryan took a second to get his bearings. First Rani and now Chan? No one else looked surprised. Was he the only one out of the loop?

As Gunner filled two glasses, Chan turned to Ryan. "How'd you make out in the lab tonight, sir? Any new insights?"

Her question took him off guard and he fumbled for something to say. "Ah, how'd you know I was out there?"

"Because you're out there most nights. And because Rani told me."

Ryan turned his scowl on Rani. "Are you spying on me?"

"No, sir." She raised her hands defensively. "Kasim was the one who told me."

"You." Ryan jammed a finger into the governor's chest. "How did you know?"

For a second, Kasim tensed, but then he relaxed and laughed. "Because you're so busy running the station, you can't see what's going on in front of your nose."

Ryan hesitated. "What are you talking about?"

"You, me, and Rani. We're having the same symptoms."

"I'm not following."

Kasim slid one glass to Chan and sipped his own. "The artifact."

It took a second for Ryan to make the link. "The three of us touched it."

"That's right," Rani said. "And the three of us are suffering the effects."

"Effects?" Ryan's mouth had turned desert dry. The drinks on the table looked very appealing.

"The dreams," Kasim said. "Don't lie to us."

Ryan took a deep breath. He felt like saying anything would be an admission of weakness.

"Every night," Rani said. "Kasim and I have made multiple trips to the artifact. We can't help ourselves. But there's no answers." She paused. "Unless you found a way to communicate with it."

It took Ryan precious seconds to beat down his inhibitions. How did one explain a jumble of colors and images that made no sense? Flashes of his own memories mixed with something so unspeakably alien he couldn't describe a fraction of it. "No, I got nothing. The dreams are crazy, just like when I touched the damn thing. I can't make any sense of it, but I can't shake the feelings, either."

"It's got a hold on us," Kasim confirmed, looking worried. "Like it's inside our brains or something."

"What are we going to do?" Rani asked. "The damn thing is driving me crazy."

"Sooner or later, someone is going to have to touch it again," Gunner said. "There is no other solution."

"Weren't you the one who advocated against that approach when we were running from Wilshire?" Ryan asked.

Gunner shrugged. "I changed my mind. The colony is balancing on the precipice of extinction. You bought us time by raiding Ceres, but that won't last forever. We can't go to Earth because the Federation vaccine doesn't work. All we have left is an alien artifact that's keeping Europa on life support."

"Much as I hate to admit it, the Neanderthal is right," Louis said. "Our colonists need to do more than just exist. If hope evaporates, you won't have to lose power to kill everyone; their spirits will be long gone anyway."

Ryan leaned back in his chair. What they said made sense. The tough part: it flew in the face of his safety concerns for the colony in the short term. "Okay, I'll think about it."

"Don't take too long," Louis cautioned. "Hope is a fragile thing."

"Speaking of fragile." Gunner poured a glass of spirits and slid it across to Ryan. "What are you going to do about the message to Lecky?"

"What's the matter, Gunner? Are you worried about what I'm going to say to her?"

"No, Ace, I'm worried about what she's going to ask of you."

# ABOUT THE AUTHOR

Michael Simon is the author of the First Command trilogy and Extinction series. He hails from Saint John, Canada, where he works as a family physician to support his writing addiction. An avid science fiction and fantasy reader, Simon enjoys spinning new tales and going where no one has gone before.